Katharine Susannah Prichard was born in 1884 at Levuka, Fiji, where her father was the editor of a newspaper. She spent part of her childhood in Melbourne and part in Tasmania before moving to Greenmount, Western Australia where she died in 1969.

Her literary output included such novels as *Working Bullocks, Haxby's Circus,* and *Black Opal* but she also wrote poetry, several volumes of short stories, and a play.

'*Coonardoo,* with the white flame of the author's creative power burning through it, is itself vital—a harsh, but a living piece of literature.'

The Bulletin

IMPRINT CLASSICS

COONARDOO

KATHARINE SUSANNAH PRICHARD

*Introduced
by Drusilla Modjeska*

ANGUS
& ROBERTSON

A division of HarperCollins*Publishers*

ACKNOWLEDGEMENTS

The letter dated 1926 from Katharine Susannah Prichard to Vance and Nettie Palmer is quoted with the permission of Ric Throssell, and of the National Library of Australia NLA MSS 1174/1/2856-7.

AN ANGUS & ROBERTSON BOOK

First published in 1929
First published in Australia in 1956
by Angus & Robertson Publishers
Angus & Robertson paperback edition 1973
Angus & Robertson Classics edition 1975
Reprinted in 1975, 1977, 1979, 1980, 1981, 1982,
1983 (twice), 1984, 1985, 1986
This edition published in Australia in 1990 by
Collins/Angus & Robertson Publishers Australia
Reprinted in 1990

Collins/Angus & Robertson Publishers Australia
A division of HarperCollinsPublishers (Australia) Pty Limited
Unit 4, Eden Park, 31 Waterloo Road, North Ryde
NSW 2113, Australia

William Collins Publishers Ltd
31 View Road, Glenfield, Auckland 10, New Zealand

Angus & Robertson (UK)
16 Golden Square, London W1R 4BN, United Kingdom

National Library of Australia
Cataloguing-in-publication data:

Prichard, Katharine Susannah, 1883-1969.
  Coonardoo.

  Modern classics ad.
  ISBN 0 207 16636 6.

  I. Title.

A823.2

Cover illustration: A Mile out of Alice Springs 1949 *by*
Margaret Preston gouache stencil on black card. 23.4 x 29.8cm
bought 1949. Art Gallery of New South Wales.
Printed in Australia by Griffin Press Ltd.

5   4   3   2
95 94 93 92 91 90

INTRODUCTION

When *Coonardoo* was published in 1929, Katharine Susannah Prichard added a preface to the novel which, in effect, justified it both as a work of the imagination, and of historical and social accuracy. 'Life in the north-west of Western Australia,' she wrote, 'is almost as little known in Australia as in England or America. It seems necessary to say, therefore, that the story was written in the country through which it moves. Facts, characters, incidents, have been collected, related and interwoven. That is all.'

Katharine Prichard took this unusual step of offering an explanation for a work of fiction because, when the novel had been serialised in the *Bulletin* during 1928, hundreds of letters were written in protest, and the publishers were anxious. The critic Nettie Palmer was quite right when she feared the response to *Coonardoo* would set back the chances for others who wanted to write seriously and imaginatively about the lives of white men and black women in outback Australia. In May 1929, after running the serial of *Coonardoo,* S. H. Prior of the *Bulletin* wrote to Vance Palmer to say they could no longer go ahead with the serial of his novel, *Men Are Human.* 'There is no chance, I suppose,' he wrote 'of your whitewashing the girl?'

Recognised as a novel that broke important ground, *Coonardoo* was published to critical acclaim as well as public outrage. Taking the latter more seriously than the former, Prior explained to Vance Palmer: 'Our experience with Coonardoo shows us that the Australian public will not stand stories based on a white man's relations with an Australian aborigine.' The problem, it would seem, was not so much that Katharine Susannah Prichard exposed the widespread exploitation of black women by white men, but that she wrote of the love, albeit unacknowledged and twisted in on itself, between a white man and an Aboriginal woman. No one denied that white men used black women for their own sexual gratification. Love, it would seem, was the real indecency.

Sixty years later, *Coonardoo* continues to make uncomfortable reading, and the challenge Katharine Prichard throws to white Australia — that we come to terms with Aboriginal Australia or perish — still comes in on target. Enough remains the same; much, one could say, is worse. But with the distance of sixty years, we can also see how much has changed. Writing about *Coonardoo* afflicts one, therefore, with a strange case of double vision. On the one hand there is the radical and passionate view from 1926, and once again I raise my hat to Katharine Susannah Prichard. On the other hand there are the assumptions and procedures she accepted and we do not, the language she could use and we would not; and the lapses and silences that would not, and could not, have been heard then, but which startle us now.

Katharine Susannah Prichard was looking for a quiet spot to finish the manuscript of *Haxby's Circus* when, in 1926, she accepted an invitation to visit the Kimberleys. By her own admission, she arrived at Turee station with very little knowledge of life in the outback, and even less of Aboriginal culture. She had set out from Perth expecting peace to get on with other work, and arrived to find herself seduced by a huge red landscape and overwhelmed by the strange and mysterious presence of Aboriginal Australia.

> It's terrifically hot [she wrote to Vance and Nettie Palmer on arrival], and the dust storms — suffocating. But I've been riding nearly every day, and am that colour of red mulga and hennaed with dust (make what you can of the verb, Nettie dear). Sometimes one of the gins rides with me, sometimes mine host, who is really a bit of the country, and sometimes Mick, a stockman who has lived here all his life...
>
> And of course I'm enciente with stories, delighted and quite mad with the beauty and tragedy of them. The only fly in the ointment that my hostess has aspirations of literary efforts ... and I'm afraid won't ever be able to do anything but the small and sentimental. I mean has no quality of language, capacity for imagery, or ability to see natural values. You know what I mean, weaving our psychology

and sentimental morality over native legends. I've been trying to show her how to do them on their own merits — to see things as the blacks see them.

And the blacks are most interesting — fair haired — and I find them poetic and naive. Quite unlike all I've ever been told, or asked to believe about them. I'm doing some character studies. But feel 'to honour bound' not to touch the legends.

It is a small irony that a writer whose working practice was to choose a subject and then research it, should stumble across one of the most powerful sources for her writing. From her time at Turee station, she wrote *Coonardoo,* a play called *Brumby Innes,* which opened to a corroboree, and two of her best short stories, "Happiness" and "The Cooboo". It was as if Katharine Susannah Prichard found there, at the edge of the desert, on the fringe of white settlement, something that touched a nerve at the heart of white Australia.

Coonardoo is detailed in its account of station life, the daily routine, the stores, the kitchen, the stockyards, the mustering, the Aboriginal camp, the homestead verandah. Perhaps it is this accuracy of naturalistic detail, always a stamp of Katharine Prichard's work, that encouraged a shocked response to the novel. At the centre of it all is Coonardoo, and although her ultimate significance is less realistic than symbolic, her story is so dreadful, and thereby memorable, that it too invited a literal reading of exploited fact. As a frame for Coonardoo's own story, the use of black women by white men extends from the predatory Sam Geary who keeps mistresses in fine clothes, to the pearling luggers that travel the coast with 'black pearl' on board, women to be used until, diseased, they were discarded.

The tragedy of Coonardoo, who ends up as a discarded *black pearl,* is not, at any rate not simply, that she is misused sexually; rather it is that her love for Hugh, and his for her, can never be acknowledged, other than with secrecy and shame, in the tiny space where his world and hers intersect. The result of this denial is spiritual death for them both. What shocked the readers in 1929, I suspect, was not so much the portrayal of the degradation of Aboriginal women, shocking as that is, and obvious as it was for a focus of outrage, but the possibility of love between Hugh and Coonardoo. It is this denied possibility that makes the other cruder forms of abuse so disturbing, because it tells us something about the failure of love, in which we are all complicit, rather than merely detailing the forms of brutality.

The point about Hugh is that he is a decent man. That is the indictment Katharine Prichard makes of him. In the 1920s a decent man believed miscegenation was morally wrong, and that the Aborigines, a dying race, should be treated fairly and with kindness. Because of his decency, this decency, Hugh denied his own feelings, and his own sexuality, and ignored, or failed to recognise Coonardoo's. Unable to acknowledge what has passed between them, he hurts his legitimate white wife and himself; he brings terrible misery to Coonardoo, and, ultimately, the destruction of the Aboriginal community on his station. He stands condemned not as a brute, but in the weakness and blindness of his own repressed obedience to unquestioned moral standards. That is a much harder indictment for a decent white Australian audience to bear. They could be shocked by the men who rape and abuse, for they were not them; or so they told themselves. Hugh was an average Australian man, better than average, a decent man like his decent readers, themselves no strangers to the failures of love.

When *Coonardoo* was published in the late 1920s, the Aboriginal situation in the north-west had been in the metropolitan news through two widely publicised incidents. In 1926 a group of Aborigines had been massacred by police at Onmalmeri in the Kimberleys as retaliation for the murder of a single white man. The outcry from the cities resulted in a Royal Commission. Then, in 1928, there was another reprisal massacre, the Coniston killings, this time some distance north-west of Alice Springs.

Coonardoo was published, then, at a time when white Australia was beginning to debate the responsibilities of government towards the Aborigines. The mood in metropolitan Australia was one of indignation at brutalities occurring on what was understood to be the peripheries of their society. So rather than assume Katharine Prichard's audience would be shocked by further revelations of brutality, one could argue that white Australia was prepared for it, even expecting it. But her readers were not prepared for a novel, ostensibly set on the edge of the desert, on the fringes of white Australia, that brought the problem right into its suburban heart. The crisis between black and white could not be attributed to isolated incidents on the outskirts, for it took sustenance from the decent respectability of middle-class Australia. Coonardoo's symbolic significance as the land itself, 'the well in the shadow', reinforced the challenge Katharine Susannah Prichard made through this novel that if white Australia, symbolically represented by Hugh, could not give Aboriginal Australia the respect of love, then both black and white were doomed to moral and cultural impoverishment.

In the foreword to the 1929 edition of *Coonardoo,* Katharine Sussannah Prichard evokes the authority of anthropology to support her view of Aboriginal culture. She writes:

> Basedow in *The Australian Aboriginal* says, 'Anthropological relationship connects the Australian ... with the Veddahs and Dravidians of India and with the fossil men of Europe, from whom the Caucasian element has sprung.' They are only a few generations removed, after all, Coonardoo and Andromache. 'In other words, the Australian aboriginal stands somewhere near the bottom rung of the great evolutional ladder we have ascended.'

From the vantage point of 1990, one registers shock at a view of evolution that is, now, thoroughly discredited. Katharine Prichard is not to be criticised for this. She was writing of her time as every writer must, and indeed in the context of twenties opinion, she was pointing out not the distance between white and black, but the continuity, as she put it, between Coonardoo and Andromache, between Aboriginal Australia and our own mythology. However, from a contemporary point of view, it is perhaps the unconscious assumptions about this mysterious black Australia, given to us through the limits of a white imagination, that tell us most about attitudes to race, then and now.

In her letter from Turee station, it is clear that Katharine Prichard, unlike her hostess, could see at once the possibility of writing about the north-west through the perspective of the blacks. There had been little enough attempt to do so in existing Australian fiction. E. L. Grant Watson, a biologist who had worked in the Kimberleys with Daisy Bates and Radcliffe Brown before the First World War, made a fictional approach to the subject in a story called 'Out There', which was received with some interest by the readers of the *English Review,* but which did not attract public attention. In *The Man Hamilton,*

Vance Palmer's hero takes a half-caste 'wife', but her point of view is well and truly subsidiary to the hero's. *Coonardoo* was effectively the first Australian novel to take an Aboriginal woman as its acknowledged subject. This, in itself, must have added to the sense of shock with which it was greeted. Approaching *Coonardoo,* however, from a contemporary perspective in which Black critics call white writers on their evasions, and in which Black writing is developing its own, very different terms, it is worth looking again to see just how far it was possible — and impossible — for Katharine Susannah Prichard to take an Aboriginal point of view.

As a writer, Katharine Prichard relied heavily on naturalistic detail, even in this, her most symbolic novel. But naturalistic detail was less available to her for Coonardoo than it was for any of her white characters. While she knew the life of the homestead verandah and could imagine it in all its moods, she did not know, and could not know the intricate and intimate experiences of Aboriginal life. We see Coonardoo almost entirely in her role with the white world, at the house, managing the keys to the store, mustering, riding, pitching camp. When the story *is* told through her point of view, it is the whites she sees, with only a glance to her own people. Her story is billed as the novel's story, and so it is, but it is her story as it bore on the life of the station, and the lives of its white owners. It is Hugh's story that is given resonance through Coonardoo, not the other way round.

The character of Coonardoo, *the well in the shadow,* the dark brooding presence of the land itself, of nature, and therefore of desire, gives meaning not only to Hugh but also to the white women on the station. It is here, displaced onto the white, that we can see unspoken assumptions about black femininity at work. There is Hugh's mother, Mumae; there is his wife, Mollie, and his daughter, Phyllis. Coonardoo spans them all.

Mumae is a figure we recognise from Mrs Aeneus Gunn, the good matriarch who rules kindly and firmly, raising Coonardoo for her part in the future, just as she raises Hugh for his. Hugh tells Mollie:

> Mother handled them extraordinarily well. It's the iron hand in the velvet glove does the trick, she used to say. Was very strict about some things. Respected them and their ideas. Made 'em respect hers. If they wanted the things she had to give, she made them do

what she wanted, obey her, wash, and not take anything without asking. They're naturally honest . . . fair dealers.

But Mumae's rule is a rule of the past. It's the rule of parent to child. And while Hugh might long for a return to that maternal certainty, Molly cannot re-create it. Hugh and Coonardoo are no longer children, and they must face what Mumae's rule denied: their own sexuality. There are hints that Mumae was once a young woman, and a little wild, but now she's a widow, and old. She is sexless herself, and while she tries to understand 'her' Aborigines' attitude to sex, 'to find in it something impersonal, universal, or a religious mysticism', she is, in all honesty, repelled. She is dependent on their knowledge of the land, and she romanticises this as natural and therefore primitive. But she rejects the sexual dimension which the novel attributes to that same notion of primitive, and close to nature. The initiation ceremonies and the corroborees trouble Mumae, leaving her vaguely dissatisfied, a dark shadow cast over her wholesome image of the station she liked to think she could control, even after death.

Frightened by his strong connection to Coonardoo, and through her to the land, Hugh marries Mollie, a woman who had proven domestic credentials, to save him from the fate of Sam Geary and his fancy black mistresses, or worse, of going bush himself. Hugh marries Mollie in Geraldton and brings her back to Wytaliba. When he steps out of the buggy he sees the child in Coonardoo's arms and knows it is his own. The child is accepted on the station as Warieda's, by Aboriginal custom the son of Coonardoo's husband. No one suspects otherwise, and Hugh keeps the guilty secret to himself. Denial accompanies his life with Mollie from the moment she arrives on the verandah. Later, at the end of the novel, long after Mollie has left 'the hard arid plains' she loathed, Phyllis realises her father took her mother 'like most men take a gin'. She could see too late that his unacknowledged love for Coonardoo was a fantasy which would turn in on itself and destroy them both.

Of the three white women, Phyllis is the only one with a sexuality worth mentioning, although there is something perfunctory about the way Katharine Prichard wrote it. Phyllis, determined to stay on the land she, too, grew up to love, falls for an ill-educated white stockman from Geary's station. That was a hard enough choice for her father —

and for the readers. In 1929 the possibility of love between a black man and a white woman was, literally, unthinkable.

Mumae, Mollie and then Phyllis are each served, and complemented, by Coonardoo. She is there, meshed into the relationship of each with Hugh, and with the place itself. Coonardoo alone in the novel is granted a full and desiring sexuality; and Katharine Susannah Prichard writes vividly of Coonardoo as a sexual being. There she is, as a young girl showing off to the young men on her way past the homestead. There she is, denied access to Hugh, living out the pain of his refusal at the other end of the verandah. There she is, with full breasts and a child in her arms. There she is, caught in her own, wretched ambivalence as Geary makes his advances.

Seeing Coonardoo in this way, again one experiences double vision. How daring of Katharine Prichard to write a fully sexual Aboriginal woman and name a novel for her in the 1920s. But there is another, contemporary view. Gayatri Spivak has shown the way in which the black woman in European literature is made to carry all that is hidden and denied in white woman: her sexuality, her madness, her suffering. All that cannot be acknowledged in white femininity is given to the black. What a burden Coonardoo must bear, taking the full impact not only of love that is denied, but its obverse, the crude desires of men; and taking also the shadow of the sexual repression white culture imposes on its own women.

Katharine Susannah Prichard made the challenge to her readers of 1929 that until white Australia could accept black Australia in love, in a symbolic sexual union that ratified their sharing of the land, both would be doomed. The unspoken challenge this novel makes to readers of the 1990s might be that there is no accommodation to be made between black and white in this country while the repressed fears and longings of the whites have to be borne by the black; for then there is everything for each of us to fear.

DRUSILLA MODJESKA
Sydney 1990

FOREWORD

THERE has been some controversy as to whether *Coonardoo* is altogether a work of the romantic imagination. Life in the north-west of Western Australia is almost as little known in Australia as in England or America. It seems necessary to say, therefore, that the story was written in the country through which it moves.

Facts, characters, incidents, have been collected, related and interwoven. That is all. The Coonardoo I knew and used to ride with, for instance, is not the gin whose life-story has been told. And Hugh is not my chivalrous host of those days, to whom, and his charming wife, this book is dedicated with a sprig of wild rosemary.

Geary exists, although the Aborigines Department has dealt with him lately. Recently, too, there has been a regulation to prevent white men from taking rooms for a gin, or half-caste, in a hotel. Nowadays, also, aboriginal stockmen usually receive a small wage as well as payment in kind by rations.

Before *Coonardoo* was printed in the *Bulletin* I asked Mr Ernest Mitchell to read the MS. Mr Mitchell is Chief Inspector of Aborigines for Western Australia. He has had thirty years' experience of the aborigines and no one in this country has wider knowledge and more sympathetic understanding of the Western and Nor'-West tribes. Mr Mitchell suggested an omission and several changes of spelling, but said that he could not fault the drawing of aborigines and conditions, in *Coonardoo*, as he knew them.

People who see the blacks only along the transcontinental line, or when they have become poor, degraded and degenerate creatures, as a result of contact with towns and the vices of white people, cannot understand how different they are in their natural state, or on isolated stations of the Nor'-West where they are treated with consideration and kindness.

Basedow in *The Australian Aboriginal* says, "Anthropological relationship connects the Australian (including the proto-Australian) with the Veddahs and Dravidians of India and with the fossil men of Europe, from whom the Caucasian element has sprung." They are only a few generations removed, after all, Coonardoo and Andromache. "In other words, the Australian aboriginal stands somewhere near the bottom rung of the great evolutional ladder we have ascended." His and our "racial development was very early disassociated from the Mongoloid and Negroid lines".

Words of the native songs are treasure really. I am grateful for them to Mr Ernest Mitchell, Mr James Withnell of Mardie and Caratha, and to his sister, Mrs James Muirdick. Only men and women like these good friends of mine who have had almost lifelong association with the aborigines, I think, can be trusted to know the sound and meaning of words in melodies sung by the blacks.

Many of the corroboree songs, or tabee, are in a dead language, it seems. Words in them are not heard in the everyday speech. The aborigines themselves do not know the exact meaning of some, or else are reluctant to give it, superstitious of unravelling the mystery of legends and saga drifted down from remote ages, perhaps. They will tell the general meaning of a song to a stranger, but not words in their rhythmic order. Only people who have had long and intimate association with particular tribes are able to garner these jewels of the primitive imagination and present them as authentic fragments.

About inspirational songs, sung by the yinerrie, inventor of corroborees, or poet and director of ceremonies, as the spirit moves him, there is not the same difficulty. Warieda's "Song of the Steam Engine" and "Perandalah willy-willeree" are improvisations of recent dates and show the adoption and growth of white man's words in the native idiom.

K. S. P.

Greenmount
17th March, 1929.

xiv

CHAPTER I

COONARDOO was singing. Sitting under dark bushes overhung with curdy white blossom, she clicked two small sticks together, singing:

> *"Towera chinima poodinya,*
> *Towera jinner mulbeena. . . ."*

Over and over again, in a thin reedy voice, away at the back of her head, the melody flowed like water running over smooth pebbles in a dry creek bed. Winding and falling, the words rattled together and flew eerily, as if she were whispering to herself, exclaiming, and in awe of the kangaroos who came over the range and made a dance with their little feet in the twilight before they began to feed.

> *"Towera chinima poodinya,*
> *Towera jinner mulbeena,*
> *Poodinyoober mulbeena."*

(*"Kangaroos coming over the range in the twilight, and making a devil dance with their little feet, before they begin to feed."*)

It was no more than a twitter in the shadow of dark bushes near the veranda; a twitter with the clicking of small sticks. Coonardoo was not supposed to be there at all. Everybody was asleep in the long house of mud bricks and corrugated iron, and under the brushwood sheds beyond the kala miah. But Coonardoo did not want to sleep.

A little aboriginal girl about nine years old in a faded blue gina-gina, she sat there, part of the shadows, with her dark skin, fair hair, and brown eyes shadowed across the cornea. Clicking and singing, she watched the plains, the wide shallow pan of red earth under ironstone pebbles which spread out before her to the furry edge of the mulga, grey-green, under pale-blue sky.

There was not a breath of wind. The windmills struck hard lines against the sky, their fans motionless, although roofs of the buggy

I

shed, harness-room and smithy shivered in the heat. Stones on the plains, glistening in the clear white light, shimmered and danced together.

A crested pigeon, on the bough of a dead tree beside the garden, seemed to be watching the plains too. He sat there under the brush of dead twigs, his tail stuck out like a rudder, tipping backwards and forwards.

Yellow moths drifted down from the white gum-blossom. Its fragrance of dry grass and honey made Coonardoo feel sleepy. And she had decided not to sleep, but to watch the plains for first sight of the horses and buggy coming from Nuniewarra.

Her eyes fluttered after the moths. She could see low brown huts down there beside the well, a deep narrow well the Gnarler had dug long ago at a little distance from the creek. Coonardoo they called it, the dark well, or the well in the shadows. Coonardoo had been named after the well near which she was born. The huts were the huts of her people.

Trunks of gum-trees were chalk white all along the dry bed of the creek, and beyond the creek, bare and red, soared the ridge of dog-toothed hills, their lower slopes tawny with spinifex. Horses and a buggy from Nuniewarra—tomorrow, they would be taking Youie across the creek and away over the ridge. Away and away by a long winding track across the plains, through those stretches of country where mulga was standing, stiff and shining as metal, so long it had been dead and bleaching in the sun. Away and away, farther than Coonardoo could think, beyond blue backs of the hills, mulga scrub, and again away, and away, to the sea.

"Towera chinima poodinya. . . ."

Coonardoo sang with sobbing breaths. It was so far that Youie was going, and for so long. She wailed with fear of it all. Her thought could not follow where he was going.

"Poodinyoober mulbeena, mulbeena, mulbeena!" she wailed, while yellow moths beat the air before her, black markings of their wings flickering, jiggling with little feet of the kangaroos, and white threads of the blossom which were falling. Little feet, fluttering wings, threads of falling blossom wreathed a cobwebby sleepiness over her. Very drowsily, the faint reedy voice twanged. Coonardoo's head drooped, the fine silky jet of curled lashes swept her cheek. Her singing ran out, and started again in a flurry.

Coonardoo shook herself and sat up. She was determined not to go to sleep.

But nothing was stirring on the wide stretch of the plains before her, except the tail of the crested pigeon in that dead tree down beside the garden gate. It tipped backwards and forwards as he sat, red legs clasping a slim branch.

"Towera jinner mulbeena. . . ."

Coonardoo's fingers grasped the little sticks she was holding tightly. They clicked faster and harder. She was very eager to be awake and ready to play with Youie when he ran out from the house.

Was he not going away tomorrow? Going to school? And they would play no more in the garden down there near the windmill. The garden with its rows of cabbages, turnips, lettuces and onions, all the bright green vegetables Mrs Bessie was so proud of. Mumae the blacks called her, because Hughie did as soon as he could talk. Mumae in their dialect meant a father, and was not Mrs Bessie, father and mother to her son, the woman master of Wytaliba since Ted Watt had died so long ago, before Hugh could speak. Soon after he was born indeed.

The pigeon flew off with a whirra of grey silken wings. What had he seen? Yukki! There was Youie running through the kitchen on to the veranda.

Coonardoo's singing bubbled away as Hugh stood on the veranda, fresh from his shower, a small boy of about her own age, tucking blue trousers over a calico shirt, torn and all the colour washed out of it.

"Tani wali (Come quickly), Coonardoo!" he called, sun-red legs wide apart, sunburnt chubby face and snub-skinned nose turned upwards. Blue-eyed, very assured and bossy, he searched for Coonardoo, knowing she was somewhere near; and saw her creeping from under the dark bushes.

"Comin', You," she called.

She started to run, and they raced together for the swing gate of the garden, lifted the wire hoop holding the gate to the fence of wire-netting which surrounded Mrs Bessie's green plot, and let themselves into the garden. Two other children trotted up from the uloo, a tall loutish boy and a little fat girl, younger than

3

Coonardoo. They pushed back the gate Hugh and Coonardoo had left swinging, and went into the garden.

"Hullo, you fellers!" Sharp and scratchy, Hugh's voice rose. "You watch me!"

He ran and turned head over heels in a patch of newly turned red earth. The black children shrieked and screamed their applause.

"Now you, Coonardoo! And then Wanna and then the little fat grub," Hugh ordered.

Coonardoo ran, her blue gina-gina wrapping itself round her thin brown sticks of legs. Over she went, legs waving in the air. Hugh shouted delightedly.

"Good man! Good man, Coonardoo!"

"Bardi? Bardi now?" cried the little fat girl, jumping excitedly.

"No. Wanna next."

Wanna, the big boy, ape-like with sore eyes, a mop of dark dusty hair, calico slacks, once white now gingery grey with grease and red dust, took his run, turned and rolled clumsily.

"Now you, Bardi!"

Bardi, who was named after the fat white grubs the blacks like to eat, could scarcely run she was gurgling and chuckling so. The other children danced and screamed hilariously as she tumbled over in the dust.

Hugh ran again to show how the thing was done. Coonardoo followed him, light and fleet; her legs waved in the air; she jumped up, shaking red dust from her fair hair.

Over and over again, with shrieks of joy and clatter of laughter, eager gleeful chatter, the children ran, threw themselves on their hands, swung over and jumped up till, wearying of the game, Hugh dashed off crying, "Narlu! Narlu!" and the little girls followed him with Wanna in pursuit.

Round and round the garden they chased, jumping the cabbages, in and out between beds of onions, turnips, and lettuces, under vines Mumae had trained against the fence, and through the legs of the windmill. Bardi was narlu, then Coonardoo, and then Hugh; and he was a very fierce wild spirit of an eagle-hawk chasing little birds, whom the blacks feared and fled in terror of, through all the fun and laughter of the game.

Suddenly, in full flight, Coonardoo stood still.

"Sam comin'," she called.

Hugh, Bardi and Wanna looked out to the horizon. Against

4

misty clustering trees beside the creek crossing, a puff of dust had risen.

"Sam comin'," they chorused all together.

In the long low house of whitewashed mud bricks and corrugated iron there was a sleepy rustle and stir. Gins who had been asleep in the shade of brushwood shelters on tall sapling posts sat up and looked out across the plains. Bandogera took a pipe from the pocket of her gina-gina, bent over, lifted a stick from smouldering embers of the fire and put it to her pipe. Meenie stood looking out to the crossing for a moment, then she stalked over to the house, a tall stately figure in her long dress of dark blue dungaree.

Mumae stepped out of her room on to the veranda and looked across at the moving dust.

"Meenie," she called sharply and walked with short quick steps along the veranda, a clear-cut figure in her white dress and low-heeled black shoes.

Dust of an approaching buggy and horses swirled across the plain. The children ran to open a gate in the fence below the garden.

"Cock-Eyed Bob with Sam," Coonardoo commented as horses and buggy jolted and bounded towards them. "Arra, other feller, maybe."

Strangers came so rarely to Wytaliba that to see a buggy and horses arrive was a game in itself. Not that Sam Geary was altogether a stranger to the children. They knew him well enough and he knew them, by name, even.

As the old-fashioned high buggy rattled and clashed to a standstill before Wytaliba homestead, he looked back at the gate and at the children running after the buggy.

"Coonardoo, old Joey Koonarra's kid, isn't she?" he asked the aboriginal boy beside Bob. "Maria, her mother . . . the one that died and there was all the fuss about, couple of years ago?"

"Eeh-mm," the boy replied, taking the reins and glancing away as Mrs Watt came out to meet Geary.

5

CHAPTER II

EARLY next morning Warieda and Chitali brought in two fresh horses for Sam Geary's buggy, and it was there in front of the veranda again.

Meenie carried out the little black tin box which contained all the clothes Mrs Bessie had been making Hugh for months, and put it in the buggy. Mrs Bessie came out, and Hughie in a suit of navy blue serge, a round felt hat and boots with tabs which stuck out behind, strutted after her. Very grand he looked in his boots and new clothes, saying good-bye to everybody.

Wanna, Mick, Bardi and Coonardoo were there to see him drive away; Joey Koonarra, as well as Bandogera, Bardi's Polly, Pinja and old Gnardadu, grandmother of the tribe.

Sam Geary swaggered out from the dining-room where he had been having breakfast, Cock-Eyed Bob beside him, a slight boyish figure in dust-stained moleskins, white shirt and the Ashburton felt and spurs, he slept in, some folks said. Sam carried himself jauntily, with an air of being master of the situation. A tall man of thirty or thereabouts, bullock shouldered, buff-coloured shirt open half down its length and moleskins the same colour tight on his thighs, tin match-box, clasp-knife and pipe on his belt, he slouched as he walked, bow-kneed, in the way of a horseman.

Sun-scorched, almost raw his face looked under the felt hat he had slammed down over his thin gingery hair; his eyes, bulbous, pale blue, stared from under pink slatted lids with straight fair eyelashes. A brush of coarse gingery hair hid his mouth, except the thick upper thrust of the lower lip and tufts of hair sprouted from the nostrils of his big sunburnt nose.

"Well, Mr Geary, I'm very much obliged to you," Mrs Bessie said.

"Don't mention it, missus," Geary replied. "Got to go south meself, and might as well take the young shaver. Bob'll look after you until our horses are spelled a bit. Then he's going out prospectin' in the To-Morrow. Reckons he can smell gold out there, and'll be making our fortunes one of these days."

"That's right," Bob murmured abstractedly, one shoulder swung over, his head askew, as if already he were following a gleam under the surface of those tumbled hills north and east along Wytaliba boundaries.

Sam lit his pipe, Warieda and Chitali stood at the horses' heads. Sam undid the reins knotted about the dash-board, gripped them in his hard sun-flayed hands and stepped carefully into the buggy. Mrs Bessie kissed Hugh and hoisted him over the wheel to his seat beside Sam. Sam's boy climbed in over the other wheel.

"Let 'm go!" Sam shouted.

The horses swayed and tussled with the traces; the big chestnut reared and plunged, threw himself about; but Sam Geary knew how to handle horses. He let them play; then they sprang forward and out, and in a few moments, buggy, horses, Hugh, Sam Geary and Arra were no more than a feather of red dust on the plains, against a sky, mother-of-pearling, in the early light.

Coonardoo, who ran down to shut the gate in the fence below the garden and windmill, after the buggy had passed through, stood to watch the last swirl of dust through the trees, at the creek crossing. The sun, rising, burnished their green and golden tips. White cockatoos flew out screeching and floated to feed on the plains, as the buggy scuttled over stones in the bed of the creek.

What was there in saying good-bye to a small boy that should drive the light and living out of a woman's eyes, Cock-Eyed Bob wondered. Mrs Bessie's eyes were hard and blue as the winter skies when she stood staring over the plains at that gap in the trees where the buggy had been.

"Oh, well," she gasped sturdily, "they'll get the mail at Karrara all right, I suppose, Bob. And I've warned Paddy Hanson to look after Hughie if Sam does get on a bender. Paddy'll keep an eye on Hughie and hand him over to Captain Frenssen, who is an old friend of mine. The school people will meet the boat."

"That's right," Bob murmured awkwardly.

Coonardoo had come to stand beside Meenie and the rest of the gins. The blankness of the world about her Mrs Bessie saw in Coonardoo's eyes.

"We'll miss Hughie, won't we, Coonardoo?" she said.

"Eeh-mm."

If ever mute devouring love lay in mortal eyes it lay in Coonardoo's. Mrs Bessie realized a suffering and endurance as great as her own. The child's shadowy eyes, her air of a faithful deserted animal, sprang a train of thought which had been haunting Mrs Bessie, hovering in the background of her mind for a long time.

She could see into the years before her, years and years, stretching mistily, filling her with fear and illimitable anguish; years which she could not touch or control, so beyond her they stretched, her son in them, man-grown, herself unable to help, reach, or care for him, so distant she had become. But the child beside her, she would be there: she could be with Hugh.

A year older, Coonardoo had looked after and played with Hugh when he was little; soon dominated by and obedient to him. Glad of a playmate for her boy, Mrs Bessie taught Coonardoo to read, write and count, as she taught Hugh.

A shy, graceful little creature of more than usual intelligence, Mrs Bessie had thought Coonardoo. But now she looked at the child as if she found something of greater value in her. Mrs Bessie prided herself on treating her blacks kindly, and having a good working understanding with them. She would stand no nonsense, and refused to be sentimental, although it was well known she had taken the affair of Maria to heart. Ted Watt was as good-natured a man as stepped, until he got drunk, everybody agreed. But he could not stand liquor, went mad, ran amuck like an Afghan, or a black, when he had got a few drinks in.

Few people knew what had happened about Maria, except Mrs Bessie, and she held her tongue. The blacks said Ted had shot Maria's dog and she was badgee with him about it, back-answered and refused to do something he told her when he was drunk. He had kicked her off the veranda. Maria died a few days afterwards; no more was heard of her. And as Ted walked over the balcony of a hotel in Karrara and was killed, a month or so later, the blacks believed justice had been done.

After Ted's death, Mrs Bessie continued to run Wytaliba. As a matter of fact, everybody knew she had been responsible for management and working of the station, ever since she and Ted bought out Saul Hardy.

Sam Geary liked to think and boasted that Mrs Bessie consulted him upon occasions. But he knew she was shrewd enough to manage her own affairs. He never doubted that it was she, and not Ted, who had snavelled Wytaliba under his nose, and Geary was willing to admit he would swap the million and a half acres of Nuniewarra for Wytaliba, any day in the week.

Mrs Bessie had her head screwed on the right way, there was no denying it, although why she married Ted Watt no one could imagine. A schoolteacher in Roebourne, she had taken up with Ted and gone off droving with him. They knocked about the Nor'-West a long time together, droving and carting from the coast to stations and scattered mining settlements along the Ashburton, the Fortescue and the De Grey.

"Ted was as rough as bags," Geary said; "a good-looking, good-natured bloke who could neither read nor write. Mrs Bessie taught him to make pot-hooks."

She had an idea if they got a place of their own she could keep him away from the pubs, and used her eyes as they wandered up and down the country. When she made Ted give up droving she planked down all the money they had saved for years to take over Saul Hardy's lease of a million acres between the Nungarra hills on the west, To-Morrow ranges on the east and tributaries of the coastal rivers north and south.

Saul Hardy had lost three thousand head of cattle, and was short of whisky when Mrs Bessie made her bargain, wrote a cheque for a couple of hundred pounds, took over his liabilities and promised another couple of hundred when that was done. She brought out her papers and made Saul sign the contract before he had time to change his mind.

Ted could never have worked out, and brought off, a deal like that. The country was dead and dry for hundreds of miles, even the mulga dying; the drought had broken Saul Hardy, to be sure. But Mrs Bessie knew what she was doing. She had seen those plains, a flowing sea of grass and herbage; and believed the good seasons would come again. And they did, bringing Saul with them. He could never live anywhere else, he said. His roots were in Wytaliba and he wanted to die there. Mrs Bessie and Ted told him to make himself at home, come and go as he pleased. He took them at their word, and spent most of his time camped on the veranda, or in a room Mrs Bessie earmarked for him.

Over eighty and deaf, Saul prowled about the garden and yards doing little odd jobs as he pleased. He had brought cattle west from the Queensland border in the early days, and tramped up and down the Nor'-West, droving, and loading stores. As a young man he spent all the money he made on sprees in the coastal towns, and went off into the back-country again when his cheque gave out. Later he had taken up that stretch of Wytaliba country, and started running cattle; but he was not cut out for a squatter, Saul himself said. He had been a rolling stone too long to sit down in one place, breed cattle and wait for them to grow.

"A rolling stone gathers no moss," he said, "but a sitting hen loses feathers." Now he was old and could roll no more, his only desire was to sit down on Wytaliba and moult peacefully.

A stiff, creaking figure, he mooched about as if the place belonged to him still; and everybody, Mrs Bessie most of all, humoured him and sought his advice. She was glad enough to have him there after Ted's death; liked to tap old Saul's knowledge and experience of the country, and to get him yarning, in the evening, as he did, sometimes, smoking, and legs stretched along the veranda.

But Coonardoo—Mrs Bessie came back from her far thinking to the child standing holding Meenie's hand before her.

Meenie loved Coonardoo as Mrs Bessie loved Hugh, although Coonardoo was not her child; but the little girl whom Warieda, her husband, would one day take to be his woman, as Meenie herself was. In the meantime Meenie had taken the place of her mother to Coonardoo.

Coonardoo's mother—they no longer spoke her name in the uloo, which indicated that she was dead. There was a mound, with bark and a small close fence of sticks round it, on the other side of the creek, where her people had laid Maria.

"We'll take Coonardoo into the house, Meenie, and teach her to be a good house-girl," Mrs Bessie said.

Meenie's dark eyes lighted with pleasure. There was no better, more faithful woman on Wytaliba than Meenie, and Mrs Bessie knew that Meenie would think it an honour for Coonardoo to be taught to sweep and wash dishes beside her, so soon. Both were fair-haired, full-blooded aborigines of the Gnarler tribe. Bando-gera, Mrs Bessie's other house-girl, whose people came from the other side of the To-Morrow ranges, had thick dark brown hair; but Meenie's hair was tow-coloured and dark only at the roots. Coon-ardoo's hair, soft, and wavy when it had just been washed, grew dull golden, like wind grass out on the plains.

Mrs Bessie had wondered at these fair-headed aboriginal women when she first came across them, thinking they were half-castes or had some white blood. She was satisfied after a while that, as far as anybody knew, they were native; among tribes which had no contact with white people there were fair-haired women. She had seen black babies with mops of golden curls, though to be sure, as a rule, the hair darkened as the children grew older. Coonardoo had been a baby like that—and all aboriginal babies are honey-coloured when they are born. Their skins darken with exposure to the air and sunshine, so that by the time they are toddling, the cooboos are as bronzed and gleaming as pebbles lying on the red earth: but their hair darkens more slowly. Mrs Bessie thought that when the women washed their heads every day, as her house-girls did, their hair remained fair longer.

Every morning, after that, Coonardoo came up from the uloo at dawn with Meenie and Bandogera; scrubbed her head with the crude soap of fat and wood-ashes Mrs Bessie made; showered in the shed beside the big windmill, put on a fresh blue gina-gina, and went into the kitchen. Mrs Bessie herself taught her how to wash dishes with boiling water, making the soap froth and foam; sweep the veranda and bedrooms, dining-room and sitting-room. At first Coonardoo laughed and gurgled, as if it were great fun, this new game she was playing. Then she missed the other children, ran off to play with them when they came near the house, or chased Mrs Bessie's white hens, forgetting to finish washing the dishes, or that there was a room she should have swept out and dusted.

Mrs Bessie spoke sharply: and when Coonardoo soiled one of her new gina-ginas turning somersaults in the garden with Bardi and Wanna, she was really displeased.

Coonardoo was slow and lazy, there was no doubt about it. She did not scrub the tables quite clean, or sew as neatly as she might have done.

"You're a bad, wicked, naughty little girl, Coonardoo," Mrs Bessie scolded. "If you won't do things properly, you had better not do them at all."

Coonardoo hung her head, scowling and sulky, eyes averted.

"What's the good of trying to teach you, if you don't want to learn?" Mrs Bessie asked irritably. "And goodness knows who's to look after Hugh when I'm gone!"

Coonardoo's eyes slanted in her direction, and away, at that.

"Of course," Mrs Bessie said, "that's why I want to train and teach you, all I can. Meenie and I can't live for ever. And who's to look after Hugh then? He'll marry some day, I suppose; but even so, I'd like to think he had some good faithful soul to look after him. Meenie's been that to me. If you're only half as good to Hugh. . . ."

As if they had made a new compact, Coonardoo went steadily about her jobs after that, no longer chasing the hens, sitting to sing under the white blossom-tree, or running off to play with Bardi and Wanna, in the morning, when she should have been busy in the house.

All day she worked beside Mrs Bessie, down at the store, in the garden, or up at the sheds mending harness and saddles, tanning skins, making soap; and at sunset she went off to the uloo with Meenie and Bandogera. Mrs Bessie in the big empty house worked at accounts, wrote letters, read for a while, yarned with Saul Hardy, or lay back to plan out her manoeuvres for the station that year and years ahead. Coonardoo saw the yellow eye of Mumae's light winking out into the night as she sat singing with her people beside their fires in the uloo.

Coonardoo would not have cared to sleep like that by herself, and every night she looked up at the white house under the starry night sky, fearful for Mumae that a narlu, or unknown evil, might swoop on her when no one was near. She was always glad to find Mrs Bessie safely in bed in the morning; pleased to stand beside her with a cup of tea before she wakened.

And Mrs Bessie was really fond of the little girl. She confessed it to herself. Imperceptibly, on quiet naked feet, with her shadowy, steadfast eyes, Coonardoo had come into a blank place in Mrs Bessie's life, a place of hunger and desolation. She set her teeth and determined to go on with the plan she had made; but for the first time in her life the yearning and ache of loneliness threatened her. She had been glad to interest herself in the child; was grateful for the eager, alert way Coonardoo tried to follow her will and interpret her wishes.

After a while it was recognized that wherever Mumae went Coonardoo went. The first time she rode out on a muster, after Hughie had gone to school, Mrs Bessie told Chitali to bring in Hera for Coonardoo to ride, and Coonardoo went with her.

By and by Mumae read Coonardoo bits from letters the school-master at Stratford wrote to her about Hugh. He was quite smart at his lessons, but a bit homesick it seemed. When Hugh's letters came, a year or so later, she read from these priceless epistles also. Once every three months Mrs Bessie sent Chitali or Warieda into Nuniewarra with letters and they brought back any mail there was for Wytaliba.

When the boys were expected in, Coonardoo watched the track over the plains, her eyes restless as birds'.

"Boys comin'," she loved to cry and race out to bring in the bag with letters. The postmaster in Karrara plastered the bags with red seals which Coonardoo regarded as movins to protect Hugh's letters from floods, winning-arras, or evil spirits, on their long journey over the hills and plains.

While Mumae was reading her letter from Hughie, Coonardoo would sit down on the floor at a little distance and watch her face. She read Mumae's face as Mumae read Hugh's letter, and knew from it whether Hugh was well and what he was doing.

Mumae would laugh and smile to herself, say, "Hughie kicked two goals in a match against High School," or "Hugh's training for the under-fourteen championship—whatever that might be!" Something to do with running, Mumae supposed. Coonardoo agreed. Youie could run, and a long way! Later Mrs Bessie looked more concerned over reports which came from the headmaster at Stratford. Hugh was not doing as well at school as he might have. He was not studious, Mr Potter explained, although strangely enough the subjects he paid most attention to were Greek history and Latin.

How Mrs Bessie laughed when Mr Potter wrote to say he had asked Hugh why he liked Greek history and Latin, and Hugh said, "Hector's one of the horses up on our place and there's Hera, Pluto, and old Diana——"

Coonardoo echoed Mrs Bessie's laughter, although she did not know why it was funny Hughie should like the names of horses on Wytaliba. Mrs Bessie tried to explain that she had named Wytaliba horses after the gods, nymphs and heroes of Greek myth and history. Coonardoo did not understand. There was a good deal Mrs Bessie talked of that Coonardoo did not understand; but she liked to pretend she understood very well; and Mrs Bessie like to pretend that Coonardoo understood. But happy as she was in the child's companionship, never in any way would she attempt to interfere with, or alter, her native faiths: turn her from the customs of her people.

Mrs Bessie would not allow any Christianizing of the aborigines on Wytaliba. She had never seen a native who was better for breaking with his tribal laws and beliefs, she said. And as long as she lived, aborigines on Wytaliba should remain aborigines. For that reason, although all day Coonardoo was Mrs Bessie's shadow, and learned to wait on and do everything for her, bring her tools, make her baths and her camp-fires, always at sunset she went off with her people and slept with the dogs by her father's camp-fire.

The seasons were good, and Mrs Bessie was very busy all those years Hugh was away at school. She planned wells and stock-yards with Charley Leigh.

The Leighs lived in a hut of corrugated iron Mrs Bessie had put up for them, at a little distance from the homestead; but most of the time Charley was well-sinking his wife camped out with him on the run.

Once a month Charley Leigh and his wife drove into the homestead for stores and Mrs Bessie kept them there, a day or two, wore her white dresses and made cakes for them, brought out her china cups and saucers and spread a white cloth on the table. She gossiped very happily with Mrs Leigh and sent her back to camp loaded up with magazines, newspapers, jam and dried fruits.

Before her first baby was born, Mrs Bessie brought Fanny Leigh into the homestead and looked after her until the youngster, a fine sturdy boy, was several weeks old. She talked wells and well-sinking with Charley half the night, costing and depths, and worked with him on a map she had made of Wytaliba, where wells ought to be sunk; where they could best be sunk. Mrs Bessie had a bee in her bonnet about wells, Charley said. It was the dream of her life to have Wytaliba honeycombed with wells.

Her dream had to keep pace with her purse. That was the worst of it; and she would not borrow money for developments. She was determined to pay off the mortgage and hand the station over to Hugh without "a monkey on it". Meanwhile she worked with an energy and obstinacy which never flagged.

A wiry, restless figure in a pair of trousers, white shirt, and old hat of Ted's, she rode everywhere, inspecting the wells and windmills Charley had made, mustering, droving, working her blacks with skill and wisdom. White stockmen she refused to have on the place, because she said they would only make trouble about their gins with Warieda and Chitali, who were the best stockmen in the country. Indefatigable, her resistless energy drove everything, everybody.

Coonardoo rode and worked with her. Wherever Mumae went Coonardoo went, and Coonardoo was a good horse-girl in no time. Coonardoo loved the cattle camps. The joy of her life was to ride out over the plains like that with the men and horses.

Mumae always took two or three gins with her when she went on a muster. Meenie looked after the packs and cooked in the camp while Wanna or one of the younger boys tailed the night horses. But Coonardoo would not stay in the camp, she liked to ride off through the wild ragged hills and pick up stray cattle. Warieda had plaited a whip and given it to her, because Coonardoo was to be his woman as soon as she was old enough. As a child she had been promised to him and sent to sleep at his fireside. In a year or so she would lie there always with him and Meenie.

Meenie had told Coonardoo, and talked to her so that Coonardoo was filled with pride and pleasant anticipation at the thought of being the wife of Warieda. Was he not a strong man, young fellow, good-looking and powerful, the best horse-breaker in the Nor'-West, everybody said. Only Mumae did not like the idea.

Coonardoo heard her talking to Meenie about it.

"Do you mean to tell me," Mumae had said, "that child's to be Warieda's wife soon?"

"Eeh-mm," Meenie murmured in her slow, tranquil fashion.

"And you don't mind?"

Meenie did not understand.

"You're not angry about it?"

"Wiah." Meenie smiled, and talked away in her own language.

"She's a pretty young girl and you've taught her to be a good wife to Warieda?"

Meenie nodded.

"Well, it's a new idea and not a bad one, perhaps, Meenie," Mrs Bessie declared crisply. "Better the devil you know than the devil you don't know, and you'll always rule the roost, I suppose."

Meenie smiled, pleased to have made herself clear to Mumae.

"Eeh-mm," she agreed placidly.

But Mumae was not pleased. She would not accept Meenie's point of view altogether. She had been careful not to interfere with her natives in any of their own ways and customs. She tried, rather, to leave them entirely to themselves in all that did not concern her. But Coonardoo—she could not accustom herself to the idea of the little girl marrying "a great brute like Warieda", as she put it to herself.

"Well," she said decisively, "I won't have it. You tell Warieda I won't have it. Not until she's sixteen, at least——"

Meenie gasped; her eyes widened. She looked disturbed, foreseeing trouble.

"Very well," Mrs Bessie said, "I'll have a word with him."

And a word she had, several words, standing up there by the stock-yards—a small sturdy woman in her white dress and a wide straw sun-hat—having looked at a mob of young horses Chitali, Warieda, and the boys had just turned into the yards.

"Warieda!" she called. The tall, handsome aboriginal with his dark and curling lashes swung over to her and stood looking down on her shyly. "They tell me you want Coonardoo. She's straight for you?"

"Eeh-mm." Warieda's brown eyes looked Mumae in the face. Mrs Bessie realized a depth and strength in his wanting of Coonardoo. Realized, too, that Coonardoo was a more suitable wife for the young man than Meenie, who was so much older than he, old enough to be his mother.

"You know, Warieda"—Mrs Bessie found it more difficult than she had expected to say what she wished—"I am fond of Coonardoo. She is my own girl. You are fond of her too, I can see. . . . I will give her to you. But the white people say it is not good to give a girl to her husband before she is fully grown."

The dark face before her gloomed and hung, sullen and heavy.

"You are mulba, strong fellow, Warieda," Mrs Bessie said. "Good man. I will give you a horse and new blankets . . . if you wait until Coonardoo's sixteen."

Warieda's eyes lighted, he grinned good-humouredly. He was almost amused to see Mumae, the woman who was like a man, as he thought of her, so concerned and making terms with him.

"And I will give Coonardoo a horse," Mumae said, "come three musters." She held up her fingers. "Tarcoodee, bullock muster."

Warieda understood he was tc wait until after three bullock musters—for three years that was—for Coonardoo. Then Mumae would give him the horse and blankets with Coonardoo. He grinned obligingly.

Mrs Bessie was well pleased to have got her own way. She trotted back to the house where the gins were waiting and watching, having seen her talking to Warieda up there by the stockyards. She was not quite sure herself why she was so opposed to Warieda taking the girl. She did not object to the idea of Coonardoo being Warieda's woman, but to his interfering with a plan she had made—a plan attaching Coonardoo to herself and Wytaliba. To take her away, give her children just yet, would have disturbed that. But Mrs Bessie had won the day; she was satisfied for the time being. Her shrewd busy brain went on with its scheming.

CHAPTER III

EVERY year at midsummer, for as long as Coonardoo could remember, the tribes for a hundred miles about had gathered for pink-eye on Wytaliba.

The milli-millis passed from Wytaliba to Nuniewarra, from Nuniewarra to Illigoogee and Five Rivers; as far as Britte-Britte, the Gap and along the To-Morrow ranges. As often as not boys who carried letters from the Rylands of Illigoogee to the manager of Britte-Britte, asking him to spend Christmas on Illigoogee, or from Britte to Five Rivers, passed on the blacks' sticks, with their fire-marked lines and dotted hoops, crossed in the end spaces.

On Illigoogee, Britte-Britte, Nuniewarra and Five Rivers the white people feasted, sang and went mad with the whisky they drank at this time. It was Christmas they called their pink-eye, Coonardoo knew. But never since Ted Watt died had there been a party like that on Wytaliba. Mumae put up green branches and lit lanterns along the veranda, to be sure, while Charley Leigh and his wife were well-sinking at Yallerang clay-pan. They came in, once or twice, and spent a few days with her at the homestead.

But most of the time Hugh was away at school, the Leighs went to the coast for Christmas, and Mumae had only Saul Hardy with her when the blacks gathered for their summer celebrations and ceremonies.

At the uloo they ate, sang and corroboreed all day. Mrs Bessie always gave her people a beast and tuckerdoo to entertain their relations, and the women cooked the meat in great stone ovens under piles of smouldering embers.

They pounded pipeclay and red ochre, mixing them with grease for the men to decorate themselves before they corroboreed. The men drew white lines, circles and dots on their thighs and breasts, each one displaying a different pattern of dots, circles and latticed lines. After a day or so, with masks painted on their faces, the older men took the boys off into the mulga thickets, at the foot of the ridge, for the bucklegarroo ceremonies which no woman was allowed to see.

The women went singing, as they gathered wood, or dug for coolyahs along banks of the creek; the air vibrated with their excitement, the ululations of their thin quavering melodies.

"Neeroo-ran neeroo," they sang, catching the man's song and singing it over and over. As it died down, somebody set the refrain going again in a higher key. The tune faltered, worn threadbare and rumbled away—to be plucked up and flayed alive by some harsh eager voice. And so it went on all day.

During pink-eye nobody wore clothes in the uloo, wandering along the creek, or hunting across the plains and through the tussocky spinifex. Coonardoo lived with her people, as they had done before the white men drove their great horned beasts in, from the distant rim of the earth where the sun rose. Her gina-ginas were hung on sticks in the shade shed beside Mumae's kala miah, although she slipped into one every morning when she ran up to the house to give Mumae her early cup of tea.

Pink-eye or no pink-eye, Meenie always put in a couple of hours doing her usual jobs. She and Coonardoo washed and dressed before they went into Mumae's house; they swept, put the kitchen in order and went down to the uloo again.

Coonardoo loved to sit and sing with the women, at night, clicking her little sticks; and to watch the men dancing with measured steps, before the fire.

How terrified she had been when a cooboo, round-eyed and sleepy, she had first seen the narlu corroboree. From darkness far out across the plain, a squat figure had come, crouched and hopping, all his bones outlined with white, a huge shield of white bark for a face. He had hopped up to the fire, peering at the women and children sitting, singing in two rows, on the other side of the fire. On his haunches he twisted and pranced, hovering as if he intended to pounce suddenly and drag some of them off into the darkness with him.

Old Gnardadu, standing up at the end of the women, had waved her stick at him, her voice rising in anger and exultation as she threatened him. The singing of the women shrilled, thrilling and awe-stricken, although they sang of their fearlessness and defiance, until the narlu quailed intimidated and hopped away backwards, disappearing far out across the plain where the stars dropped into the earth.

The women's singing wavered, died away: one after the other, voices guttering and murmuring, until the silence flowed again.

Coonardoo gurgled and smiled to herself as she thought of it; but she was very proud of being allowed to sing in the corroborees. Her childish voice rose, shrill and high, above the voices of the women.

She liked best of all the white cockatoo corroboree, and told Mumae about it.

"White cockie, he blackfellow one time, always singing, making corroboree," she explained. "Other blackfellow, movingar steal 'm corroboree, change blackfellow always singing, making corroboree into white cockie. Now . . . all blackfellow make 'm white cockie corroboree."

Mrs Bessie had seen the corroboree. Watched Chitali, who was always chief performer, come from a screen of bushes, and dance down to the fire, under his pipeclay diagrams, flecked with down. Graceful, agile, stepping from one foot to the other, coming down on both together, with knees turned out, he played the young man "always singing", making his corroboree, boldly, gaily. Old Joey Koonarra, a tuft of emu feathers tied on for a tail, strutted and pranced behind Chitali, waving his arms and shaking himself with small jiggling steps, until Chitali fled back to the screen of bushes.

After a few moments the rest of the men led by Chitali came from the shelter, stuck all over with down and wearing cockatoos' feathers in their hair. They wheeled in before the fire like a flock of white cockatoos alighting, making a rustling as of wings, while the women's song kept up a refrain of the cockies' harsh grating cry, "Pee-taerda! Pee-taerda!" The men crouched, fluttering, and hovering beyond the firelight; then wheeled away, waving their arms and making the stiff rustling sound of wings. The women screeched "Pee-taerda! Pee-taerda!"

And how Coonardoo sang for the fire corroboree! When Warieda gave the rhythm and air of the song, in a low melodious alto, clicking his kylies and the women began to sing, Coonardoo's voice quivered with her excitement, stretched shriller and higher to the strange magic words, and fell, creaking, whispering when Chitali came from the screen of bushes behind which the men were hiding.

A red mask painted along his brows and under his eyes; rows of lines and dots between, patterned red on his middle, and in upright shields on his thighs, he sprang, high-stepping, short-stepping, with knees turned out to the fire burning to ember, snatched a stick with smouldering ends from the fire and whirled it about his head. He seized another stick, shot it like a rocket to the sky; then, taking two sticks from the fire, whirled them so that they showered sparks. Dancing into the fire he kicked out the embers.

The rest of the men, done up with red too, darted out from the dark bushes and, imitating their leader, sprang from one foot to the other. Rhythmically, and in unison, they shuffled, beating their feet against the earth. Each seized sticks from the fire, whirled them about his head, and kicked out the cinders, so that red sparks flew in every direction; while the women sang, wrought to the highest pitch of admiration and ecstasy by the grace, agility and daring of their men.

A year or two after Hugh went to school Coonardoo began to realize her growing importance in the camp. She was ten years old. Meenie told her that she would be a woman soon, and Coonardoo had heard the women exclaiming at the way her breasts began to thrust themselves out from her slim upright body.

Then one morning during a pink-eye, Warieda had told her he knew where there were bardis in a tree not far from the creek. Coonardoo went off with him to find it. Several men streaked out from the uloo after them and walked a little distance over the plains.

Shy and a little afraid, when she found herself so far from the other women, Coonardoo hung her head and turned to go back to them. But Warieda commanded her to sit down on the ground. He sat down before her, and all the rest of the men sat in a half-circle round them.

Warieda had put his hand on her breast, and smoothed the round pointed bulbs with gentle fingers. He began to sing in a low, far-away murmuring voice. He was talking and singing about her breasts, Coonardoo understood. She sat quivering and filled with excitement and mystery. Her fair head drooped, the round head cropped like a boy's with little drakes' tails of curls, twisted and turned up all over it. She knew very well that Warieda was singing to make her a woman. His hands moved round her breasts, moulding and kneading them. He pasted red ochre mixed with emu grease round the nipples, singing to make them grow quickly, be strong and full of milk to nourish her children.

The rest of the men, who were nuba to her, men to whom her father might have given her, had not Warieda obtained his promise, repeated his words and kept up an accompaniment to his singing, clicking their kylies, swaying, and muttering rhythmically. In a swooning of bewilderment and sensuous confusion, without raising the fringe of her lashes, Coonardoo could see the fierce faces of her kinsmen in all the exultation, lust and reverence of their excitement. As Warieda put his mouth to the ruddy nimbus he had made on her budding breast, Coonardoo knew that he was drawing all the thready instincts, deeply buried in her body, towards him.

"Goodness, what on earth have you been doing to your gina-gina, Coonardoo?" Mumae asked next day when she noticed red smudges on the child's blue dress.

Coonardoo hung her head and did not reply.

Mrs Bessie looked at Meenie, who smiled, nodded her head, covering Coonardoo with a glance of tender affection.

Mrs Bessie knew of this "singing to make a woman business", as she called it, and did not like it. Wandering along the far side of the creek once, she had come on a half-circle of men squatted before a little girl, and singing to her breast. They looked as if they were worshipping her, squatted there on the wide plains under the bare blue sky. And they were in their own way, she imagined, venerating the principle of creation, fertility, growth in her.

Mrs Bessie had fits of loathing the blacks. Although she had lived and worked like a man, so long in the Nor'-West, without the least respect for conventional ideas which hampered her in anything she wanted to do, her white woman's prejudices were still intact.

She was disgusted by practices she considered immoral, until she began to understand a difference to her own in the aboriginal consciousness of sex. She was surprised then, to find in it something impersonal, universal, of a religious mysticism.

From her birth every girl was destined to pass, Mrs Bessie knew, within defined lines of tarloo and descent to mateship with one of her kinsmen. Families on the creek were Banniga, Burong, Baldgery and Kurrimurra. A Banniga woman might be given to a man who was Kurrimurra. Their child would be Burong and could not mate with either a Banniga or a Kurrimurra. Beyond that there was room for choice. The men who were nuba, or noova, to her might never touch her; but they were permissable husbands in case of the death, or absence of the man to whom her father had given her. Her husband, by way of hospitality, might lend her to a distinguished stranger, or visitor, to the camp; but any children she might have would be her husband's children. The blacks, unenlightened by white people, do not associate the birth of children with any casual sex relationship.

Mrs Bessie resented these pink-eye courtesies when they touched the women of her own household, Meenie or Bandogera. After a while she began to see the aboriginal point of view, and to acquire a faint respect for the man who did not attach much importance to lending his wife's body, yet was jealous of her deeper function. Although she did not deceive herself, the aboriginal motive was probably quite practical. A cooboo was property, whether girl or boy, and added to the man's sense of power and importance.

And Mrs Bessie hated the initiation ceremonies which were performed during midsummer pink-eyes, sensing a sadism in them, a whipping-up of sexual excitement in the cruelties practised by old men on boys and girls.

On the hottest days of summer, under bare, pale-blue skies, drifts of the men's singing came to her from grey smoke-misted thickets below red bare peaks of the ridge.

> *"Neero-ran, neeroo
> Ora kaljee kaljee. . . ."

She knew that was one of the bucklegarro songs. And there was another:

> †"Choongoo choongoo cheriegoo,
> Wannerjettie gnadegoo
> Yeralger mundanie."

Whenever she heard those chants, and the murmurous boom of a coolardie, Mrs Bessie knew what was happening. Old men of the tribes away from the camp were preparing youths, by crude rites of circumcision and mutilation, for the standing of men in the camp.

* Called the Kramadee, meaning chiefly "cut".
† Meaning "Cut! Cut!"

She was always restless and irritable while that singing was going on, more particularly if one of her own boys was with the men.

"Devils! Old devils!" she muttered to herself, trying to read or sew. And was as relieved as women in the camp when men returned at sunset with, or without, the lad. Sometimes he was left in the bush to recover. It depended a good deal on the stage of his initiation and whether he had done his period of isolation from the women.

Mrs Bessie could see from her veranda when the men brought a boy back to camp, leaping about him and singing, while the women ran out to meet them with wild lamentations and gleeful, exulting cries. Mrs Bessie herself always made a fuss of Wytaliba boys when she saw them looking wan and a little exhausted after their ordeal. To the amusement of the gins, she had fed Wanna up with beef tea and large pieces of juicy steak, as she rationed men and women on the strength of the station.

Lonely and curious, occasionally, she went down to the uloo to watch the corroborees. Sitting on the far side of the fire, at a little distance from Warieda, and the rows of women, children and dogs huddled together, she had marvelled at the beauty and significance of these legendary dances done on the vast plains, under blue, star-scattered night skies.

After the fire corroboree, one night, just as she was going away, Warieda asked Mumae to stay and see the corroboree his people had never before permitted a woman to watch. Appreciating the honour implied, Mumae sat down on the earth beyond the fire again.

Part of the shadows, sitting there in the dark, she had glimpsed another world, the world mystic, elusive, sensual and vital of this primitive people's imagination. A presentiment of being part of the shadows, of the infinite spaces about her, and of the ceremonial dance itself, she banished peremptorily.

Coonardoo, crouching with the rest of the women, her head in the dust, had seen Mumae, for a moment, sitting there on the far side of the fire in her white dress. But not for worlds would she look again, believing that if she caught any sight of the forbidden dance, she would be pursued by evil spirits, haunted by bad dreams until she died. She sang with the rest of the women; Mumae could hear her childish treble among the low throbbing voices under blankets Warieda had thrown over the women.

24

Chitali danced before the fire in a head-dress like a gigantic spider-web with a veranda out from it. The spider-web, bound with white down, stood high up and jutted out from his forehead. His body streaked and patterned white and red, Chitali had gestured and danced, knees wide over the fire.

"What was it all about?" Coonardoo heard Mumae say to Saul Hardy, next day, although she dared hardly confess the eavesdropping to herself even. "I don't know. It had some sex significance, I suppose. Fire is male. They believe smoke caused by the men in these dances impregnates some female spirit of things which dispenses life—for birds, beasts, coolyahs, bardis. The abos themselves, I think."

Now and again during a pink-eye, Coonardoo had seen the gins dancing in a long line behind girls from Britte-Britte and Nuniewarra. There was a mystery and ominousness in it all which she did not fathom, until she found herself dancing, scared and naked, at the head of a long line of women under a clear starry sky.

The women danced and kept on singing until Coonardoo was ready to drop; but Bandogera with hands on her hips pushed her on, giving her little smacks on the back. When Bandogera let her go, Coonardoo had fallen asleep by her own fireside, to be awakened again by that wailing song of the women, led out by them under the starlit sky to dance in a long line before the smouldering fires again. Coonardoo was awed and a little disturbed by it all; but she would not show fear. She tried to sing and dance as well as the other women. A vague idea of what was happening had flitted across her. She was being made a woman, and must not show herself weaker, less worthy of her people than girls from Britte-Britte and Nuniewarra.

It seemed to Coonardoo that she had been dancing and singing all day and for days, all night for nights; she was worn out and half dead with sleep; but she knew it would soon be morning, stars were so faint in the sky, when the men sat round her in a ring and she was spread out on the ground before them. She remembered the time when the men had sat round singing to her breasts. Then in a flash of pain, she heard her own cry, shrill and eerie like the note of a bird.

In the morning, when Coonardoo stood beside Mumae's bed with her cup of tea, Mumae had exclaimed, "I've only just gone to sleep! They were making a terrible hullabaloo at the uloo last night, Coonardoo. What was it all about?"

Coonardoo shook her head. It was forbidden for her to speak of what had happened. And Mrs Bessie knew her people too well to press their reticences.

The child looked queer, she thought; there was a new wide-awakeness, something sombre and wise and old in her eyes.

"Oh, well, you were asleep, I suppose," Mumae said. "I'll be glad when all this pink-eyeing is over."

From Meenie she heard what had happened.

"Make 'em Coonardoo woman," Meenie explained, smiling slyly.

She was very pleased and happy about Coonardoo being a woman, it seemed.

Mrs Bessie understood what that meant. Girls of some of the Nor'-West tribes were subject to a preparation for womanhood as the boys were for manhood.

"But, why, Meenie?" she asked. "Why do they do that?"

Meenie shook her head. Perhaps she did not know, perhaps she was reluctant to talk when she sensed disapproval in Mumae's face. Mrs Bessie was clearly annoyed; her white woman's prejudices inflamed.

"Oh, well," she declared, "I think its perfectly disgusting for an old man to destroy a girl's virginity with a stone, like that."

But her anger went deeper. Mrs Bessie realized that however she might teach and train Coonardoo in the ways of a white woman, teach her to cook and sew, be clean and tidy, she would always be an aborigine of the aborigines. Not that Mrs Bessie wanted to take Coonardoo out of her element. She did not, but she was jealous of an influence on the child greater than her own. She did not wish to lose Coonardoo. Her people did not wish to lose Coonardoo either. She was theirs by blood and bone, and they were weaving her to the earth and to themselves, through all her senses, appetites and instincts.

Before Coonardoo was sixteen Mrs Bessie realized her people were right. Coonardoo was marriageable. She ought to be married. But obstinately, Mrs Bessie kept to her bargain with Warieda, and Warieda kept his bargain with her, although it was not easy.

Wiry, well-fed, lithe and graceful, her eyes as dark and velvety as a moth's wing with glittering irises, Coonardoo swung between the homestead and the uloo, disturbing both by her youth and roguishness.

As handsome and spirited as an unbroken filly, she tempted every man who saw her to the breaking and handling, knowing very well no one dared attempt it. Was she not promised to Warieda and had not Mumae forbidden him to take her? Coonardoo swaggered with a light-hearted independence and impudence, very galling to her own people. Meenie scolded; and Warieda followed her with watchful eyes, his lust glowing and blazing.

Mrs Bessie herself saw what was happening. She watched Coonardoo swinging down to the uloo one evening when she had left her gina-gina in the shade miah. Her slight brown body, straight-backed, long legged with pointed breasts, was a nymph's, cast in bronze, against the twilight sky. Coonardoo had walked, swaying, jerking her small rounded buttocks and casting sidelong glances with back-flung words at the men as she passed.

"The minx!" Mrs Bessie exclaimed to herself.

Desirable, unattainable, Coonardoo had enjoyed herself very much in those years.

After pink-eye, when she was fourteen, a young man from the hills twisted a slit stick in her hair and tried to run away with her, and there had been a fight in the uloo about it. Coonardoo held Warieda's spears, as she was entitled to, when the man from the hills stayed to fight him for her. The spears flew swiftly, silently; both men too clever and skilful to be caught by each other's weapons. The man from the hills was much younger and slighter than Warieda. He had no woman and was eager to fight for Coonardoo. She, thrilled and impressed by the strength and vigour of Warieda, had screamed and screeched furiously at the stranger.

But he was clever on his feet and smart with the kylies. His first shied past Warieda's temple; his second missed Warieda's left cheek; but Warieda's third kylie caught the young man's forehead, gashing and splitting it open, so that he lay bleeding for a long time, and slunk away to the hills next morning, as soon as he could walk. Not that the fight was over. He promised to come again and steal Coonardoo when he was stronger, Warieda growing fat and less agile.

Meenie was angry about the whole business. She blamed Coonardoo for it: said that she had been naughty and mischievous

—a hussy, in fact. But she was sulky with Mumae too, and told her no good would come of keeping Coonardoo unmated for so long, after she was ready to go to her man. At the camp, Warieda saw that nobody interfered with Coonardoo, and he was keeping his word to Mumae, the horse and blankets looming for ever in his eyes. Mumae laughed at Meenie's objection, pointing out what a fine, strong girl Coonardoo had grown.

But she was more concerned than Meenie when a messenger came from Sam Geary offering old Joey Koonarra, Coonardoo's father, a rifle, blankets and tobacco for the girl. Joey was more than tempted. He found it impossible to refuse so much wealth. It was so long since Warieda had made his bargain, and a rifle— Joey's eyes glistened.

Warieda himself dealt with the messenger, packed him off with his gifts, and came to Mrs Bessie about it, trembling with wrath and indignation, his eyes ablaze. Warieda knew well enough he would need Mrs Bessie to help him against Sam Geary, particularly as for a bottle of whisky, forbidden though it was, and a gun, Joey would do anything in the world.

Mrs Bessie sent Coonardoo to the uloo next time Sam Geary came to the homestead, and she herself gave him a piece of her mind.

"Oh, well," Geary said, "if you won't marry me yourself and let's run Wytaliba and Nuniewarra in double harness, I might as well take Coonardoo. Sarah's getting a bit old and frowsy. Besides, I thought you'd be glad to get the baggage off your hands before Youie comes home."

"I'll thank you to let Wytaliba manage its own affairs, Sam Geary," Mrs Bessie cried.

Geary guffawed. There was nothing on earth he enjoyed so much as baiting Mrs Bessie, and he had never succeeded in rousing and riling her so much as by trying to take Coonardoo away from her.

To increase his fun, as much in jest as earnest, he sent a couple of boys and an old woman to kidnap Coonardoo one night, when he knew the men were away from the camp. But she had kicked and screamed and bitten so effectively that she aroused all the women. Sam's messengers were whacked and bludgeoned into flight. And for weeks afterwards Mrs Bessie kept Coonardoo locked in the homestead bathroom at night.

Mrs Bessie would not acknowledge defeat, but she was really relieved to present Warieda with the chestnut colt on which his heart was set, after the next April muster; and to hand him a pair of grey blankets with broad green and red stripes. To Coonardoo she gave the bay mare Thetis, a little bag of boiled lollies, and a red woollen jacket to wear in the cold weather. Coonardoo was more than pleased with her presents and the importance being Warieda's woman gave her.

CHAPTER IV

BEFORE the boys mustered along the To-Morrow ranges, the following year, Coonardoo was walking about with a cooboo in her arms. A little girl, with hair of cocoon floss and tawny skin. Charmi, they called her, and very happy and delighted the young mother was with her baby.

Mrs Bessie had arranged for Hugh to do a course of engineering when he left Stratford. The Leighs were anxious to make a move. With three young children, Mrs Leigh was finding life on Wytaliba too hard and lonely. She was so discontented that for years relations between her and Mrs Bessie had been hostile and unfriendly.

"I think I've given you a fair deal, Charley," Mrs Bessie said to Charley Leigh when they discussed the trouble, "but your wife's made up her mind she needs a change. I think she does. And the children'll have to go to school soon."

And so it was decided that the Leighs would leave Wytaliba, when Hughie came home. Hugh was disappointed to find he was not going home as soon as his schooldays were over. His mother had foreseen the advantage a knowledge of machinery, the making of wells and windmills and how to keep them in order, would be to him. So when he left school, Hugh had gone into an engineering and windmill contractor's workshop in Perth for twelve months.

Very hard and meagre the life on Wytaliba had been all those years Mrs Bessie was making the station for Hugh. She earned the name of a regular skinflint. Fanny Leigh was quite right, Mrs Bessie was mean and as hard as nails, it was agreed. If a drover or prospector strayed into Wytaliba there was no whisky. And Mrs Bessie was doing well, she had mustered three hundred fats that spring, and Don Drew swore she did not get less than £10 a head for them in Karrara.

A little woman, wrinkled and weathered, with eyes of the flame in her, blue-green, clear, shining, unquenchable, she had steered the station through dry years and dust storms, rains flooding the creeks and clay-pans: good seasons and bad. But with a growing bank balance she was beginning to wear out. "It's time for Hugh to be coming home," she said.

Coonardoo and the gins knew why. For days at a time Mrs Bessie scarcely ate anything. She lived on milk and green vegetables, a little broth, and Meenie and Coonardoo had seen her doubled up with pain. Mrs Bessie tried doctoring herself: she had taken castor oil and pain-killer, but always the pain was there. She moaned and groaned half the night when she went to bed.

Everybody at the uloo was troubled. The men went about, not knowing what to do when Mumae was sick. They wandered from the stock-yards to the shade miah, from the shade miah to the harness sheds, the uloo and back again, beginning one job and going on to another.

Mumae had them up to the veranda, and gave directions for wood-gathering, burning charcoal, and trapping dingoes.

"Got 'm guts-ache," she explained impatiently, using the phrase she knew they would understand, and forbade anybody to talk of it.

Joey Koonarra trotted up from the uloo to have a word with Mumae about her sickness. As the oldest man in the camp, he was entitled to talk to her as a man and an equal. Fat and dirty; grey hair matted with grease and dust, in the grimy rags of a white shirt and once blue trousers, he came and sat down on the edge of the veranda. His eyes, namma holes in viscid orbits, glittered at her, as he swung his naked feet. Clearly, he did not like the look of this sickness, and suggested getting the moppin-garra over from Nuniewarra to try his magic on it.

"I'm not as bad as all that," Mrs Bessie declared. "I reckon I know what's the matter with me, Joey. I'm going to lie here for a bit and drink milk. Then I'll go down south, see a doctor . . . white man's moppin, that is . . . and bring Hughie home."

"Eeh-mm." The old black nodded his head, his eyes glinted through the smoke from his pipe.

Satisfied he had accomplished a good day's work, that Mumae had taken his advice about seeing a moppin-garra and getting Hughie home, he stalked away again down to the uloo.

Coonardoo's second baby was born a month or so before Mumae went south. Taller and slighter, Coonardoo was then, the restless glitter gone from her eyes; that roguish aloofness of the days when she walked with swaying hips and back-flung words. Very happy and pleased about the baby, she brought the fat, curly-headed little one to see Mumae. Warieda was disappointed the baby was not a boy; but Coonardoo gurgled happily, telling Mumae they called the child Beilaba, because she had eaten beilaba—as the little fat lizard was called—before the baby was born, and it had made her sick.

Mumae went south, as soon as she was about again, leaving Saul Hardy in charge, although she gave minute instructions as to what she expected done in her absence. A new well was to be dug at Britte-Britte, fences and yards swung out from it.

Chitali and Warieda drove her over to Karrara in the buggy with four horses. From there she would get a mail-car to the coast and go down to Fremantle by boat. Mrs Bessie told Chitali and Warieda to meet her again at Karrara in three moons.

When the third moon was a slim gilt kylie in the sky, Chitali and Warieda drove the three hundred miles in to Karrara to meet Mumae again. She was there, waiting for them; Hugh, also, a tall towny-looking young man of nineteen or twenty. And there was a girl with Mumae, who she told the boys was to be Hugh's woman some day—perhaps. Her name was Jessica.

Mumae herself looked stranger than Warieda or Chitali had ever seen her. Smaller, more shrivelled and bowed, in her black dress, new black hat and a dust-coat the colour of withered leaves. She trotted about very pleased to see them again; excited and eager to be going home, asking about everything and everybody. How was the country looking on Wytaliba? Had there been any rain? Was the well finished at Britte-Britte? And how were Meenie, Bandogera, Coonardoo and the children, Mick, Wanna, and old Joey? Flame leapt and spurted in her eyes, playing over the boys, keener, hungrier, happier, although they read something tragic and doomed in the small energetic figure.

Hugh himself looked very pleased to be going home again. The boys knew that by the way he hailed them. "Hullo, Warieda! Chitali!" And went to the horses' heads, looked the leaders over and wanted to know about them.

"A Pluto isn't he? Cripes, a good cut of a mare, that, Warieda!"

The boys grinned, delighted with Hugh for praising Wytaliba horses. It seemed but yesterday he had gone away. They knew him so well, although he had been magicked into this shape of a tall young man.

32

"Lord, Mum"—Hugh looked up at Mumae, laughing, eyes glistening—"it feels good to see them again!"

In a great hurry to be off Mrs Bessie would scarcely wait to spell the horses. She borrowed another buggy and horses, and insisted on leaving at dawn next day.

Hugh wanted to drive, of course, but knew his Nor'-West horses too well to try at the start-off. Mrs Bessie herself did not offer to take the reins. She climbed in beside Chitali, and had the luggage roped on under a dust-sheet behind her, giving Hugh and Jessica the more comfortable buggy with Warieda to drive.

Mrs Bessie had planned the journey by easy stages, so that Jessica would not be too tired, she said. Her cavalcade camped beside the wheel tracks at night, but stayed one night at Five Rivers and another at Illigoogee Station, took the fresh horses Warieda and Chitali had left on their way to Karrara, and went on. Although she passed within a few miles of Nuniewarra homestead, Mrs Bessie would not call in there. Sam Geary had been known as "a gin shepherder" for some time and a family of half-castes swarmed about his verandas. Mrs Bessie could forgive the children; but she would not meet a gin as mistress of a white man's household, or spend a night under Sam Geary's roof, if she could help it.

After ten days on the road, Hugh and Mrs Bessie looked happier and better pleased with each other and everything they saw. The girl pretended to be as pleased and as happy as they were; but Warieda and Chitali heard the uncertain note in her laughter, and saw how dismayed she looked, as the horses beat their way farther and farther over the wide plains of red earth with drifts of wind grass, yellow as the chickens Mrs Bessie was carrying in an old dress-basket.

Across the sandy swales of dead rivers, beyond the blue wall of distant hills, lying straight as if ruled against the sky, the horses plodded, the buggies lurched and swayed, coming at last to bare red hills of the Dog Toothed Ridge, the creek crossing, and to first sight of the white roofs and scattered buildings of Wytaliba homestead.

They were great days, the first days of Hugh's homecoming, from the moment Mrs Bessie stood on tip-toes on the veranda to kiss him and say: "Welcome home, my laddie. It's all yours." She waved her hand to the wide plains and far hills. "I've done the best I could with it for you."

Hugh in the grip of his joy and pride could not speak. Next morning he went round the stock-yards, store, smithy and harness sheds with Mrs Bessie, Saul Hardy, Charley Leigh, and Jessica, who stepped daintily beside him in a white muslin frock and white shoes, holding a pink silk sunshade over her head.

Mumae told Chitali, Warieda and the rest of them that Hugh was master of Wytaliba now. They were to serve and obey him as they had her, and all would be well with them. There was no word in the native dialect which meant master or boss; but the boys understood very well what Mumae wished to say.

Never again did she ride out with them. Never again gave orders. Suddenly she had shrunk into being a little old woman who wore skirts always, and rarely left the homestead verandas and garden. The blacks did not know what to make of it except that Hugh had come home.

Work of the station went on as usual. Mrs Bessie saw to that; she went over it all with Hugh and worked at her stock-book and ledger of accounts. Mrs Bessie looked very happy and satisfied with herself and the way everything was moving about her; although Meenie and Coonardoo, who knew her best, were not at all easy in their minds. They had seen new and strange bottles of medicine in Mumae's room, and knew that the pain which she had gone away to cure, still plagued and devoured her.

"My work's nearly done," she told Meenie one day. "There's just a little more I want to fix up, put in order, and then I can go. But mind you, if ever you behave badly to Hugh, any of you at the uloo, I'll come back and haunt you. . . ."

A flock of cockatoos rose from the plains and wheeled, their white wings chequering the blue sky, as they eddied towards the creek gums.

"I'll come back, like that . . . a white cockie . . . and give you bad dreams . . . guts-ache, and a pain, eating your inside out, like I've got. Do you hear, Meenie? Coonardoo . . . you'll live longer than she will. You're to look after Hughie . . . no matter what happens . . . when I've gone."

CHAPTER V

MUSTERERS were returning with a mob of young horses from the To-Morrow.

Jaded, crawling out from clouding red dust against a pale blue sky, the horses came on, swarming. Chitali, riding out in front, his big black gelding prinking and pranking as though he were leading an army, turned into the stock-yards. Coonardoo, Warieda, Mick and Hugh, stiff and stocky as wooden figures in the distance, rode in against the mob, moving it after Chitali.

Dust swirled up before the stock-yard rails, as the horses shied off from them, trying to make off over the plains again; but the stockmen chivied them a bit, hustling and jostling the strangers into the yards. Rough-haired and spent, there was not much mischief left in them. Only Warieda's chestnut stallion, resentful of being separated from the mares and young things, bucked and rooted out across the plains.

Children ran up from the uloo to meet the musterers, and Coonardoo came down from the stock-yards to them. Slight and lithe as a boy, in her faded blue trousers and shirt, red with dust, she stepped lightly over the stones, her feet bare, her hair waving back from her face, as the horses' manes had done. Gleaming like ironstone pebbles her skin was, her eyes laughing under their heavy curled lashes.

Very happy and pleased with herself, Coonardoo looked. Had she not been out on a muster with Youie and the men? She picked up the smallest of the children, her cooboo, and went to the kala miah; the children trotting along beside her.

Yes. She had been out beyond the ranges, Coonardoo explained, behind the hills where the sun went down. Blue as the dungaree of a new gina-gina they were, very far away, mysterious and impenetrable, with trees curled thick as the hair on your head all over them. Through trees and trees she had gone, up and down the steep hillsides, along them and the dry creek beds. Already she was telling the children about it. The horses she and Warieda had chased; the rock holes by which they had camped.

35

There had not been a horse muster on Wytaliba for two or three years. And when he came home, the first thing Hugh wanted to know was how many horses there were on the place, and what they were like. Mumae had bought a new stallion while she was away and Hugh was anxious to weed out crocks and old entires.

A dry year, and then Mumae's illness, was why there had been no horse muster. This was a good season in the To-Morrow, Coonardoo explained. The grass—her hand went out to the height of the grass—and she had seen a great koodgeeda among the rocks. Colour of the rocks he was, so that you could scarcely see him until he moved, then he coiled himself up. Yukki! But she was frightened.

Chitali and Mick were taking the stock-horses down to troughs near the big windmill to drink; Warieda, Wanna and Bardi moving about the shed where the saddles and bridles were hung. Hugh, turning down from the sheds, walked slowly, crooked and stiff after his first days of hard riding, his tan trousers and shirt rusty with dust, his face sun-red, and eyes a deeper blue in his face.

Mrs Bessie, coming out from the low whitewashed wood and iron of the house among dark trees, heard Coonardoo talking to the children.

"Good muster, Coonardoo?" she called.

"Eeh-mm," the girl answered. Her eyes and Mrs Bessie's met and smiled. It was a dream come true for Coonardoo and Mrs Bessie that Hugh should be at home and mustering on Wytaliba.

Coonardoo stood with her baby in her arms to watch Hugh take off his hat to kiss his mother. A neat small woman, Mrs Bessie moved beside her son's dust-stained bulk, eyes light-filled and faded to gimlet pupils as she looked into his face. Hugh's spurs made a slight silvery tinkling as he walked.

"Sam Geary's here, Hugh," she said, "and Cock-Eyed Bob. Sam's got Sheba driving the ration cart; I won't have her at the house. Like his cheek to bring her here at all."

Out from the narrow dark shelf of the veranda Sam Geary lurched towards Hugh Watt and his mother, tawny earth-stained shirt and trousers held under a heavy belly by his leather belt. Cock-Eyed Bob sidled along beside him, slight and neatly turned out, his trousers clean and shirt sun-dried.

"Youie, by God!"

Heavy and slouching, Geary steered towards Hugh, hesitated and stood, as if to walk farther were not worth the effort; and Bob stood beside him.

"Hullo, Mr Geary!" Hugh hailed him. "How's things, Bob?"

"Not too bad, Youie," Bob said.

They went on towards the veranda. Mrs Watt explained crisply, "Sam and Bob's been out prospectin', Hugh. Been out a couple of months and are on their way into Nuniewarra."

"Any luck?" Hugh asked.

"Not too bad——" Bob began.

Geary's reluctant growl rumbled. "But we near done a perish for water, You."

"The gold's there all right," Bob said, in his thin, nervously sharpened voice. "We got one good lump, Youie, and scratched about all round. But Sam got the wind up about there being no water and the camels clearin' out. So I reckoned best thing we could do was to come in for stores."

"You can have it on your own, young feller," Geary growled. "I'm through with prospectin'!"

"Misses his three square meals a day and sting," Bob explained.

"Many's the good gold-mine we've walked over—if only we knew it," Mrs Watt chirped.

The little gate, in the netted fence making an enclosure about the house clicked. The men went on past the row of shrubs, bird plant, and punti with its little yellow flowers, to the veranda.

Geary made for one of the easy bag chairs, with a framework of saplings, and Bob seated himself on the edge of the veranda, his back to a post. Hugh sat down opposite to him. Mrs Bessie trotted off along the veranda, her feet in nailed shoes rapping the boards with a quick, measured tread.

"Oh well, Youie," Geary remarked, "a good deal's happened since you went away to school——"

"Everything looks just the same," Hugh said.

"But it isn't," Sam replied. "Not by long chalks. Though I don't mind sayin', Youie, you'd have had a darned side more up-to-date property, if your mother'd let me have a finger in the pie."

Casting his eye back he discovered Mrs Bessie coming along the veranda, and Meenie behind her with a tray and glasses.

"By God, she's comin' on, your mother, You," he chortled.

37

Meenie put the tray down on a little table near Geary's chair. Mrs Bessie poured the whisky herself and passed round the glasses.

"Well, here's to us all, Youie," Sam Geary lifted his glass. "You're boss on Wytaliba now, Mrs Bessie tells me, and this is a good sign. There's been a drooth on the land, as you might say, while you've been away." He drank with gusto, put his glass down, squinting expectantly at Mrs Bessie. "And they tell me you've brought a woman home with you?"

"Not so fast, Mr Geary, if you please," Mrs Bessie objected. "They're not married yet."

From the far end, where small green three-cornered leaves of Nor'-West creeper screened the veranda from afternoon sunshine, Jessica came eagerly.

"Is that you, Hugh?" she called.

Hugh stood up.

"Come along, Jessica," Mrs Bessie replied. The girl came towards her, a slight pretty creature in a white frock sprigged with little flowers.

"Mr Sam Geary of Nuniewarra Station and Bob Hall, Jessica." Mrs Bessie jerked a hand towards the recumbent figure of Geary, and on to Bob. "Miss Jessica Haywood, to whom Hugh is engaged, Bob, and Mr Geary."

Geary struggled out of his chair, shook hands with Jessica and sat down again. Jessica said, "How do you do?" limply, shrinking from him. She disliked big unshaven men like this, and the way they seized your hand and shook it. Bob sidled over, took her hand, wagged it, and Jessica sat down beside Hugh on the edge of the veranda.

"Miss Haywood has come up to spend the winter with us. See how she likes the Nor'-West," Mrs Bessie explained.

"She has, has she?" Geary glanced from Mrs Bessie to Hugh and the girl sitting there on the edge of the veranda, looking at each other. Sam Geary saw very well what Mrs Bessie was at. So well that his eyes brightened. He gurgled again. "She has, has she?"

Mrs Bessie poured another whisky for him, fearing what he would say next and anxious to distract his attention.

Bob said no to a second drink, and Hugh had been taught to watch whisky like the devil, Sam guessed from the way he handled his glass. Mrs Bessie drove the cork into her bottle when she had poured a third glass for Sam.

"Here, missus," Geary protested, "what are you doing with that bottle?"

"No, you don't, Sam Geary," Mrs Bessie replied. "I know you of old. You're not boozin' up on my whisky—and you can say what you like about hospitality on Wytaliba."

She went off along the veranda, carrying the black bottle by the neck, as if it were a fowl whose neck she had wrung. Bob and Hugh laughed.

Sam Geary looked after her with thirsty, yearning eyes; then he laughed too, recovering his good humour.

"Great little woman, your mother, You," he said, "but she is sewed into her pants, isn't she? Remember when first she came out here, drovin' with your dad. Not more than seven stone, she was, and him more like seventeen—a big, good-lookin' bloke, but no good with horses. And she was a great horse-woman, Mrs Bessie. Met 'em once, when they was droving down Illigoogee way, and he had a young horse. 'I'll take a twist out of him, Ted,' she says, in the morning, hopping on before him. And she did too. . . ."

"You'll just have time for a shower before tea, Hugh," Mrs Watt called, returning to the kitchen.

"Right, mother!"

Hugh stretched the long legs he had laid along the veranda, dropped them to the ground and stood up.

Jessica rose when he did, sighed and tripped away again into the shadow of the Nor'-West creeper.

From his chair, Geary watched Hugh go in a leisurely swinging stride to the shed beside the windmill where the men showered.

He chuckled with derisive satisfaction.

" 'They're not married yet,' she says. What's the bettin' she means 'em to be, Bob? Mrs Bessie knew what she was doin' when she asked that damned young silver-tail to spend a winter on Wytaliba before Youie puts his head into any matrimonial noose."

CHAPTER VI

I~N~ a finely netted cage on the veranda Mrs Bessie fussed over the spread table, scolding Meenie for having left the door open and let flies in. She clouted at flies, while Sam Geary and Bob gazed at food on the table behind them, cold beef and lettuce-leaves, jam, cheese and a big round loaf of fresh bread. It smelt good. For weeks they had not eaten anything but salt meat and damper.

Meenie brought a huge enamel teapot and put it down beside cups and saucers at the end of the long table. Then she went off to the uloo. Sam Geary and Bob heard Mrs Bessie calling after Meenie and Coonardoo, and their fluted replies as the girls drifted away over the darkening earth.

Sunset passed from glittering brassy light to amber and ember behind the blue-black humped backs of the hills. Hugh strolled to the veranda in white moleskins and pale-blue shirt. Jessica fluttered up from her room.

"Come along!" Mrs Bessie called. And everybody walked across the veranda into the dining-room.

Seated at the end of the table, with its white cloth and array of china dishes, Hugh served his mother and Jessica, carved huge junks of beef for Sam and Bob, loaded their plates with salads, and cut slices of bread for everybody.

Mrs Bessie chatted happily, lifting the heavy teapot and pouring out cups of tea.

"By God, it's good to see a feed like this, missus," Geary said, and ate steadily.

Cup after cup of tea Mrs Bessie poured, and Hugh carved again for Sam, who slapped fresh bread with butter, his jaws working, tongue thrashing up and down, as he ate and talked.

On the veranda, again, stretched and smoking, he swapped yarns and gossip of the countryside with Mrs Bessie. Hugh went out from the veranda a little and threw himself flat on the earth. Jessica brought a cushion and sat down near him. Bob perched on the veranda, where he could stare at Jessica without her noticing. So lovely and rare a creature she seemed to him.

The moon, rising over the dark edge of the plains, was large as a dray-wheel, red-gold. It moved through a sky clear green with the glimmer of still water, extinguishing the stars, chasing them to depths of the high dark. The stock-yards, sheds and windmills were clear in the moonlight; corrugated-iron roofs and fans of the windmill had a white radiance. Huts of the blacks, just visible, were low mounds against the earth near the creek; their camp-fires, red jewels in the distance. A subdued murmur and drift of singing, clicking of kylies came from them.

"You live well on Wytaliba, missus," Geary grunted. "Time was. . . ."

"Yes, Sam," Mrs Bessie said. "Time was, that's why."

Geary seethed to his reminiscence; his eyes rounded and gleamed.

"Remember when you and Ted was drovin' for Weelarra?"

He looked across at Hugh, where he lay looking up into the sky.

"Ted'd drive the ration cart and she'd drive the bullocks with a couple of boys—black imps—about ten and twelve," he said. "And when some of the chaps got on to Ted for letting Mrs Bessie ride after the bullocks, she said, 'Here, what are you chippin' about? When Ted's with the ration cart I know where he is, and when I'm with the bullocks he knows where I am.'"

Mrs Bessie chuckled. "Well, it was the truth, wasn't it?"

"Too right, it was the truth, missus," Geary agreed. "But it was rough on the roads those days." He liked watching Hugh's face, the pride and shame of it, as the boy listened to these stories of his mother. "Damper and salt meat was all we had to eat, with a bit of 'roo steak or wild turkey now and then. She'd cook, too, Mrs Bessie, but she didn't like cookin'. 'Here,' she'd say to Ted, 'you get the breakfast, and I'll get the bullocks.'"

"Course," Geary continued pleased to have the floor, "she could do pretty near anything, Mrs Bessie. When Ted was well-sinking she'd wind dirt for him, or shovel down the well. But she didn't like cooking!"

"Oh, go on, Sam Geary!" Mrs Bessie exclaimed. "I never had any wages for cooking till we worked for you."

"How about the morning Gingee got up to his tricks?"

"How about it?" Mrs Bessie exclaimed, and Geary laughed, his laughter rattling and rumbling through him.

"By God, I never laughed so much as when Ted told me about it," he said. "They were bringing cattle down from Weelarra, during a drought. Poor as sticks, they were—and didn't need watching at night. Ted had them black imps with him; Gingee used to wear an old coat of Ted's the sleeves coming right over his arms . . . and he was full of tricks."

"No matter what clothes you gave him, he'd manage to lose or swap them for something else," Mrs Bessie protested.

"One morning she went out after the bullocks: they'd mooched off a bit," Geary went on, "and took Gingee with her. Sent him one way and she went the other, and when she'd rounded up her mob, thought he'd be joining her, what did she do, but find him playin' round where she'd left him . . . and the bullocks gone to glory."

"I was that mad," Mrs Bessie explained, "I rode right into camp and told Ted."

"And he was so mad, he grabbed her horse and rode after the kid," Geary said. "Gingee guessed he was in for it, when he saw Ted coming, and lay on his back . . . flapped his arms, with ends of the sleeves coming right over, at the horse. The horse shied, propped and shot Ted fair over his head. The kid, quick as greased lightning, jumped on to the horse and galloped back to Mrs Bessie. 'Don't let him give me a hiding,' he yelped. She was much too anxious about what had happened to Ted to worry about him. 'Well, you get after them bullocks, and I'll let you off this time,' she said. She went for Ted, and the kid had the bullocks moving along the road towards midday."

The yarning went on and on. Geary liked the sound of his voice, and Mrs Bessie enjoyed talking about those old days of hers.

Jessica, wearying of the talk and Hugh's absorption in it, walked along the veranda to Mrs Bessie's sitting-room, in which a carbide light fluttered and flared faintly. As she began to play the old piano there, Bob stalked off to the harness shed, where he and Sam had left their packs.

Moonlight, drenching the plains with dim silvery light, lay pure and hard on the veranda; an angle of the roof and the bush miah cast black diagrams.

Jessica was singing as she played. The piano gave out a feeble rattle of loose keys, and she sang in a high, light, melancholy voice:

> "In the garden of tomorrow
> Will the roses be more sweet,
> Will there be relief from sorrow?"

Mrs Bessie disliked the song. It annoyed her unspeakably, its sentimentality, moping and groping after something you had not. And Jessia was always singing and wailing as if she meant it:

> *"Oh, I'd so much rather*
> *All life's roses gather in the garden of today. . . ."*

Little fool! Who wouldn't? Mrs Bessie asked herself. But was there any chance of gathering all life's roses in the garden of today? She hated weaklings, a poor spirit; hoped to goodness Hughie did not mean to marry this girl. It would be disastrous if he did.

Yet she could not ask Hugh not to marry Jessica. That would be foolish, she realized. Mrs Bessie had set herself boundaries in her dealing with her son. There were barriers she would not break down. His life as a man, his man's life, she left to him. She did not intend to interfere, butt in, if all was going well with him. Long ago she had decided she would have no right to. She had tried to influence Hugh as a child, give him a compass of common sense, and cleanliness, moral and physical, to steer by. That was all. She did not inquire how he applied them; she could only judge, and was fairly satisfied.

Bob walked in from the moonlight beyond the garden, a violin and bow in his hand. He sat down on the veranda again, plucked the strings and turned keys, trying to tune his instrument.

"Give it a bone, Bob," Geary cried.

"I like a bit of music myself," Hugh murmured.

"Near drove me silly out there in the To-Morrow," Geary growled. "He was worse than the blacks with his yowling."

"You two 've had it your own way, yarning," Hugh said. "How's it for a tune, Bob?"

"What'd you like, Youie?" Bob looked up, his thin face eager. He was vain of his music, loved the wooden instrument he had made himself when Geary, in a drunken frenzy, had smashed the fiddle which was the joy of his life.

"What he wants to be always twiddling and sawing away at that thing for, I don't know," Sam said.

Bob's music was flat and strayed from the air it was after, as often as not. But Hugh found in it something Bob found, the voice of a mystery beyond them. Bob's music was Bob, all his hurt, wistful, sentimental soul, lying, swaggering, fighting to preserve the decencies, fend for itself.

43

With his instinct of a countryman to read tracks on earth and faces, Hugh knew why Bob clung to his violin—and to Sam Geary. Any mate is better than none when a man has nothing and nobody to attach himself to.

The marvel was what Bob had done with his life. A weak and sickly child with a shrunken limb and one side of his face twisted, he had been left on Illigoogee when his mother died there. She had been working as cook and housekeeper for the Rylands, and as nobody knew to whom to return the child, or anywhere to send him, Bob grew up on the station learning to do any odd jobs and make himself generally useful as he grew older.

He had come to be a good horseman and handy about a cattle camp: prided himself on his feats with cattle and horses and lied about them so whole-heartedly, clanking about with spurs on and the largest size in Ashburton felts, that he was known as Bob the Liar, almost as much as Cock-Eyed Bob.

If you asked for Bob Hall, folks east of Karrara scarcely recognized whom you meant; but everybody knew Bob the Liar, or Cock-Eyed Bob. He had knocked about the country with teamsters and Afghans, camel punching, and learnt a good deal, prospecting with old miners round about Nullagine and the Bar. After a while the will-o'-the-wisp gleam of dull metal in dry creek beds, and on the shingly ridges, drew him away from the road and the cattle camps. Bob was haunted by dreams of the gold he would find one day in rich deposits; the fortune he would make.

Hugh admired and respected the grit and spirit in that slight, crooked body. He could make allowances for the swagger and lies with which Bob bucked himself up; and watched curiously in half-hearted affection as Bob bent over his instrument, trying to pick up the air Jessica was singing. She came to the door of the sitting-room to see who was fingering a violin.

As she stood in the doorway, Bob looked up; but no one else turned or glanced in her direction. Jessica wondered whether Hugh and his mother had heard her singing even. Very delicate and blossomy she looked, there in the darkness with the pale light flickering behind her.

"How'd the muster go, Hugh?" Mrs Bessie asked.

"All right." Hugh's voice spurted lazily. "There's a lot of poor stuff in the mob. Some good young things too. But we had to get 'em!"

"Shirked mustering horses these three years." Mrs Bessie smiled across at him.

"A mob led Chitali and me up a steep hill once, all rocks," Hugh said. "We rode them to a standstill on the top. 'Got to get 'em down now,' Chitali said. And away he went——"

"Case of every man for himself?" Saul grunted.

"That's right, Saul," Hugh said.

Jessica walked over and sat down beside Bob, asked him about his violin, and he played to her while Hugh talked.

"Warieda and I got ahead, steadied and held 'em," Hugh went on. "We waited for Chitali, waited and waited, but he didn't come. Thought something had happened to him. After a bit I went back looking for him . . . and there he was on the top. His horse had gone sulky, wouldn't gallop any more."

"Saturn, I'll bet," Mrs Bessie said. "He's like that, a sulky brute; but Chitali thinks no end of him."

"What do you know about that?" Geary murmured.

"Got the rest of the mob next evening," Hugh drawled. "Most of them, at any rate. But we had to turn in some coaches."

"Wild as hawks them To-Morrow horses," old Saul muttered. "I told your mother, Youie, we'd oughter mustered them before."

"Oh, well, we'd a great go," Hugh said. "Knocked up most of our nags. Hermes was tenderfooted, and so was Coonardoo's mare."

"Coonardoo?" Geary exclaimed. "Great horseman, isn't she? Been after that gin since she was so high."

"Mr Geary!" Mrs Bessie spoke sharply. "I think you forget where you are."

Geary chuckled, delighted to have vexed Mrs Bessie.

"Your mother, Youie," he rumbled, "don't approve of me emulating the patriarchs. But what I say is, man was not made to live alone. And in a hot country. . . . Monogamy's all right for cold climates—perhaps. But when climatic conditions approximate to the Biblical, well, I say, it's all right to do as Solomon did, or Abraham, or David. . . ."

"We know what you think, Sam Geary, and we are not interested," Mrs Bessie declared.

"All self-taught," Bob was explaining to Jessica. "And I made this fiddle myself."

"Just fancy," she murmured. "Why?"

Geary wrenched himself from the comfortable sagging bottom of his chair.

"Don't mind if I do, Youie," he said, squinting broadly at Mrs Bessie. But she refused to produce any more whisky. And Sam trundled off, muttering and grumbling, to the shed where he insisted he would sleep better, although Mrs Bessie was aware he would make in a roundabout way for the creek, and stretch under the ration cart with Sheba. Sam liked to sleep in the open without a stitch on during the hot weather, she knew. Hugh pulled a bed for Bob on to the veranda.

CHAPTER VII

I$_N$ the big yard of the stock-yard the horses Hugh and the boys had brought in were moving restlessly. Slender stalks of legs, bodies chestnut, bay, brown and black, crowding, hustling, seething; heads alert, turned and glancing, wild eyes slewing, startled; manes and tails tossed and waving, an ace, arrow-head or splash of white flashing out from dark foreheads. Blowing and snorting, the mob went round the yard, backwards and forwards, raising a fog of dust.

When Geary and Cock-Eyed Bob walked up to have a look at the horses with Hugh, the boys were turning mares and foals from the mob into the next yard. Warieda and Chitali singled out the foal they were after, ran him round the yard until he was separated from his mother, then the gate of the crush opened. The young thing found himself between the high rails of a narrow yard just big enough to hold a horse. A gate at the farther end opened; he bounded into the round yard; Wanna slammed the gate and swung a chain across the posts.

Geary and Bob stood up against the rails, inspecting the horses.

Hugh had his horse-book. A fire was smouldering in a log beside rails of the pound. Branding irons were in the fire. Caught by a running noose in the hide rope Chitali and Mick held a colt against the fence. Warieda, on the other side, passed an iron through to Hugh, who held the brand to the colt's near shoulder. Wanna swung the gate and the colt galloped back to his dam.

"Cooked him that time, Youie!" Geary yelled jocosely.

Hugh, entering the name and description of the colt, with the number of his mare, in the horse-book, did not speak.

The boys had a chestnut filly ready for him. He jabbed her shoulder with the T.7W, numbered her on the neck and entered name and number in his horse-book.

Children from the uloo had come to play in the shade of the brushwood shed. They dashed behind Sam Geary and Bob, limbs gleaming through the torn rags of their garments. Charmi had picked up the horns of a dead bullock and, with it on her head, was rushing the other children. Eddy and scream of the children's laughter flew out from the shadow of the thatched shed, going all through the breaking and branding.

"He's a good-looker, Youie," Geary called as a four-year-old stallion, dark bay, galloped madly round the pound, snorting, stopping to gaze with wild terrified eyes through the barred circle of the yard.

"Not too bad," Hugh agreed.

Caught by the flying noose of Chitali's hide rope the horse galloped more madly than ever. Banging against walls of the yard, throwing himself down in the dust, he squealed like a pig. The brand fixed, black on his hide, with tail stuck out, head held stiff and straight up, stepping short and high, he was turned from the pound into the next yard.

All the morning Hugh and the boys were busy branding and gelding. While Bob gave a hand Geary stretched on the ground of the shed watching the horses and children.

"Coonardoo's kids aren't they, the two little girls?" he asked.

"Eeh-mm," Hugh replied, busy with his book.

A filly, flashing and sprightly, dashed into the pound. She rushed round the yard, banging the walls, trying to jump them, scrambling up and falling back, squealing and blowing.

"What'll we call her, Warieda?" Hughie asked.

"Coonardoo's mare Thetis grow'm."

"She did, did she?" Hugh looked up. "Let's call her Thetis, the second, then . . . and give her to Coonardoo, from me."

Warieda grinned.

"Mother's a darn sight better at names than I am," Hugh explained to Geary. "I'll have to read up these Dago goddesses a bit."

At midday the talk round the dinner-table was all of breaking, branding, and the horses in the yards.

"Wild as hawks, they are right enough, missus," Geary told Mrs Bessie. "And not much good. I noticed a couple of bumble-foots among them."

"Drought foals," Saul Hardy muttered. "They get it gallopin' when the feed's scarce. Youie says there's a few good Hera colts, though."

"Too right. I liked the filly he gave Coonardoo!"

"Coonardoo?"

"It was to please Warieda. . . ." Hugh looked across at his mother.

48

Gift of a horse from Sam Geary to a gin, her father, or husband, would mean that he expected her to be sent to his camp, Mrs Bessie knew only too well. She knew, also, nothing of the sort was in Hugh's mind when he told Warieda that Coonardoo might consider the Thetis filly hers. Hot colour flamed in Hugh's face as he glared across at Geary. He was young enough to detest Geary's insinuation. A boy with a swag of ideals, Hughie was still, Mrs Bessie realized.

"Warieda said the filly was out of Coonardoo's mare, Thetis," Hugh went on. "And the mare got fairly knocked up while we were out. I reckon——"

"Coonardoo's fairly earned this filly," Mrs Bessie broke in. "So do I, Hughie."

"Well, I reckon you treat your gins pretty well on Wytaliba," Geary said. "Not long before you're treatin' 'em as well as we do on Nuniewarra."

"Aw, shut-up," Bob muttered.

He smiled at Jessica vaguely, and she smiled at him sensing something infinitely delicate in his feeling for her isolation among all these strange people.

"Are you going to give me a horse, Hugh?" Jessica asked, in the awkward silence about her.

Geary spluttered.

"Come up to the yards and choose one for yourself this afternoon," Hugh said.

His glare at Geary held fire. Mrs Bessie caught his eye and held it, her gaze wavered to Jessica. Hugh understood and controlled himself. He was sitting at the head of his own table and recognized what was expected of him.

"I'll have something to say to you when we've finished dinner, Mr Geary," he said.

Jessica's gaze passed from one to the other of the men, as if they were talking in a language she did not understand. She glanced at Mrs Bessie, whose eyes lay on Sam Geary, cursing him, if ever a curse lay in grey-blue eyes with a clear and steady stare. Geary, however, looked as if he were thoroughly enjoying himself. His raw pink face glowed; his eyes popped and swam joyously, as he sat there, teasing Mrs Bessie and appreciating Hugh's discomfiture.

Chitali had a colt in the pound when Mrs Bessie and Jessica

went up to the yards, after their afternoon rest. A mad, wild young thing, well made, big in the bone, with short back, deep barrelled, he beat round and round the rails, scarcely visible for dust.

In the yard behind, Warieda and Mick were singling the Thetis filly from a score or so of mares and young horses. Turning this way and that, the mob surged and swayed. Over and over again the filly with swift cunning dashed past the gate into the crush which Wanna held back for her. Then Warieda cut her off; there was only the open crush-gate to make for. Wanna slammed the gate on her dancing quarters, and the filly found herself jammed in the narrow yard before she knew where she was.

Geary, Bob and Hugh were standing talking, out from the stock-yard, as Mrs Bessie and Jessica came up from the house. Hugh opened a gate for them, and they went across to the brushwood shed. Mrs Bessie spread the little camp-stool she liked to sit on while she watched the boys and horses in the yards and Jessica sat on a log beside her.

Chitali had let the young horse in the round yard go until he was blown. Tall and spidery, long legs in blue trousers, greyblue shirt tucked into his belt, elastic-side boots pulled over the end of his pants, and felt hat tucked under at either side, he approached the horse.

Standing in the centre of the yard, a long pole in his hand, Chitali stretched it out and laid it on the back of the young horse. But away the colt flew as the pole touched him; Chitali swung round and round with the pole and the galloping horse. He rubbed the pole over the horse, up and down, down and up; then he slipped a halter on the end of his pole. As the horse stood trembling and blowing, Chitali rubbed the halter on the end of the pole, over his wet dark back, dropped the halter over the horse's head, threw the pole round which the rope had been twisted to the ground, and held the colt by a hide rope. Away the wild thing went again.

The Thetis filly was throwing herself about frantically in the crush between the pound and the big yard, although there was not room for her to turn in it.

"Yukki!" Coonardoo called, watching her with the children, from the far side of the big yard. And there was the filly, clambering and scrambling over the high rails of the crush. She raced round the outer yard and was over the six-railed fence like a bird, away and flying across the plains. Warieda and Wanna went after her, taking saddled horses from the outer fence of the stock-yard.

"She's a bird, not a horse, Coonardoo," Mrs Bessie called.

"Sooner you handle 'em when they're wild and gallopin' the better!" Geary shouted.

Hugh lit his pipe and pulled on it. He had only just taken to a pipe. It comforted and soothed him to smoke; a pipe gave him a sense of age and assurance. He had said his few words to Sam Geary after dinner, and felt better for them.

"See here, Mr Geary"—Hugh had not beaten about the bush at all—"I'll thank you never to speak again at my mother's table, and before a girl, as you did today."

"What are you givin' us, Youie?" Geary expostulated. "Have I got to mind my bloody p's and q's when I open me mouth on Wytaliba these days?"

"Too right you have," Hugh assented.

"You're one of these god-damned young heroes. No 'black velvet' for you, I suppose?"

"I'm goin' to marry white and stick white," Hugh said, obstinate lines settling on either side of his mouth.

Geary laughed.

"Oh, you are, are you?" he jeered. "What do you think of that, Bob? Well, I'll bet you a new saddle you take a gin before a twelvemonth's out—if ever you're in this country on your own."

From the grey fringe of the mulga Warieda and Mick had turned the filly and were bringing her to the yards.

Jessica left her own log by the fence, and climbed to the top rail of the stock-yard to watch them. Hugh went to stand near her. Through Jessica he intended to keep faith with himself. Beside her he felt safe from Geary's sneer.

"No stud gins for mine—no matter what happens," he swore to himself, disturbed and irritated.

Slowly, carefully, with infinite patience and perseverance, in the round yard, Chitali had imposed a bridle on the colt he was breaking. The colt, moving restlessly, shifted the saddle, bucked it off. But at last Chitali had crupper and saddle in position; girth and surcingle were fastened. He crawled over the horse. Wanna opened the gate. Horse and rider dashed into the big yard. Up and down it the colt went, slewing, rooting, pig-jumping, while

Chitali sitting back, grinned complacently. Anticipating every move, swerve and dive, he rode until the horse stood in his tracks.

"How do you like it?" Hugh asked Jessica.

"Oh, it's fascinating, isn't it, Hugh?" she cried breathlessly. "But I'm scared to death. Are you sure he won't get hurt?"

"Chitali?" Hugh laughed. "This is child's play to him. He's broken more horses than any man on Wytaliba; but Warieda's better than he is, really. How would you like this horse?"

"I'd love him!" Jessica gasped. "But I'd never dare to ride him."

"He's called Nessus," Hugh said, "and he's yours. Chitali'll handle him until he's fit for you to ride. We brought in old Hera yesterday. Coonardoo says she's as good as gold yet; can be trusted to behave herself. What about going for a ride tomorrow?"

"Oh, Hugh." Jessica hesitated. "I'd love to! But you know I'm terrified of your horses up here."

"You'll soon get over that." Hugh was watching Chitali through the rails.

"You got him where you want him now, Chitali," he called. "Of course, we ought to mouth 'em a bit first," he added to Jessica. "Let a young horse stand with roller and ticklers for a day or so before he's ridden. The boys are just showing you what they can do."

Chitali dug heels into the colt's sides, let him play about, kick and screw till he was tired, then rode him into the yard and let him go there, to chew over his bit. Taking a pipe from his belt, Chitali lit up, and swung over towards the round yard into which Warieda had turned the Thetis filly.

Pressed against the fence, near the killing yard and the gallows, Coonardoo too was waiting to see Warieda handle the bright bay filly with jetty mane, tail and socks. The boys had told her Hugh said the Thetis cooboo was to be hers. In her dark-blue gina-gina, eyes wide and radiant, Coonardoo watched the filly bend nearly double racing round the pound, beating the earth into a haze. Twice the filly tried to climb the fence, and the third time, scrambling and clambering, over she went, alighting on the far side; but the boys had her before she could fly the fence of the outer yard, and turned her back into the crush and the pound again. How everybody laughed and exclaimed! It had been done before, but not many horses contrived to scale the high rails of Wytaliba pound.

In the centre of the yard Warieda stood watching, as the filly dashed round and round, becoming giddy fell in the dust, picked herself up and went on again. Gradually her pace slackened. As if she had got used to sight of the man, standing there in his blue trousers, striped shirt and old grey felt hat, the little mare stood off from him, blowing and snorting, dripping sweat, wild-eyed and apprehensive

Warieda held himself quite still, waiting and watching her. He spoke quietly, moved towards her. The filly shied and fled from him; but again and again Warieda went through the same movements, uttered the same word.

At last, arresting, magnetic, with a greeting, like a brumby boss, head thrown back, eyes challenging the wild bright eyes before him, his own as wild and bright, Warieda went up to the horse, his arm, the dark sinewy arm of a black that was like the branch of a tree, stretched out before him. Imperious, irresistible, he approached, something swaggering, gallant, of a triumphant lover, in his attitude. His hand going straight to brain communicated the spell of the man, in language of the flesh, an old forgotten flow of instincts. Warieda was nearer to the horse than any of the white men about him. Handsome, aboriginal as he was, that was perhaps the secret of his power.

Warieda's hand reached the forehead under the forelock of silky black hair. The filly quivered and broke away; but came up again when Warieda held out his arm with thin fine fingers stretched. Talking quietly, Warieda moved closer to the horse. Gently, every gesture slow, restrained, he rubbed her between the eyes, under the forelock, along the nose; the little mare snuffled the dark hand, so caressing, reassuring, sleeking and rubbing her. It passed over and over her thick-haired pelt which had known no touch but the wind's, or a leafy branch, on the hills.

With her sensitive nose the filly sniffed Warieda; nostrils, flaring scarlet butterflies, went over the man; her lower lip quivered.

And Warieda talked murmurously.

"Wiah! Wiah! Menoo, yienda Thetis cooboo!"

Rails of the stock-yard were hard and dark against the light-blue fall of the sky, as Warieda stood there talking to the horse, caressing and rubbing her, while she quivered to him, her tail stuck out, the long tail of a wild two-year-old.

"It's a miracle," Sam Geary said. "I never seen anything like

Warieda's horse-breakin' in all me born days, and I seen Jim Penny and some of the best of them."

"Warieda was Jim's boy for years," Mrs Bessie said, "and learnt all he knows of horse-breaking from him."

The filly and Warieda stood caressing, embraced. He put his arm over her head: she seemed content to stand smelling him.

"If anybody told me that could happen to a horse, jumpin' the stock-yard rails half an hour ago, I'd have said he was a liar, a bloody liar," Sam remarked cheerfully.

After the bridle was on, carefully, steadily, Warieda lowered a saddle across the mare's back. She shivered, and shied the saddle off. Fled, but returned as Warieda called: came up to him again.

She threw the saddle, and again and again, with infinite patience, Warieda went over each gesture and movement, fondling and rubbing her, until the saddle sat forgotten on her back. Catching the swinging end of the girth with a piece of hooked wire lying on the ground and holding the filly by one ear, he tightened the girth and surcingle; then adjusted the crupper. The filly jumped and kicked. Warieda fell to miss her swift-flung heels, as she dashed bucking and rooting round the pound.

"She'll deal you a full hand, Warieda," Hugh exclaimed.

Warieda smiled.

"A Thetis filly all right, eh, Coonardoo?" Mrs Bessie called.

Coonardoo smiled at her, the slow, equable smile of her pride and happiness.

"Thetis was by Ironstone. You remember the big bay Ted got off Britte-Britte?" Mrs Bessie said to Geary.

"Remember?" Geary growled. "Didn't Ted lend him to me once, the brute. He'd go for a bit and start buckin' again."

"Had a horse once, bucked for a mile," Bob said. "It was when I was on Illigoogee. He'd begin with a flyin' root and a couple of high bucks . . . and go on buckin' and rootin' in a circle. Knocked himself up buckin'. Did in his fetlock and had to be left out on the run."

"Go on?" Hugh's eyes were on the yard where Warieda had left the Thetis filly against a fence to chew over her bit, and get used to the feeling of girth and crupper before he rode her.

Nobody believed Bob's yarn, or took much notice of it. It passed for one of Bob's lies and fell flat. Bob looked apologetically towards Jessica and seemed to shrink a little. He knew he was lying and

54

that everybody else knew he was lying. But Jessica—he hoped she did not think so. It was for her he had told the story; to loom a little in her eyes.

Mrs Bessie got up, shaking her white skirt, folded up the stool she had been sitting on while she watched horses and men through the rails.

"Oh, well," she said, "I'd sooner watch Warieda horse-breaking than do anything I know."

CHAPTER VIII

IT was washing day and the gins were sitting beside wash-tubs on the shady side of the veranda, rubbing dirty clothes with coarse station-made soap on which the caustic soda had rimed.

They rubbed and slapped trousers and shirts, handkerchiefs, sheets, towels, and table-cloths, slowly, lazily, talking together, looking out over the plains, seeing all that was going on at the sheds and at the stock-yard, nearly half a mile away, where the boys were still handling and breaking young horses.

Meenie, Bandogera, Bardi and Coonardoo, they were all there. Coonardoo's laughter could be heard, every now and then, a ripple and throwing out of merry little sounds. Bardi laughed too, but slowly, with a flat low gurgling. Only Coonardoo's laughter danced and sang.

Meenie looked across at Coonardoo with eyes which spoke for her, and Coonardoo's eyes made talk with Meenie's, the affection and understanding between them deep and placid. Only old Bandogera, the wild turkey, did not smile; she went on pounding and thrashing dirt from the clothes as if it were solemn and awful work she was engaged in. Her thin brown stalks of fingers writhed and twisted among men's garments, blue and buff trousers and shirts, very greasy and stiff with dust, which would not come clean without a tussle. Meenie had Mumae's white dresses and underclothing in her tub, and Coonardoo swished the soft muslin things, silk and laces, Mumae had given her to rinse through rain water, with softer soap, in one of the flat tin milk-dishes.

Bandogera chased off children from the uloo who had come to play round the wash-tubs. Coonardoo suggested they should look for eggs the white hens might have laid in the wood-heap, and the little ones ran off, throwing a word or two back to her over their shoulders.

Coonardoo's laughter rippled, as she held up Jessica's dainty garments. Meenie and Bardi exclaimed and laughed with her. Only Bandogera went on rubbing grease and red earth from

Hugh's and Saul Hardy's trousers, as if this was the only part of the washing that mattered at all.

A little distance out from the veranda, an oil-drum of water steamed over a fire, between large stones. Meenie took her tub of light white things out to it.

Up at the sheds Geary's camels were standing ready to move off. Bob mounted first and swung away, against the sky, great tawny beast moving slowly, a younger camel strung behind. The camel Geary was to ride crouched on the ground waiting for him to seat himself. Already Sheba and the ration cart were at the creek crossing. She had driven off as soon as Bob brought the camels in.

The gins talked about Sheba and Sam Geary as they rubbed and wrung clothes in their wash-tubs. Sheba had been with Geary two or three years now. She kept the keys of the store-room. Before Sheba there had been Sarah and Tamar. Now Sheba and Tamar both had corrugated-iron huts on Nuniewarra, although Sheba spent most of her time at the homestead with Sam. She made tea for visitors, and Geary took her with him when he went into Karrara, engaged rooms for her at the hotel and gave her money to buy silk dresses. She went to the races with him. But here in Wytaliba, Sheba had to eat at the kala miah with the other gins.

All the evening before, Sheba had crouched in the dark by the wood-heap, while Sam sat talking with Mrs Bessie and the men on the veranda, too afraid to stay after dark beside the ration cart, and waiting until Sam should say good night and stalk off, to follow him, make a fire and go to sleep herself under the ration cart.

Wytaliba women laughed at, exclaimed over, but did not envy Sheba.

From the other end of the veranda Jessica and Mrs Bessie watched the camels swing away, the great, slow, unwieldy beasts, their heads raised as though scenting the distance.

Hugh walked out from the barred rails of the stock-yard, waving his hand to Bob. Bob waved and called back to him.

Geary shouted, swaying to the slow lurching gait of his camel, "A new saddle to a case of black and white, Youie!"

"What does he mean?" Jessica asked.

The words had floated to the veranda on the still clear air.

"Oh, it's a bet, I suppose," Mrs Bessie replied testily. She had heard that bet before, but never of a young man winning his saddle.

"I wish it were me! I wish I were going too," Jessica cried, watching the camels dwindle, obliterate themselves in low clouds of red dust.

She began to cry.

"I can't bear it, Mrs Watt!" she exclaimed. "I really can't!"

"Oh, my dear——" Mrs Bessie's voice was very quiet, though her joy suffocating. "I'm sorry. You'll have to tell Hugh."

"It's not a bit of good. I could never marry him and live here!"

"Poor child!" Mrs Bessie did not know quite what to say. She did not wish her joy, or shrewd reckoning, to be obvious. And she was sorry for the girl who had not found beauty and peace in the long quiet days and work of Wytaliba. Bare and hard the life was; but Mrs Bessie loved every phase of it, every line of the trees, every light and colour of red earth and pale-blue sky, dove-grey mulga, and white-barked creek gum-trees with their long dark pointed leaves.

"It's so ugly and—empty," Jessica sobbed. "There's nothing to do . . . nowhere to go. Even Hugh isn't the same . . . and I don't see him for weeks at a time."

"I understand." Mrs Bessie was dying to say, "I thought you'd feel like that about it." But she would not allow herself to.

Jessica said it for her.

"I believe you're glad," she gasped. "I believe you knew I'd feel like this."

"Well," Hugh's mother murmured gently, "I wanted to be sure. Hugh belongs here and loves the country. So do I; but it isn't easy to get used to—if you really don't like it."

"I'd like to like it. I have tried to get used to it," Jessica cried regretfully. "Mother'll be awfully cross with me."

The fibres of Mrs Bessie's being tightened. She knew, of course, what was at the back of all this. Hugh was being made a convenience of.

"Oh, well," she explained crisply, "you'll have better chances than Hugh, I'm sure, my dear. You see, this is a very poor station really, heavily mortgaged. It's never done more than pay its own way. And we've had bad seasons and bad seasons on end. Sometimes I wonder if it's ever going to rain again."

Jessica's forehead wrinkled to her perplexity and concern.

"Mother thought, of course, you were wealthy. All station people have pots of money."

58

As they washed and chattered, the gins had seen Mumae and Jessica talking, near the shadowy screen of the Nor'-West creeper, hung with the tiny yellow and vermilion lanterns of its seed-pods. Looking under their eyelashes at Mumae and the girl who was to be Hugh's woman, they guessed something was wrong, exclaiming and gossiping together.

Meenie and Bandogera exchanged ideas on the subject. Coonardoo stared at Jessica who had dropped into one of the bag chairs and was crying helplessly. This girl did not want to be Hugh's woman. She was filled with amazement. She, Coonardoo, had thought any girl would be proud and very pleased for Hugh to take her.

Jessica wept and wept.

"Wiah!" Coonardoo exclaimed to herself, ashamed because Jessica could be so stupid as to cry like that.

The satisfaction of her morning was shadowed by the shadow threatening Hugh. She knew the ways of white men were different from the ways of her own people. Jessica had talked of going away. Was Hugh to lose his woman?

"Mrs Leigh says she doesn't think I ever would get used to it!" Jessica's eyes wandered to where the Leighs lived in that small square house of corrugated iron, at the back of the homestead veranda. There was no scrap of green, no tree about it. Only a shade shed of rusty leaves at one side, a bough screen on posts rammed into the earth before it, for a veranda. "The sweat-bin", Mrs Leigh called it, and Jessica believed, as she said, living in it must be too awful for words.

"No," Mrs Bessie replied grimly. Hugh had taken Jessica to see the Leighs, and Jessica had gone over once or twice to have tea and talk to Fanny.

"They're going down in a day or two, aren't they?" Jessica ventured.

"Would you like to go with them, Jessica?" Mrs Bessie inquired politely.

"Mrs Leigh says, if you wouldn't mind—they could make room for me and. . . ."

"Of course, my dear!" Hugh's mother was kindness and consideration itself. "I'm only so sorry you've had such a dull time. But I warned you, didn't I, what it would be like up here?"

"Oh, yes, you did, Mrs Watt." Jessica's tears dripped. "But I never imagined I'd be so lonely . . . that station life was anything like this."

How would Hugh take what Jessica had to say, Mrs Bessie wondered.

He was so restrained; so reserved always. Eagerly, closely as Mrs Bessie studied her son, she could never quite tell what was going on within him. Hugh had escaped her in those long years at school. The wonder was he had come back with a hunger for the country and work of the station.

His mother did not know how much of Jessica had got beneath Hugh's skin; whether it was just an inclination for women which had presented itself in her, or whether there was something in this shallow, dainty creature appealing to him more than that. Hugh was sufficiently her own son to elude her, Mrs Bessie discovered.

He had seemed little more interested in Jessica than in half a dozen other girls, although Mrs Haywood declared Hugh and Jessica had been great chums for years—ever since Tim had brought Hugh to spend summer holidays with them, when the boys were at Stratford together. Mrs Bessie had heard of the Haywoods and Moores in Hugh's letters, of course; but she was surprised to find him with such a bevy of friends when she went south.

"I'd no idea you were such an attractive young man, Hugh!" she exclaimed.

She had taken rooms at the Savoy Hotel while she was in Perth, and entertained all the people who had been kind to Hugh, with eager high-handedness, by way of reaction from the long years of parsimony she had endured for his sake.

A queer, frumpy little woman, Mrs Bessie thought she looked, when she saw herself in the long hotel mirrors, talking to Hugh's smart friends in her old-fashioned black dress with a neat tucker of white net, flat black hat and low-heeled shoes. But Hugh was very proud of his mother. The way she walked, striding, with the lurch and sway of a horseman, swore absent-mindedly, and apologized with such charm, her eyes smiling.

"Oh, Hugh, she's priceless, I think, your mother!" Jessica had cried, when she first met Mrs Bessie.

"She is," Hugh replied, annoyed by the girl's little laugh. "There's nobody like her."

Older men had said that to him, acquaintances of his mother.

They liked to talk to her and point her out to each other, in the lounge and hotel dining-room: "Mrs Watt . . . Mrs Ted Watt of Wytaliba, a great little woman, nobody like her," Hugh had heard them say. And he realized it himself in those days of their holiday, so manly his mother seemed to Hugh, yet as fresh and sprightly as a young girl. And how happy they had been together.

Mrs Bessie had enjoyed being taken about and introduced by her big handsome son. Not that Hugh was so big or handsome, but solid and clean-looking with bumps over his brows, a bony sensitive nose, and blue eyes which gave you a straight, clear gaze. "Oh, a nice lad! A dear boy!" everybody said.

"Quite like one of my own sons! I don't know what we shall do without him," Mrs Haywood had purred. And Mrs Bessie knew what that meant when Hugh told her he had asked Jessica to marry him. Was it calf love, she wondered? A schoolgirl and schoolboy affair? It did not even look like that—rather an arrangement Hugh had slipped into, something comfortable and convenient, which pleased him quite well, fitted in with ideas of his own. And yet his mother did not know. Perhaps Hugh cared for the girl more than he seemed to. She was very pretty.

Mrs Bessie let Jessica break her own news. Leaving Hugh with Jessica in the garden under the stars, she went into the dining-room to write letters, knowing Hugh would be driving Jessica down to Nuniewarra with the Leighs in a day or so. But Mrs Bessie could not write, hearing Jessica's voice, it's exclamations, staccato and broken. She was crying. What Hugh had to say, his mother did not hear. His voice was so low; it moved on a word or two, gravely, quietly.

As Mrs Bessie tried to write, moths whirled in the light about her. Then Hugh stood beside her; some hurt in his eyes.

"Jessica would like to go down—as soon as possible," he said.

"I know."

His mother tried desperately to read on the quiet surface what was going on in the man's body and mind Hugh had acquired. But it was no use. Already habits of solitude and independence were ruling him; he had closed in on himself as most men of the country do.

After all, Mrs Bessie discovered, with Geary's bet ringing in her ears, she was less pleased than she had thought she would be for Hugh to lose his sweetheart.

CHAPTER IX

His mother was dying. Hugh had no doubt of that when Meenie rode out for him to the To-Morrow well where he was mustering. She had been two days and two nights on the way, and Hugh knew she would never have dared the nights alone in the bush unless there was need for it. He knew how terrified she was alone, among the trees at night; and how desperately she must have picked up his tracks and followed them. For a long time his mother had been ailing, Hugh knew; but he did not think she was seriously ill.

It was nearly a year since the Leighs and Jessica went down, and Hugh had been busy overhauling windmills and pumping gear, away from the house a good deal. Saul too was away from the homestead, with Cock-Eyed Bob, on the trail of colours, near the head of Wytaliba creek.

"Mumae sick feller. Tell 'm yienda buckunma (you come quickly)," Meenie said.

Hugh knew from the gin's eyes that she was afraid; she could see farther than he.

He told Warieda to carry on with the muster, mounted and was away in a few moments. All the way back across the ranges he had beaten into Wytaliba, riding all night and through the next day. Catching a fresh horse at the Half-Way well, he came in through the Five Mile gate towards sunset.

Mrs Bessie was lying on her bed, along the shady side of the veranda, Bandogera beside her, fanning the flies away. She had made the gins carry her bed out of doors, Hugh guessed. Scarcely conscious, muttering, and calling out as spasms of pain clutched and racked her, she lay, her head turned towards the road by which he would come in from the hills.

Very little, withered and worn, she looked as Hugh gazed down on her. She had taken her false teeth out and her mouth fell in. Wrung with grief for her suffering and what was befalling them, Hugh stood beside her, unable to speak.

His mother's eyes turned to him. Strange ringed eyes, shallow and faded, almost phosphorescent they seemed, with the fires of her flickering spirit. Her lips moved to the twist of a smile.

"Knew Meenie'd find you," she gasped. "I've been waiting for you, Hughie . . . but it's damn bad . . . have to go now. Been hanging round me a long time. Cancer, you know. Wouldn't let Dr Kairns tell you when we were in Perth . . . made up me mind to see it out, up here."

Hugh knelt beside her.

"Mother," he cried, "don't leave me."

"If you knew what the pain's like you'd take me out and shoot me like you would a horse," she said. "I've stood it as long as I could for you, Hughie. But listen . . . I want to go like this, out here. It might be a day or two . . . don't try to take me away. I'd like to die like an old gin, under a tree."

"I'll send one of the boys into Karrara for McCarthy."

Bessie Watt moved her head wearily.

"It couldn't make any difference. Ask Bandogera, she knows . . . been howling for me at dawn already, haven't you, Bandi? No, let me have peace in my time, Hughie. And afterwards, you can put me down there near the creek, under one of the big gums . . . I've showed Meenie and Bandogera the place. . . . I can watch all they're doing from there. If they steal the sugar or tea . . . when you're not looking and have nobody to housekeep for you, I'll haunt them . . . and give them a guts-ache like I've got when they eat, and. . . ."

The sturdy spirit was battling with its pain and ultimate disaster, sweat dewing on her forehead.

"Can't I do anything?" Hugh gasped.

"There's these." She glanced at the hypodermic syringe in a glass of water and phial of morphia tablets on a chair beside her. "The doctor in Perth gave me them when we were down; but they're not much good now——"

"And you never told me!" Hugh was aghast.

"What was the use? Water, Bandogera."

Hugh moved to go for the water.

"No, you stay here." The cold bony hand clung to him. "I feel better while I can look at you, Hugh. Joy of my life, that's what I've always called you to myself. Joy of my life . . . and I wanted to make this place for you."

The old gin trotted back along the veranda, carrying a glass and jug of water on a tray.

"Dilute the pill in a little water and draw it into the syringe," Mumae directed. Hugh filled the syringe. She held out her arm, his eyes winced from sight of the withered forearm freckled with tiny punctures. Then he injected the morphia, laid her arm gently beside her and put down the syringe.

Mrs Bessie lay back on the pillows for a while with closed eyes. When they opened to gaze at him, her eyes were mild and calm. "I've loved it, Hugh," she said. "I've wanted to be here and stay here. But if you don't like it, I don't want you to stay."

"I like it all right," Hugh said.

"It was a lie . . . what I told Jessica," his mother went on, a smile, sly and whimsical, on her lips. "There's no mortgage on Wytaliba now, Hughie. You can sell out if you want to——"

"I won't sell," Hugh said.

"But I couldn't 've borne you to marry Jessica, Hugh. She's all right in her way . . . but not for here . . . and not for keeps. I'd rather you took a gin than a white woman like that for keeps. White ants are not in it with them. They suck a man dry. Look at all the men up here, married women down south who don't like the Nor'-West. . . . Won't live in it. What sort of a life have they got? If I could 've found a woman for you before I left, Hughie— a woman like Jim Ryland's wife, will face hardship with a man, stand by and fight through with him."

"Don't worry about me, mum," Hugh begged.

"It's a man's country . . . and you're a man, Hughie, not a boy any longer," his mother continued. "It'll be lonely when I'm gone. I don't want you to go mucking round with gins. But I'd rather a gin than a Jessica. Oh, my God——"

The lightning of pain passed. She went on breathlessly, faintly, "It's no good, a man can't live on himself. There's the drink, of course. You can fill up with that; but it's no good to you. Out here, in this country, the blacks are right. Life's got to be straight and go on. You've got to keep in tune.

"It's no good stewing in your own juice. You'll go sour or mad. When I'm gone, you go away for a bit. . . . Take this mob you're after now to Midland yourself, and keep your eyes open on the stations and farms down south. There's any amount of good girls

64

wanting a husband. See if you can't find one you like well enough to bring back with you."

"I think you're right, mum. I'll do as you say," Hugh answered. "Don't you think you'd better rest a while now?"

Mrs Bessie shook her head.

"There's a letter over in my desk there. I asked Kairns to give me for you—when we got as far as this—just to assure you it really is . . . hopeless, and to tell you how to help me over the last stages. . . ."

Hugh went to the desk in her room, found and read the letter from Archibald Kairns whom Mrs Bessie had consulted when she was in Perth.

". . . Only a question of time," the letter said. "Cancer of the stomach"; and there were instructions as to how to administer morphia so that the last hours of agony would be diminished as much as possible. Dazed and aghast, Hugh realized how long his mother had suffered and defended him from knowledge of the sorrow which must befall him.

"There." She smiled faintly. "That's the lot. Everything's fixed up nice and tidy. Henderson and Crowe's my lawyers . . . and you won't ever think your mother's been a bad woman, will you, Hugh?"

The weary, murmuring voice paused.

"Tell you what I've found out. . . . Sex hunger's like any other. Satisfy it and you don't think about it. I mean . . . it won't get out of proportion. Work's the thing . . . not sex. . . ."

She fell asleep, talking, hand in his. And Hugh sat watching her frail, withered face against the pillows, going over the long, fighting trail of her life as far as he knew it. His feeling was very little a son's for his mother, but a man's for his workmate, comrade in arms. He had scarcely any sentimental tenderness; personal affection for her, but a passionate admiration, and sense of physical need. It was her companionship he was going to miss, the intimate association of interests in common. Through all he did and said, the thought of her was woven.

Windmills clanked as they turned slowly, out from the house, struck against the night sky.

In the sheening quiet, from distances of the plains, Hugh could hear a thunder of hoofs. A mob of horses was coming into drink at troughs beyond the stock-yard fence. Hugh could hear them long before he saw any movement on the dim starlit plains. That low, thudding thunder of horses in the distances, how familiar it was! How it had always stirred him: and her. So often as they sat on the veranda in the evening they had listened to it, coming nearer and nearer. Watched the mob swing into sight, bunched, and turn to the well, spreading out, blowing and snorting after a long gallop.

Hugh could not believe it would no longer be part of his mother's life, to sit on the veranda in the evening and hear the horses come in to drink.

"Coonardoo, I'd liked to have seen her," Mrs Bessie wakened to say once. "But she's out on the To-Morrow with the boys, isn't she?"

"I'll send for her," Hugh said.

Mrs Bessie shook her head. "No, let her get on with muster, Hugh. Cattle's high just now—and we don't want to lose the market. I've said all I wanted to her.

"I don't suppose . . . anybody can live long enough to do all they want to, Hughie. There seems so much I haven't done, I wanted to do. But Saul'll stand by you—and his advice's worth having. Sam Geary . . . don't trust him farther than you can see him. He's always wanted this place and Coonardoo. I couldn't bear him to have either of 'em."

Mrs Bessie lay for two or three days wrestling with her pain. Crying out as it clutched and racked her. The drug had lost its power to give her rest or oblivion: her pulse was a slow, thready knocking on its arterial walls. Then one morning, while a cool wenda was calling, and Hugh lay asleep near her, she called him. He went to her and caught the last flickering breath of her sigh, as she lay looking out to the edge of the mulga under a grey sky shell, blistered by the first light.

CHAPTER X

IT was very quiet and lonely on Wytaliba, all day, before the blacks carried the wooden box Mumae had made Joey Koonarra put together for her, and laid it in the grave Hugh and Joey dug under a tall white-barked creek gum.

Very frail and light his mother's body felt as Hughie lifted it into the rough wooden box still smelling of redgum.

There had been wailing in the uloo at dawn. Hugh gathered all the flowers he could find, punti and little green bird-flowers, with trails of Nor'-West creeper and its red and yellow lanterns, to spread over the box, when he had nailed down the lid.

Cockatoos, scattered snow-white on the ground, flew off with a rustle of stiff silken wings as Hugh, Bandogera, Meenie and Joey Koonarra carried their burden towards the creek gum and the place they had prepared for it.

After the box was lowered, Hugh shovelled red earth and stones over his mother. The blacks wailed and howled, Meenie and Bandogera cutting themselves with sharp stones, as though it were one of their own people who had died.

Hugh sent the blacks away, and stayed himself under the tree. He lay there a long time stretched out on the sand. People in the uloo watched him, but were afraid to go near. Then towards sunset Hugh got up and walked across to the house. He called Joey, Meenie and Bandogera, handed out stores, and told them to keep the dogs away from his mother's grave. Doors banged; keys were turned in flour and sugar bins.

Then Hugh rode out, and away along the track back to the To-Morrow where Warieda, Chitali, Coonardoo, Bardi, and the rest of the boys were mustering. There was no need to tell them what had happened.

In the morning before dawn a fierce wailing went up. Hughie listened. Coonardoo was wailing for his mother, he knew; and all day, as he rode, the sorrow of her dark eyes followed him. At night whenever he awakened Hugh heard Coonardoo crying, sobbing and beating her breast.

67

Warieda's fire glowed red through the darkness, at a little distance from where Hugh himself lay, watching the dead branches of his fire smoulder, and fall into ashes.

"Coonardoo," he called, when it was morning and the camp astir again.

She came to him. Hugh had barely spoken to anyone. Warieda and Chitali watched him, staring away into distances of the hills, forgetting to eat, starting suddenly and riding off as if to escape some torturing thought. Coonardoo went to him. She hung her head. Thin, and sorrowful as Hugh, Coonardoo looked as she stood there before him. Hughie went to her, parted the shirt over her breast, saw the raw red gashes sharp stones had cut in her brown skin.

"You know Mumae sick long time?"

"Eeh-mm."

"Why didn't you tell me?"

"Mumae say not."

"If you had told me," Hugh said harshly, "we might have saved her. She might have been here now."

He knew he was unjust; that Coonardoo had done as she was told. It gave him some satisfaction to see her shrink away as though he had kicked her. He turned his back on her, picked up his saddle and went over to the well where the boys were watering the horses, saddled Demeter, the mare Wareida had brought in for him, and telling the boys to meet at Yallerang clay-pan that afternoon, rode off into the ranges.

Next day, cut off from the rest of the men, while they were scouring the shelving hill-sides for strayed cattle, Hugh rode up to Coonardoo as she went drooping over her horse, scarcely looking in his direction.

She was like his own soul riding there, dark, passionate and childlike. In all this wide empty world Coonardoo was the only living thing he could speak to, Hugh knew; the only creature who understood what he was feeling, and was feeling for him. Yet he was afraid of her, resented a secret understanding between them.

But Coonardoo the playmate—Coonardoo whom he had seen long ago under the shower, young and slender, her lithe brown body, wet and gleaming, brown eyes laughing at him, her hair, wavy and sun-burnished, lying in wet streaks about her head.

Coonardoo? Why should he hurt her by a harsh, indifferent manner he showed no one else?

It had been funny to find her one of Warieda's women with a kid of her own when he came home from school. But sentimental about a gin Hugh had promised himself never to be. His regard for Coonardoo was a relic of their old playmateship, his admiration of her horsemanship. Every finer, less reasonable instinct he had stamped on, kicked out of his consciousness.

"What's the matter with you?" he asked roughly as he came up to her, leaning against her horse. "Warieda beat you?"

"Wiah." She looked at him with deep, beautiful eyes.

"Is it—about Mumae?"

The gesture and movement of her head reproached Hugh.

As if he had forgotten how to sleep, he lay by the side of his camp-fire, throwing wood on, watching the stars, listening to the horses feeding with tinkle of hobbles out over the plains; or wandered about restlessly at night.

The blacks exclaimed among themselves at his worn, wretched expression, his distraught gaze. Hugh was liable to fits of anger, unfathomable dejection. There was no pleasing him. He became gaunt, almost unrecognizable under the rough beard and in the filthy clothes he was wearing.

But wherever he wandered at night, a slight dark shadow streaked after him. Wherever Hugh went, Coonardoo followed, terrified though she was in the darkness, of the gliding death which might strike her feet at any moment; of the narlu, flapping from tree to tree and fixing her with ghost eyes. But Coonardoo was more afraid of what might happen to Youie while he roamed about at night only half conscious of what he was doing.

Hugh wore her and himself out. The blacks were becoming afraid of him; that he was bewitched. "Baba" they cried to themselves when they saw him streaking past their camp-fires at night. The spirit of Mumae had come back to pursue and possess him, it was said. She intended to take Hugh with her, whither she had gone. Nobody doubted he was becoming mad. He had been heard calling and talking to Mumae, as though she were with him, when no mortal eyes could see anything but the air before him and silver writhen shapes of dead mulga in the starlight. And Coonardoo—everybody recognized it was her right to watch over and look after Hugh as well as she could. Had not Mumae commanded her to? Warieda was as anxious as Coonardoo herself to save Hughie from the recklessness of his misery and the evil threatening.

From an agony of fitful sleep Hugh wakened one night to find Coonardoo watching beside him, a still, dark figure on the other side of the dying embers of his fire. She sat looking towards him.

"What are you doing there?" he asked.

"Warieda send 'm," she murmured humbly.

"Well," Hugh snarled angrily, "you go back to Warieda and don't come hanging round my camp again. Do you understand?"

Coonardoo stood uncertainly before him a moment, humbly with prayerful eyes; then moved away through the darkness of the slender low-growing trees.

It was a few nights later that Coonardoo found Hugh wandering so far from the camp that he did not know where he was. He had walked off restlessly, absentmindedly, along a saddle of the ridge. Scrub was thick there, low-growing trees tufted sootily against the sky. Hugh turned to go back the way he had come, and after walking a while sat down on the earth near a clump of dead mulga whose branches shone in the starlight. He recognized the trees, so lustrous they were, like giant candelabra in the gloom. He had passed them several times, and knew he was bushed.

"Show 'm track, Youie," Coonardoo said, moving from the shadow of the trees.

"Coonardoo!" Hugh started to his feet.

He understood what she had been doing as she wavered there against the thronging tree stems, afraid to come near him.

"Do you mean to say you've been following me?" he asked.

"Eeh-mm."

"All the time. Ever since Mumae—went away?"

"Eeh-mm."

Hugh sat down again. A trembling seized him. He had a swift vision of passion and tenderness stalking him through all the lonely misery of his wandering. When he looked up he saw Coonardoo was still standing there in the shadow.

"Sit down," he said. And a moment later, "You must be tired too. We've come a long way, Coonardoo?"

She nodded and sank down on the earth at a little distance from him. Her fingers, as a matter of course, went after the sticks lying about; they piled leaves and twigs. Hugh struck a match and set a flame spurting over the leaves and sticks. He saw then how tired she was, her body sagged; she was half asleep already as she sat beside the fire.

"We'll rest here a bit," Hugh said. "Then you can show me the way to camp again, Coonardoo."

She nodded, smiled and stretched to sleep on the far side of the fire. Hugh sat watching her. Years fell away between them. She was Coonardoo, the old playmate; he felt about her as he had when they were children together. This was a childish adventure they were on. His gratitude shook him as he thought of how she had followed and watched over him during the last weeks. It yielded to yearning and tenderness. Deep inexplicable currents of his being flowed towards her.

"Coonardoo! Coonardoo!" he murmured.

Awakened, she came to kneel beside him, her eyes the fathomless shining of a well in the shadows. Hugh took her in his arms, and gave himself to the spirit which drew him, from a great distance it seemed, to the common source which was his life and Coonardoo's.

They slept beside the fire near the clump of dead mulga until it was morning. Hugh started up to find Coonardoo stirring embers of the fire. They had walked back into the camp then.

"Lost me tracks. Was fair bushed when Coonardoo found me," Hugh told the boys. No more was said of the matter.

He was more like his old self that day, quieter, saner; and for two or three weeks went about his work picking up and cutting out cattle for the road, much as usual. He did not seem to be grieving in the same way for Mumae. The boys believed Hugh's fibres had been snatched at and attached to the earth, so that Mumae could not draw them away.

Then suddenly he became sick, could not eat, rolled about with a pain in his stomach; his eyes and hands blazed feverishly. Hugh declared he had eaten or drunk something which disagreed with him. But Warieda, Chitali and the rest of the boys were sure Mumae had come back, entered into Youie and was struggling to take his spirit away with her.

CHAPTER XI

WHEN Hugh became so ill that he could not move as he lay by his camp-fire in the morning, Coonardoo made the boys take him into the homestead.

Warieda and Chitali slung Hugh's ground-sheet on two stout poles, and they and the two other boys took it in turns to carry Hugh. Coonardoo watched, riding beside them. She would not let them travel during the heat of the day, kept wet rags laid across Hugh's forehead, and hung branches of green leaves over the pole to keep flies away.

For days and nights Hugh raved and talked incessantly. Coonardoo, who had learnt the ways of white people since she was a child, cared for Hugh as she had seen Mumae care for him when he was a small boy and had a touch of the sun.

At the homestead she used the keys Hugh gave her, to open closed doors and food bins. She rationed her own people, and slept on the veranda to watch over and look after Hugh.

People at the uloo said Mumae had been there. They had seen her little figure, in a white dress, trotting along the verandas, and a white cockatoo screeched about the house every morning at dawn.

Coonardoo believed Mumae could see and would know all she was doing. She kept a fire burning beside the veranda at night, and in the kitchen during the day. She had made the boys go out and bring in a cow with a young calf, and milk her, so that she could feed Hugh on milk and water.

Warieda objected when she declared that someone must go into Nuniewarra and tell Saul Hardy that Hugh was ill. Saul and Cock-Eyed Bob had come into the homestead a few days after Hugh went back to the mustering camp, Joey Koonarra said. They had gone on to Nuniewarra. Saul would know what was the matter and what to do for Hugh, better than she did, Coonardoo explained. Warieda guessed Sam Geary would return with Saul and Bob, and did not want him on Wytaliba.

"Do you want Youie to go with her?" Coonardoo asked angrily, and pointed out that if they did not drag Hugh from the grip of this sickness he would die as Mumae had done. Then Sam Geary, or some stranger, would come and take possession of the uloo and Wytaliba.

Chitali rode over to Nuniewarra. Much as she hated Geary, Coonardoo had realized that a white man would know what to do for Hugh better than she.

When Sam Geary, Saul and Cock-Eyed Bob appeared, driving out from the dust of the creek trees, Hugh was better, conscious; but so weak that he could not sit up in bed. Coonardoo was satisfied he was not going to die. He could tell her what to do for him now, look at her gratefully, smiling, and saying, as he used to, "Good man! Good man, Coonardoo!"

She, worshipful and devout, smiled back, scolding him. "Silly cowa-cowa yienda, nothing look out make 'm sick fellow."

When the Nuniewarra buggy pulled up and Warieda took the horses, Sam Geary stamped along the veranda, full of bluster, and proud of his own importance. Old Saul and Bob followed when he walked into the shaded room where Hugh was lying.

"Now then, what's all this about?" he roared, looking from Coonardoo in the doorway to Hugh.

"Oh, I see!" His eyes hung on Coonardoo.

Hugh half raised himself, angry colour flaming, his eyes flashing. "You see a damned sight more than there is to see," he gasped.

"Seein' double, am I?" Geary jeered. "Well, I don't blame you, Hughie."

Hugh fell back weakly. Coonardoo's eyes flared their rage and loathing of Geary.

"By God!" Sam exclaimed, "he is bad, isn't he? What is it, Coonardoo?"

Hugh had closed his eyes, lost consciousness for a moment.

"Here, get me some whisky!" Sam said.

Coonardoo went out of the room.

"Bad business this, Bob. What do you think it is?" Geary glanced from Bob to Hugh, the gaunt limp figure he made on the bed.

"From what the boys say, looks like sun or ty. or both," Bob said.

Coonardoo came into the room, a glass, bottle of whisky and jug of water on a tray. Geary took the bottle, poured whisky into the glass and, stooping over Hugh, held it to his mouth.

Hugh revived under the spirit. Geary had helped himself and was standing, glass in hand, as Hugh looked up.

"Well, Youie," he said, "looks to me as if you was done for. You're a dying man if ever I saw one. . . ."

Hugh looked at Geary's swaying figure, and at Bob and old Saul beside him.

"You're a liar, Sam, " he said quietly. "I'm going down to the coast in a day or two—I'll see you out and half a dozen like you!"

"That's right, Youie." Bob said. "Course you will."

"What's that? What does he say?" Saul muttered.

Hugh was determined not to die and give Geary the chance he had been waiting for to mop up Wytaliba. It roused every resolute and fighting nerve in him to think of Geary on Wytaliba; what he would do with the homestead, those bare white rooms, the long shady verandas with their screen of Nor'-West creeper; what he would do with the blacks and Coonardoo.

An instinct chivalrous and perverse sprang to defend her. He had heard from his mother how Geary had tried to take the girl. Over and over again he had made overtures for Coonardoo to Warieda and her father, promising rugs, a horse and goodness knows what not. But always Mrs Bessie had thwarted the bargain. And Hugh instinctively sprang into the breach. Not as long as he lived, and could help it, would Geary get either Wytaliba or Coonardoo.

CHAPTER XII

G EARY and Bob camped on the veranda for the night: Saul went to his own room. Mrs Bessie's door remained locked. Hugh did not have it opened, though neither Bob not Geary would have cared to sleep in Mrs Bessie's room.

In the morning Coonardoo grilled steaks and made porridge, tea and toast. It was difficult to believe Mrs Bessie had not superintended getting of the breakfast as usual.

Expecting the buggy from Nuniewarra, Warieda had gone out after a killer, cut up the beast and given everybody in the uloo his or her share.

"Oh well, Youie, have it your own way," Geary said, smoking over his meal. "I only come thinkin' I could do something for you —take you down, maybe."

"Thanks, Sam," Hugh replied. "My own boys'll take me down in a day or two."

"And who'll look after the place while you're away?"

"Saul, of course! Cripes, he would be sore if I left anyone else in charge—though Warieda and Chitali know as much about running things as I do. Besides, I won't be so long gone."

"The blacks say Mrs Bessie's still keepin' an eye on the place."

A faint wispish smile moved Hugh's lips.

"She seems to have thought of everything."

"Coonardoo says Mumae told her what to do if ever you were sick," Bob said.

"She would," Hugh agreed.

"Well, we'd better get a move on, if you won't come along with us," Geary remarked. "We're mustering just now, Youie, and I left the boys holding a mob on the Gidgee well."

"It's damn good of you, Sam," Hugh replied, "but I'll get the boys to rig up a stretcher in the buckboard and go down in a day or two."

Coonardoo had washed and ironed clothes, packed them in a suitcase as Hugh told her, and fixed the tucker bags. She would have liked to go to the coast with the boys. But Hugh said no to that. He knew the life of the coastal towns too well to wish her to go near them.

She had lain on the floor near him, wakeful, watching, or sleeping lightly, all the time he was ill, and had done every service for him. As she helped him to wash that night before he was going away, Hugh said, "What pretty hands you've got, Coonardoo!" So elegant and delicate the slim brown fingers were. "I'd no idea you had such pretty hands—and feet."

He glanced down at the small brown feet which were as straight and well-shaped as her hands.

Coonardoo looked shy at the words of praise. Her eyes covered Hugh with unfathomable tenderness.

And next day she watched him go, lying on a mattress on the floor of the buckboard. She had filled his waterbag and put Mumae's umbrella beside him to keep off the sun, warning the boys to travel slowly and rest during the heat of the day.

With Meenie, Bandogera and Saul Hardy, Coonardoo stood looking on, while the fresh horses Warieda had brought in, swirled and plunged, then turned, carrying the four-wheeler away over the plains. She watched till her eyes could not see clouding red dust and creek trees through which the buggy disappeared.

As a child she had suffered to see Hugh go away. And something of the old desperate anguish returned to her now. It was as if her entrails were being dragged as the distance grew between her and Hugh. When she could not bear the tension any more, a fibre snapped in her. The intensity of her following sense failed; it was as if life had receded from her.

Coonardoo felt that Hugh would not die. She had guessed the fighting instincts Geary roused. If she had not done the right thing in sending for Saul Hardy, she had done well in bringing Geary to Wytaliba. Coonardoo guessed Hugh was determined to get well if only to defeat Geary.

Hugh would come back to Wytaliba. He would come back, well and strong; not so much a stranger as before; but part of it; of the country and of her. He belonged to them.

Instinctively Coonardoo knew these things as she sat gazing out to the sky that was blue-grey, iridescent, with fuchsia-coloured mists against the hills like the bright feathers in a crested pigeon's wing.

He would bring a woman with him, as he had done before—not the same one. She would be different. But he would bring a woman. The spirit of Mumae would rest more easily under the white-barked gum-tree near the creek. Coonardoo would be there also. Always she would be there, where Youie was, to watch over and care for him as Mumae had said she must.

The white woman would come and would go, Hugh's woman; but Coonardoo would be there. Always she would be there where Hugh was. The happiness of the thought comforted her. Hugh would return, Coonardoo told herself. She must sweep the verandas, brush down the spider-webs and chase fowls from the veranda; keep the house as Mumae would have liked it kept for Hugh's woman, the white girl he would bring back with him for a wife.

Hugh never remembered that journey to the coast, except as a nightmare, in which he had swayed and jolted endlessly across the plains, up the steep walls of tablelands, red and bare where the surrounding country had subsided from them, through the grey seas of mulga, stretching away and away under dim, pale-blue sky.

Bare red earth and ironstone gravel, black under the sky film, thin, blue-grey and green, clear as water, he had seen through half-open eyes. Brush of mulga, with narrow leaves, withering, grey-green and brown, upstanding, scratching the sky, and quandongs; thick stunted shapes of dwarf firs. He closed his eyes on those drought-stricken stretches of country where the mulga, bare and beaten by sun and sand through years of dryness, shone like silver through hard white light. Every germ seemed to be sterilized in the still air. Only a hill in the distance, lumped like a giant blue whale along the horizon, promised life and hope.

Snippets and scraps of the country he passed through wove a patchwork over Hugh's brain. He saw wind-grass growing among the rocks, tufts as fine and yellow as mulga blossom, beaten away and driven to dust against the shingle. Coming to ruckled earth of a river flat, the wind-grass flowed, luxuriant and wheel-high, under bloodwoods and light scrub. Wild flowers, magenta and mauve, swirled to the foot of rugged hill-sides, as if a brightly patterned old-fashioned shawl had been thrown down there.

Creek gums whose trunks looked newly white-washed sidled and swayed nymphishly beside the dry sand of their water-courses.

The green, soft and young, of their crests, telling of water beneath the creek bed, coolness and shadow there: flash of birds, the blue wing of a butterfly.

Through the dust and heat of the long journey Chitali and Warieda drove by turns. While one had the reins the other sat beside Hugh, put wet rags on his forehead, moved Mumae's black umbrella so that it shaded him from the sun, and sang or told him aboriginal legends of stones and hills they passed.

There was the story about that crag at the end of Nungarra range, a mass of granite which could be seen against the sky, miles away.

"Before my mother grow," Warieda said, "before her mother, weary bugger years"—he waved his hand, vaguely for a long time ago—"big blackfellow kill people and eat 'em. Wallabee come. Old fellow tell 'm hide in trees, kill all blackfellow and eat 'em. Young blackfellow make smoke, tell other blackfellow. Old blackfellow see smoke, very sulky. Chase young fellow, want kill 'm and eat 'm too. Young fellow movingar, make cloud, send lightning, tear up old fellow, send him into earth. He make stone . . . big stone over there in hills, Nungarra."

Warieda first saw a steam-engine galloping along rails one time when he had gone to Karrara with cattle for Mumae. He made a song about it and sang the song to Hugh, often as they bumped on over the long track to the coast:

> "*Me-ra-rar ngar-rar ngular-gar gartha-gara!*
> *Calling with steaming head!*
> *Mooranger! Nar-ra-ga! Mille-gidgee!*
> *Coming! Passing! Gone!*"

Each day Hugh became weaker, more exhausted. He could only drink the water he had told the boys to boil and cool off for him; and, although the fever abated, his heart seemed to swim all over his body, his breath came in such faint windy gusts, that he lay without speaking more than he had to. At Illigoogee and Karrara the boys got fresh horses and drove on again, more anxious than Hugh, and set on getting him to the coast without loss of a moment.

A dream it had all been; but the horror and oppression lifted always by the presence of those two dark protecting figures.

Towering as trees, they had loomed before Hugh sometimes, and merged with the darkness shrouding his brain. But how they had cared for and attended him—with such gentleness and sympathy, patient and alert, singing and talking to while away the time!

Lala station, a hundred miles from the coast, was reached at last. The Burnhams of Lala owned a truck, and insisted on lifting Hugh on his mattress into the house, and feeding him with beaten eggs and milk, before taking him on into Onslow.

Hugh sent Warieda and Chitali back to Wytaliba from Lala, and told them to obey and work for Saul Hardy as they had when he owned the place. They would get on very well with Saul he knew: there was nothing to worry about on that score.

John Burnham and a couple of his boys carried Hugh on to the boat; and those days on the freshening blue seas to Geraldton were like lying in a cradle and being rocked to sleep after the long journey from Wytaliba.

There was no milk on the boat; but oranges, plenty of oranges. Hugh ate oranges. He sucked at the golden rind, lying gazing over the blue dancing expanse of southern ocean, sleeping, dreaming, not thinking.

Wytaliba was a mirage on the horizon of his consciousness. All the distraught passion, loneliness and suffering, beyond the flowing miles of plain and tableland.

He could hear the blacks singing beside their camp-fires in the dark, the frail eerie melodies winging over the dark plains, under a wide sky on which the stars were dim as rock crystals. That throbbing on one note, flight, fall and reiterated rhythm and melody quivering, infiltrating had always stirred and excited him. He told himself he liked to hear the blacks on Wytaliba singing, because it showed they were happy; life was good to them.

But there was more in it than that. The blacks' singing was a communication, a language of the senses, remote and aboriginal. Infinitely, irresistibly Hugh felt it. Always he could hear Coonardoo singing above the rest of the women.

The *Centurion* made her way to Geraldton with leisurely lurch and stride. The land looked dark and menacing, after the peace of the sea. White lines of surf and beaches flashed from the lightning bluffs and headlands. Hills, trees and green swardy slopes, grew out from them. Sea birds, swooped, screaming, about the steamer as she bumped piles of the jetty.

79

There was nobody he had seen before in the gaily coloured little crowd which assembled to meet the boat; but Hugh felt as if he knew everybody; everybody was glad to see him. Geraldton was a place you dreamt of, and talked about a great deal, on Wytaliba. Coming to the township again was like dipping into his childhood. Hugh had been there before when he was going down to school. Eustace Fairweather, the doctor in Geraldton, an old friend of his mother's, had come to the boat and taken him away for the day.

Hugh asked the steward who had been looking after him to send for a car as soon as the boat arrived, and told the driver to take him to Nurse McGillvaray's cottage hospital which he remembered having heard his mother speak of.

In a bed of the neat small house, tucked away behind plumbago hedges and pink oleander bushes, with a stout middle-aged woman, and a girl who was learning to be a nurse, fussing about him, Hugh began to feel really well—to laugh at himself for all the fuss he had made, about "a go of fever and a headache", he said.

But Dr Eustace Fairweather, who overhauled him, was not amused. He realized the experiences of his patient, and that he had come nearly five hundred miles for treatment.

"Oh yes," he said, "you've had ty. all right, my boy. You ought to have died."

"That's what Sam Geary said," Hugh told him smiling. "But I wouldn't—to spite him."

CHAPTER XIII

How many moons was it since Youie had gone? Coonardoo had seen the slim kylie of a new moon in the sky, wane silverly, belly and wither ten times. She scarred the bark of a creek gum with a sharp stone for each new moon, and watched every dust wind that puffed and swirled beside the creek, where the track dipped to the crossing and was hidden among trees, grey-misted against blue, pale sky.

Her eyes were birds which had a nest there, so they hovered and whirled round the place. She knew every tree and rut at the crossing; how horses came down the steep red bank opposite, pebbles slipping and flying under their feet; a buggy rattled across the stones, jolted and bumped as it climbed the soft ruckled earth, rising steeply and veering on the other side.

Eeh-mm, Youie would call to his horses, fling out his whip, making it crack joyously, as he drove over the creek. Birds would fly out from the trees, and the horses which had been waiting at Lala all these months, smelling the home drinking-troughs, jaded though they were with their long plod through the ridge, would swoop out and in to the lower gate, coming to a standstill before the house, red dust baked with the sweat on them. Youie would be red with dust, buggy, wheels, harness, the ground-sheet over the luggage roped on at the back of the buggy; everything near and beside him would be powdered with red dust of the plains.

He was not dead, although he did not come, Coonardoo was sure. Mumae's house began to look as if nobody had lived in it for a long time. Saul Hardy lived in the Leighs' hut for a while when Hugh was away. Not for more than a month or so, however. Wytaliba those days gave him the creeps, he said. Saul swore, as the blacks said, the place was haunted. He had seen Mumae trotting along the veranda, in her white dress and low-heeled black shoes, and the white cockatoos nearly drove him demented. They screeched round the house so.

Once during Hugh's absence Saul had come over from Nunie-warra, bringing Sam Geary and Cock-Eyed Bob with him.

They camped in the Leighs' hut. Saul called up the blacks, dealt out flour, sugar, and tea; then all three, Saul, Sam and Cock-Eyed Bob, had driven back to Nuniewarra in Sam's new motor-car. Saul declared Mumae was calling him all night. She had trotted up and down the veranda, crying, "Saul! Saul!" just as she used to. Even Sam Geary said he could not stand it. Wytaliba had such a deserted air; there was something uncanny about it.

Meenie and Bandogera swept round and scrubbed the verandas of Mumae's house now and then when the white hens made a mess of them. But they were afraid to go into the rooms. Spiders wove their grey films there and red dust was heavy on everything.

Every morning at dawn, white cockatoos rose in a cloud before the house and flew off screeching against the sun. They roosted in the white gum, beside the veranda, and in the old tree down near the creek under which Youie had laid Mumae. Coonardoo believed, as did everybody in the uloo, that Mumae's spirit had taken possession of a white cockatoo and was always flying round the place.

No one from the uloo would have dared to go into the house, or break open the store, although everybody was hungry waiting for Youie to return. The tribe had gone back to its old way of living, hunting kangaroos, snaring bungarra and birds while the gins husked and pounded grass seeds or dug for coolyahs. Once Warieda had killed a bullock; but the white cockies screeched so, and almost everyone had pains, or was sick from eating too much meat. Meenie declared, and everybody agreed with her, that Mumae had made the food disagree because she did not approve of a beast being killed without leave.

Warieda explained Youie had told him to bring in a killer and feed the uloo as usual; but Bandogera and Meenie were sure Mumae was against it.

All through the long hot days the uloo waited and watched for Hugh. Red haze of dust storms hid the homestead, and winning-arras spun, dancing in long unsteady columns from over the plains.

One of the windmills had broken in a storm and flapped its fans forlornly. Coonardoo tried to mend it. Climbing the iron stays to discover what was the matter, she had caught the fan, and with a piece of wire, swung and fixed it into position again.

The mill kept water running, in little channels, through the garden, so that the green things there would not die. Coonardoo weeded and guarded them from the sun with brushwood screens as she had done for Mumae. By and by, when food was scarce, she rode out and brought in a cow with calf and milked her. There was no harm in that, in taking some of the milk from the calf, the old women decided, though they would not have done it themselves. It was then, they declared, Coonardoo had been caught in a winning-arra, and a cooboo dropped into her. It grew quickly during those summer months, the baby in Coonardoo's body. Before the rains, she and Bandogera had walked away from the camp along the creek together.

Bandogera made a fire in the warm sand of the creek bed, and she and Coonardoo sat down at a little distance from the fire. Bandogera had made Coonardoo lie down on the warm white sand and rubbed her body all over with thin persuasive fingers, singing and muttering movins against any evil spirits which might be hovering near.

Coonardoo had gazed through the leaves of river trees, fluttering their long dark fingers, sooty and innumerable, out of the night about her. She had looked up at the stars, the glittering crystals of stars which made air of the sky, all shining as a wide stretch of water. The stars had fallen into her, darkness, and those fluttering fingers of the leaves. As Coonardoo writhed and cried out, Bandogera chanted more fiercely. She warmed her hands at the fire, took a handful of dead ashes still warm, and rubbed them over the child struggling against Coonardoo's body.

It was a sturdy little creature Bandogera laid in the sand and covered with warm ashes. Coonardoo exclaimed with delight when she saw him sprawling beside her, so fat and vigorous. Bandogera too was pleased with the result of her labours. She knew everybody in the uloo would agree it was a fine cooboo the winning-arra had given Coonardoo.

Warieda, with two little girls, had desired a son. It was an old trick of the winning-arra this, to drop the spirit of a child into a woman. It had been done before. Warieda was well pleased the winning-arra had given his woman the spirit of a man child.

Overjoyed with the baby herself, Coonardoo sang to him, wandered along the creek hunting bardis and honey ants, digging for coolyahs. The days were not so long; her eyes watched the plains less for dust flying out from the mist and shade of trees by the crossing.

Pink-eye on Wytaliba that year was not as lively and uproarious as usual. The moppin-garra came from Nuniewarra, and milli-millis sent before Mumae died to tribes within hundreds of miles, brought a great gathering along the creek, at the time white people on all the stations were pink-eyeing too, after their fashion, eating, drinking, singing and giving each other presents.

Usually Mrs Bessie had been generous with rations for pink-eye. She had given bags of flour and sugar for the gathering, content that her people should not wish to wander. In all her years on Wytaliba they had not been away on pink-eye once. Now and then old Joey and his gins would go bush for a month or so. Chitali had roamed off several times, and come into the uloo wild, naked, and hungry-eyed. But Coonardoo, Bardi and several of the younger boys and girls knew no country beyond the station boundaries.

This year there was no Mrs Bessie to give flour and sugar, and blacks from other stations had become accustomed to these food-stuffs. Visitors were for raiding the store-room, but Joey Koonarra would not hear of it. No man or woman of the Gnarler would con-sent to break Mumae's law. They told how her spirit still watched over the place, and what the vengeance would be, should her will be disregarded or disobeyed.

But food was scarce; and hunger cast a gloom over celebrations and ceremonies which had been carried along so often before on full stomachs, with the strength and glee of a well-nourished priesthood. The men had gone out hunting and brought in a kangaroo or two, but most of the kangaroos were so poor that they could not be used and had to be hung on a tree as a warning to the spirit responsible for growing kangaroos that this was all the goods provided were fit for.

The Nuniewarra moppin saved the situation by declaring Mumae's spirit had come to him and told him that Wytaliba men must go out and bring in a fat bullock, as they had always done for the pink-eye. It was Mumae's wish.

Great was the rejoicing when the beast was brought in, killed, and his flesh divided among the families from far and near. After roasting and eating the fresh meat someone made a song about the red steer and the spirit of Mumae. Always, the song said, the spirit of Mumae had decreed, a red steer was to be brought in, roasted and eaten during the midsummer pink-eye on Wytaliba.

The rains came early that year. For days and days it rained. Nobody doubted Mumae had sent the rain, knowing how badly it was needed. Water fell sluicing down out of the sky, and flooded the plains. Soon the creek was running.

Coonardoo with her children took refuge in the big shed near the stock-yards. She watched the showers, laughing, running about excitedly with the naked children. Every hut in the uloo had water lying in it, and all round. The roofs were sieves through which the rain poured. In an interval of the showers Coonardoo tried to patch up open places in the roof of her wongo with leafy boughs, pieces of tin and hide. The huts looked all festive, as if her people were celebrating the rain by garlanding their shelters with fresh green branches.

Coonardoo knew how pleased Youie would be. She did not like the rain much herself. Not if it lasted too long, and there was no dry place to lie down in at night. Under the corrugated-iron roof of the buggy shed with its open sides she was very comfortable. She could hang up her wet clothes and Warieda's trousers and shirt to dry.

While the men were sheltering on the veranda of Mumae's house during a willy-willy and thunderstorm one day, Warieda made a song about the rain. Everybody joined in while he was singing, following the lead of his clear mellow voice; in subdued accompaniment at first, clucking and chuckling. For hours, they sang, smoked and sang, one man picking up rhythm and melody as another dropped it, striking a higher note, singing above the others, until all joined him. Warieda turned the melody into a minor key and the voices flowed with him, repeating each phrase again and again. Warieda sang and the men chanted after him:

"*Perandalah gnunga, willy-willeree, wilbee-wilberee, chidelah*
  tarra-murra,
Wonga coolah, kangee, weerungunoo babba, bookerilla munda,
Yirri-billee moolungoonah.
Coonderilla, yierra barnmunma, yierra barnmunma,
Gnieba yierra, midgeleerie-midgelerrie
Wonga cubba yiding-garra."

(Verandaing while it is willy-willy, in gusts, rain running from the roof and springing up from pools on the ground. Loud thunder shakes the earth; lightning, through rain, dazzles the eyes so that we can't see the hills over there.

All happy, clicking teeth, one after the other, enjoying looking on, smoking, showing red tongue, white teeth, talking all in a row!)

All happy, indeed they were sitting there singing and smoking while thunder rumbled and cracked among far hills of the To-Morrow ranges, lightning flashed and threw glittering mysterious koodgeedas across the sky. Warieda's new song was a great success. For days men and women went singing. Thin and high, through the nose, fretted and quavering, fragments drifted:

"Perandalah gnunga, willy-willeree, wilbee-wilberee. . . ."

In the distance somebody would tune up and go on:

"Wonga coolah, kangee, weerungunoo babba, bookerilla munda. . . ."

The rain had made a great inland sea of the place where Mumae's house stood. The house and the trees were like a little island in it. But still the white cockatoos roosted there, screeching wildly. "She's afraid what the water will do to the house," Coonardoo thought, knowing how Mumae had loved the white roof and walls of her home.

Long ago this place had been all water. There was a song about it. Wytaliba homestead reared itself from the floor of a dead sea really. There were hills all round still, and the sea had been made from waters draining out of them. Pebbles on the ground were still water-worn.

Coonardoo sang and played with her children under the roof of the buggy shed until the sun shone again and rain water disappeared, soaking down into the earth, where it whispered to seeds of the grass. Soon there was green down everywhere on the plains.

Did Youie know there had been rain? If he knew there had been rain on Wytaliba, he would come quickly, Coonardoo guessed. Soon he would be coming.

White cockatoos had taken possession of the homestead. Always they were shrieking and flying restlessly about it. Feeding in drifts in the garden, they rose with that swift silken flash of wings against the light, so that Coonardoo was dazzled, afraid, and cried "Yukki!" as they turned and wheeled in the air past her.

The day came when, about sunset, Coonardoo's glad cry roused the uloo.

"You comin'!"

Dogs flew out barking; men and women, young and old, ran down to the gate.

Dust at the creek crossing swirled and swung in.

Coonardoo stood where she had first seen it. The Wytaliba buggy which had been waiting for Hugh at Lala threw off its clouding red dust. Coonardoo knew the horses Hugh was driving, the bound and swing of Nessus and Paris, the punch and plodding sway of Demeter and Saturn.

Wanna and Mick flung the lower gate open and the buggy drove on. Coonardoo's head swam and her eyes would not see. Then they got Hugh in mass and outline. He was not alone. She had known he would not be. The woman she had thought he would bring was there beside him—Youie's woman.

White cockatoos feeding in the garden flew up and away, whirling against the sky with their thin shrieking cries. They would feed no more in the garden, roost no more in the gum-tree beside the veranda, Coonardoo knew.

As she went down to the house, her cooboo in her arms, the joy of her life was pressed into this moment. Youie had come again; she would see him. He was well and strong; she could hear him shouting out to Joey and Meenie, as people from the uloo came swarming up to the garden in front of the veranda to meet him, a dirty draggled crowd, their clothes in rags.

Coonardoo was pleased to remember she had been to the shower-house under the big windmill that morning. Every morning lately she had been down to the shower-house because she knew Hugh might come any day now, and he would not like to find she had not washed, or soaped her hair and dried it in the sun, as Mumae made the gins do every day before they went into the house.

Hugh threw the reins to Warieda, who stood to the horses' heads.

"Hullo, Warieda! Chitali! Meenie! Bandogera!" Hugh had jumped out of the buggy and was calling to everybody. "Joey!

Wanna! Mick! Toby! Pinja! By God, what's the matter with you all? You look half starved. This is—the new missus!"

The bundle of clothes which had been sitting beside Hugh on the seat of the buggy, under a green gauze veil and big hat, stood up, lifted her veil; and a round, good-natured little face looked out at everybody, eyes laughing.

"Hullo!" she cried. "Who's who, and which is which, Hugh? This Meenie? Which is Bandogera? And where's Coonardoo?"

Coonardoo had come up behind the others, her eyes filled with Hugh, seeing nothing but Hugh, his back and shoulders in the white red-dusted overalls he had been driving in, his new wide-brimmed felt hat. He was talking to Warieda.

"Yes," he said, "where's Coonardoo?"

His eyes sought among the blacks for her.

"There you are, Bardi. My word, that one fat feller." He pinched the round brown cheek near him. "But where's Coonardoo?"

The others fell back, and Coonardoo moved towards him, carrying her baby.

Hugh's heart moved with a strange sharp beat when he saw her.

But Warieda, grinning happily, gave the situation its rhythm again.

"Coonardoo grow 'm cooboo," he said.

"Cripes." Hughie went to Coonardoo and stood looking down on the cooboo. "That's a surprise for us! Coonardoo's the fond mother of three now," he explained to the sonsy young woman who had hopped from the buggy, and was standing like a brilliant parakeet, a little bewildered and aghast at the dreary and dilapidated aspect of her new home, with this horde of dirty ragged blacks about it.

"Winning-arra, boy coobinju," Warieda explained proudly.

"A jolly fine one at that!"

Hugh stood beside Coonardoo, looking down at the child, knowing as he did so that this was his son, knowing what the blacks did not suspect, as if someone had twisted the fibres of his being, giving them a sudden wrench and tightness. Coonardoo looked at him, and then down at her baby; but Hugh had seen her eyes, waiting for him, asking nothing, expecting nothing, ready, he knew, to serve his wife, this white woman he had brought to live with him, as tenderly and devotedly as she had him and his mother.

88

"This is Coonardoo," Hughie told his wife. "You know I told you, she was mother's pet girl and looked after me when I had fever. She's Warieda's woman, and Meenie there, too. But they help with the housework. Meenie, Bandogera and Coonardoo are the house-girls. Bardi there, the little grub, she's too fat and lazy."

Hugh was gazing at the long verandas, the closed doors and dust-dimmed windows of the house before him, white of the walls and roof under red-ochre dust.

"Lord, doesn't it look neglected!" he exclaimed.

But plants his mother had set were blossoming in the strip of broken earth out from the veranda, punti showering fragile trails of little flowers like yellow boronia, fragrant and exquisite. Bird-bush held branches of green flowers as if small birds were clustered and swaying all in a row; and at the end of the veranda oleanders, tall and dark-leafed, dropped under milk-white bloom.

"They have kept the verandas scrubbed, and swept round the house," he added. "If there'd been a chance to send word and let 'em know we were coming, so as they could clean up inside, Mollie, I would have. But I don't know whether they'd have gone into the house, anyhow."

"Why on earth?" Hugh's wife asked.

Hugh laughed. "You see mother thought she'd put the fear of goodness into them, and told them she'd always be watching over the place, looking after it . . . and if anybody took advantage of her being away, to pinch sugar or tea, and didn't behave well to me, they'd better look out for themselves. She said her spirit would jump into a white cockie, and always she'd be flying round to see all was being done as it ought to be—until another white woman came. Then she'd leave Wytaliba in peace. And they would have to obey the other white woman as they had her. So, as a matter of fact, everybody's very glad to see you."

Hughie walked along the veranda, throwing open the doors; went into the rooms and unlatched the windows.

"Tomorrow everything'll be fresh and sweet as a new pin," he said.

"Here you fellows, how about some rations?"

The blacks crowded to the kitchen door. "Here Joey, Warieda, and you, Meenie!" Hugh called, naming two or three to come into the kitchen and pass on food as he portioned it out. When he opened the flour-bin, moths flew out, spiders had woven their webs over the sugar. But they were liberal rations every man, woman and child on Wytaliba got that evening. There were apples and boiled lollies in the packs on the buggy, and Hugh dispensed them with tobacco and tins of jam, promising new boots, trousers, hats, pipes, gina-ginas and goodness knows what not, when he visited the store next morning.

CHAPTER XIV

STARS were still in the high dark, as a coolwenda called from the fringe of distant mulga. His two notes in the silence rang, pure and slow, far over the plains.

Coonardoo, beside the embers of her fire, stirred and sat up. Already streaking across the rough stony earth towards the homestead, she saw the tall straight figure of Meenie, and Bandogera, stooping a little as she hurried. She was getting old, Bandogera. So quickly the light grew, Coonardoo had no more than raised her baby's head to her breast and he, shaking his round fair head and bucking, settled in against her, than the sun jumped over the far edge of the trees.

At the same time everybody in the uloo was awake. Warieda stretched and stalked away down to the creek. Fires were kicked, embers thrown together; there were exclamations; dogs yelped, stirred from sleeping bodies. Coonardoo saw a breath of smoke go up from the kitchen chimney.

"It breathes; it breathes again!" she cried to her baby.

She knew every detail of the morning's work up there at the homestead, and was eager to be at it with Meenie and Bandogera. When they had lit the fire they would pump at the little mill, carry kerosene buckets of fresh water from the mill to the house, fill a kettle on the stove; leave one bucket beside the fireplace and take the other to a brush shed beside the kala miah where they would scrub their heads, make a lather of soap, plaster their bodies with it, and stand while each poured water over the other. Meenie would pour it over Bandogera, shrieking with laughter, while the old woman gasped and suffered the breaking and splash of the water over her head, and as little of her body as possible.

Their morning wash was a real hardship to the old women; but Coonardoo had showered in the shed under the big mill since she was a child, and laughed at Meenie and Bandogera taking their wash by the kala miah.

But where were the white cockies this morning? Already they had flown off and were feeding out on the plains.

Coonardoo could see Hugh striding about the verandas, his legs in blue trousers, stepping briskly. White shirt, blue trousers and the pink blob of his face, she could see them coming and going from the rooms to the veranda, from the veranda to the kitchen.

Coonardoo laughed and pulled a milk-sweet nipple out of her baby's mouth. To be sure he had sucked until he could not move, the little fat pig. And she must hurry to make morning tea for Hugh's woman. Already day was growing; the sun was moving across the sky.

The air smelt hot and dry. It was going to be a day which would bring blossoms down from the white gum-tree beside the veranda, showering white threads, and yellow dust. Coonardoo would sweep them away, and she would sit and sing in the shade of the tree when Pinja brought her boy to her during the morning. For it was understood that the old woman would mind the son of a whirlwind while she, Coonardoo, swept the dust from Hugh's house; scrubbed and washed dishes as Mumae had taught her.

Coonardoo must make tea also, and take it to Hugh's woman while she was in bed. Everybody knew that. Who but Coonardoo knew how to arrange the little tray, set a cup and saucer on it, with sugar and milk, and a flower? Happily there was milk; a cow with calf in, Meenie had been making Coonardoo herself drink cow's milk. Coonardoo could see her going up to the stock-yards with a bucket now, and Bandogera tramping after her to help bail and leg-rope the wild red heifer. Hugh himself would milk, most likely, after today.

Coonardoo set her boy in the coolamon she had scooped with sharp stones from the elbow of a river gum and took him to sleep beside her grandmother, warning her, as she laid a leafy branch over the child, not to delay bringing him to the house when he wakened and cried for another meal. Then she ran up to the kala miah, seized a bar of yellow soap which lay on a log there and went down to the shower-shed with it.

How she scrubbed her hair. Was not Youie home? Happiness grew in her until she screamed with glee as she let down the showers of well water, starting and gurgling, when her nerves curled and quivered under it. Was not Youie home? And did he not expect that she should wash like this every day? There was the gina-gina she had worn when he left, hanging in the shower-shed waiting for her to put on again.

Coonardoo slipped the long straight gown of faded dungaree over her body and, with short hair dripping still, went up to the kitchen to make tea. How carefully she measured tea from a red caddy into the big enamel teapot, and poured boiling water over the leaves as she had done for Mumae.

She called to Meenie for milk, and when Meenie brought the bucket, strained milk into a shallow pan, taking some in a little jug for the tray.

Then on silent bare feet, carefully, she carried the tray to the shady side of the veranda. Hugh had hauled the big bed out there, the bed his father and mother once slept in. She was lying on it, the little woman with straight dark hair and grey-green eyes, whom he had brought back with him. Lying there, she looked about her curiously, dismayed, hopeful and adventurous, taking everything in. Her pink gina-gina! Coonardoo could not take her eyes off that.

She stood beside Hugh's wife holding the tray. Too shy to look up, seeing the gina-gina under her lashes—soft silky stuff like that flush in the sky before sunrise—and the plump little woman under it.

"Coonardoo, isn't it?" Hugh's woman queried. "Thank you, Coonardoo."

Coonardoo's eyes flashed to her from under their long curling lashes, deep beautiful dark eyes, promising love and devotion.

The morning passed like a happy dream. It was what Coonardoo had thought of so long. Hugh's home-coming and getting the house ready for the woman he would bring with him, to live in it. Coonardoo had not wondered whether she would like the new-comer. She knew that she would. Was she not Hugh's woman?

She told the other gins about the pink gina-gina Mollie wore when she was in bed, as they drank their strong black tea, sweetened with plenty of sugar, and ate the bread and jam Hugh had doled out to them. He was as gay and generous as when he had been a little fellow. Everybody ate until they were full, and very happy, smoked and gossiped about Mulli. What was it he called her? They tried to get their tongues round the name, and laughed at the queer sound it had.

Hugh himself cooked the breakfast that morning, and his wife came to eat with him in the dining-room, a gown over the pink gina-gina, at which Coonardoo opened her eyes wider and wider. So many birds and flowers were scattered over it, and fruit that you could almost take off with your hands! She stood transfixed in awe and admiration; and Meenie beside her gurgled and exclaimed.

"What is it?" Mollie asked.

"They like your kim," Hugh explained.

Meenie put out her hand to see if the apples on the chintz of Mollie's kimono would come off, giggling and cuddling herself shyly when she found they were only coloured drawings.

Hugh said all the dishes in the kitchen were to be washed in boiling water with plenty of soap, the veranda must be hosed down, every room had to be swept and scrubbed out. The gins went eagerly about their work, treating it all rather as a joke, laughing, and exclaiming to each other.

And Mollie, sitting beside her trunk on the veranda, unpacked, strewed the worn jarrah boards with ribbons, frocks, under-clothing, lace, pictures, bright scarves, shoes, scented soap, and silver-backed brushes; trinkets and wedding presents of all sorts. She took out a bottle of sweets and called the girls to her; poured a handful of small boiled lollies into Coonardoo's hand and into Meenie's; gave Coonardoo a long piece of blue print for a dress and Bardi a necklace of red beads.

Hugh came stamping along the veranda.

"Now then, you fellows," he called; and the gins, from watching and exclaiming over the treasures which poured from Mollie's box, scattered about their work.

Hugh had fastened spurs to his boots, and was itching to be out with the boys after the killer they were going to bring in that afternoon.

So the morning passed. Hugh opened tins from the store for lunch, and made damper.

"Most people don't let the blacks cook for them," he said. "Mother used to do most of it herself. But please yourself about that. She taught Coonardoo and Meenie to do nearly everything. They can sew and cook quite well. But Bardi's a lazy little swob . . . not too clean. I don't know that I'd trust her——"

"Oh, I can cook," Mollie replied.

Hugh laughed and kissed her.

"It'll be awfully strange and lonely at first," he said. "But you're a brick, little woman. I hope you'll like being here."

"It isn't what I expected," Mollie confessed. "But the abos are different—nicer than any I've ever seen before."

"That's because they're Pedongs, for the most part—haven't had much contact with white people," Hugh said. "A good deal depends on how you treat them. Mother handled them extraordinarily well. It's the iron hand in the velvet glove does the trick, she used to say. Was very strict about some things. Respected them and their ideas. Made 'em respect hers. If they wanted the things she had to give, she made them do what she wanted, obey her, wash, and not take anything without asking. They're naturally honest . . . fair dealers."

"Who's that laughing?" Mollie asked, as merry girlish laughter rippled again and again from the wood-heap where the blacks were eating their midday meal.

"Oh, that's Coonardoo," Hugh said.

When he rode up to the veranda on Hector a little later, Hugh looked as full of exuberant vitality as the chestnut.

"I've got to go out after a killer. You'll be all right?" he called.

Mollie looked up, startled. Was he going away already? Far? And would he be long?

"Be back before sundown," Hugh cried gaily.

Hector had not been ridden for months and was bounding and reefing under him.

"Isn't he gorgeous?" He swung and posed the horse for Mollie's admiration.

Mollie gasped, watching the chestnut with more fear than pleasure.

Coonardoo, going across to the gum-tree beside the veranda, where she intended to sit in the shade and feed her baby, stood a moment to watch Hugh and his horse. She smiled to herself, knowing he was showing off, to let the horse play up like that. Hugh seeing her, and knowing Coonardoo would guess what he was doing, laughed across at her.

"Coonardoo'll look after you!" he shouted to Mollie as Hector swung and danced out, tail stretched and neck bowing. "Won't you Coonardoo?"

Coonardoo's eyes, their steady gaze, met his. There was no need to reply. He knew, and she knew, how loyal her caring for his wife would be.

Warieda, Chitali, and Mick were cantering down from the shed. Hugh turned and rode out to them.

Mollie went back to unpacking and stowing clothes and wedding presents from her boxes, to drawers and cupboards in her new home.

Coonardoo sat down under the gum-tree, opened her gina-gina and gave her breast to her baby. He clutched and clung to her.

She sang as he sucked, watching the blossoms fall:

> "*Towera chinima poodinya*
> *Towera jinner mulbeena. . . .*"

The words of her little song bubbled and burbled together. White sweet blossoms on the tall tree waved and fell over her. The tree became dark. The blossoms were stars in a dark sky, and drooping, as her baby dropped from her breast, Coonardoo stretched to sleep there in the shade under the still blue sky.

CHAPTER XV

MOLLIE laughed when she heard Hugh telling the gins what to do about the house next morning. At first she had not been sure enough of herself to ask for anything, much less give orders. But she was beginning to feel at home.

"This is my home," she told herself. "These are my servants."

Looking round the edge of her door she saw Hugh, spurs and hat on, a sturdy figure, not very tall, of average height, standing there on the veranda, the gins before him as he gave instructions for the day's work. She thought he looked "the master", every inch of him, and very nice in his white moleskin trousers, faded blue shirt, big-brimmed felt hat, stock-whip looped over one shoulder, a brass match-box and clasp-knife on his broad leather belt, his pipe tucked through it. She was very proud of being his wife; still a little excited about it and the adventure she had embarked on.

Not that Hugh's courtship had been at all what she imagined a courtship should be. There had been no love-making about it. In the most matter-of-fact way he had asked her whether she thought she would like to marry him and live outback on a rather rough and lonely cattle station. Maid of all work in a boarding-house in Geraldton, where Hugh stayed for a few days after he left the hospital, she had thought he was joking. He declared he was quite serious, and she supposed he must like her, more than he said, to be wanting to marry her.

If Hugh had not been much of a lover before they were married, he was the most lover-like of husbands. Mollie found herself thoroughly enjoying being Mrs Hugh Watt, during the long journey from the coast to Wytaliba. Hugh was good to look at, gentle and courteous; and being waited on, considered, looked after—the experience was so new to Mollie, who had run about, waiting on and looking after other people as long as she could remember, that she lapped it up greedily. And Hugh, she felt sure, was liking her much better than he did when they started out on the journey.

He smiled gratefully to her for "cracking hardy", pretending she was not tired when her back ached and her head swayed giddily on the long days driving, and gazing through dust and blinding sunshine, over the ever-widening, ever-distancing plains.

"It's quite romantic, after all, isn't it?" Hugh asked happily when they camped by the roadside. He made a fire and spread their mattress under the open sky. "You and I to be driving away like this!"

"It is, isn't it?" Mollie replied.

Hugh did not pretend to be "gone on her": "wild about her". "I want a wife," he had said, "a good sensible girl like you, Mollie, to come and be mates with me out there. We'd get on well together, I think. You've had a hard life . . . and I'll try to make up. Be good to you."

"Don't be a fool," her aunt who kept the boarding-house advised. "He's the best chance you'll ever get. Even if you're not in love with him, you can easily be."

Aunt Emily was right, sure enough, Mollie reflected. And Mrs Fairweather, the doctor's wife, said Hugh had chosen her from among several of the prettiest girls in Geraldton, who would have been quite willing to go and live with him on Wytaliba.

Mollie had heard Eustace Fairweather congratulating Hugh, on the day Hugh and she were married.

"I think you're right, my boy," he said. "You've chosen well. She looks sound in wind and limb—a good, commonsense little creature, who will be grateful for all you do on her behalf."

Hugh hoped that Mollie was as pleased with their companionship as he. There was nothing he desired so much as to make his wife happy and satisfied.

Looking through the doorway, she thought it was funny to see him standing there, ordering the gins about.

"Here," she called, "that's my job."

"Right." Hugh turned to laugh back at her. "You can have it."

He went over to the door of her room; Mollie was standing half dressed, twisting up her hair, before a small square mirror.

"I've got to get out and do some branding, or we'll be short of calves this year," Hugh said.

"I'll be all right."

Mollie's smile and her cheery assurance brought Hugh across

the threshold. He kissed her bare shoulder and went out of the room again.

She heard him whistling as he swung along the veranda to the kitchen. There he made a great noise about tucker bags which had not been washed or could not be found; rationed the blacks, carved hunks of meat from a huge joint and put tea, sugar and flour in their tins.

"Can you make bread?" he asked when Mollie trotted into the kitchen, fresh and eager-looking in a lavender-checked print dress.

Prowling round shelves against the wall, she lifted pie dishes, milk tins, saucepans. Every second one had a hole in, and some were plugged with scraps of dirty rag. She sniffed and explored.

"You see," Hugh apologized, "mother was a bit mean about these sort of things. She didn't know quite what I would do. We'll make a list and send down for all the new things you want."

Mollie's face lighted.

"I'll make it while you're away," she replied promptly. "You'll see how different the kitchen will look presently. You won't know the place."

"The gins will do all the hard work, scrubbing and washing," Hugh said. "Meenie knows what mother did, or Coonardoo. But they'll do just what you tell them. Be firm, and then carry on as if you were having rather a good joke together."

Hugh went off a few minutes later. Mollie saw him riding with the boys towards hills which looked as if they had been dipped in a blue-bag.

She set to work to put her kitchen to rights. She had spent so much time working in other people's kitchens, washing their dishes, scrubbing their floors. And this great barn of a place was her kitchen, filthy and ramshackle as it was, no curtain on the window, glass cracked and quite out of one square, no newspaper on the shelves. "No nothing," as Mollie put it to herself.

Whatever else Hugh's mother was, she wasn't much of a housekeeper, Mollie decided. She might have been able to run a station; but Mollie bet herself, any money she liked, she would run rings round Mrs Bessie, housekeeping.

And fancy having so many servants! Elated at the thought of her dignity, Mollie bustled the gins about as Mrs Armstrong had bustled her about so often. On the whole she was rather glad Mrs Armstrong had bustled her; insisted on her doing things properly. She would show Hugh how a house should be run, and the gins too, Mollie promised herself. This slow, lazy, go-as-you-please way of doing things would not suit her.

For the first time in her life Mollie had a sense of ownership. Her proprietorship in this kitchen, these pots and pans, was a new sensation. It was her kitchen, these were her pots and pans. Mollie was very proud of herself, disdaining them, sending them to the rubbish heap, ordering the gins about, getting their wide eyes of awe and amazement, hearing their exclamations.

All day she spring-cleaned the kitchen enthusiastically, giving herself and the girls only time for a cup of tea and some bread and butter at midday.

Hugh left her keys for the hut of mud bricks with a thatched roof, at a little distance from the homestead, and Mollie had jingled the keys importantly and gone down to the store, taking Coonardoo with her, to show where things were.

The store had been a revelation.

"Why, it's a shop, isn't it?" she exclaimed delightedly when the big key Coonardoo fitted into a huge lock grated and groaned; the barred door swung back.

"Wiah!" Coonardoo breathed anxiously, as Mollie stepped into the store.

"Why, what is it?" Mollie hesitated on the threshold, realizing the warning and fear in the girl's exclamation.

"Koodgeeda." Coonardoo gasped. "Koodgeeda lie down here."

"Oh!" Mollie understood. It was better to wait in the doorway until her eyes were accustomed to the dark of the windowless hut after the brilliant sunshine out of doors.

Taking a long stick from the outside wall, Coonardoo beat the floor. Mollie heard the thatch rustle as a snake slipped away through the roof.

She remembered Hugh had warned her, "Be careful when you go down to the store. It hasn't been opened for a long time, and sometimes a stray snake or two goes to sleep down there."

Mollie was terrified of snakes. She did not know whether she would go into the store after all. But Coonardoo walked into the hut on her bare feet, and glanced back, smiling, as if to say, "It's all right. You may come in now."

Once in, Mollie was thrilled by the store. It was a shop really, a little shop in the dark, very dirty and badly arranged—shirts and men's blue trousers hanging up all together; rows and rows of tins in gaudy wrappers, jam, cocoa, coffee, tomato sauce, fish, along the wall; bags and bins of flour, sugar and tea piled at one end.

Mollie was thoroughly pleased to think that a shop went with a station. She understood the shop better than the station, and looking about, promised herself a good time arranging and putting it in order when the house had been disposed of. Meanwhile, she was a little chary of putting her hands among the bales and packages, not knowing when a swift, gleaming body might not slip from among them.

"Salt and whitewash," she told Coonardoo. "And what's that? Green paint? Let's have some of that too."

Coonardoo foraged for and found the salt. She took a tin of green paint from a high shelf. But "whitewash", she shook her head, smiling, and trying to tell Mollie that came from a creek bed some distance away. You pounded the soft limestone to dust, and mixed it with water. She would send the children for some.

Mollie did not quite understand; but nodded her head, realizing Coonardoo knew what she wanted and would get it for her.

Thrusting her hand into a tin which held nuts and raisins, Coonardoo brought out a handful and held them to Mollie with eyes which gleamed and laughed, as much as to say, "See this is where the treasure is hidden!"

Mollie took a raisin, and shook her head.

"No, you eat the rest," she said.

Coonardoo's slim fingers curled over the nuts and raisins. She did not eat them herself, but clutched them carefully. Later, Mollie heard her calling children from the uloo, and saw her giving the nuts and raisins to Charmi and Beilaba.

Two old women had come over from the uloo and asked for tobacco and gina-ginas. Mollie did not know what to do about them. Coonardoo scolded angrily and sent them away again.

She helped Mollie to carry the salt, green paint, coffee, cocoa, jam and tinned fish they had raided from the store.

Very pleased with herself and her possessions, Mollie walked over the rough stony earth to the house again, thinking how homey it looked, crouched there among dark shrubs on the red earth, against the background of tumbled blue hills, trees, thick and curled, in dense scrub upon them. The kurrajongs in a row beside the fence had fluttering crests of light-green leaves. No other homestead she had seen beyond Karrara looked as comfortable and homely.

But she was not so pleased when she found Meenie and Bandogera had taken advantage of her absence to have a smoke and yarn together at the wood-heap; and scrubbing of the kitchen floor was not much farther on than it had been an hour before.

When Hugh came in towards sunset the gins were hosing the veranda and Mollie putting the last of a few pieces of crockery and enamel-ware, considered worthy, back on the shelves. From the heavy sullen faces of Meenie and Bandogera Hugh guessed what had happened. He stood, head flung back, laughing at them, as he stepped on to the veranda.

"Nabi, silly cowa-cowa! Look at the sun!" he exclaimed, pretending that they had forgotten it was time to stop work. "Finish 'em quick feller, and come along for tucker."

As the gins scuttled away, taking the hose and brooms, Mollie came from the kitchen, conscious somehow of having done the wrong thing.

"Oh, Lord, womanie," Hugh explained, "we never work them as late as this. After midday, as a rule, they never do a tap."

"But, Hugh," Mollie protested. He saw the kitchen behind her newly whitewashed, the shelves with their newspaper runners cut and fringed, Coonardoo still arranging dishes and plates on the dresser.

"My word, you *have* been going the pace!" he exclaimed.

Mollie was not sure he was altogether pleased, but she was too satisfied with her effort to have room for wondering how Hugh felt about it. Naturally, she thought, he would not like things altered, upset. But she intended to be boss in her own kitchen. She had made up her mind about that.

"Everything was in an awful mess. I'll get the place to rights gradually," she apologized.

Hugh's sympathy and compassion welled as he kissed her.

"You're a brick," he said.

But he laughed as he had on the veranda when, turning to Coonardoo, Mollie said, with a lofty air, "That will do, you may go now."

Coonardoo said, "Yes, ma'am." And with a dignity and grace, inimitable, turned away and went out of the kitchen.

Hugh laughed as though that were the best joke he had ever heard.

"What's the matter?" Mollie inquired.

"You can't have her calling you that," Hugh explained.

"What?"

"Why, 'ma'am'. The whole countryside will have a fit."

A shade of that obduracy which was the bedrock of Mollie's character set on her face.

"I didn't think there was anyone in the countryside to have a fit. Besides——"

"They'd soon know at Nuniewarra, and you may be sure Sam Geary'd let everybody hear of it for hundreds of miles around," Hugh said.

Mollie jerked herself away from the arm he had thrown across her shoulder.

"Two old women came down to the store when I was there and said, 'Gib it gina-gina, Mullie,'" she explained. "And I said, 'Here, you mustn't call me Mullie.' I didn't know what to tell them to call me, so I said, 'You say ma'am.' When Coonardoo and the others started to Mullie me, I told them to say, 'Yes, ma'am! No, ma'am!' when they spoke to me, like I had to say to my mistress."

"I see." Hugh understood, and very tenderly went about soothing the wounded pride which had gone into this explanation.

"But we don't feel like that out here," he said. "The blacks always called my mother Mumae, because they used to hear me calling her mummy, I suppose, when I was a kid. But Mumae means father in their dialect, too, and mother was proud of their name for her. It meant mother and father really. And they've always called me You, or Youie. I've grown up with most of them . . . besides, I don't know any man in the Nor'-West who works his own place doesn't like to be called his Christian name by the blacks. We sling off at the man who makes his abos 'sir' or 'boss' him. He's a new-chum, or a sleeping partner."

"What are they to call me then?" Mollie inquired. "I never heard of a woman's servants calling her by her Christian name."

"But these people are not servants," Hugh told her, "not in the ordinary way. We don't pay them, except in food, tobacco, clothing. Treat them generously, feed them well, give them a bit of pain-killer or a dose of castor oil when they've got a bingee ache, and they'll do anything in the world for you. But you must never work them too hard—specially gins. They're not made for hard work, can't stand it. Look at their little hands. Coonardoo's—I've never seen any woman with as pretty little hands as Coonardoo's."

Mollie stared at him curiously, her brows lowering. She could see her idea of a nice orderly home threatened; but she was not beaten. She intended to be mistress in her own house. She did not mean Mrs Bessie's way of doing things to rule Wytaliba for ever. But she would go warily.

"Anybody been through while I was away?" Hugh asked Warieda, who had come to the kitchen for the blacks' ration of meat and flour.

"Sam Geary and Cock-Eyed Bob come with Saul one time," Warieda replied. "Sam got motor-car. Sheba drive 'm."

"He has, has he? A car?" Hugh cut chunks of the dark wooden-looking meat. "What did he want here, anyhow?"

Hugh had heard about Geary's car, and that he had taught Sheba to drive, so that when he was drunk she could take the wheel and deposit him wherever he wanted to go.

"Oh, just walk about. See everything all right."

The black was grinning. He knew as well as Hugh how Geary hankered after Wytaliba; how he had been scheming for years to get possession of the place.

"Want you to go over and do some horse-breaking for him?" Warieda nodded.

"And you wouldn't go, Warri?"

The black shook his head.

"Wiah!" he said. "Tell 'm Wytaliba boy. You comin' close-up now."

CHAPTER XVI

COONARDOO's face writhed and twisted. Her eyes flashed fear and hate.

Sitting under the shade miah, she was nursing her baby. Dust, blowing in a straight line along the back road, rushed towards the lower gate of the paddock which enclosed the homestead and uloo. Meenie and Bardi, sleeping in the shade, grunted and stirred at the muttered curse. Warieda wakened where he had been lying near Coonardoo. Chitali, and the boys beside him, stretched and sat up quickly, quietly, as is the aboriginal way, at any suggestion of fear or danger.

Everybody knew Coonardoo had uttered that fierce low imprecation, and why. It was Sam Geary in the low red cloud of dust spinning towards the homestead—Geary in his new motor-car.

On the shady side of the veranda, where he lay stretched on the boards for his afternoon nap, Saul Hardy got up. He had returned to Wytaliba as soon as he knew Hugh was home again. His glance swung from the wood-heap and shade miah to the road from the Five Mile gate.

Geary's car rushed out of the dust it raised, and stopped suddenly, a little distance from the house. Mollie came out from her room at the unusual sound.

Sam Geary got out of the car and walked past the wood-heap. He saw Coonardoo nursing her baby, strutted over and looked down on the child in her arms.

"So that's it, is it?" he crowed, bloodshot eyes alive with a gay ill-humour. "Where's Youie?"

Coonardoo glared at him and turned her head away. Geary went on to the house.

"Hullo, Saul." He greeted the old man exuberantly. "How's things? Come to call on the bride!"

A visitor and motor-car! Mollie could scarcely believe her eyes. But there was Geary's new Ford, already red with dust and looking as if it had spent many years on the road, standing out beyond the guardian line of kurrajongs, and a woman with him. Mollie could not see more than her pink dress, in the car.

She did not know who the man was. Hugh was working in the smithy with the boys. Mollie was very delighted and excited to see a visitor, put her hand to her hair; and wished she had time to change her dress.

"How do you do, Mrs Watt," Geary hailed in a thick, jovial voice.

Mollie came towards him across the veranda.

She put out her hand.

"My name's Geary, Sam Geary. We're neighbours."

"Oh, yes," Mollie fluttered. "Won't you come in, Mr Geary? But," she added, "won't you bring in the lady too—Mrs Geary, is it?"

Sam Geary looked back at Sheba.

He guffawed. The light in his eyes rippled, broken into little waves by the tides of alcohol and amusement.

"No," he said. "No, I don't think I will. She'd rather stay where she is. That's Sheba, the Queen of Sheba. Haven't you heard of her? Oh well, you will. She gives 'em something to talk about in this part of the world. Don't you think I'm rather a good Samaritan to give 'em something to talk about?"

"Of course," Mollie agreed nervously.

Geary sat down in the little sitting-room which held the enlarged photograph of Mrs Bessie, disconcerted by catching a glimpse of her staring at him, grey and wraith-like, from the walls. He did not know what to say next. Mollie did not know what to say. She sat down opposite him, taking in the huge slack bulk of the man, his red perspiring face, thin wet hair and cunning eyes.

"But where's You?" Geary asked. "We been to Milli-Milli races. Should 've been there, missus. It was a great turn-out, Saul."

The old man had steered his way to the door of the sitting-room, and stood looking in, some vague idea of propriety disturbing him. What did Geary want with Hugh's woman? But the sitting-room looked too small to hold anyone else.

"Won't you sit down, Mr Hardy?" Mollie inquired politely.

But Saul had seen Hugh coming down from the smithy and harness sheds. "No," he said; "no, I don't think I will."

"Got back all right, Saul?" Geary gibed. "Youie left him in charge, missus, but he wouldn't stay by himself. The place gave him the jim-jams, he said. Mrs Bessie kept calling and calling him. Bad as the blacks, Saul is. Lived so long among 'em; gone native, as you might say."

The old man cursed under his breath; his stunted creaking figure moved off along the veranda.

Mollie heard Hugh's step. His head and shoulders shut off the light as he stood in the doorway.

"Hullo, Youie." Geary heaved himself out of the chair. "How's things? Came to pay me respects to the bride."

"Good day, Sam."

Hugh's greeting was short. It was evident that he was not the least pleased to see the visitor.

"Comin' along the track from Milli-Milli races, thought we'd better turn in here," Geary made conversation obligingly. "My, it was a great meeting. Should 've been there, Youie! There was about a hundred turned up and Milli-Milli homestead isn't no bigger than this. Where they put everybody to sleep, Gord knows. Found meself turnin' in with a mother and twins, and wasn't there a hullabaloo! Should have heard it! They haven't stopped laughing on Milli-Milli yet, I'll bet.

"We don't get many festivities in this part of the world, missus. Make the most of those we do get! A Nuniewarra colt won the Creek cup, You. . . ."

Geary babbled on, refusing to notice Hugh's lack of cordiality.

"Staying the night, or pushing off?" Hugh asked.

"Oh, well, since you are so pressin'. . . ." Geary's malicious humour was equal to even that. "But perhaps I'd better be moving on."

"You'll have some tea, though?" Mollie jumped up to go to the kitchen.

"That's all right, missus," Geary replied suavely. "Youie knows better. There was a corner in her own special cupboard Mrs Bessie kept for me."

"Bring a couple of glasses, Mollie," Hugh said.

Mollie went to the kitchen for the glasses.

Hugh opened the little old-fashioned chiffonier in which Mrs Bessie kept whisky, and put a bottle on the table. Mollie reappeared with glasses, a jug of water, and a biscuit barrel on a tray. Geary poured himself out a drink, and lifted his glass to her.

On the whole Mollie did not think he was as bad as he looked. He had a kind of rough and kindly geniality.

"You might find it a bit lonesome up here, missus," he said. "See Youie don't forget to give you a run over to Milli, some time. They'd be real pleased to see you. I'll run you over in the car, Youie, you and the missus, some day. Takes a week or so with horses; but we do it in a couple of days in the car. Or you might come over to Nuniewarra. I got one of these ding-dong gramophones up, and we could have a bit of music."

"Oh, thank you! Thank you, Mr Geary," Mollie exclaimed, feeling grateful to him for thinking she might be lonesome some time, and would like a run over to Milli-Milli creek or Nuniewarra.

Through the door of the sitting-room she could see the blacks standing round the car, talking to the woman Geary had called Sheba. Warieda was there, Meenie, Bardi, and the children. They got into the car and she drove out across the plain with them. Through that narrow opening of Mrs Bessie's sitting-room Mollie watched the car turn and come towards the house again, the girl in the bright-pink frock and red hat with flowers, having given folk from the uloo a ride in Sam Geary's new and strange vehicle.

Going down to the gate Geary stumbled; Mollie heard him swear and pull himself up.

"By Gord, Youie, lucky devil, aren't you? Real sonsy little woman, I call her. But, I say——"

Stalking away from the wood-heap, Coonardoo's lithe figure caught his eyes. Coonardoo, carrying her baby, was going down to the uloo so that she would not see Sam Geary again.

Standing with Hugh at the gate Geary seemed to be enjoying himself hugely. Laughing and chuckling, he jogged Hugh's elbow. Mollie could not hear what he said; but she guessed Hugh was angry about it. He wrenched himself away from Geary, and stood, so taut and square, confronting him.

"But how about Coonardoo?" Geary burbled. "How about Coonardoo, Youie? And Coonardoo's cooboo? By God, that's as good a joke as ever I heard. Give you my word. Now there's some of us don't pretend to be saints, good Lord! But them as do—ain't no better than the rest of us. And I reck'n you owe me a case of whisky, You!"

"Look here, Sam." Hugh glanced across at the veranda where Mollie was standing. "Stop that—once and for all. Do y' understand?"

Geary chuckled.

"That's all right, Youie, me boy! Eleven, I've got, eleven of 'em! Talk about the patriarchs. But I know when to keep me mouth shut. Understand? I understand. She's a real decent little woman and I don't blame you. Rather have Sheba, meself, or Coonardoo. Gins work out better in this country. They don't rouse, and you know where you are with 'em. They know where you are when you've got a bit in. No, I wouldn't do you for your wife, but I've always had a fancy for Coonardoo, you know. I don't mind takin' on Coonardoo, any time you like."

Sheba drove up to the gate again. Warieda and the children scrambled out of the car, chattering and exclaiming at the wonder of it.

Judging that he had reduced Hugh to a state of speechless fury, Geary took his seat beside Sheba. The car jerked, snorted, and swung off.

"Why, Hugh, what's the matter? What did he say?" Mollie went over to Hugh, as soon as the car moved away, and gazed with amazement at his torn and passion-wrought face.

"Oh, he's a foul-minded brute!" he told her. "I loathe and detest him. What he wants to come here for I don't know—except that he likes to make me mad. He always has, ever since I can remember. God, how I hate him! If ever I murder a man it'll be Sam Geary."

"Hugh, for goodness' sake!" Mollie was frightened, although she was curious too. "But the girl, was she a half-caste? She looked it; she had a pink silk dress on, and did you see her wristlet watch and the gold chain round her neck?"

"I didn't," Hugh said.

"Is she a half-caste?" Mollie insisted.

"No. Oh, no, she's pure-blooded all right," Hugh said bitterly. "That's Sheba, the Queen of Sheba he calls her. Geary gives all his gins Old Testament names."

"Goodness!" Mollie gasped. "But I never thought they treated gins like that."

"Some do," Hugh said bitterly, "and some just clear out and let 'em starve."

"But fancy his giving her silk dresses and a wristlet watch!"

"Why shouldn't he?" Hugh rasped. "She earns 'em, goodness knows."

"Some men don't give even their wives a wristlet watch, or silk dresses," Mollie said. There was a sting in her word.

Hugh looked after her as she trotted back to the house. More than once he had glimpsed the small mind whirring as if a wasp had built its clay nest within that neat compact body.

For weeks afterwards Mollie talked of Geary; asking questions about him, and about Sheba, or Tamar her predecessor. She asked Hughie what happened when you went to Nuniewarra. "You don't go to Nuniewarra," Hugh said. "At least white women don't."

By careful inquiry Mollie heard that Geary had one house for Tamar and another for Sheba. Tamar was old and looked after the youngsters, though some of the boys went out with the stockmen now and girls had been given to passing teamsters, or drovers.

Sheba looked after Geary, cooked for him and washed his clothing, or saw that Tamar and some of the girls did it for him. She was his favourite woman for the time being. He could not get along without her, Saul Hardy said. She was manager of Nuniewarra really, kept the store-room keys, and guarded the whisky and tobacco when Sam was drunk.

If a man went to Nuniewarra it was Sheba who came out to meet him, did the honours, showed him to a guest-room in which she kept clean sheets, a towel, soap and hair-brushes. She was a remarkable woman, everybody agreed, intelligent and useful; drove Sam's car for him. When he went to the port he took a room for Sheba in the best hotel in the township.

On one famous occasion, of which there was still gossip, he had taken apartments at a pub for both Tamar and Sheba. There was no room for Charley Leigh and his wife and children when they came along. The gins got on quite well together, were quiet and unobtrusive, and Sam Geary's custom was worth too much for a publican to offend him.

But Mollie could not get over it. So much fuss to be made about a gin! Of course, at most places where there were white women, Sheba did not come into the house. She had to go to the wood-heap with the other blacks. Mrs Bessie, Mollie understood, would not have Sheba to sleep in the house. She had to go to the kala miah, or uloo, at Wytaliba, and Mollie decided that was one rule of Mrs Bessie's she would always enforce.

She had tried pumping the girls about Geary. Meenie, Bardi, and Coonardoo, in turn, she plied with questions; but could get nothing out of them, except Meenie. She said, with pride, that Geary had wanted Coonardoo: he had offered a horse, rugs and a gun to Joey Koonarra for her. But Coonardoo had been promised to Warieda and Joey was afraid to displease Warieda and Mrs Bessie, who had said Joey was not to give Coonardoo to Sam Geary. When Youie was away Geary had come and offered Warieda a rug and horse for Coonardoo. But Warieda would not give her. It was before the cooboo was born.

Coonardoo scowled as she heard Meenie talking.

"She doesn't like him, Coonardoo?" Mollie asked.

Meenie shook her head, laughing, the glimmering light of sunset in her wise eyes. "Coonardoo, Wytaliba girl," she said.

"And he's after Coonardoo, the old blackguard," Mollie told Hugh. "Meenie says. . . ."

Hugh's face, heavy and thoughtful, stirred under the skin.

Mollie watched him suspiciously.

"You'd never be a gin's man, Hughie?"

"No." Hugh got to his feet, feeling for the pipe in his belt.

"I remember," Mollie remarked, "you told me some men, out here, go with gins. But you've tried to keep yourself clear of that sort of thing. You'd never——"

"No." Hugh faced the inevitable lie, fairly and squarely. "I've never gone with a gin."

The gin has come with me, was the cynical saver he gave his conscience. But why make trouble for himself? It was impossible to say, "Coonardoo's child is mine also. She doesn't know. Nor anyone, except Geary. He guesses."

Mollie could not be expected to understand or like it. She would resent the sight of Coonardoo about the place. Would demand that she be sent away.

And Coonardoo could not be sent away from Wytaliba. Had she not grown there? And Warieda. It would mean losing him. The station could not afford to lose Warieda. Wytaliba came first with Hugh; but he had so assimilated the aboriginal point of view that he felt no need for hostility between himself and Warieda, because of Coonardoo. Hugh had a real affection for the big handsome aborigine. Almost all he knew of cattle, tracks and country he had learnt from Warieda in the great open book of the plains and the ranges. His feeling for the black was more respect and admiration than anything else. Had not Warieda stood by him in his great need; sent Coonardoo to him even? There was no deception about that, although Warieda believed Winningarra was his own son; any child of Coonardoo's would be his son.

Through his love of the country and of Wytaliba, Hugh realized, was woven regard for the people who had grown in and were bound to it. To the country he had attached himself with a stubbornness there was no thwarting or denying; and the people who served and fought it with him, claimed his loyalty, protection. Saul Hardy told terrible stories of shootings, and the abuse of native women in the early days. There had been native retaliations, of course. There still were; but on these inland plains the tribes were peaceful and conservative, avoided contact with white people, other than those they knew and had become accustomed to. Neither Saul Hardy nor Mumae had ever experienced trouble with Wytaliba folk. Generous, kindly their relationship had been, in an overlordship imposed, gradually and imperceptibly, until the blacks recognized and accepted it, by conditions of work for food and clothing.

The aboriginal sense of justice recognized the bond. It had never been broken. That was why Hugh believed Wytaliba people were different from the blacks on so many other stations. Poor degraded wretches, treated like dogs, worse than dogs, they were, on stations farther south and nearer the coast. Dirty, diseased, ill natured, lost to their tribal laws and customs, he had seen them, remnants of a dying race, drifting about the up-country towns and settlements along the coast. As Saul and his mother had dealt with Wytaliba folk, so he would deal with them, Hugh promised himself. He would keep faith as they had kept faith with him—and the Gnarler sing round their camp-fires in the uloo, through the years ahead, as they had done for all the years he could remember.

"It's a good sign, Hughie," his mother used to say, when she heard the blacks singing round their fires in the evening. "I'm always glad when I hear them singing like that. Shows they're happy and content."

And Warieda was chief singer, leader in the corroborees. Hugh remembered his song of the steam-engine; how it had remained with him and haunted him while he was ill, on the boat, and in Geraldton.

> *"Me-ra-rar ngar-rar ngular-gar gartha-gara!*
> *Mooranger! Nar-ra-ga! Mille-gidgee!"*

He went about trying to whistle it, and caught the gleam of Warieda's eyes, lighted to pleasure and amusement.

CHAPTER XVII

WINTER on Wytaliba was no more than a season of keen cold winds. For a few months after the rains the air cooled and freshened each day. In the early morning and at night it was so cold that the blacks went shivering in their thin clothing. The old women wandered about carrying fire-sticks to warm them.

Mollie laughed to see Bandogera driving the big red and patchy white cows Hugh had brought in for milking towards the yards at dawn, crouched over the glowing end of a fire-stick. The old woman scuttled over the stones on her bare feet, throwing stones at the cows to make them hurry, a drab, stooping figure in an old coat and felt hat which had belonged to her man, long ago.

But Mollie was glad to huddle into a woollen jacket and stand over a fire, herself. She spread meals in the kitchen, shutting the doors and windows to keep out the wind. The wind was keen all day, during June and July, sometimes, although usually sunshine played brilliant and warming at midday; coats and jackets were shed, and a sky, soft as smoke from the blacks' fires, deepening towards the zenith, spread over the plains, hills and trees, finely etched, delicately toned, in the still bright air.

After the dust storms and first rain, clouds floated, white and hard, from behind Nungarra peak, drifted across the sky, like pieces of wadding, scattered and vanished. There were days of diminished light and a tepid greyness during the rainy season. But a cloudy sky over the wide plains, how everybody watched and exclaimed at it! From the moment small clouds broke flowering, at sunrise from behind the bluff of Nungarra, until they massed, threatening and thunderous, reflecting the sunset, all eyes followed their pageant.

Sometimes the clouds brought rain, hail-stones, thunder and lightning; and sometimes the beautiful white vapours just piled up and curled across the sky for days, wreathing beasts, mysterious landscapes, colossal towers with shadows, mauve and tawny-grey of the smoke from bushfires. Hugh called Mollie to show her a gigantic polar bear pawing the air; and a snow-white peacock with long splayed tail, star-eyed. Lake lands, alps, avalanches, glaciers; silver, glittering, immaculate forests and seas of islands, gleamed and misted away.

When the clouds played about like that the blacks said they did not mean business. There would be no rain. Coonardoo told the children stories about the great koodgeeda who lolled there in the clouds and rolled out of sight. After a few days of bare blue skies the clouds would come again; but darker, hustling and jostling each other from beyond the hills, late in the afternoon, usually, and pursued by thunder. Lightning cast wriggling electric worms across a screen of sky, smoke dark, the blue of volcanic basalt. Showers slanted, veiling the hills. The first drops sped outwards, and down came the rain, sluicing and splashing with a low moan in the distance, rattle and clatter of hail-stone striking pebbles far out across the plains.

It was warm and comfortable in the big kitchen at night during the cold weather.

When Hugh and Saul Hardy had finished their evening meal, Mollie washed the dishes. Hugh took a towel and dried them for her. Saul pushed wood into the range, making a fire big enough to roast a bullock, and he and Hugh sat yarning and smoking before it, while Mollie fixed up her yeast, and the sponge for bread-making, next day.

A carbide light on the table flickered over her busy hands, fluttering and spluttering. Broad ruddy gleams from the fire struck the dresser of china on one side of the room, the piece of chintz she had nailed over a small square window beside it, and the huge wooden bins of flour, sugar, and tea in the darkness of the room behind her. If the room got too hot and stuffy with the smoke of mulga, minnerichi, and tobacco, she opened a door, and its black woodwork framed a panel of night sky, clear blue-green, and starry.

"I don't know what's the matter with this bread," Mollie remarked when her bread would not rise during the cold weather.

"The last lot of hops we got off old Ben was real bad," Hugh comforted her.

"Mrs Bessie used to put rice water in her yeast, or the water she'd boiled potatoes in," Saul remarked, sitting on a straight-backed chair, hunched over his knees and staring into the fire. "She used to put the sponge in a blue billy on the end of the mantelpiece here, this time of the year, missus. It's parky just now, though ordinairely she would just leave it on the corner of the table like you do."

"Oh, well, I don't suppose bread could be expected to rise, if I didn't make it just the same as Mrs Bessie," Mollie exclaimed tartly. She put the sponge in a big blue billy on the end of the mantelpiece, and went to the dresser for her basket of sewing.

"Where's the teams now, Mr Hardy?" she asked.

"Been near three months on the road," Saul meditated. "I've known 'em sixteen weeks comin' from Karrara."

"No wonder Ben Alsop says loading for Wytaliba don't pay." Mollie settled herself before the fire to sew.

"At ten pounds a ton . . . ." Hugh murmured, his chair tipped, legs stretched and heels on the bricked sides of the range.

"Camels bogged down be Five Rivers, I suppose," Saul went on. "They was stuck there for two weeks once. Cock-Eyed Bob was camel punchin' with Ben then. Ben cleared off to the pub and left Bob with the camels. You should 've heard Bob curse, when he was tellin' about it. But he pulled the wagon out of the river and on to the road again."

There was nothing Hugh liked better than to get the old man yarning, as they sat beside the fire in the kitchen, and a keen wind blowing over the plains thrust its way under the doors and up through the flooring boards.

"Ever have any trouble with the natives—out here, Saul?" he asked once.

Saul shook his head; he smiled into the fire.

"Mind, I don't say I didn't get one or two scares." His eyes glittered in the firelight and he smoked as the memories stirred. "Was lookin' for stray cattle up in the To-Morrow soon after I settled here. Had gone out with old Bandogera's man, Stinker. We separated, followin' tracks, and I managed to get slewed. Camped for the night, made a fire and was boiling me quart when I looked up —and there was a mob of niggers all round me."

"Goodness!" Mollie glanced aside from her sewing.

"They had spears enough to sink a ship," Saul said. "Where them blacks come from Gord knows, though Stinker'd been a bit nervous and scary the day before. I'd hobbled me horse out and they could have made a pincushion of me any moment they liked. There was nothing to do. I didn't even have a gun. Why, I don't know . . . except, I thought I knew the country and the people. But these were strangers. I wongied 'em a bit, and shared out me tucker—though there wasn't much of it. Then I sat down by the fire and went on eating as if they weren't there. They watched for a bit—then lit out.

"When I lay down by me camp-fire I never expected to leave it alive. But Gord, I was that sleepy I dozed off. And that was the last I see of 'em—till next pink-eye here on Wytaliba. Caught me horse in the morning and rode off. They were Pedongs, it seems, some of Bandogera's people."

"You were so helpless they didn't think you were worth bothering about, I suppose," Hugh commented.

"The blacks are like that, I reck'n," Saul agreed. "They never kill for sport—only for food or vengeance. I've always treated 'em fair and honest, let their women alone—and never had any trouble with 'em."

"You don't know when you may be reaping some other man's vengeance," Hugh observed. "That's the worst of it. If you get a reputation for square dealing yourself, you'll be all right, mum used to say."

"That's right." Saul moved to his memories. "And the blacks has plenty of reasons for vengeance, Youie. Thirty years I've been in this country, and there's things I've seen. . . . No black ever did to a white man what white men have done to the blacks."

Mollie wrinkled her forehead. She was impatient of the way Saul went on talking, laying down the law. Coming from one of the coastal towns, she had acquired the belief that it was a divine right of white men to ride rough-shod over anything aboriginal which stood in their way.

"But, Mr Hardy," she said, "the abos are filthy and treacherous. I thought you had no time for them."

Saul looked at her. Words formed to contradict her flatly; but he was timorous of getting to holts with a woman, more particularly this one. He watched the obstinate little mug Mollie had drawn her face into, curiously. He was no sentimentalist, old Saul: a shrewd hard-doer he had always been; but something of dismay struck him at the make-up of the little woman sitting there, stitching with quick steady flashes of needle and forearm.

Hugh stared at Mollie too. He did not know why she had interrupted. She knew nothing about the blacks really. She had wished to assert herself, he decided. She often spoke like that quite irrelevantly and off the subject, in a way which made you hopeless of reaching her mind, combating what she had said.

"No, girl," he said quietly, "they're not treacherous—except when they've been treacherously dealt with. And filthy? You never saw a wild black look as dirty as a native about the towns. And cripes, when Coonardoo's done up Warieda's white moles, you'd hardly call him filthy, would you?"

"But you're quite right, missus, I don't like 'em. Never did," Saul put in eagerly to save Mollie discomfiture. "I don't know why. It's just being different, I suppose. All the same, you can't help seein' when a thing's as plain as the nose on your face. You can't help seein' the blacks' point of view. White men came, jumped their hunting grounds, went kangaroo shooting for fun. The blacks speared cattle. White men got shootin' blacks to learn 'em. Blacks speared a white man or two—police rode out on a punishing expedition. They still ride out on punishin' expeditions. . . ."

"Didn't police in the coastal towns get one and sixpence a head for abos they brought in?" Hugh asked.

"Reduced to a shilling after a bit," Saul replied. "The police was makin' a good thing out of 'punitive expeditions'. Used to bring the niggers in, in chains, leather straps round the neck, fastened to their stirrup irons. Twenty or thirty like that, and I've seen the soles of a boy's feet raw when he came in. Never spent eighteenpence a nob on 'em either. Police'd let one or two men hunt for the rest, bring in kangaroo.

"And there was black-birding too. . . . I've seen blacks brought in, in chains for the pearlers' crews. Only on a certain part of the coast though. One crew of Swan Point boys, a pearler I knew black-birded, was so dangerous he had to drive 'em overboard when he got to sea. He and his mate, with loaded guns behind the nigs."

"You never went unarmed when you were working along creeks the pearlers put into, Saul?" Hugh asked.

The old man shook his head. "Remember I was loading for Weelarra station once and the pearling lugger that brought stores up the river was late. I was waiting for her—had a moppin lad with me. Moppins are born, as well as made, it seems. . . . This youngster, Jacky I called him, was the only survivor of his tribe. His father, the old moppin, fell on and covered him during a set-to between two tribes. When the boy was found alive he was brought up by the old women who said he was moppin, knew the things other moppins knew. Moppins of different tribes can talk together although the rest of the natives stand round and don't know what is being said. When the old men took him away to make a man of him, they agreed the lad was a moppin and taught him some more tricks. 'T any rate he was with me that time I was waiting for the Weelarra loading. And there was a mob of blacks waiting for that lugger too. . . . I gave the blacks fifty pounds of flour and went on. Weelarra was forty mile up the river; they came after me and next night the moppin lad warned me.

" 'Look out, Saul,' he says. 'Got no women with 'em.' "

"How many blacks would there be?" Hugh asked.

"Must 've been between two and three hundred camped in the sand-hills, all round." Saul squinted over the bowl of his pipe. "And there was me, lyin' awake beyond me camp-fire, a fourteen magazine Winchester rifle beside me. Jacky wongied 'em to say I had a gun could fire all night and all day, without stopping, because he'd never seen me load it. And next morning he said, 'Women come, Saul!' which meant it's all right, they're not goin' to fight. I doled out some more flour and we made long tracks."

"What's all this talk about black beef?" Hugh asked.

Saul brooded. "There's parts of a dead man his relations or enemies eat sometimes, that moppin lad told me. But it's sort of eating in memory of, to get strength or cunning. Tell you something funnier than that, Youie . . . the blacks believe white men are cannibals, particularly parsons. Heard two boys arguin' about it, once. The one who had been to missions in Broome was describing a gathering of folks for the Communion and came to me wanting me to bear him out that it was really the body and blood of Christ white people were eating in the Blessed Sacrament!"

"My God!" Hugh gazed into the fire. "We don't seem much farther on, for all this talk of evolution, do we, Saul?"

"That's just it; we aren't," Saul said.

Sometimes Mollie sat and sewed before the range when Hugh and Saul were yarning, or moved their chairs to the table for a game of cards. As often as not, though, she went to bed as soon as Hugh took the pack of cards from a corner of the kitchen mantelpiece. She hated cards, could not play five-hundred, and a game with Hugh was the joy of Saul's life.

Hugh and Saul sat playing cards in the kitchen far into the

night. Mollie wakened to hear them laughing, chiacking and black-guarding each other good-humouredly. She wished she could enjoy herself as thoroughly, turning over a pack of greasy cards. Hugh and Saul were as happy as a pair of small boys playing marbles, as they sat smoking and scoring against each other. They got no end of fun out of their game and roared hilariously over the turn-up of a card.

The teams had been sixteen weeks on the road when they reached the homestead, that first year Mollie was on Wytaliba, and it was Ben who carried word to Milli-Milli, Illigoogee, and Roebourne that Hugh Watt's missus was a "pepper-pot, by God!"

Hugh had got up in the night when the camels went prowling round the house with their bells on, and the missus could not sleep.

"If you don't take the bells off those blasted camels, Ben," he roared, "I'll cut their throats!"

Ben promised to cut Hugh's bloody throat with a bloody stirrup iron and chased camels half the night. But there was a reason for the fractiousness and uncertain temper of Hugh's good lady, he intimated up-country and round about. She would be going down to Geraldton before the hot weather set in.

CHAPTER XVIII

From her first trip to the coast Mollie returned very plump and pleased with her baby, a fat rosy little blue-eyed girl.

She felt thoroughly important and satisfied with herself. She had stayed with her aunt in Geraldton; and ever so many people had called on her, Fairweathers, Munroes, Castlereaghs, Carewes, bringing little gifts for the baby. Phyllis had bibs, bonnets and bootees enough for a dozen babies. Mrs Fairweather had taken Mollie under her wing, helped her to shop, and drove her about in her car to afternoon teas.

Curious perhaps, but not unkindly the attentions were. Everybody who ever had a baby gave Mollie advice about feeding and clothing the child, and she thoroughly enjoyed being the object of so much interest, deference and courtesy.

"As a social experiment, Mollie is quite a success," Eustace Fairweather wrote to Hugh. "That's the difference between girls in this country and a girl in the old country who might have had her experience. Mollie has no sense of inferiority because she might have washed dishes for some of these people. None whatever. She is very common sense and natural about the difference in her position now and then, taking all the amenities shown her as a matter of course. An admirable little mother, healthy, unassuming, with just sufficient realization of her importance as Mrs Hugh Watt of Wytaliba."

Hugh had gone down to Nuniewarra to meet Mollie and he was very delighted to find her so handsome and pleased to be coming home again. It had been lonelier than he expected without her in the neat orderly house she left him. And the baby, his daughter—he was filled with awe and an adoring reverence for her. Was this really his daughter, the small fat fair-skinned little creature in muslin and lace whom Mollie displayed so proudly? Any lingering regret he may have harboured that she was not a son disappeared.

A son, of course, would have belonged more to him. There was the cooboo who played about the stock-yards with the black children, his skin just a shade lighter than theirs, honey brown. With what agony Hugh thought of him, sweating at night. To Coonardoo, in all that year before Mollie went to the coast, he had scarcely spoken. Only once in the shed when he was working at the forge, a furnace going between them, and the children were playing about, running in and out of the shed, Hugh had glanced from Winni to Coonardoo, and said, "Take care of him, Coonardoo."

And Coonardoo, her dark eyes unswerving, had answered, "Eeh-mm."

"By and by, when he's a big chap, I'll take him out with me," Hugh said. "We'll give him a horse, eh, Coonardoo? Teach him to ride?"

Her eyes gleamed. She understood Hugh was attached to the child; that he would like to look after him.

"Eeh-mm," she murmured again, and turning her eyes from him went down to the house.

Mollie's baby, fresh and pink-and-white, was a fairy creature. Hugh loved her; but she was less real, much less his own than that son of a whirlwind. Always as he leant over, played with and held the baby, he thought of Winni. His affection for the boy plagued him.

Was it because he reproached himself for the existence of the child? Perhaps. Hugh could not tell. Did he reproach himself really?

Coonardoo had been the one sure thing in his life when his mother went out of it. He had grasped her. She was a stake, something to hang on to. More than that, the only stake he could hang on to. He had to remind himself of her dark skin and race. Hugh had never been able to think of Coonardoo as alien to himself. She was the old playmate; a force in the background of his life, silent and absolute. Something primitive, fundamental, nearer than he to the source of things: the well in the shadows.

It was very easy for a school-master to preach virginity in the playing fields of a boys' school; but here in a country of endless horizons, limitless sky shells, to live within yourself was to decompose internally. You had to keep in the life flow of the country to survive. You had to be with it, and of it, in order to work, move as it did. After all what was this impulse of man to woman, woman to man, but the law of growth moving within them? How could a man stand still, sterilize himself in a land where drought and sterility were hell? Growth, the law of life, which brought beauty and joy in all the world about him? No wonder the blacks worshipped life, growth—sex—as the life source.

From the moment she saw Mollie's baby there was no one more devoted to her than Coonardoo.

She had exclaimed with wide eyes at the lovely little creature. At first Mollie would scarcely allow the gins to touch Phyllis; but after a while, when the child was fractious, teething, or having digestive upsets, she was glad enough to hand the baby to Coonardoo to mind and look after for a while.

Coonardoo took the baby for walks, or put her to sleep, while Mollie rested in the afternoon. Coonardoo did all the washing and ironing of Phyllis's small clothes. Neither Meenie nor Bardi would have dared to touch them.

Phyllis was just toddling when Mollie knew another baby was coming. The winter had been long and dry, and she was nervy and exhausted by nursing Phyllis, who was a big healthy child. As the hot days lengthened and bore down on her with their breathless stillness and dust storms she was glad enough of any excuse to leave the wide dry plains, bare blue skies, and promised herself a breathing space among the small bright shops and comfortable homes of Geraldton. She longed to be able to put on a light frock and go visiting, talk with other women. The baby, she hoped, would be a boy this time. She supposed she ought to have a boy, and it might be as well to get the business over as soon as possible.

When the baby arrived and was a girl Mollie was annoyed as well as disappointed. Everybody sympathized with her. When Mrs Fairweather came to see the baby, cheerily, consoling, she said, "Never mind, my dear, the next will be a boy."

"Don't talk to me about any next," Mollie cried.

"But of course, my dear, there must be a next. You don't imagine Hugh is going to be happy until he has a son?"

"I suppose not," Mollie moaned.

"And it's natural enough, surely." Mrs Fairweather looked down on the soft, chubby-cheeked little creature she was nursing. "This is a darling, of course. I'd give anything in the world for her myself. But a man needs a son. Hugh wants a boy to be a com-

panion in his old age, to work with him, and to hand on Wytaliba
to——"

"Wytaliba! Wytaliba!" Mollie exclaimed petulantly. "It's all
Wytaliba."

"But surely, dearie," Mrs Fairweather protested, "it's your job
to be a good wife and mother. Why, if ever a woman was built
for mothering, you are. . . . You're robust; Hugh's a good, clean-
living fellow. Aren't you proud of your babies, the dear fat fluffy
things?"

"It's always the people who haven't got children think they
want them," Mollie declared waspishly.

The sensitive face of the doctor's childless old wife quivered.
For a moment she wondered whether Eustace was right; whether
the marriage of two physically fit and suitable young people,
without any psychological bond, was going to be the success they
had hoped.

"Oh, I know I'm ignorant and common!" Mollie snapped, something of Elizabeth Fairweather's revulsion of feeling reaching and
stirring the resentment which had been fermenting within her.

Coonardoo was much more at the homestead than out on
the run while the children were little. Her own cooboo was five
years old when Mollie's third daughter was born. There was so
much to do for Mollie's children, Coonardoo had no time for
babies of her own, Meenie and old women in the uloo said.

And as for Coonardoo, she loved to walk off with one of Mollie's
babies, and spend the afternoon in the shade of the creek trees,
singing to her; telling the children stories, making tracks for them
in the sand, showing them how to copy the footprints of wild
turkey, kangaroo and dingoes.

As often as not Winning-arra and her own little girls joined
them. Winni would throw toy kylies of curved tin, or dig in the
sand for water and bungarras with Charmi and Beilaba to amuse
Phyllis.

Hugh had seen Coonardoo down at the creek with the children,
and heard her singing her little song of the kangaroos to them:

> "Towera chinima podinya
> Towera jinner mulbeena. . . ."

One day he came on them while she was telling the story of the emu and wild turkey.

"Turkey bin argument with emu, which one better woman," Coonardoo said. "Turkey say, emu go walkabout all day; got no kids. Emu say, 'Eeh-mm, got weary bugger (plenty) kids.' Emu go bush, come back with plenty kids. Turkey got only cootharra (two) kids. Turkey say emu can't run so fast; emu run to creek and come back again. Say turkey can't run so fast. Turkey run to creek, little way, go up, fly . . . leave kids with emu."

Coonardoo's laughter and gurgling with the children was as merry and fresh as theirs. Everybody enjoyed the joke.

"Turkey want to go away, Coonardoo?" Hugh said.

"Eeh-mm," she murmured with downcast eyelids.

In her sickness, weariness and dissatisfaction Coonardoo was the person Mollie talked most to.

"I don't know what on earth I'd do without you, Coonardoo," she said. "I don't really."

Coonardoo had taken over the bread-making. She looked after the cooking and the children. When Mollie went away to the coast for her fourth baby, the children were left in Coonardoo's care. Mollie's fourth and fifth daughters were as much an excuse to get away from Wytaliba as desperate bids for a son. But Betty was a last attempt. Mollie swore she would do no more child-bearing; neither would she live in the Nor'-West all her days. She had no patience with the new baby—was weary to death of babies, she said; never wanted to set eyes on another as long as she lived.

Coonardoo took the baby in her arms and walked off with her. When Mollie had not slept at night, was tired out and hysterical, Coonardoo made the children play in the garden or up at the sheds until she was ready to take them away to the creek. Often she carried a bag of mending with her and sewed while the children played, or slept, curled up beside her in the shade.

Although Meenie and Bardi still washed, scrubbed and swept about the house, Coonardoo did everything for the children at that time; bathed them, cooked and sewed for them, put them to bed. Mollie had grown to depend on her for every little service.

"Coonardoo! Coonardoo!" she was always calling.

Through all the nervy restlessness and fury of Mollie's discontent Coonardoo was her slave. Silently, with slow grace and dignity, she waited on and worked for Hugh's wife, very often not getting the rest at midday with the other gins, it was so difficult for her to go without. An expression of suffering and fortitude deepened on her face.

Meenie muttered and scowled until Hugh wondered what on earth was the matter with her. He understood at last, she was concerned for Coonardoo.

"Here, Mollie," he cried roughly one day, "you're working that girl to death. Can't you see?"

"Who?"

"Coonardoo!"

"Of course," Mollie exclaimed. "It's always some one else you're thinking of. Never of me!"

"You go and have a bit of shut-eye, Coonardoo," Hugh called, as she was taking the children for their afternoon walk. "I'll mind the kids today."

He played with them quite happily, leaning against the trunk of a big white-barked gum where black shadows of its leafage sprawled and fluttered across the brilliantly lighted red and yellow earth. He watched Winni, as well as the little girls who chattered and played so delightedly beside him. Winni's skin was the colour of dark honey; his hair not duskier than the locks of Mollie's little girls. Yet he was a pure-blooded young aboriginal to look at: his eyes brown and shy, with jetty curled lashes.

Days and years fled, so much the same, the heat waning and growing, rain threatening and fleeing, showers and thunderstorms flashing, but never dispensing the good slow drenching which would have revived and saturated the dead earth. Mollie stayed a year through on the station; but before next summer her trunks were packed. She counted the days until she and the children could drive away to the coast for the hot weather.

A long drought had driven Hugh to the banks. Wytaliba fell again under the dead hand which Mumae had struggled against so long. But what could be done? Hugh was desperate at the prospect of losing more stock. He had to sink wells to save cattle, and money was needed for that. Every year Mollie's journey to the coast cost more than a well or two. When there were babies about, it was all very well; but afterwards, he thought, she might face out a hot season. The children were sturdy; heat did not affect them.

126

Mollie loathed the station. She wanted Hugh to sell out and buy a shop in Geraldton. She could not understand his faith in the place, his loyalty to it.

"No," he said, "I'll never sell out, or give up."

There seemed nothing between them at last but endless arguments and bickering.

Saul Hardy tried to pour oil on the troubled waters, but his efforts at peacemaking usually amounted to a siding with Hugh and singing the praises of Wytaliba and station life generally. Like a barnacle he clung to piles of the homestead, and Hugh's way of deferring to, humouring, and making a fuss of the old man were constant sources of irritation to Mollie. Saul had his quagey old man's ways of course. Mollie found them very trying; although he was wonderfully good natured with her and with the children.

Wild imps they were, but Saul was really fond of "Youie's five queens" as he called them, allowed them to plague him and scramble all over him to their heart's content. Only now and then he complained bitterly when they tore his papers—he was a great reader, old Saul—hid his pipe or tobacco, and made drawings in coloured chalk all over his *Riddle of the Universe*.

Mischievous, and full of a gay restless vitality, her daughters were growing up no better than youngsters from the uloo, Mollie said: particularly Phyllis. Whackings and squalls were noised along the veranda almost every day, as she punished them for fighting and scratching each other, playing about the stock-yards when a beast was being cut up, or running off with Winni, Charmi and Beilaba along the creek.

Saul could not bear to hear the children cry.

"You're a bit heavy-handed, missus," he would object in his blunt way.

"Mind your own business, Mr Hardy," Mollie would reply sharply, over and over again. "I must bring up my children in the best way I can."

Saul laughed at the children's rough, rude ways, she said; encouraged Phyllis and Cora to play up. And Hugh was as bad as Saul. It was no use expecting him to correct the children, or make them behave decently.

Hugh was away in Karrara the morning the friction between Mollie and Saul took fire. Saul had chased the children out of the garden and locked the gate, because they trampled on some seed-beds he was watching anxiously.

Phyllis, picking up a stone, threw it after him, screaming at the top of her voice, like an old gin, "Walyee mari, minyinbulla nunki-nunki chungee-chungee booketera kundi-kundi spa!"

Mollie, who saw and heard, called to her from the veranda. The child went to her, beginning to cry. Saul hurried to intercede for Phyllis.

But Mollie seized the child and hustled her, kicking and screaming, to her room from which the slaps of a piece of flat board resounded on Phyllis's little bottom.

Old Saul sat down on the edge of the veranda, pulled out his pipe and smoked miserably. Phyllis was dear to him in a way no one had ever been. Since she was a baby she had snuggled up to him, pulling his beard and hair, and rubbing wet kisses all over his face. It made him groan inwardly to hear her cry, and to be the cause of her punishment.

"You oughtn't to beat her like that, missus," he said when Mollie reappeared. Phyllis, howling and sobbing, had thrown herself on the floor in the room behind them.

"I'll thank you not to interfere, Mr Hardy," Mollie cried furiously. "You're always interfering . . . and it's no business of yours. Do you think I'm going to let Phyllis use that filthy language? Over and over again I've told her she's not to . . . and she goes on just the same."

"You're right, of course," Saul said. "It's not nice for a little girl to be usin' them blacks' swear words. But she doesn't know the meaning of them . . . and then, too, she'll forget every native word she ever knew when you take the children away to school."

"We're not gone yet," Mollie exclaimed in her despair and impatience. "And anyhow I'm not going to have Phyllis growing up defying me the way she does——"

"It's your nerves, missus," Saul said. "Things have got on your nerves a bit, and that's why you're banging the children about. They're not bad kids, real nice little nippers, the lot of 'em, I think, and there's no need to whack 'em really. Only——"

"See here, Mr Hardy"—Mollie's temper was rising beyond the point at which she knew what she was saying—"I've stood you about as long as I can. Things have got on my nerves, as you say.

You among them. I won't have you interfering between me and the children any longer. I simply won't have it. And the sooner you understand that the better."

"I understand." Saul rose on his slight old legs. Very little and old he looked as he stood before her. "I'm a bit of a nuisance, hanging round."

"Too right, you are," Mollie said and, turning her back on him, walked away.

Late in the afternoon she saw Saul pottering about in the stock-yards and watched him ride out on his own old white mare which one of the gins had brought in. Coonardoo said Saul had asked for some flour and tea for his tucker bag, and told her to tell Hugh he was going out to camp with Cock-Eyed Bob for a bit.

Hugh came in after several days and Mollie described to him what had happened. Hugh said little; but he prepared to go out again, taking Warieda with him.

"I wouldn't for worlds have the old chap's feelings hurt," he said. "You don't know what he might do if he thought we didn't want him on Wytaliba. He's got nowhere else to go. . . . Besides, I do want him. What's a station veranda for, if an old chap like Saul Hardy can't camp on it———"

"Of course," Mollie cried. "That's what you would say. And it doesn't matter what I have to put up with."

She was distressed, all the same, when Hugh and Warieda returned without Saul a week later.

"We followed his tracks out to the edge of the sandhills," Hugh said. "Found him sitting under a thorn-bush. He never even tried making for Cock-Eyed Bob's. It's what he always said he'd do, ride out there east, where what they call the sandy desert begins, and let his horse go. We buried him under the thorn-bush."

There was no money for Mollie to go to the coast that year. Hugh was sorry; but it could not be helped. If she thought less of herself and more of her work about the place, he said, she would feel better. His mother had worked through years on Wytaliba—a scrap of a woman.

The five little girls fluttered about that summer after Saul Hardy's death, shrieking and screaming, much as they had always done. Hugh was on good enough terms with them. He was really soft about the little blighters, he assured himself, although they were the joke of the countryside, his "poker hand". He had his secret solace after all. There was that son of a whirlwind who was ten years old and could go out with him now, ride like a demon and look after the pack-horses.

Wherever Hugh went Winni went. It was recognized that Winning-arra was Hugh's boy, made his camp-fire, spread out his rugs. He slept with the blacks; but everybody in the uloo knew Youie's affection for Winning-arra.

CHAPTER XIX

BLUE of the sky thickened and faded. On the horizon mirages blotted out trunks of the trees. Smooth polished stones, black and red, lying over the plains, shone with the light of dull metal.

The air, at a little distance, palpitated, thrown off from the stones in minute atoms, visible one moment, flown to invisibility the next. Weaving, with the sun for shuttle, the air spun heat which was suffocating. The sun, an incandescence somewhere above and beyond the earth moved electric, annihilating. And stillness, a breathless heaviness, drowsed the senses, brain and body, as if that mythological great snake the blacks believed in, a rock python, silvery-grey, black and brown, sliding down from hills of the sky, were putting the opiate of his breath into the air, folding you round and round, squeezing the life out of you.

The summer began early and showed no sign of relenting after eight months of brilliance and dust storms. There was a thunderstorm towards the end of January which cooled the air for a night or so and scattered futile showers; then the days went on bare and dry, or swept by the scurrying columns of the winning-arras.

Hugh was anxious. The blacks were talking of a long drought. Leaves of the mulga hung sere and dying for miles.

Away from the homestead for two or three weeks at a time, he moved cattle from dry water-holes on to windmills, droving night and day wherever there was feed and water. Eyes narrowed to slits against the fierce white light, sweltering through thick red dust, he kept the bullocks going across sun-blasted stretches of hills and plain. Drovers and beasts plodded, drooping and drowsing; the boys swayed half asleep as they rode.

At midday, after they had boiled their quart pots for tea, eaten a hunk of damper and some salt beef, Hugh and the boys threw themselves in any shred of shade beside a clump of karrara bush, or thicket of mulga to lose consciousness of heat, dust and dryness in a few moments' sleep.

Hugh took his rest as the blacks did. No chance of the bullocks wandering too far those days. They were so poor they would scarcely move unless pushed on by the horses and cracking whips.

Year after year, when the hot weather began, Hugh had sent Mollie and the children to Geraldton, and she had come back to the station after the rains. But with continued dry seasons he could not stand the expense of the long journey at last.

"Keep busy, and you'll be all right," he advised cheerily.

"Keep busy?" Mollie wailed. "I can hardly stand."

She loathed the hard arid plains, the blacks, and every eyeful of grey withering trees and red earth. Dawns came without a breath of cool air, light glancing from a sheening sky as from metal at white heat. Red dust stood in the air from the day before, until the winning-arras caught and whirled it, in long leaning columns, half a dozen of them at once, across the plains, to topple and break, deluging the house and veranda.

While Hughie was out moving cattle, a fan of the big windmill broke. There was no water for the beasts who came in to troughs on the outer fence, and hung moaning and blasting their savage cries round it all night. Coonardoo and Bardi sat at the little mill waiting for water, it drew so slowly.

There were no baths when the big windmill got out of order. And if Hugh was away with cattle for a fortnight or three weeks, Coonardoo took his gun and shot pigeons or galahs for a meal. As often as not there was no man at the homestead but Joey, and Joey could not see well enough to shoot those days.

The children thought it great fun to go shooting with Coonardoo, hide by the fence in the garden and run to pick up the pigeons as they fell. They carried the limp, dangling bodies in with gleeful cries, plucked fuchsia-coloured wing feathers from the soft blue-grey plumage of the little birds, and gobbled their pigeon pie hungrily. Mollie was glad to have pigeons to give the children to eat. She had no sentiment about crested pigeons, pretty little creatures though they were, with their black helmets, red legs and red-rimmed beady eyes. Flocks of them flew round the garden every morning; but she was furious at having to fall back on pigeons for food.

"Why not a little game, now and then?" Hugh asked. "If we were paying half a crown a pair for pigeons—we'd reckon they were a treat."

He found it difficult to forgive Mollie for not playing the game better, standing up to the drought, heat and hardships everybody else was fighting with such grit and good humour. It went to prove what Sam Geary was always talking about, the weakness and unfitness of white women for the hard and lonely life of the Nor'-West.

The life was rough on a woman, Hugh agreed. Mollie had had a crook spin when the children were little. But he had done his best to make up to her, lighten her burden, give her a fair deal.

There were women like his mother, and Mrs Jim Ryland of course, who stood by and worked through good and bad seasons with their men. And had not Mrs Withnell, the pioneer woman of the Nor'-West, brought up a large family on a lonely staation, without sight of another white woman for years at a time? Hugh had hoped Mollie would be of that stuff.

But for years now, she had been wailing and complaining at every hardship and difficulty that cropped up. There were the children, of course. . . .

Hugh blamed himself for the children. Mollie said she had had too many babies, one after the other, and was worn out nursing and rearing them, coping with the difficulty of food when a loading was late and the anxiety of their ailments so far from a doctor. She had been distracted when the babies suffered from summer diarrhoea, and Phyllis would have bled to death when she cut her foot on a broken bottle had not Coonardoo plastered the wound with clay and ashes, aboriginal fashion.

There was a good deal of truth in what Mollie said, Hugh admitted. He understood her point of view and tried to be patient; but he had not patience really with her yearning for the life of a small town as for Paradise.

After a while he put on his hat and went out to avoid the rattle of her voice, its incessant clatter and fault-finding. He could hear Mollie grousing, unmoved, at last. Let her grouse; he could stand it; he would stand anything, Hugh assured himself. There was nothing else to do, for the children's sake—and Wytaliba. He would not give up Wytaliba.

At the uloo Coonardoo had heard Joey Koonarra suggesting Hugh should take a stick to Mollie. But that was not the white man's way, she knew. He might take her by the shoulders and shake her till her neck was nearly broken, or put his hands round her throat, threatening to strangle her. But a stick, or a boot, he would only use on a gin. Mollie would never get those.

To Coonardoo herself Mollie wailed and complained a good deal.

"I wish I were you, Coonardoo," she cried. "I wish I was a gin and didn't mind the beastly place. Didn't want to see shops and places, talk to people . . . wear nice frocks and dance sometimes, or go to church and the races, like they do in Geraldton."

Coonardoo had listened impassive and unsmiling.

"Oh, it's man's country," Mollie wailed. "What they all say is quite right. It's only what a man wants, matters out here. A woman can go mad, or clear out, for all anybody cares."

For days after a row Mollie sulked. Hugh did not speak to her more than he could help, and she, as often as not, did not reply when he did. They sat at meals together. He said thank you when she passed his tea. He asked whether she would have more bread or beef. She said "Yes" or "No, thank you" and that was the end of their conversation for a day.

Hugh found his balance restored as soon as he turned away from the house, swung into his saddle, and left the long white lines of the homestead with all its sheds, buildings, windmills, and green-leafed trees far behind. But for Mollie repression meant a fermenting and rotting of every decent instinct and impulse. She was poisoned by the fever of her discontent; brooded over her grievances and misery until they burst from her, with the violence of physical nausea.

Hugh's indifference, bitter cynical humour, infuriated her.

"Why did you marry me?" she screamed. "Why on earth did I come here? I was better off really scrubbing pots, being a servant, than Mrs Hugh Watt of Wytaliba station. My God, I work like a gin. I look like a gin. But I'm not as well off as one of Geary's gins really!"

"Perhaps you'd like to change places with Sheba," Hugh said.

"At least he knows how to treat a woman," Mollie retorted.

"All right." Hugh stamped off the veranda. "Go where you'll be appreciated. Go to Geary and stay with him, or go anywhere and stay anywhere, so long as we get a little peace again."

"Give me the money and I'll go, all right," Mollie screamed.

Hugh came back, walked into the sitting-room, sat down, took his cheque-book from a drawer and wrote a cheque for five hundred pounds.

Coming back on to the veranda, he threw Mollie the strip of paper.

"There," he said. "That's all the hard cash I've got in the world. Take it and go, for God's sake . . . you're like a maggot in my brain. You'll drive me mad, woman."

He walked off towards the shed, slamming his hat down over his head.

CHAPTER XX

WINNI had mounted a ruddy bay colt Warieda was breaking, and Warieda was riding out from the yards on his own gelding, beside the colt. The colt threw up his heels, a little distance from the yards, twisted, started bucking, rooting and prancing. He flew off at a gallop, propped, bucked, and Winni flew to earth. Up in an instant he swore after the runaway.

"I stick 'm! I stick 'm!" he cried.

Warieda galloped after the colt, who with tail stuck out, head up, and barrel bouncing on short stiff legs, was making for the distance.

Warieda brought the colt back and heaved Winni into the saddle again.

Winni swung as the colt swung, clapped like a spider to his sides, stuck and weathered a spasm of rooting, while Hugh and the rest of the boys at the stock-yard fence watched, crowing gleefully.

"Winni's fair shook on riding this colt!" Hugh exclaimed.

Three times the colt threw him and three times Winni jumped up, shrieking furiously, and mounted again.

Hugh was for stopping the contest. But Warieda would not have it.

"Best let 'm finish, You," he said.

And Hugh, gazing at the youngster, mastered his fear. He watched the boy wrestle with the colt, humour and outwit him, until the wild thing knew and settled down to that light weight on his back, slim strong wrist on his jaw.

"By God, he's a kid to be proud of, isn't he?" Hugh called to Warieda. "Be as good a horseman as you are, Warieda!"

Warieda's dark eyes lit to their pleasure and satisfaction.

"Good man, Winni," Hugh yelled as the boy rode in, showing off a little, careless and cock-a-hoop in his excitement and triumph.

It was next day the colt took his vengeance. With a flying root he sent Winni to earth, so that he lay, crumpled and unconscious, on the stones out from the stock-yard.

Hugh was first out and beside him, picked the lad up in his arms, and sent Wanna flying to the house for whisky. He carried Winni to the buggy shed and knelt over him until the curled lashes fluttered and the imp's dreaming, fathomless eyes looked into his own.

Bewilderment, wonder and rage returned to Winni's eyes. He started up, looking for the colt.

"Where is he? I stick 'm!" he cried.

How they had laughed, Warieda, Chitali, and the rest of them, standing about, and glancing out to where Mick had tied the horse against the stock-yard fence.

But Winni fell back unconscious again, blood streaming from the wound in his head, as he moved. Hugh saw Coonardoo bending over him.

Mollie had gone into the half dark of the big shed while Hugh was there, watching the boy.

Coming from the brilliant sunshine, she could not see at first. Then Hugh's white shirt and his face as he crouched beside Winni impressed themselves on her.

She saw Coonardoo, a tin of water beside her, holding a wet rag to Winni's head, Warieda, Chitali, and two or three of the other boys standing silent, aghast at the back of the shed.

"What's the matter?" Mollie asked sharply. "He's not dead, is he?"

Hugh got up from his knees.

"No," he said, "he'll be all right now."

Hugh wheeled out of the shed. He walked towards the house, steering unsteadily as though he were drunk. Mollie went after him.

"What on earth's the matter?" She looked at Hugh curiously when they stood together in the sitting-room, under the enlarged portrait of Mrs Bessie. "I've never seen you so upset in my life."

"Oh . . . thought the kid was killed," Hugh muttered. "Seeing him crumple up like that . . . and the crack, as he hit the ground."

He opened the cupboard, took out a bottle of whisky, poured himself a stiff peg, and went along the veranda for the waterbag.

Mollie stared after him. His wrenched face, the suffering of his eyes, surprised her.

" 'Pon my word"—her thought formed slowly—"anybody'd think it was your own child had been nearly killed. You weren't anything like so upset when the buggy horses bolted and Phyllis and Cora and I were bumped out."

Hugh stared at Mollie as she spoke, as if an idea had just come to him. He drank his whisky, standing a little away from her, walked into the sitting-room again, put the bottle back in the cupboard, shut the folding doors and went into the kitchen with his glass.

He could not talk just then. It would not be safe, he realized, still under the shock of knowing Coonardoo's boy mattered so much to him. He had kept an eye on the lad, seen he was well fed and got a new pair of trousers now and then. But the rush of fear and anguish which assailed him when Winni lay where the colt had thrown him was too passionate and overwhelming to be reasoned about. It was there to be reckoned with; that was what he had to get hold of. He was sick, and shook to the fear which had pierced. They were mad to have let the kid try a young horse like that. He had spirit all right, but Hugh promised Warieda a piece of his mind for giving Winni such a "roughie" to ride.

The thought brought its cooling reminder. After all, it was for Warieda to say what the boy should do. But no, Hugh argued with himself, the blacks knew he would not allow unfair chances to be taken with boys in the stock-yards, Mick or Wanna, any more than Winni. And Mollie—what was it she had said?

That was a different matter. He guessed what the thought she had put up would do in her mind.

"Anybody'd think it was your own child," she had said. And Hugh saw the suspicion stirring in her grey-green eyes.

She would brood over it, pump the gins, try to worm the truth out of him. What was there to do? Nothing—except lie consistently. Hugh would have liked nothing better than to claim the youngster, treat him as his son, make a fuss of him, give him clothes, have him taught to read and write, as he would in any other circumstances. But there was Warieda, his pride in the boy. Were his love and pride greater than Warieda's, Hugh asked himself? He was fond of the kid; but could he do for Winni what Warieda was doing, teaching him to handle horses, fit him for an independent life in his natural surroundings? Warieda was on his own with horses. And how would Warieda take shattering of the belief that Winning-arra was his own son.

Hugh did not know whether the belief could be shattered;

138

but he determined that never in any way would he allow it to be tampered with, if he could help it.

Next morning Winni was up at the yards, his head swathed in bandages, ready to mount and ride the colt again. But Hugh said harshly, "No, you're not to ride today."

He had stalked off down to the house. The blacks looked after him, wondering. They knew Youie too well to disobey. Winni understood he could not ride if You had spoken against it; but he felt shamed and discredited, broken in his pride of horsemanship.

He lay in wait for Hugh as he went up to the yards next morning and begged to be given the colt again.

"I stick 'm, You," he begged. "I stick."

Warieda and the others laughed, hearing the youngster. Hugh looking over to them caught their good-humoured amusement at the boy's spirit and his concern.

"What do you say, Warieda?" he asked.

"Got to have few busters," Warieda replied. "We'll give Pan a turn in the yard first."

"Right."

During the morning Hugh went up to the yards. He watched Warieda handling and humouring the colt, teaching Winni how to make friends with a horse, keep out of the way of his heels. The youngster followed his movements with an assurance and boldness which amazed and delighted everybody.

"Beat you for your own job some day, Warieda," Hugh cried.

He joked with the boys and Winni about the fall. Asked Winni what he had done to the colt to make him carry on like that, bluffing out the buster in the high-handed genial fashion these goings-to-earth of a good horseman were usually the occasion of.

The boys grinned and joked back with him. Winni hung his head, sulky and shamefaced. He wanted to mount the horse and ride again next morning. But Warieda knew better than that; no need for Hugh to give him a piece of his mind. Warieda had judged and condemned himself, although Hugh was there to see that the roughie, as they called him, got more riding and handling before he went out of the yards again.

When Warieda went out with Pan, a week or so later, Winni rode the colt and rode him well.

Hugh was surprised at Mollie's silence. That it was as sultry as the day before a storm he recognized, and prepared to leave the homestead. He arranged to go out to one of the wells until she had time to forget and gather a crop of new grievances. Mollie waited and watched. She had gazed, long and curiously, at the son of a whirlwind next time she saw him. And saw Hugh stamped all over him. But questioning Meenie and Bardi about Winni, she met only the blank wall of their stupidity, feigned and invulnerable.

Winni was no darker than many a Greek or Italian in fruit and fish shops, or oyster saloons, in Geraldton. His features were aboriginal certainly, but with a refinement; and his ears were Hugh's ears, his finger-nails the finger-nails of a half-caste. Mollie did not mean to ask Hugh any questions. She had rummaged out all the facts she cared for. They were sufficient.

Mrs Bessie's death . . . Coonardoo in charge . . . Hugh's illness and Coonardoo nursing him at the homestead. The baby in her arms when Hugh came back from the coast. His name even, son of the whirlwind. Hugh had lied to her. Of course he had lied. Mollie knew her Nor'-West well enough to know now that on this subject most men lied to their wives.

But so sour and hostile had her mind become towards Hugh that she found pleasure really, a secret mean joy, in following the suspicion which had risen against him, and piecing the evidence for and against it. There was much more for than against. She realized her knowledge would mean power. It was a whip she could use over Hugh. She knew well enough how to scourge him with it.

When she told Hugh that she knew what he wished to hide, she could make terms, Mollie decided. Her own terms. Terms, he would not, could not, consent to. She knew what almost any woman in her position would do. She would declare it was a shame and a disgrace for Coonardoo and the boy to remain on Wytaliba, while she was there. They must be sent away. But where? That was not her business. After all there was Nuniewarra and Geary. Why couldn't Coonardoo go to Geary?

Mollie could not quite persuade herself she was justified in asking Hugh to do that. She knew very well he would not do it. Her natural good sense assured her she would be asking him to do what even she could not imagine his doing. But she was determined to go away; to make him suffer for all the suffering she had endured because he refused to live anywhere but on Wytaliba.

She did not arouse herself to much wrath and virtuous indignation about what had happened before she married Hugh. He had a strict code of what he called honour, she knew. After they were married she was quite willing to believe there had been nothing between Hugh and Coonardoo. She could not trace anything to lay against him on that score. In fact, Mollie was sure, the more she thought of it, that Hugh prided himself on being "a faithful husband". She had driven him from her so often with perverse pleasure in thwarting his passion and to reap his gratitude and remorse. It was a vague perception of that, now, which incensed her.

She wondered vaguely whether Hugh had married her to escape Coonardoo. She knew enough of him to understand he had some queer idealisms locked away at the back of his brain. He loathed Sam Geary and the way he lived with native women. It was for fear he should ever become like Sam that Hugh had resolved to take a wife back to Wytaliba after he was ill, Mollie guessed. "A wife?" And she was that. Hugh had been very good to her; they were happy enough; got on quite well together for the first years.

But latterly, under the strain of the long summers, in the throes of her dissatisfaction, Mollie had reproached and abused him for her ill health and the children, until Hugh swore never to touch her as a wife again. He did not come near her room. And for so long he had kept his word that Mollie was consumed with a resentment she could not explain. She liked to have this sound grievance against Hugh, it seemed; and to remove it removed her good ground for upbraiding and humiliating him.

When she spoke she was sure of herself. She knew just what she was going to say.

The girls were playing in the garden, and Winni, strolling down from the stock-yards—a slender figure already with the gait of a horseman—stood to watch them. He leant over the fence, a white rag still tied round his head, showing under his hat.

"Good man, Phyllis," he called as Phyllis threw a hand-spring and picked herself up in good style. She shook red sand out of her hair and ran over to the fence.

Winni considered himself too much a man to play with the little girls and youngsters from the uloo any more, although he would have liked to show them what bonny somersaults he could throw; and walk on his hands as well.

The horses were ready and he was going out with Hugh. Winni would have charge of the packs. He had come up to the house for Hugh's tucker bags and pack.

Hugh came out from the kitchen where Coonardoo had been stowing tea, flour and sugar in the bags. Mollie, stretched in one of the hessian chairs on the veranda, knew well enough he was going out to avoid the scene which he suspected she had in store for him. She did not intend that he should escape.

"Hugh," she called, as he walked across the veranda, his spurs chinkling.

Hugh stood and looked towards her. Seeing she had more to say, and knowing the morose concentration of her gaze, he went towards her.

"Well?" he asked.

"What are you going to do about it?"

"About what?"

Mollie's glance strayed to the garden where Winni was still leaning over the fence talking to the children.

"Winni?" Back to him those grey-green angry eyes swerved. Hugh gathered his forces for what he had resolved to say. Mollie stopped him with a passion, vindictive and uncontrollable. "I know what you're going to say and it's no use! You've lied to me before. Winni's your own son and Coonardoo's his mother. I know. It's no good saying he isn't!"

Hugh looked back along the veranda. The gins were in the kitchen.

"Hold your tongue, for God's sake!"

"I've held my tongue long enough, though I believed you really, until a day or two ago. I've been a fool, but not——"

"You're mad," Hugh gasped, "to say what you're doing. Even if it's true."

He was in no mood to deny; make a fool of himself for Mollie's benefit. "They don't know." He jerked his head to the kitchen. "You know what the blacks believe. Warieda——"

"I understand all that." Mollie was almost blithe in the realization of her power. "But what are you going to do about it? That's what I want to know."

"Do?" The resentment of his long repression was in Hugh's muttered undertone. "What I have always done."

"That's all?" Mollie queried. "Oh no, that's not all. You don't mean to say you imagine you're going on, just as you've always done. You don't mean to say you think I'm going to stay here with your gin and her half-caste brat——"

"Mollie!" Hugh sweated under her outpouring.

"No," she continued. "That's one thing I won't stand. It's an insult. No decent man would ask his wife to live in the same house as his gin. They've got to go, Coonardoo and her son. You've got to send them away."

Hugh gazed at her. What had happened to the woman? Had she lost her reason?

"Don't be absurd," he said. "You know it's impossible. Coonardoo was born here. She grew here, as they say. It would kill her to go away. Wytaliba folk are not like others. In all the twenty years we've been here, they're never been off the station, once. And Warieda——"

"Let him go too."

"Warieda?" Hugh could not grasp the idea. To send Coonardoo and her child away was impossible, of course, preposterous. They could not be sent away. They belonged to Wytaliba; were part of the place as the air and the trees were. But Warieda, the pride of the station, the best horseman and breaker in the Nor'-West, what would the place be without him? And to send him away—Warieda who had resisted every tempting offer made him to work for bigger, wealthier stations? Warieda, who boy and man had served Hugh with a loyalty and friendship beyond understanding; in all the time after his mother's death, the long years of mustering, droving, and breaking, through the droughts. It was unthinkable. He would sooner chop off his right hand, Hugh told himself. How on earth could Mollie suggest it? What had happened to the woman? She used not to be unreasonable like this.

"Have you thought," Hugh asked, trying an appeal, "what you've said yourself about Coonardoo? You could not get on without her. What she has done for you when the children were little? Have you thought what it would mean to her?"

"Have you thought," Mollie flashed, "what it means for me to see her, and that boy, about the place?"

Hugh entreated; he tried by every means to reach Mollie's good nature, to make her understand the situation as he saw it. He promised he would do everything within his power to make her happier, more comfortable.

But Mollie, with all the obstinacy of a small mind, realized her power. She had found the stick to beat Hugh, and was beating him to her satisfaction.

Either Coonardoo and Winni must go—or she would, she said, taking the children with her.

Hugh tried every way he could think of to move and soften her. But Mollie had planned her campaign. She knew what she wanted; and how she was going to get what she wanted.

"It was when I was alone up here, after mother died," Hugh explained, pleading with her, throwing himself on her mercy. "I'd have gone mad or died but for Coonardoo and Warieda. And never again, I swear, Mollie."

"You've lied to me before," Mollie reminded him coldly. "I would not bother any more, if I were you."

"But I say, old girl, you don't believe, you don't think . . ." Hugh protested.

"Coonardoo's been here all the time I've been away."

"But I say. . . ." Hugh despaired of making headway against her resolution.

"I like Sam Geary's way better, after all," Mollie declared. "At least he doesn't ask a white woman to live with his gins."

"By God!" Hugh sprang to his feet, his face tortured. "I haven't asked you to live with gins. You've had the best I could give you always—and if that's not enough, then go and be damned to you."

He seized his hat and turned from the veranda.

The day was hers. Mollie was satisfied with the result of the conflict.

"Very well," she said. "When can you take us down?"

"As soon as you like."

Hugh could see Mollie's point of view, he assured himself. Almost any other white woman would have carried on as she did—except, perhaps, his mother . . . and she had loved the country more than her husband. Nothing would lead her from it. Ted Watt could do anything he pleased, so long as he left her in peace to run the station as she liked.

Of course, Mollie was entitled to feel herself outraged. The women in Geraldton would agree with her when she told them the story. They would say she was quite right to refuse to live on Wytaliba with Coonardoo and Winni.

Perhaps Mollie was right; he had lived so long among the aborigines, Hugh told himself, he was seeing black; thinking black. He felt things as Warieda and Coonardoo did; saw their right to live and work on Wytaliba as long as they wished. He could see nothing but wrong in Mollie's demand for them to be driven off. It could not be done. Should not be done. Hugh could not do it. He would not. He had promised himself to keep faith with the aborigines on Wytaliba, as they kept faith with him. Was he to be less scrupulous observing the unwritten law between them than they? Was the honour of a white man not to be equal to an aborigine's? Hugh swore his should be. He would keep faith if he died for it.

Riding out over the wide tawny plains, the scene with Mollie re-enacted itself. Over and over again it flitted, pursuing and tormenting him.

Wytaliba without Warieda, Coonardoo, Winni. What would it be? Hugh was devastated by a sense of utter loss, irretrievable disaster. The possibility was not to be thought of.

If Mollie went, and the children went, after all what difference would it make to Wytaliba? He had a sense of relief in the thought of being able to face the homestead without the feeling of walking into a shindy. There was rarely anything to look forward to at the house, these days, except a row or unpleasantness of some sort. The prospect of going in through the garden gate and having the old homeliness, quiet and restful, comforted him. He could see himself stretched on the veranda, reading and sleeping at midday.

The more he thought of it, the more reconciled Hugh was to the idea. After all, it should be less costly for Mollie to stay down in town, put the children to school, than for them to be coming and going every winter. When he returned to the station, he had become so accustomed to the idea that he was almost pleased Mollie had thought of it, disposed to be kindly and complaisant. He would tell Mollie, Hugh decided, he was going to make her as generous an allowance as the station could stand. That might please her; perhaps they would part good friends.

Before he left the homestead Hugh warned Mollie against showing Coonardoo any ill will.

"If you do, you'll have the place on your hands until you go down," he declared. "Nobody'll do a turn for you."

"Coonardoo, Coonardoo!" Mollie jeered. "Can't you think of anybody but Coonardoo?"

But Hugh guessed Mollie was shrewd enough to realize she must treat the gins as she had always done, if they were to continue doing the work of the household, until she went away.

That the tongue-banging at the homestead had something to do with Coonardoo the uloo guessed and resented. For so long Coonardoo had been the person in favour there. She had done everything for Mollie for years, growing gaunt and docile in her service. And from her power at the homestead Coonardoo had attained a position quite unusual for a gin, in the uloo. Of course, she was Warieda's woman, and Warieda was the most powerful man in the camp. But he, too, respected the way Hugh, Mollie and the children deferred to, and depended on, Coonardoo.

Humble and untiring at the house, Coonardoo in the uloo was a different person. She ruled the camp with an intelligence and authority which were unquestioned, although she was wise enough never to let it be seen or guessed she ruled except through Warieda. As the person with influence over Hugh and Mollie she was obeyed; her requests were attended to. Had she not the giving of flour and sugar, issues of namery and tuckerdoo in her keeping? But Coonardoo out of favour: everybody was whispering and wondering about it.

CHAPTER XXI

THE two heavy, old-fashioned four-wheeled buggies were piled with boxes and bedding strapped down under a ground-sheet when Mollie and the children went south. The gins knew she had collected all her pictures, stowed away china ornaments, tray-cloths, and books which they remembered she had brought with her when she first came to Wytaliba.

They did not ask questions. But the uloo knew very well that this going of Mollie's was different from any other. She was going away for a long time.

Mollie gave the gins some old dresses and woollen jackets, talking quite affably, a little more to Meenie than to Coonardoo. A very little, but Coonardoo noticed it, and felt the change in her manner. She knew her name came a good deal into that last row between Hugh and Mollie on the veranda. She had heard some of it, and sent the other women out to the wood-heap so that they could not hear. Mollie tried not to show any difference in her manner to Coonardoo; but all the gins knew she was not pleased with Coon-ardoo. Coonardoo had something to do with this going away of Mrs Watt.

Mollie did not look at Coonardoo when she gave her an old dress with the other gins. She did not call her to do as much as she had always done. Coonardoo moved with the same straight back and easy swinging gait, her face quiet and heavy when she was at the house. She played with the girls as usual, took the baby away down to the creek so that Mollie might rest in the afternoon, told the children stories, mended their frocks and knickers while they hunted for bardis, climbed trees, dug for water, or played narlu through the acacia and thorn-bushes.

Phyllis coaxed Hugh to let Coonardoo take her for a ride the day before they went away. A wiry, sun-brown little creature, utterly fearless, she had climbed on Hugh's own mare, Demeter, finding her saddled beside the fence one day, and galloped off over the plains on her. Winni had gone out after her and brought her and the mare in. But Hugh himself scolded the child soundly.

It took him all his time to handle Demeter, and how Phyllis, who was nine years old at the time, had managed to hold her and hang on he did not know. She had pulled up the stirrups before starting, it seemed, and prepared to thoroughly enjoy herself. The joy of her life was a ride across the plains with Hugh or Coonardoo. Phyllis had a natural seat on a horse, and hands made for handling reins, but she was too daring. Hugh was afraid every time she got on a horse, he admitted. Even Winni could not boast so many spills from horses as Phyllis, and the most serious punishment Hugh could threaten her with was that she should not be allowed to ride out to one of the wells with him when a windmill or pumping gear was out of order.

The other two little girls who might have ridden, were as nervous as cats and could scarcely be induced to go near a horse. Hugh gave each of his daughters a horse when he branded young things during the year of the child's birth, and it was understood a horse might be claimed as soon as its owner could ride. Phyllis demanded Persephone after her first jaunt on old Hera with Hugh.

When the dust of the buggies had gone, swirled away beyond the line of the creek trees, the scowl lifted from Coonardoo's face. She went about her day's work at the house, sweeping and scrubbing, clearing and putting the place in order as she had always done when Mrs Watt went away for summer holidays. She shut the door of each room where the wardrobes were empty, folded mattresses and blankets on the little girls' beds, and carried soiled sheets, pillow-cases and towels to the washing box. She locked the food-bins Hugh had left in her charge and hung the keys on a nail beside the kitchen door.

Her face wore its old peaceful dreaminess; its serenity and waiting calm. When Meenie and Bardi stretched to sleep under the shade shed at midday Coonardoo sat, legs doubled under her, gazing over the plains, and smoking, as if she were allowing realization of the quiet at the house to soak into her. So absorbed was she that she did not notice Winni for a while.

In the men's shelter he stretched, sulky and wakeful. Wanna and Mick were sleeping like logs there. But to Winni had come disturbing thoughts and he brooded over them. He had expected to go with Warieda to Karrara. Always, wherever Hugh went, Winni went to look after his baggage and horse. To be left behind like this had never happened to him since he was working as a man. He was Hugh's boy; wherever Hugh went Winni went.

Winni did not understand it. He brooded over his grievance. Hugh must be displeased with him. He had been very offhand when he said, "No. You're not going, Winni."

Hurt and disturbed, the lad did not know why he had been thrust aside like that. There was something about this whole business of Mrs Watt's going away which hurt and disturbed him. She had stared at him in such a cruel, humiliating fashion, turned her back and walked away when he went to say good-bye to her. And she had always been kind and jolly. Winni did not understand it at all. His restless movement, a grunted exclamation, drew Coonardoo's eyes.

What was troubling him she guessed; called, and Winni slouched over and sat down at a little distance from her.

Coonardoo went on gazing over the plains. She was thinking, disentangling her memories out of the distance, gathering and puzzling over threads of the talk she had heard between Hugh and Mollie, reviewing beliefs, native superstitions and the ideas white people had given her. She had heard what Mollie said to Youie and what You said to Mollie.

Coonardoo picked up her son's hands and examined them closely. She laid her own beside one of his. Winni's nails were white shells laid on the darker skin. Her own nails were of darker horn. And his ears—she pushed back the soft loose hair over his ears. Small curled ears, flat to his head, they were; but she recognized them. Her eyes smiled into his eyes, the troubled turgid eyes of adolescence. Smiled with the wealth of her knowledge and tenderness. She was very proud of, and pleased with him, though the mystery was beyond her understanding.

"Why did you not go with You?" was something of what she said to him, and got the hurt of it.

"But he will come back," Coonardoo said when she had heard that Hugh did not want the boy. "He will come back; and she has gone."

Winni gazed with wonder at his mother's face.

"Always now Youie will take us with him," Coonardoo said. "But she did not want us. She said to Youie, Warieda, Coonardoo and Winni must go away, anywhere. Go from Wytaliba . . . go to Geary's place. Youie said, 'No . . . Warieda, Coonardoo, Winni not go away . . . not go away from Wytaliba. Coonardoo, Warieba, Winni grow here, belong here.' Mrs Watt say she will go away if Warieda, Coonardoo, Winni not go away. She has gone. Out of the winning-arra you came to me, but it was the spirit of Youie in the winning-arra. . . ."

"Wiah!" Winni exclaimed, wide-eyed.

Coonardoo nodded.

The boy looked at her with the eyes of his aboriginal intuition, instinctive wisdom, his white man's intelligence, reasoning. He sensed the mystery; her reluctance to unveil it farther. The feeling of power and joy Coonardoo herself had, she communicated to him. Winni understood she had revealed to him something of which he must never speak, he had it for himself, to know and to hold on to. He was not unhappy now. He looked out over the wide plains as she did.

"Youie will not send us away." Coonardoo's voice had the throb and cadence of a song. "We will stay here, take care of Youie and he will take care of us, as Mumae said."

When the buggies came back to the homestead, dogs from the uloo flew out barking to greet them; but the house was quiet; no one moved out from it. Hugh stayed at home for a day or two, pottered about the sheds and the veranda, reading or sleeping. The gins came up in the morning, swept and scrubbed and washed dishes, gossiping and laughing as usual. Coonardoo made bread and cooked. She did not raise her eyes to look at Hugh unless he spoke to her, then the shaft of her devotion was deep and tranquil.

Coonardoo packed the tucker bags. Hugh was going out beyond the Koodgeeda gap. There had been no rain for months and he was anxious about the cattle that side of the range. It was more than likely he would be away from the homestead for weeks, moving stock.

When Hugh went out he took most of the horses and all the men, except old Joey, out with him. Coonardoo remained at the homestead to ration the uloo.

Before Hugh returned, three weeks later, Don Drew had been and gone with a loading, earlier than anybody expected. Warieda found tracks of his camels beyond the Five Mile gate.

The stores had been stowed away in Saul's old hut and everything was in order at the homestead except that Don had taken Bardi with him. Hugh was wild about it. Warieda and Wanna were for going after him and bringing the girl back; but the old women insisted Bardi wanted to go. She had run after the camels and joined Don's camp, although Coonardoo shut her up one night in the bathroom at the homestead. Don had left a couple of blankets for Chitali, whose woman Bardi was, and Chitali seemed to prefer the blankets.

Coonardoo handed keys of the store-room and bins to Hugh. But he, weary and red with dust, gave them back to her.

"You keep 'em, Coonardoo," he said. "If you're not to be trusted, nobody is."

He slept a night on the veranda, showered, and ate the meal Coonardoo prepared for him, while the boys killed and cut up a beast they brought in. As soon as the meat was salted, the packs were ready, and horses spelled, Hugh rode out with Warieda, Mick, Chitali, Wanna and Winni again.

All through the summer and dust storms it was like that. Hugh was away droving cattle, would come in to the homestead for a night or two, to sleep, get fresh clothes, replenish his stores, and then be off and away in the ranges for weeks.

Coonardoo slept at the uloo, coming and going to watch over the house, windmills and store miah, giving flour, sugar, tea, meat and jam to her people, and making a note of what she used in the store-book, as Mrs Bessie had taught her.

"See," she said when Hugh came in from the back hills that first time after Mollie and the children had gone south, "Mumae come again." A flock of white cockatoos flashed up from the earth before the veranda.

Hugh laughed to see how the myth his mother had made held still. He wondered whether Coonardoo really believed Mumae's spirit was there among the white cockatoos. She bore all the surface marks, "outward and visible signs" of his mother's influence; but her mind moved still with the traditions of her people, he thought; even if there was a smile in her eyes when she told him about the white cockatoos.

From Geraldton had drifted north the reason for Mrs Hugh Watt's leaving Wytaliba. Hugh had taken a gin, it was said, and Mrs Hugh refused to live on the place with her and her children.

Don Drew and Sam Geary carried word of Coonardoo's reigning at the homestead. It was generally understood she was Hugh's woman. Hugh got the tail of the gossip in a letter from Geary, intimating that a case of whisky long overdue might be forwarded at his convenience. He paid no attention to it. Coonardoo looked after the stores, kept the house in order; managed the washing and cooking for him. He was grateful to her; but in those first years after Mollie and the children went away, he had no personal feeling of any sort. No passion or desire, except to beat the drought. Every breath and thought he was spending on moving cattle, trying to save beasts by travelling at night and turning them wherever a picking was to be got.

CHAPTER XXII

THERE were only forty-three points of rain that year after Mollie and the children went south. But the following year a downpour in January and February revived the earth and brought new life to men and beasts, inland along the tropic. Not that all the stations fared alike. Illigoogee and Britte got only the tail end of a couple of thunderstorms. Wytaliba benefited sufficiently to right herself and steer a steady course for the following years.

Hugh mustered four hundred fats and got a good price for Wytaliba beasts in the Midland yards.

Mollie had taken a house in South Perth and the children were going to school. Hugh was pleased with the cheque he could send her, and that their lives had arranged themselves and were moving in a more or less comfortable and satisfactory fashion.

Three years wheeled with days, so much the same that but for the almanac with dates fixed for meeting a drover with cattle, for mustering with Sam Geary, or Milli-Milli, Hugh would scarcely have known how they passed, when the weeks slipped into months, the months into years.

Once every three months, if no loading was due, he sent Chitali and Wanna into Geary's for newspapers and letters, which the mail-man dropped into a box on the Nuniewarra boundary, though few letters came Hugh's way except from agents for cattle sales or warehouse accounts, and occasionally a note from Mollie to say her expenses were heavy and he must increase her allowance.

Hugh saw few people but his own blacks. Once he had gone into Nuniewarra for mails; but every encounter with Geary raised the fur of an internal irritation. Cock-Eyed Bob was the only other man to talk to. Bob had been out prospecting in the To-Morrow with two camels and came in to get water and stores now and then. He had found a mate in a wild cut of a young chap named Billy Gale. Gale was droving in the Kimberleys before he bought out Big Otto, who had taken up a few thousand acres on the northern boundary of Wytaliba.

The days went tranquilly, at a leisurely pace. Stock were

mustered, young things drafted and branded, fats put on the road; horses rounded up, branded, broken and gelded.

Wells were sunk, tanks and mills repaired or erected. When Hugh set up a new mill he taught Winni all he knew of the job, and found the boy as eager to master the mechanism of windmill construction as he had been to know and tame horses.

But Warieda—that was the severest blow those years dealt Hugh. How it happened he did not know. Warieda and Chitali were moving cattle from the top end of the run to the Fifty Mile well. Hugh was farther east with Winni and two of the other boys. Warieda had found a patch of good feed for his cattle and the mob was mooching along, coming in by way of Nuniewarra, when the boys fell in with some of Sam Geary's blacks, and camped by the creek with them. Old Munga, the moppin-garra, was there.

One of the Nuniewarra boys warned Warieda that the moppin had pointed a bone at him. Warieda went sick almost immediately, would not eat, said he had guts-ache, moped disconsolately, and felt he was going to die.

Chitali brought him into the Wytaliba uloo. In a day or two Warieda had lost flesh, was weak and would do nothing but lie about his own fireside. Nothing Coonardoo or Meenie brought him made any difference; he refused to eat.

Chitali himself rode out to find Hugh and tell him of the calamity which had overtaken the camp. Warieda had been "boned" and was dying. Hugh came in from the back hills, travelling night and day, for two or three days, to reach the camp. He tried jollying Warieda out of the belief that he was going to die, and sent Chitali into Nuniewarra for the moppin-garra to come and take his magic off Warieda.

Warieda wandered about like a lost soul until Munga arrived. From the good-looking stalwart man in his prime, he grew thin; every bone in his body stuck out. He was dying slowly on his feet; dying of the idea that he was to die.

In a few days the moppin appeared from among trees along the creek bank. It was well known he had a grudge against Wytaliba people because he was not as welcome among them as at the uloo on Nuniewarra. There was trouble too about Beilaba, Warieda's younger daughter. Charmi had been given to a man on Milli-Milli, and Beilaba was promised to an old man of the Banniga on Nuniewarra, who had died during the year. Wanna, Banniga also, and straight for Beilaba, a Burong, begged Warieda to let him have her. Munga's son, next by tarloo right to the dead man, claimed her; but Warieda gave Beilaba to Wanna.

Munga had threatened Warieda, the most powerful man in the camp, by the Coonardoo well—Warieda, the maker of songs, breaker of horses, and master of ceremonies. This was his revenge.

A half-crazy skeleton of an old man, naked but for the ashes of a camp-fire in which he had been sitting, and a hair string with tassel dangling round his middle, down and wild turkey feathers stuck through his hair, eyes as bright and glittering as a hawk's, he hopped up to the camp; and everybody got out of his way. Everybody, except Coonardoo, and she standing beside her man, watched the moppin with an unmoving quiet gaze.

Hugh had told Winni and Chitali to let him know as soon as the moppin-garra arrived. He went down to the camp when Winni told him Munga had come, to find the old man crouched beside Warieda.

"Make him better, you understand," Hugh said sternly. "Warieda not die. What do you mean scaring the life out of my man? I'd rather lose anything on the place than Warieda."

The moppin-garra, his lean snake-wood legs twisted under him, leant over Warieda, muttering, making a queer clicking noise deep in his throat, taking no notice of Hugh. His eyes glittered, a crazy, malicious smile writhing and twisting in and out of his face.

"Tell him," Hugh said to old Joey, trying another tactic, "I'll give him rugs and namery . . . a pipe and new hat, any damn thing he likes if he'll take the bulya out of Warieda."

The moppin sat beside his patient. Shook his head, signifying that nothing was to be done. Warieda was to die. He was a crazy old brute, Hugh decided; had seen men die in this way before, and rather liked to see them die as evidence of his power.

Ordinarily the moppin-garra would be sprawling all over a sick man, kneading and scrabbling him with frenzied fingers. Then, putting his mouth to the body, he would suck out the poison, spitting for everybody's amazement such a collection of rubbish, sticks, gravel, chewed bark, that exclamations of horror and amazement went up. A bone, or a stone, exhibited gleefully, as cause of the illness might be presented to the sufferer, who usually responded to the suggestion that he was going to be quite well now.

155

Finding Munga was not trying any of his tricks on Warieda, Hugh chased the old man out of the camp, promising he would shoot him if ever he found him pointing a bone at any Wytaliba folk again. Old Joey and Bandogera did not like this treatment of the moppin; but they were too overcome at the disaster which had overwhelmed the camp to do more than mutter.

Hugh sent Coonardoo for whisky and tried to make Warieda believe old Munga was no moppin-garra really. Knowing it was forbidden for a moppin to eat anything hot, Hugh swore he had seen Munga eating hot meat; and drinking hot tea the gins gave him. His magic had left him, therefore.

Warieda smiled faintly.

"Bloody liar, Youie," he said.

"You tell the old blackguard to go hell, Warri," Hugh begged, "like Mumae did when he wanted to throw water over Coonardoo that time she had pneumonia. You remember, long time ago? 'Throw water over 'm; put the fire out!' he said. And Mumae wouldn't let him. Coonardoo got well. I make you well."

But there was no moving Warieda's mind. He had been willed to die by rite and magic: believed it inevitable that he should die, and die he did, within a few weeks of the moppin's movement against him.

When the uloo wailed at dawn there was no one who, in his own soul, wailed more than Hugh. Boy and man, Warieda had stood by him. He had been his right-hand man. There was no one like him with horses in the whole countryside. Chitali, probably, was a better tracker, better with cattle. But Warieda, who made songs which Coonardoo said the jinki told him; Warieda who understood and talked like a white man—Hugh was going to miss him as much as anybody.

It was a shock too, that this trick of the moppin-garra could have got Warieda. Hugh thought Warieda had absorbed white men's ideas and ways too much for a boning stunt to affect him. Yet his superstitious fear went so deep, it had annihilated him. Hugh knew, of course, that a black ordinarily would succumb to a "boning". But Warieda—it seemed unbelievable he could be done to death by a crazy old loon pointing a bone at him.

The mourning for Warieda lasted for weeks. Every morning before dawn Hugh could hear Coonardoo, Winni and Meenie crying and howling. But every morning Coonardoo brought in tea, made porridge, cooked and, with Meenie, washed and swept as usual. Majestic and silent, she moved about, not looking at Hugh unless he spoke to her, her face a mask of sorrow. He had no doubt that, under her gina-gina, her body bore the gashes made by sharp stones as a mark of grief for her man.

In the camp she would live silent and retired for weeks, as a widow; Meenie also. Neither of them, as far as Hugh knew, plastered their hair with mud or whitened their faces. At the house they went about their day's work much as they always did.

Coonardoo? Hugh wondered what would happen to her. He knew Warieda's brother, who was one of Geary's boys, was entitled to claim her. Hugh did not intend to surrender Coonardoo. Or Meenie for that matter. But Meenie was old now. It was not likely she would be sought or demanded.

Before he went back to the well where Mick and Wanna were holding beasts they had mustered, Hugh called Coonardoo and gave her the keys of the store-room.

There was nothing for it, Hugh realized, if she was not to go to Nuniewarra; if Warieda's brother was not to demand her, and pass her on to Sam Geary, he must claim her, himself.

"You will be my woman, now, Coonardoo," Hugh said. "Sleep in the room at the end of the veranda. Winni can go to the buggy shed."

"Eeh-mm," Coonardoo replied quietly.

A few weeks later Warieda's brother claimed Coonardoo. He left Wytaliba with Hugh's gifts, a horse and pair of boots, a hat and silver-mounted pipe.

Sam Geary, hearing that Coonardoo was established in the homestead, came to call on Hugh, congratulate and crow over him.

"Oh go to the devil!" Hugh muttered. "Come and have a drink."

Coonardoo lived on the veranda at Wytaliba and was regarded as Hugh's woman. Only she could not imagine why Hugh did not take her as his woman. His woman, he had said she was to be. She watched and waited, knowing his loneliness, the deep surge of his drawing to her.

Sheer cussedness, Hugh thought, deterred him from doing what everybody expected him to. A sullen anger grew in Coonardoo's eyes because of it. She had come one hot night and laid her head on his feet and Youie had pushed her away. She did not understand it. Hugh's hunger was in his eyes when he looked at her;

he did not wish her to go away, and yet he would not touch her; moved away if she stood near him.

He was kind to her; gave her keys of the store, and gina-ginas of bright new dungaree. His eyes lighted as he sang out, coming in from the back hills or Karrara.

"Hi, Coonardoo! Coonardoo! Anybody at home there?"

And always her dark quiet figure appeared from the shade of the white flowering bushes, or on the kitchen veranda, with eyes which shone their welcome.

"Eeh-mm."

No surprise; no elation. Only the deep eyes and that murmur with its flowing joyousness.

Next year Wytaliba missed the rain. Hugh watched the thunderstorms working behind Nungarra hills, flash along the ranges, and sweep west to Nuniewarra, beating along the horizon. Scarcely a shower to lay the dust fell on Wytaliba. Sometimes the ranges caught a few points when not a drop fell on the plains.

Dust storms blew up, dark and threatening. Nobody complained. Hugh held himself with a tense insistence, praying with every instinct for the rain which sometimes followed dust storms. But again and again the dust passed, moving in columns like smoke along the creek bed and towards the river.

Years moved slowly, implacably, with bare blue skies, deepening and fading. The earth rose into the air, of its dryness, and hung there in red mist.

Hugh himself became gaunt as his beasts: his eyes were bloodshot with the stinging dust. His brain surged sun-stricken and would not sleep. Sam Geary, and Billy Gale, whom Sam had taken on as head stockman, finding Hugh almost insane on the roads, hauled him over to their camp.

"Look here, me boy," Sam said, "you've got to let go somewhere. I know this country. You've got to get drunk and blot out or you'll go mad on it."

Hugh drank their whisky, emerged from the darkness and oblivion it gave with relief, a sense of relaxation. He had come to believe, as Geary said, "You can only weather this country . . . you can only beat it on its own terms. Serve for it like Jacob served for Rachel. Wait for her—seven years if need be. If you're too hard on yourself, too strenuous, you won't stay the distance."

In order to fight the drought Hugh had to increase his overdraft;

there was nothing to do but sink wells, keep those he had in good working order, if he was to beat the dry years. The banks had taken over Illigoogee and Karrara Downs, Jim Ryland was working as manager on his own place. But, "One good season will compensate for seven bad years," Hugh assured himself.

That the argument was sound he never doubted. He had seen country, beaten bone-dry for years, flourish green as river flats after two or three seasons of decent rainfall, restock and throw off any "monkey" the banks had on it. You needed faith in the country and courage to hang on, that was all.

He had the faith, Hugh told himself. Wytaliba was worth waiting for. He would hang on: there was nothing else to do. He could not keep up the fight at the pressure he had been putting on himself, though; relaxed and made a habit of drinking off a depression, when the outlook was too bad.

So for seven years he lived and worked on Wytaliba, with Chitali, Wanna, Mick and Winni, who mustered and drove with him: Coonardoo and Meenie, who loooked after the homestead, cooked, sewed, washed and kept the place in order. Ben Alsop stayed a few days when he arrived with a loading, and Cock-Eyed Bob had been in, now and then. Hugh met other white men at the sales in Karrara, and Roebourne, or during station musters. For the rest, his life swung between the homestead and cattle camps on the plains or in the ranges.

CHAPTER XXIII

MELLOW light lay on the plains; the red wall of the ridge had mists, azure and magenta, in its broken sides, the evening Coonardoo coming down from the little well, a smoke-blackened kerosene bucket of water on her head, stopped suddenly, and glanced behind her as though someone had called.

Tall and straight, in her blue gina-gina, dark as the hills, she stood listening.

"Car comin'!" she called.

Hugh rose from the chair on the veranda in which he had been stretching, and looked out across the plains. He heard the distant hum and bluster of a car; its rattle and burr, as it crossed the creek stones, two miles away, climbed the opposite bank and turned towards the homestead.

Children from the uloo were running out to open the lower gate. As the car swung in, Coonardoo knew it was not Sheba driving; nor was Geary in the car. Hugh himself exclaimed.

The car, heavy with dust and way-worn, rocked over the pebbles. A woman was driving. When it came to a standstill before the veranda, Hugh went down to meet her, and, to his surprise and consternation a girl looked out at him.

"Give you three," she cried, as he stood before her, "and you won't guess who I am."

She jumped out of the car, hatless, a fawny-grey dust-coat over a dress the same colour. Hugh glimpsed naked-looking silken-clad legs and a short frock. There was a suitcase in the car. She had come to stay, no doubt. Her black hair was straight, and cut like a boy's; she had greyish-green eyes; there was something vaguely familiar about her mouth and jaw.

"Phyllis!" It was Coonardoo who uttered the little cry; and the girl turned to her.

Standing at a little distance from Hugh, Coonardoo's eyes were filled with joy.

"Coonardoo," Phyllis cried, "of course you would know."

She went up to Hugh, put her arms round his neck, and kissed him. "I've come to stay with you, Youie! Bolted? Yes. . . . All by myself. How many thousand miles is it from Perth? Thought I'd never get here. Was bogged on the Gascoyne. But, Lord, I wouldn't have missed it for worlds. It's been great fun, everybody's been so kind telling me the tracks, and I smelt my way along from Nuniewarra. Every inch of the road was familiar. Felt I knew it all the time——"

"Phyllis, Phyllis," Hugh murmured, unable to accustom himself to the idea that this was his daughter, this pretty young thing who had, if she was to be believed, motored over a thousand miles to see him.

"A cup of tea would save my life," Phyllis told Coonardoo.

Coonardoo turned and went back to the house. Putting her arm through Hugh's Phyllis stered him to the veranda, flopped into one of the big chairs there, felt in the pocket of her coat for a cigarette case, and took out a cigarette, while Hugh gazed at her, too bewildered and at a loss to offer a match. She lit up, crossed her legs and smiled at him.

"There, that's how it's done, You darling," she said. "If you want to see a parent bird you haven't seen for years and are rather devoted to, nick a car, and—make your own arrangements. Say you're glad to see me. I don't believe you are, but——"

"Of course, you know, my dear, you can't stay here."

"Why not?"

"Oh, well," Hugh hesitated, "of course, they've told you the sort of old blackguard I am. . . . Living here with a gin . . . all that sort of thing."

"Do you?"

Phyllis looked him over, her young eyes reading more than anyone had done in Hugh's, an obscure principle for which he was immolating himself. She found something heroic and absurd about him; his stoutish figure, round pink face and greying hair. Stupid and sentimental she thought he might be; but altogether lovable in his humility and stand-offishness.

"Wytaliba's not a fit place for a young girl these days." There was bitterness in the slow gentleness of Hugh's voice.

"You think it's fitter down there?" Phyllis asked. "I'm fed up with it all, daddy. You don't know how fed up. I really can't stand it any longer, being cooped among houses, your eyes full of walls, walls and walls. I've ached to be home again. I'm sick for Wytaliba really."

What queer happy dream was it, Hugh wondered, to hear his girl talking like this? As she lay back in the chair, she looked as she said, as if she had been sick for the country. Her eyes, wandering over the plains, took in their vastness, the silence, with an expression he understood.

"I've always wanted to come back. You don't know how I've wanted to come back. I love being here."

"Yes." Hugh remembered her spirit.

"Mum wouldn't let me come. She likes living in town, of course. So do the girls. And you didn't answer my letters, so I just saved all the money I could get hold of for petrol and repairs —and here I am."

"By God. . . ." Hugh gazed at her admiringly.

"Sent mum a wire to say I'd taken the loan of her car to come and see you," Phyllis went on, smiling. "You see, dad, it was the only way. You don't know how awful it is tracking round with her, these days. . . ."

Hugh smiled his sympathy and amusement.

"Five of us, and mum always trying to marry us off—me particularly. And I won't be married off. I loathe every young man she trots along and is nice to. If a man speaks to me she's so nice to him I could kill him, 1 hate him so. The married men aren't so bad. . . . I can bear them because they don't think you want to marry them. I get on with them, well enough—too well . . . that's the worst of it. . . ."

Phyllis knocked the ash from her cigarette, doubting whether to go farther in this confidence.

"Your mother's rather a social success, I understand?" Hugh's eyes had a quizzical gleam.

"She's on every charity ball committee," Phyllis told him. "We hang round Government House, cadge race tickets and theatre passes—dance, play bridge, tennis, golf. Cora makes her own frocks, and ours sometimes. She's pretty . . . everybody likes her. But I can't sew . . . am damned useless in the whole business, dad. It makes me mad to play bridge in the afternoon. I smoke myself sick, lose my money, and when Garry Macquarrie suggests a sail on the river, or out to the islands, I'm so grateful——"

"Garry Macquarrie?" Hugh tried to remember and associate the name.

"Ever hear of him?"

"Garath Macquarrie? I've heard of him, all right."

The reputed millionaire, owner of a string of popular stores, a racing stable and considerable interests in mining properties, had recently been divorced by his wife on sensational evidence, to the tune of handsome alimony.

"Oh, yes," Phyllis exclaimed lightly. "Garath Macquarrie! I've been getting myself talked about, as they say, with him. Garry's such a damned fascinating man. . . . Oh, well, the end was in sight, old dear, when a girl I know rather well. . . ."

Hugh was looking so pained and uncomfortable, Phyllis faltered. It was funny to feel so sorry for him. She laughed; the flow of her confidence veered inconclusively.

"She told a few tales about Garry—and here I am." She hesitated, then went on, "I've always thought of you as more like a decent sort of elder brother than a father. I ought to have been a boy really. I hate this female life so. Let me knock round with you?"

Hugh felt a host of new and tender sentiments stirring.

"You could——" he began.

"I couldn't," Phyllis interrupted, "stay in at the house and look after the cooking. I want to be out and away with you. Do you remember the times you took me out camping in the To-Morrow? I'm as strong as a bullock really. If I were a boy you'd let me. And I ought to have been your eldest son."

"There's Winni," Hugh said.

"Oh, yes." The thought did not disturb Phyllis. "Well, won't you do as much for me as you do for him? He goes everywhere with you, they tell me. Let me knock round like that. Forget I'm a girl. How would you have liked it if grandmother had wanted you to stay in Perth, go to the uni, be a lawyer or doctor, or something?"

"I wouldn't have stayed."

"Well, I won't."

In the silence between them the windmills clanked, Phyllis could hear water gushing into troughs beside the outer fence where horses and cattle came to drink. A flock of white cockatoos rose from a patch of earth beyond the garden fence and wheeled, the flakes of their white wings sequined and glittering against the twilight sky, as they flew to roost in one of the creek gums.

"There she is!" Phyllis rose, looking after the white cockatoos. "If you knew how I love them! Do you know what mum says?"

163

Hugh waited for her to go on.

Phyllis played her trump card.

"I get all this hankering after Wytaliba . . . the life here, to be with you, from her."

Hugh's eyes had all the stirred tenderness of his new emotion. It was as if the gay and lovely companion he had dreamt of in his youth had been given to him when he was past hoping for her. And that she should be his own daughter!

"Your grandmother liked being here," he said.

"And to think of her having made the place, worked it and given it to you, like it was." Phyllis looked out over the plains, where the moon rising was like a fire on the mulga. Round and golden, dinged on one side, it came slowly over the dark of the trees.

"I've always felt I ought to be a son to you, for her sake, dad. I've wanted to be. And all I've done is drain all the money I could out of you . . . with mother and the girls. Think of it, all the years you've been up here, through the heat and the droughts—slaving for us! And all we've ever done is squeeze you for every penny we could get—to play the fool, drink, dance, chatter. . . . Oh, it makes me mad!"

"The place is heavily mortgaged, my girl," Hugh said, "and every day things seem to be getting worse instead of better. I had to write to your mother—explain to her that her allowance would have to be cut down."

"I know, that's why I came. Do you know what I've been dreaming?" Phyllis's voice was very eager. "That I can do what grandmother did, help you to make the place again—throw off the mortgage."

Hugh smiled into the young face which was so serious now.

"You've got her spirit, Phyll. There's more of my father in me. I haven't half the grit she had. . . ."

Phyllis took possession of the big bare room which the little girls had regarded as theirs. It still held the chest of drawers made from fruit boxes, with a faded cretonne curtain sagging along a string in front of it. The pegs on which their small clothes had hung were still screwed beside the window, and some of Phyllis's and Cora's first alphabet scratchings in coloured chalks, and drawings of birds and pointed houses with smoke coming out of the chimneys, stalked gaily across the pale-green wash on the walls. The bullock-hide stretcher, on which any stray man who was passing through Wytaliba had slept since the children went away, stood ready with clean sheets and pillow-cases as Coonardoo always kept it.

"But you can't stay here. You can't stay here," Hugh groaned as he looked round the bare, shabby room, bringing Phyllis's suit-case in and putting it beside the box cupboard with a small square wooden-framed mirror on top.

Phyllis sat down on the seat under the wide-open windows at the end of the room.

"The trouble is, my dear," she said, "you can't get rid of me —unless you want me to make that trip to the Argentine Garry's been suggesting."

Hugh gazed, confounded and aghast, at the young, pretty thing before him—his daughter—who looked more like a good-looking, rather effeminate boy, with her short hair and long slender legs.

Phyllis took a comb-case from the pocket of her coat, pulled a little comb from its gold-monogrammed tortoiseshell case and raked back the wave of her black hair. Then she went up to Hugh, put her arms round his neck and kissed him.

"We're going to be cobbers, old dear, aren't we?" she begged. "I'm going to work with you, learn to run the place like gran did."

Hugh stared at her abashed and wondering. He admired her so, was so touched by her way with him. A passion of tenderness gripped and shook him.

"It seems too good to be true," he said. "Wytaliba's your home. You'll stay here as long as you want to—of course. I'll try to make the place fit for you, Phyllis."

CHAPTER XXIV

IN the morning Phyllis came from her room, stepping jauntily in buff-coloured riding breeches, a white blouse, and tan boots over the end of her pants. Her hair was wet from the shower, and her eyes as eager as a child's.

Hugh could scarcely believe his eyes; he felt foolish with happiness every time he looked at Phyllis; as if he must break into a silly giggling. It was so unexpected, to see her there and remember how she had come.

Phyllis sat at the end of the breakfast table and poured out tea. They ate and chatted together. She took a cigarette case from her breeches pocket, passed it to Hugh, lit up and smoked.

"Chitali and the boys are out after a horse for you," Hugh said. "We'll ride over to the Fifty Mile, if you feel like it. The mill wants looking to."

Phyllis laughed happily. "The old Fifty Mile still playing up, is she?"

Coonardoo's eyes lighted to a smile as she carried off a pile of dishes.

"Is Coonardoo coming too?" Phyllis asked.

"Not today."

"Remember the day Persephone bolted with me, Coonardoo, bumped me off into a karrara bush, and we came home double-donkey on Thetis?"

"Eeh-mm."

Coonardoo was as pleased and surprised as Hugh about the girl. "What happened to her, dad?" Phyllis asked.

"Thetis? She's out at the Pool. We don't work her now."

"And Persephone?"

"She's there, too."

"Who am I going to ride?"

"Oh. . . ." Hugh hesitated. "Chitali's bringing in Daphne and Damon, and——"

"None of your old crocks," Phyllis warned.

"Boys comin'!" Coonardoo called from the veranda.

In morning sunlight flooding the plains, the distant line of mulga was grey and misty blue, acacias, the young green of almond-trees, against a clear, fine sky. Phyllis watched the rosy dust moving in from the horizon, knowing it held Chitali, Wanna, Winni and the horses.

"Come on, dad," she exclaimed eagerly. "I'm dying to see everything and everybody. Let's go up to the yards. And, tell me, what sort of a season has it been? The country's looking good down by Five Rivers. I was bogged out from Nuniewarra. They came and pulled me out. Decent of old Sam; but it was his manager really, I suppose, a long thin slab of a man?"

"Gale," Hugh said. "That'd be Billy Gale."

"Is that his name?"

"I'll fix up the tucker bags; then we'll go up to the yards," Hugh said.

Phyllis stood on the narrow ledge of the veranda watching the horses come in. When Hugh returned from the kitchen she had taken one of his old felt hats from the pegs.

"I've bagged one of your hats, dad," she cried, and glanced over at him.

Hugh had on a clean pair of white moleskins and a pale-blue shirt, more faded than his eyes. His feet looked small in neat oiled boots with elastic sides. He walked with a sharp firm step, his spurs clinking on the rough shingly earth.

"That's one of the first things I can remember," Phyllis said. "The chinkle of your spurs, Youie, and I've always thought of you in a pair of old white moles with a shirt to match the sky."

Across the shingly earth to the yards they went, Hugh striding easily, Phyllis swinging along beside him.

At the yards the boys were waiting; Chitali, long and straddling, with the turned legs of a horseman; Wanna, Mick, Toby, and Winni, hanging back shyly, hardly daring to look towards the girl in her man's trousers, although she called to them gaily, "Hullo, Chitali! Wanna! Toby! Mick! Winni! What have you got for me? Something decent, I hope."

The boys let down one of the rails for Phyllis and Hugh to walk into the yard beside the end run where the horses were.

"Beauties, aren't they, dad?" Phyllis cried excitedly. "He's a Hera, isn't he? The chestnut there with white feather under his forelock?"

"Dionysus," Hugh said. "I thought you could have him, but Chitali won't hear of it. Says he bucked like blazes the other day, threw Wanna and Mick——"

"Oh, I say," Phyllis protested. "I could ride a bit once, you know. Couldn't I, Winni?"

Winni looked up shyly from the strap he was buckling and unbuckling.

"Course you could, Phyllis," he said.

"Chitali thinks you'd better have Coonardoo's mare, Thetis the second."

"Youie!" Phyllis protested.

"What do you say, Winni?" Hugh asked. "Which'll we give her?"

"Brought Persephone in," Winni replied, hanging his head.

"You did, did you?" Hugh laughed. "Of course, there she is."

Looking through the rails, Phyllis picked out the horse she had ridden and galloped about on when she was a child.

"She looks fit, and must be nearly a hundred," she cried. "How old is she, Winni?"

"Sixteen," Winni said. "Pluto out of Juno by Hector from Ceres."

"She's a bit gone in the wind and shies like old billy-oh," Hugh said. "But perhaps she'll do for today."

Phyllis agreed. "She'd feel hurt, perhaps, if I didn't ride her today. But tomorrow I want Dionysus. You can't expect me not to be crazy about a horse like that, dad."

Hugh looked at Winni. They understood each other very well on that glance.

"He's yours, Phyll," he said. "But you'll give me your promise not to ride him till Winni say's, won't you? He's horse boss now."

"I see." Phyllis smiled between them. "Winni'll take the steam out of Dionysus, first of all? Well, I don't want any broken bones, dad. It's a go."

Coonardoo had kerosene buckets of water boiling on the stove when Phyllis and Hugh rode up to the veranda in the evening.

Phyllis threw a leg over her saddle and alighted before Hugh could reach her.

"It's been great, Hugh," she said. "I feel as if I've been starved and am devouring the sight of it all . . . plains, wind grass, and those dark hills. The 'wild To-Morrow ranges', I say to myself.

They look so mysterious and impenetrable. It's got a taste for me, dad, the sight and sound of everything. Food for my soul, that's what it is. Oh, I'm as happy as larry and we're going out mustering presently, aren't we?"

Phyllis had seen what Dionysus could do, the first morning Winni took him out of the yards. He rooted and jumped about, slewing and swinging round, bowed up, head through his legs, while Winni sitting back let him show off. Then he belted the chestnut about the shoulder with his hat, encouraging him to buck till he was tired.

"Let him show us what he can do, eh, Winni?" Hugh crowed.

"If I could ride like that." Phyllis exclaimed.

All that week Winni worked Dionysus. He took no end of pains with the horse, teaching him to stand, and calling Phyllis to hold and handle him, ride beside him, so that the horse would know her voice. Phyllis was impatient to be up and away on Dionysus, long before Winni would hear of it.

"Winni knows his job." Hugh laughed. "I can trust him to let you ride when Dion's ready for it. Winni knows what he's doing all right."

He was proud of the lad and his horsemanship, conscious of the care he was taking to break and gentle the gelding before giving him to Phyllis. Winni made Coonardoo try Dionysus even before he would allow Phyllis to mount, although she had the easy, natural seat of a child who has scrambled over horses almost as soon as she could walk.

They had been out all day and were coming in behind a mob of cows and calves the evening Winni handed Dionysus over to Phyllis. She had been working with Hugh and the boys as though she had done nothing else all her life. Winni himself had been riding Dionysus.

Phyllis rode the chestnut to the gate of the Five Mile paddock, and brought him in proudly, although there was no one to see but old Joey Koonarra, Bardi's Polly, Pinja, Meenie, Bandogera, Mick's and Toby's gins, the children and dogs in the uloo.

"But I'd cry my eyes out if he didn't buck any more," she confided to Coonardoo. "It's the dream of my life to sit a buck like you and Winni do, Coonardoo."

Coonardoo's dark eyes gleamed.

"You sit 'm buck long time ago," she said.

169

"I did, didn't I?" Phyllis exclaimed gleefully. "But who's that?" she asked, her glance wavering to a gin, very dirty and dejected looking, crouched against the wall of the bathroom.

"Bardi!" Coonardoo replied. "She come home . . . run away from Don Drew . . . walk all way."

"Bardi! Hullo, Bardi!" Phyllis called. "You get homesick like me, eh?"

Bardi looked up and gurgled. Her eyes were sore and bleary; she was very sorry for herself, hungry and footsore, and she knew Chitali would beat her as soon as she went along to the camp.

But in a day or two she had settled down into her old place at the uloo, and was going about the homestead, laughing and chugging like a well-greased engine, as fat and jolly as if bygones were always bygones, and she had never been away from the fireside of her man and the native well on Wytaliba.

CHAPTER XXV

WHEN they were setting out for a three weeks' muster in the To-Morrow, two or three days later, Dionysus put his head down and bucked, light-heartedly. Phyllis sat back, feeling as gay and light-hearted as he in the clear morning air. There was no doubt in Hugh's mind as to whether she could handle the chestnut he had intended to ride himself, after that, although Winni had two other horses for Phyllis to ride, in the mob he was taking for night work and cutting out, in the hills.

Coonardoo, Bardi and six of the boys went out on the muster and there were twenty horses. Wanna had charge of the packs; Winni and Chitali, Toby and the rest of the boys were riding with the spare horses. Phyllis and Hugh led along the long winding track to the hills. They were going across the range to the Weelarra gap and working back in towards the homestead again.

On the plains beyond the first gate wind-grass was still green, Mitchell grass rusty, salt-bush, fringing the red earth and gravelly track, flowed blue-grey and soft as smoke to the edge of the hills.

Trees stretched out from the foot of the hills, acacia, thorn-bush and mulga; gidgee, round, dark-green and glossy-leafed, the water-tree, from whose roots, if you were bushed, you could get water. Mulga gave the sky between the web of its twigs and branches, with leaves fine and tough, grey-blue of the wild pigeons' breasts. A flock of kangaroos, gingery-red as the earth they hopped over, forty perhaps, young things, does and an old boomer or two, scattered away through the trees or over the plains. Java sparrows flew off with faint sweet tinkling cries. The mulga now and then was hung with pale-yellow tasselled blossom, and long flat seed-pods. Paper-daisies spread in drifts under the trees and away over the flat land. Trails of the desert pea spilt new bright blood beside the track.

When Hugh swung off his saddle to have a drink from the waterbag hung round his horse's neck he picked a spray of desert pea. Phyllis stuck it through her hatband, and they went on again at the quick walk stock-horses travel by.

When they boiled the quart pots at midday, Hugh threw an old log of sandalwood on the fire, and its dry, smoky fragrance drifted far out across the plains and through the hills.

Phyllis exclaimed, delighting in it all, the wide blue skies, frail and exquisite, the air so fine and dry with that faint incense of paper-daisies and sandalwood.

"I've dreamt so often of doing this, Youie," she explained. "And I can't tell you how it eases some queer pain in me. You seem able to breathe and think better in the bigness out here."

On the hill-sides, where the earth under thick, wide-spreading scrub of mulga and thorn-bush was bare and shingly, Hugh's eyes were skimming for cattle tracks.

"Chitali'll find 'em," he chuckled. "He'd find cattle where no one else can. Tell you a stray, unbranded bullock in the tracks of a mob. Out in the back hills two or three years ago we were short of a couple of hundred beasts and couldn't pick 'em up.

" 'Find 'em Koodgeeda well,' Chitali said. None there. No tracks. Pointing to a hill farther on. 'Over there, maybe,' Chitali said.

" 'Far, Chitali?' I asked.

" 'No, not far.'

"We rode on ten miles. Nothing. No tracks. There was a soak a bit farther on.

" 'Cattle Weelarra soak,' Chitali said.

" 'Far, Chitali?'

" 'No, not far.'

"Rode another four miles. Then I saw he was right. We got tracks.

" 'How far away are they, Chitali?'

" 'Not far.'

"We got the beasts about five miles farther on."

Phyllis laughed happily, enjoying Hugh's yarn. And just before sunset, as sketchy outlines of an old wooden windmill were darkening against the sky, Hugh and she came to the well where they were to camp for the night.

The boys had hobbled out the horses and the camp-fires were going when Hugh and Phyllis rode in. Coonardoo, who had started ahead, was spreading the packs. Phyllis insisted that she should not be treated like a young lady on a picnic. But there was nothing to do. Winni took her horse and Hugh's. Coonardoo and Bardi had opened out the tucker bags and ground-sheets. Phyllis was to sleep beside Hugh's fire, and she was glad enough to stretch there, after her long day in the saddle, eat huge chunks of meat and slabs of bread with butter slapped on, half an inch thick, and to drink the hot tea without milk, he brought her.

When she lay down against the earth, for a while she was too excited and happy to sleep, listening to the clink-clink of the hobbled horses, watching the stars, crisp fires of silver run, thick and bright in blue-green of the sky. Through the warm dark came the creak of the fire as the embers fell apart. A kangaroo hopped up to the glow and away again; a bird cried, startled by the horses feeding as they strayed through the trees.

And, before the first flush had crept into the sky, behind the rampart of the range, the camp was stirring again. Boys went out after the horses. Coonardoo stoked the fires, stood quart pots round the embers. Raw meat, grilling and frizzling put smoke and a harsh savouriness into the fresh morning air.

From the roll of her own gear Phyllis took a towel and soap, splashed her face and hands in a bucket of water Coonardoo had set beside her, took the small tortoiseshell comb from her trousers pocket, and raked back her hair.

She was anxious not to appear fussy, or to make more demand on time and convenience than anybody else. After a meal of steak, hot from the embers, and a hunk of bread, with a mug of hot coffee, the blacks saddled and slung the packs. Hugh gave his directions for the day, and they rode on again.

After riding for three days, Weelarra soak was reached, and next morning the camp broke into parties of two and spread out fan fashion, to ride mustering along the range. Hugh and Phyllis were to go north. Coonardoo and Winni south and east. Toby, Mick and Chitali west, turning their beasts to the camp where Wanna held the packs and horses for cutting out.

When they rode out in the morning, through the scrub, spread out and feeding, Hugh and Phyllis passed cattle, ruddy and rusty young bullocks with great horns, and a few cows and calves. Hugh turned them and gave them a start in the direction of the camp, so that he could pick them up on his return. He was going to the head of the creek, and making over the range, to round beasts from that end towards the old yards on the clay-pan.

He camped at midday to make a fire, and put on the quarts.

Phyllis and he ate a piece of meat and some bread from the tucker bags Hugh had strapped to his saddle, while the horses nosed through the herbage. But the meet was for four o'clock, so Hugh skipped his midday stretch and snooze in the shade, smoked, and saddled up again.

It was easy going, this end of the range, and the cattle moved off slowly towards the plains whenever they were turned.

"We don't want to rush 'em," Hugh said, and Phyllis knew her job was to ride in on stragglers and, without exciting them, get them going down the range.

Chitali, Coonardoo and the boys had their beasts on the flat when Hugh's mob came in. Circe was standing saddled beside the fence of one of the oldest yards on Wytaliba.

"They're looking good, eh, Chitali?" Hugh scanned his three-year-old and four-year-old bullocks with satisfaction.

The black's eyes glimmered to a smile in the shadow of his hat-brim as the mob swayed and turned restlessly before him.

"Couple of S4G calves," he said.

Phyllis never enjoyed anything more than watching Hugh cut out on Circe, and holding her end of the swaying cattle. Winni had brought her an old stock-horse for the job.

"Give him his head, Phyll," Hugh said. "Damon knows his job. He'll steady 'em." Hot, sweated, and red-grimed with dust as the men, Phyllis worked until sunset with Hugh and the boys.

Warieda had trained Circe for cutting out years ago. She did nothing else and had been at the game for twelve years.

It was a treat to see the sturdy little bay mare go into a mob after a beast. You would think she knew the bullock as well as Hugh did, the way she cut out that beast, walking behind him, following on his tail until, on the fringe of the mob, she shot him out before he realized what had happened. Then Chitali swung in behind and turned him off among the fats Wanna and Mick were holding for the road.

Cows, calves and stores had been turned back to the hills again, and fats were in the yards so that there would be no watching for the first night, when Cock-Eyed Bob came into the camp. He said he was camped on the other side of the range, had seen smoke on the table-top, guessed Hugh was mustering and come in for a bit of sugar and a wongi.

Cock-Eye was glad of an invitation to eat and camp with Hugh for the night. Sprawled before the fire, he gave more of the gossip of the countryside, although he had been in the ranges for nearly three months, than Hugh had heard in years.

"Still got that little mare of yours, was such a wonder cuttin' out, Hugh?" he asked.

"Too right I have," Hugh agreed.

"Never saw a better except Misstake. You remember little Misstake they had on Ashburton Downs?"

"Circe's by Misstake," Hugh said.

"You still hear 'm talk of him, along the river," Bob went on. "Remember that muster at Milli creek in 1901, wasn't it?"

"Nineteen one?" Hugh cogitated.

"Best muster ever I was at," Bob said. "There was sixty men and about two hundred horses, six horse tailers——"

"Turn it up, Bob! Six horse tailers?" Hugh murmured with gentle derision. "Sure you weren't seeing double?"

"They had Misstake down from the Ashburton, and there wasn't a horse a patch on him cutting out. Men blew along from Illigoogee, Nuniewarra, Five Rivers. We were to meet at Milli well. There'd been four inches on the creek a month or so back and the feed was good. I was on Illigoogee at the time. . . ."

Hugh smiled to see Phyllis listening intently to Bob's yarn, although she knew it had to be taken with a grain of salt. Stretched on her stomach, at a little distance from the fire, she listened, smiling, and chaffing Bob as he talked.

"Four inches, Bob?" she queried. "They've got all the luck on Milli, haven't they?"

"We'd brought along a mob of young horses," Bob continued, not to be stopped. "Worked 'em on the way . . . and there was some fun in the mornings. They'd go rootin' and bucking all over the ground. Here was a bloke takin' a stretch out of a horse and there was another sitting the hump of a buck. You'd see the horses go kicking and comin' down on all fours, head between legs, so as you were gazing straight down on the ground. I had a fair cow of a horse called Grasshopper. My, he could go to market! The only thing to do was to sit back and hang on. But he could keep the corkscrews going until your head was near jerked off of you. . . ."

"Go on," Hugh murmured amiably, knowing Bob was letting off steam for months of silence and dreaming by himself.

"Bill Gale was there," Bob said. "Never seen a man sit a horse like Bill does, as if he was glued on. He's on Nuniewarra now. Did y' know?"

Hugh nodded.

Phyllis looked up, her eyes full of the firelight.

"Billy Gale?" she queried.

"Sam calls him his manager," Cock-Eye explained; "head stockman he is, I suppose. Bill doesn't mind what he calls it. The pay's good and he runs the rule over old Sam, they tell me. I reck'n Bill Gale's the finest stockman in the Nor'-West."

"Go on."

"Seen him stand in a yard with a couple of young steers, and let 'em charge at him. He stands stock still and swears ninety per cent'll think he's a stump and swerve aside."

"How about the other ten?" Phyllis asked.

"It's them you got to look out for, Bill says."

Hugh's face was varnished by the glare of the fire, as he stooped over for a stick and relit his pipe with the glowing end. "I've seen him. It takes some doing, all right."

"But, Lord, you'd've laughed," Cock-Eye went on. "I seen Bill get once! My godfathers, didn't he get. There was a big cow in a mob we was branding on Nuniewarra last year. His horse wouldn't stand, and Bill called me to take him off while he held the cow's head. I hear the boys yell when I'm ridin' a good way off, looked round and there's Bill, going hell-for-leather, the cow after him. Rode between and separated 'em. The cow come after me. But it was a near go for Bill all right."

"How's the fiddle these days, Bob?" Phyllis asked.

"Going strong," Bob replied eagerly. "Like a tune?"

"Rather!"

He hobbled across to where he had thrown down his pack, and was back in a few minutes, sat down beside the fire, tuned up, and presently, absorbed and happy, was playing and singing the scraps of sentimental ballads and rag-time he had picked up in mustering camps, from drovers, teamsters, miners, and cracked gramophones, grinding out their tunes in hotel bars.

Phyllis, half asleep by the fire, heard him laying a white rosebud on his "sweetheart's gr-y-ave" and wakened to the trot and taunting melody of "La donna e mobile".

"Where did you get that, Bob?" she called.

"Bill. He's always singin' it," Bob murmured. "Was prospectin' with me a bit last year. Got it from a Dago woman he was gone on in Roebourne . . . and you should 've heard him beef it out. We was singin' and playin' half the night sometimes."

The fiddle wailed and he sang in a broken nasal voice:

"Oh I'd so much rather
All life's roses gather—
In the garden of today.

"Remember that, Youie?"

"Blest if I do," Hugh drawled lazily. "What was it all about, Bob?"

"Only set eyes on that girl once," Bob said. "And I've been gone on her ever since. Jessica, her name was. You remember, Youie? 'Course you do. She was up at your place. You were going to marry her."

"Cripes, yes," Hugh murmured.

Phyllis shook herself from the drowsiness which had been creeping over her.

"I'll turn in," she said, starting up. She stood a moment before the fire, stretching. It was good to be having this life; to be part of it; to feel serene and sleepy.

"Good night, dad. Night, Bob."

She swung off; sat down on her ground-sheet a few yards from the fire; had a good look round to see there were no ants about, stood her saddle up behind her as a break-wind, took off her boots and blouse, pulled a woollen jumper over her head, placed her felt hat over her boots to keep the dew out, and was asleep in a few minutes.

CHAPTER XXVI

Mick and Toby were tailing the fats. Chitali, Coonardoo, Winni, Hugh and Phyllis riding into the hills, next day, mustered a rough and rugged stretch of country. The meet was for four o'clock, five miles farther down the creek.

It was harder riding than the day before, and the cattle were wilder. Late in the afternoon Hugh joined up with Coonardoo, Winni and Chitali, bringing in about two hundred and fifty beasts.

As they rode up to the bend of the creek where Wanna and Bardi had a fire going, Chitali exclaimed, "Billy Gale come in!"

Hugh did not look pleased. He rode over to the camp where a man was standing beside his horse.

A tall, rakish young man with the slouch and bend of a horseman, Billy Gale stood waiting as Hugh and Phyllis approached him. There was ease and assurance in his bearing, something free and untamed. He had the air of someone belonging to the country.

His trousers, the worn buff and earthy red of the clay-pan, covered him as if he grew them: his shirt rolled back from sun-red neck and breast, was tawny and dust-stained too. His spurs, the ends of his narrow pull-on stockman boots and his big Nor'-West hat were struck against the light behind him. The thin, hard brown face, in the shadow of his hat, was only a shade less dark than Winni's or Coonardoo's.

Phyllis remembered the face she had seen on a Papuan carving, a queer, sensitive, faunish face, with oblique eyes, three-cornered eyebrows. Mouth hooked over the pipe he was lighting, his eyes smiled into hers, a shy, restless, glittering smile. There was a lazy, unconscious grace about the man as when he had helped to dig her car out of the mud at Nuniewarra.

"Thanks for your message, Mr Watt," he said. "As y'r mustering, thought I'd better ride over and see if there's any of our young stuff about."

"Bound to be," Hugh replied. "There's always some of your young stuff about. Damned funny none of Sams' old stuff fancies runnin' with my cattle."

"Go on." Bill Gale laughed. "I'll see you get a fair crack of the whip now, Mr Watt."

Winni had brought Circe saddled for cutting out. Hugh changed horses, turned and rode out to the mob the boys were holding.

Hugh cut out on Circe while the boys held the mob, and Billy Gale stood off watching. Phyllis resented the curious, amused stare with which he followed her.

There were no yards and the fats had to be held during the night. Hugh set the watches. Chitali and Wanna for the first, then Coonardoo and Winni. He took the dawn watch himself with Mick.

After they had eaten from a hot-pot of salt beef, Hugh yarned with Billy Gale for a while, sprawling beside the fire, and Phyllis, lying on her back, gazed up at the stars, listening and smoking.

"Bought out Otto But-Not-of-Roses," Bill was saying. "Supposed to be fifty thousand acres . . . three or four hundred cattle, and open country around."

"Go on!" Hugh muttered drowsily.

"But all I ever mustered was eighteen beasts, and they were dead round a dry water-hole."

The blacks were singing round their camp-fires. Phyllis could hear Coonardoo's voice and Winni's. The melody on its low rhythmic beat wailed through her consciousness with a breath of earth and the aeons of space above her.

"Catchy-Catchy Downs, Otto called the place," Billy's voice drove on. " 'Cause he'd stocked up on the catch-as-catch-can principle, and branded anything came his way. Liked to talk about his station. An empty tank on a mulga ridge, it was. Lived there with a couple of blacks and their gins for Gord knows how long. . . ."

Phyllis wakened to see the mob hunched dark upon the plains in the starlight, to hear the boys going round the cattle; Chitali on the inside, riding half-way and then back; Wanna riding to meet him and back, the horses swinging with easy movement to the wavering air of the blacks' low singing. Phyllis was not to go on watch for the first night or two until the cattle were more or less settled down. But, sleeping lightly, she heard the watches changed: Chitali waken Coonardoo, and Winni come to Hugh. She had seen Hugh pull on his boots and go over to the kerosene tin of coffee by the fire, dip in his quart pot and drink.

"How are they?" he asked Winni.

"Moochin' all round. Won't settle at all," Winni said quietly. "Keep your eye on the white-faced bullock on the far side."

Hugh had swung into his saddle on the night horse Winni brought and moved slowly over to the mob. Winni, beside the blacks' fire, squatted a moment taking off his boots, then stretched. The camp-fires creaked and flickered again, while Hugh went on with the air Winni had been singing, in a low voice, very flat and out of tune, wandering off after a while into:

> "Trust him not, oh gentle stranger,
> Though his voice be low and sweet. . . ."

And keeping that going until dawn.

At five o'clock, when Hugh came off his go, he wakened the camp. Chitali and Mick went after the day horses, Hugh made a wagon-wheel of damper. He was faddy about his damper and liked to mix it himself. Coonardoo brought the tins of water, put one down beside Hugh's pack and another beside Phyllis's.

Phyllis washed in her tin of water as Hughie did, combed back her hair and was ready to eat and drink with Hugh and Billy Gale.

Gale was going with Hugh as far as the boundary of Nunie-warra. He insisted on taking a go at night. The cattle were restless, would not settle at all. The boys had a busy time with them. Phyllis had wakened to hear the crack of the stock-whips like rifle shots in the starlit night. She had seen Winni streaking after a white-faced bullock which mooched off, looking for his mother; watched the runaway brought back to the mob and heard Billy Gale go on with the boys. He sang some of the songs Cock-Eyed Bob had sawed out of his violin a few nights before, as he went round the cattle, "La donna e mobile", "It ain't goin' to rain no more", "Horsey, keep your tail up", and "The Desert Love Song".

In and out of the camp for ten days, Phyllis saw the tall rakish figure of Sam Geary's stockman. He sprawled by the fire with Hugh in the evening. They ate and drank their hot tea together; but Bill was off with Chitali and the boys all day, and took a watch at night before Phyllis went on with Coonardoo and Winni. She admired the easy, unconscious grace with which he swung about, riding and walking, or standing to light his pipe, and liked to watch him move off in the morning on the Blackguard, exclaiming with the blacks when the big gelding bucked and disported himself in the keen air.

"They're well matched," Hugh said. "A pair of them, I reck'n."

"What?" Phyllis asked.

"Blackguards."

"You don't like him?"

"No, I don't like him," Hugh said.

He did not seem to dislike Billy Gale when they yarned beside the fire in the evening, and Phyllis lay on her back, smoking and listening to them. She threw a word into the talk now and then; but Gale rarely spoke to her; if she found his eyes on her, he averted them quickly like a black of her own age.

Phyllis did not wish to be aware of him, of that queer faunish gaze of his, although she liked to listen while he was going round the cattle at night. There were notes in his voice, which came to her through the darkness, that dim light from the stars, and dropped into her:

> "Till the sands of the desert grow cold,
> And its infinite numbers are told. . . ."

Bill sang:

> "Love, I'll love thee,
> Till desert sands grow cold. . . .
>
> "Love me, I'll love thee,
> Till sands of the desert grow cold. . . ."

His voice moved, low and murmuring, as if he were thinking to himself, half singing, half talking. Phyllis wondered about the woman in Roebourne.

"You've got a great collection of songs, Bill," she said one evening when she and Billy were alone beside the camp-fire for a while.

Billy grinned lazily.

"Sam's gramophone," he drawled. "He bought it a couple of years ago when he was in Karrara. Got a lot of fun out of it till he poured a bottle of whisky down it one night. It's been a bit rusty ever since. That's where I get most of my songs."

"Not the one about women being changeable?"

"No." He looked at her with narrowing eyes. "How did you know?"

"Cock-Eyed Bob! The Dago woman in Roebourne, Bill . . . was she a plume swaying in the wind?"

"Cripes." Billy pulled himself up on his long legs. "I'll screw Cock-Eye's neck when I see him."

"Oh, I say——" Phyllis protested. But Billy swung off into the darkness.

Phyllis did not see him again that night. She unfolded her ground-sheet, looked around to see there were no mingas and went to sleep until she heard Billy singing in the small hours. Why on earth should she always waken when Bill Gale was going round the cattle, Phyllis wondered, disturbed and vexed with herself?

Billy was singing:

> "Till the sands of the desert grow cold,
> And its infinite numbers are told. . . ."

Over and over again he sang the love song. He sang nothing else during his last nights in camp.

Time flowed from the coolwenda's first notes before dawn, breakfast of coffee, damper and salt meat, mustering all the morning, with stretch, and a quart pot of tea, under bare blue sky and a vertical sun at midday, to cut out in the afternoon, off saddle and meal when a rosy glow was on hills and plains; turning out of day horses and bringing in of night horses; a sprawl, smoking and yarning beside the camp-fire for an hour or so, then sleep under the stars until your call came to go on watch round the cattle.

Then the tramp round the mob, restless and unbroken to the road still, singing softly and watching the big horned four-year-old bullocks who were giving all the trouble.

Phyllis swayed sleepily as she sang sometimes. She liked to take up the song of the man she was following, tried to imitate Coonardoo or Winni, teased Hugh by singing "The Gipsy's Daughter" all flat and out of tune as he did, and lightly, mockingly, for Bill's benefit burbled "La donna e mobile":

> "Plume in the summer wind,
> Waywardly playing, ne'er one way swaying
> Each whim obeying. This heart of womankind every way bendeth,
> Woe, who dependeth on joy she spendeth."

She had no idea that Bill watched through her watch, until the white-faced bullock got away one night. Phyllis went after him; but not before she had heard the flash and jerk outwards of the long figure from Bill Gale's fireside. He passed her on the spare night horse, headed and turned the beast.

"Damned swine!" Phyllis gasped, venting her rage and chagrin.

"He'll get away yet," Billy declared cheerily. "These suckers're more bother than they're worth. We should have kept his mother in the mob. Better let me go on with you."

Phyllis shook her head. She could not have endured the beast to get away, yet she wished Bill had let her manage by herself.

"Hugh'd sack me, if he didn't think I was up to the job."

Billy went back to his rug and fireside. Phyllis looked after him, troubled and a little afraid. Happy to be sex-free; to be living in the rough hard way of men, with a sense of independence and exhilaration in the courage and skill required for the work she was doing, she had sunk into her place in the camp. Even Hugh was beginning to forget she was a girl. She took her watch with the men; had worked all night when the bullocks rushed at Perry's Pool, and stuck it when the watches were double-banked for two or three nights afterwards.

CHAPTER XXVII

"WE'RE mustering on Nuniewarra, twenty-eighth," Bill said when he was turning off through the pass by the Nungarra rock. "Sam said to tell you, and say you're welcome to come over."

"Thanks." Hugh was remembering the number of S4G calves running with his cows. "We'll send a couple of boys—if I can't get over."

Gale's eyes were following the mob Chitali and the boys had moving over the plains, feeding as they went, and Phyllis riding with them on her chestnut. Hugh's resentment went deeper. He understood the dazed dreamy stare Gale put after his daughter. Helpless with rage, he glared at Billy.

"I'm all in, Hugh," Bill said steadily, earnestly. "Rough as bags and all that, but——"

"Nothing doing, Bill," Hugh stopped him.

"By cripes—isn't there?" Billy Gale's eyes slewed to him. Hugh looked short and stoutish nowadays, dour and bossy. "We'll see isn't there!"

Billy lifted his reins, rose in his stirrups and cantered to where Phyllis was riding. Hugh saw him pull in his horse, rock to, beside her. A moment later Bill was cantering across the plains towards the tumbled masses of Nungarra rocks, after his boys.

"Curse him. Curse his damned impudence!" Hugh smouldered, following his own beasts.

He had a presentiment Gale was right. He would see that lathy good-for-nothing walk off with Phyllis; walk off with her under his nose. And there was nothing to do. That was the worst of it. Wasn't there though? Hugh went over the tales he could tell Phyllis about Gale.

There was the woman in Roebourne, Geary had talked of; but she was mad about Bill and married after all. And the girl in Karrara—no, that wouldn't do. Hugh could not see himself tale-telling, spouting and moralizing. But, by hook or by crook, he intended to prevent Geary's stockman from marrying his daughter. He was not going to see his girl taken possession of by a man who took orders from Sam Geary. A man Sam Geary took orders from, was what the countryside was saying. Still, who was he, Bill Gale? Phyllis Watt, eldest daughter of Hugh Watt of Wytaliba station . . . to Bill Gale, by God knows who or the devil knows what, and cares less. No. Hugh set himself against the idea with sombre anger and resentment. If Billy Gale dared to come between him and his daughter. . . .

Hugh watched Phyllis, trying to discover whether the young man had made any impression on her. But from her quiet face he could discover nothing. Very soon Phyllis had acquired the habit of closing up on herself, and gazing out over the plains, with far-seeing eyes, absorbed in her own thoughts. She no longer chattered as they rode along together, or when they stretched beside the camp-fire in the evening.

That first night after he had left them, Phyllis found herself awake and listening for Billy Gale to go round the cattle. Thought of his singing, his shy virile grace and avid, dreaming eyes stirred and moved her.

"He's clean and straight, surely, dad," she said next evening.

"Who?"

"Bill Gale."

Hugh laughed shortly.

"Sam Geary's man? Big Otto's successor on Catchy-Catchy?"

On one pretext or another, with cases of fruit, books or papers, Bill had ridden and driven over from Nuniewarra several times during the year. Offhand, and determined to "nip this thing in the bud", Phyllis let him see clearly she did not wish to be regarded as a young woman who might be laid siege to and courted. Hugh was delighted that she was "taking a tumble", as he put it to himself, and would stand no nonsense from the young man.

But Bill, stalking a mate, had lost his awe of Phyllis and of Hugh. The shrewd faun in him leapt, making fun of the boyish gear Phyllis liked to wear; her attitude of indifference. Becoming reckless, he made love to her gaily, defiantly.

When he rode over with letters, on a young horse, Hugh groaned.

"The devil! The cunning devil!" he exclaimed to himself, watching Phyllis, the glow and admiration in her eyes as Bill, lithe and strapping, swung to every plunge and gyration of the chestnut stallion he was riding.

Bill on his own, she could have resisted. But Billy Gale on horse-back—Hugh despaired of being able to hold Phyllis against him. The country and youth were on Bill's side too. Phyllis had no companion of her own age.

Every time, after Billy had been, Hugh saw himself losing ground: realized that Gale was gaining it. Phyllis watched the creek-crossing when he did not appear for weeks at a time, was restless, and asked questions about him. Hugh was afraid Billy had won when she put on a light frock one evening, after he arrived, and powdered her nose.

He would not leave Gale a moment alone with Phyllis. When Phyllis herself suggested a walk in the moonlight it was the finish for Hugh. The stone end, he told himself. She must go away. She must go back to town for a while until this affair blew over. There was nothing else for it. Propinquity and the loneliness of the country were doing their work. What they could do, he knew very well; and yet there was the stuff in Phyllis to resist all that, if she chose. If she chose. If she didn't. . . .

Hugh boiled at the thought, all his love clamouring against withdrawal of the girl from himself. His being surged with incomprehensible fury and antagonism to the man who was taking his daughter. "To have and to hold. . . ." He remembered the marriage service, distracted by the thought of what it would mean now to be without the companionship which had come into his life, releasing him from the bitter loneliness of so many years.

With the coming of Phyllis Hugh lost sight of his own problem. Phyllis had banished his loneliness and bitterness of spirit. Her coming to him, and adoption of the life on Wytaliba, had been so unexpected, so surprising and miraculous. His thought, all his tenderness, surged, turning to admiration and pride as he settled down to acceptance of her, a confidence and happiness which at last he believed in and took for granted.

Connardoo moved about the house and the verandas as she had done when his mother was there, working for, obeying Phyllis, anticipating what she would like done, tranquil and happier-looking than she had been for a long time. As the dark mirror of his soul, Hugh realized, in a vague half-conscious way, Coonardoo reflected his moods, the happiness and peace which had come to him.

And in Coonardoo Phyllis found not only the faithful woman who had served her mother and her grandmother, but something more. What, she did not quite know.

At the house, in her blue gina-gina, Coonardoo was silent and reserved. She went about her work in a slow, dignified way, without approaching in the least familiarity. But riding together, on the plains and in the ranges, as they often did, it was quite different. Coonardoo in her faded dungaree trousers and an old shirt, naked feet in the stirrups, her hair still fair and glinting in the sun, was the most fascinating companion. She laughed her merry girlish rippling laughter, and talked about trees and landmarks they passed, telling Phyllis stories of Hugh when he was a boy. Of Mumae and Warieda she never spoke, unless asked, a shadow lying across her face in full sunshine at mention of the dead.

"Do you remember . . ." Phyllis would ask.

And Coonardoo with lighted eyes would gurgle assent.

"What was that story you used to tell me about the emu and wild turkey?" Phyllis asked.

"Emu and wild turkey bin argument which one better woman?" Coonardoo inquired.

"Eeh-mm." Phyllis had fallen into the aboriginal murmur of assent. They laughed over the legend together.

Coonardoo pointed out a tree beside the track, from which a snake had dropped and almost fallen on her and her horse as they rode beneath, one day, long ago.

"Goodness, what happened?" Phyllis asked. Coonardoo was very frightened of snakes, she knew; would not speak of a koodgeeda after dark.

"Youie kill 'm," Coonardoo said.

The year had swung round and Phyllis with it. She looked leaner, harder than twelve months before; but she was more sure of herself. The days had lost some of their glamour and interest for her; but she had settled down into the life of the station, satisfied to be part of it, to be taken seriously as Hugh's right-hand man.

Wearing the spurs she won after her first muster, she clinked and clanked about with a free, buoyant tread, very like Hugh's

187

own. Sometimes her spirit was stronger than her back. Coonardoo had seen Phyllis knocked out after a long day, now and then, although she kept going with obstinacy and a stiff upper lip.

Hugh seemed to remember she was a girl only when Billy Gale rode up to the stock-yards. He hated to see Phyllis in the green linen frock she put on to please Billy, and to find Bill, spruced up, hair slick and oiled, stretched out talking to her on the veranda.

"God damn his eyes," he said to Cock-Eyed Bob when Bill brought Bob along with him one evening, and they had spent the evening singing to Bob's fiddle on the veranda.

"What's up, Youie?" Bob asked. "Bill's been tellin' me you gone sour on him——"

"Never was sweet," Hugh stormed. "What the hell does he want to come hanging round my girl for?"

"Why shouldn't he, in Gord's name?" Bob asked. "What's the matter with Bill anyhow? I reck'n I'd be shook on him all right if I was a girl . . . and he's no worse than the rest of us. Better than most, if the truth was known."

Bob's admiration for Billy Gale was very downright.

"Oh, I suppose I'm a cantankerous old snoozer, Bob," Hugh said. "I can't endure the idea of him or any man getting Phyllis."

"Well, somebody's got to get her," Bob observed. "And it might as well be Bill, Youie. Better put that in your pipe and smoke it."

The idea was smoke-dried in his mind already, Hugh assured Cock-Eye. He had tried to reason himself out of the absurd jealousy with which the sight and thought of Gale possessed him, although he felt powerless against it.

"I reck'n we'll muster the To-Morrow—first week in April," he told Gale next time they met. "I daresay you'll get your usual haul."

The year had been hard, dry and strenuous, moving cattle from played-out water-holes to wells and stretches of country between the hills where the feed was good. Only an inch and a half of rain fell in January; but thunderstorms scattered showers throughout the back hills, and Hugh was hoping to have a mob on trucks before cattle from the Kimberleys reached the sale-yards.

Billy Gale rode into the mustering camp the day after Hugh reached Weelarra. Lounging beside the fire in the evening, after he had eaten with Hugh and Phyllis, Billy yarned lazily.

Darkness was gathering, stars glittering in green of the sky, when Hugh mooched off to see the boys about a mare which had fallen during the afternoon.

"Been out prospectin' with Cock-Eye," Bill said. "He's on a good thing. Not got it yet; but he's right, I reck'n. You can smell gold all round where he is. He's got a bag of specimens. And there's a mountain of asbestos, out there at the head of the creek. . . ."

"It'd never pay to work."

Phyllis had heard that said so often. It was easy to repeat without thinking, and she was not thinking of what Bill was saying. Her mind was full of the dry season and a talk she had been having with Hugh that morning.

"The numbers 're up, Phyll," he said. "Looks as if we couldn't keep goin' much longer. Ought to have done better last year. The season was good, but we missed the market somehow, with that last mob you mustered with us."

If the bank foreclosed what would happen? What would Hugh do?

She was worried and depressed. It did not seem possible to think of Hugh leaving Wytaliba, and yet he would have to go, he said. Unless the bank kept him on as manager, he would have to get managership of some other station.

Billy went on talking of Cock-Eyed Bob and his mountain of asbestos.

"I brought in this for you." Bill leant over, holding in his hand a piece of asbestos, silver threads glistening in green matrix.

Phyllis took it from his hand idly.

Billy, lying stretched on the earth before her, covered her with his eyes. She looked up from the stone which he had cut and polished to the shape of a heart. Her eyes glanced off from his, as though she had taken fright at them and the sight of the stone in her hand.

"You know about asbestos," Billy said, "how it'll stand fire, drought and rain, any old thing. And the harder you use it, the better it'll be. That's me for you, Phyllis."

"Bill!"

Phyllis knew that what she was seeing in Billy Gale's eyes was as shining and old as the stone in her hand.

"I'm rough as bags. I'm not up to you, Phyllis," Billy said quietly.

189

"But I sort of feel we're straight for each other, like the blacks say."

"Yes." Phyllis was surprised to find herself discussing so calmly what she had determined to put away. "I feel we're straight for each other, Bill. But——"

"I know," Bill interrupted, sitting up, the flame leaping in his eyes. "Youie'll hate it like poison. But, by and by he'll get over it. You see"—he leant over again, smiling, with that queer, faunish lift of eyebrows and slanting eyes—"I been schemin' like hell. Never before I saw you, Phyll—never planned, looked ahead, acted cunning in my life before. Just lived from hand to mouth, all me born days, as they say."

"Go on." Phyllis smiled.

"Then I saw you, and wanted you. And how was I to get you? How in God's name was I to get you? Worked it all out. Told Sam I wanted a rise straight away when I went in after Wytaliba muster last year. Made a bargain with him. He agreed to pay me a percentage on his profits . . . and I been stocking Catchy-Catchy—Big Otto's place, you know. This year I warned Sam I was clearin' out and going to work me own place soon. He begged me to stay . . . and I put it to him. . . . I'd stay and manage Nuniewarra for him until he pegs out—see he gets all the sting he wants, if he'd make a will in my favour. . . . And I got him into Karrara to fix it all up in writing."

"You didn't lose any time." Phyllis said.

"Why should I?" Bill asked. "Sam's gettin' on and he's got no one belonging to him, except Sheba, Tamar, and the rest of them and their kids."

In the shadowy world about them the mulga whispered faintly; the blacks murmured about their fires a little distance away; Phyllis could hear the boys' droning chant as they went round the cattle.

"Will you be my woman, Phyll?" Billy Gale asked.

"Billy!" Phyllis's voice quavered between tears and laughter. "I'd like to, but I don't see how I possibly can."

"If you'd stand by me . . . like your grandmother did her man, we could make a place as fine as Wytaliba."

Phyllis smiled, knowing how subtle he thought the appeal. "But how can I desert Hugh?" she said. "I wanted to help him and things are bad now, I can't leave him when he's so down on his luck."

Hugh came to the fire again. And after a few minutes, Gale drew up his long legs.

"Good night, Phyll," he said.

Billy swung over to the fire his boy had made on the other side of the blacks' camp. His saddle and ground-sheet were there.

Phyllis sat down on her own rug, shook it out, pulled off her boots, took off her blouse, and thrust her arms through the woollen jumper she slept in, and lay down.

Looking up at the stars, she found herself pinned to the earth by swarming currents, a magnetism which shivered, dancing, acclaiming, and overwhelming her. Just a little distance away, beside his own fire, Bill had thrown himself on the ground. It was that she felt through the earth, Phyllis knew, the force and tumult of him; his every nerve and instinct, wirelessing, had fastened and was feeding on her.

CHAPTER XXVIII

PHYLLIS admitted to herself that Gale had a magic for her. She knew when he was about as she did when a thunderstorm was brewing. Felt him like that; her body stirred to him. There was oppression in the atmosphere, before he came; then, as he looked at, or brushed her ever so lightly, electricities, jagged and tingling, flashed and played through her. As she watched the sky behind the hills, during a storm, fearing yet delighting in the lightning which promised rain to the dead earth, she thought of Bill. It was pleasant to feel him like a thunderstorm on his horse, to know she might be her own moppin-garra and call down the lightning and rain when she wanted them. But after all that was not how it was going to be. Bill was to blow over—as so many thunderstorms did on Wytaliba.

You could see them coming, were sure the dusty clouds would break on the purple-dark backs of the hills, break and toss rain to deluge the plains. But as often as not, lightning flashed for a while, played across the screen of the sky and withdrew on a muttering of thunder which meant nothing. The clouds misted away and the long still days of heat and bare skies went on again.

"I suppose I'm in love, really," Phyllis told herself, "to get all dazzled and fussed-up like this when Bill's about!"

Riding with Coonardoo one day, she asked suddenly, "What's the matter, Coonardoo? Why doesn't Youie like Bill Gale?"

Coonardoo's eyes swung on her, the bright beautiful eyes of a wild animal in their thick yellowy whites. A child's eyes, yet wise and old.

"A dog must have a bone to chew," was Coonardoo's quick muttered reply.

"*Un coeur cela veut un os à ronger.*" The phrase flashed from a crevice of memory with glimpse of a classroom of girls doing French compositions. Mademoiselle Meunier, translating, expounding, her grey hair tightly curled about her head, her bright bird's eyes darting, ear-rings of filigree gold dangling beside her face. Her waist was so small your hands would nearly meet round it over the gown of striped black velvet she wore to display her figure.

"A heart must have a bone to gnaw." Mademoiselle Meunier and Coonardoo! Phyllis smiled to think of them; so different, yet saying the same thing.

She herself was the bone in the case, she realized, Hugh's bone. The bone he was holding to himself and chewing over. And Coonardoo had known that. Phyllis guessed there was no other reason for Hugh's objection to her marrying Bill Gale. The others were smoke he put up to hide his loneliness and fear. Coonardoo had detected the real reason, the bone to gnaw. Oh, well, he should have his bone, Phyllis promised herself. Not for Billy Gale, or a dozen Billy Gales would she take his bone from Hugh. Particularly now when he was so down on his luck.

She had come to a good understanding with Bill. When he came to Wytaliba on some pretext or other, they fraternized, yarned in gay, free, unromantic fashion.

"Of course," Phyllis said, riding in from the Fifty Mile well with him one evening, "I can imagine any white man falling for Coonardoo."

"Can you?" Billy squinted across at her, his eyes in the shadow of his hat-brim. He wondered what she was getting at, how much she knew of the gossip about Coonardoo and Hugh. There was scarcely a white man in the district who did not disapprove of Hugh Watt's having his daughter on Wytaliba. Billy among them, although he woud not have dared to hint as much to Hugh. He was a queer chap, Hugh Watt of Wytaliba, it was agreed, and you never knew where you were getting to with him.

"She's a remarkable woman, Coonardoo," Billy observed. "Sheba's another at Nuniewarra. I'm not shook on gins myself. They're a repulsive lot, mostly. Not that I've been any better than most men who've lived a long time in this country, Phyll."

Phyllis smiled into his glittering faun's eyes. She imagined he was relieved to have got so much off his chest.

"I know, of course," she said, "what the countryside thinks about Hugh and Coonardoo. There's nothing in it, as far as I can see. Might have been once. Winni's a sort of stepbrother of mine, I suppose. Hugh says as much himself. It seems to me Coonardoo and Winni, as far as Hugh's concerned, were an accident."

"Gins are, as a rule."

193

"Hugh's been decent about them," Phyllis persisted. "So decent that people would hardly believe if he told them, and he wouldn't bother to explain. He's like that, Youie—awfully decent, inside. He's got a high standard of his own. 'I believe in honour,' he says. 'Honour, courtesy—and keeping yourself clean.' And he reads any old paper-covered novel and—*The Iliad*. Whatever else there is or isn't in his pack, there's bound to be *The Iliad*. He lies stretched out, reading by the camp-fire, spouting yards of it."

Phyllis laughed with the tenderness of her vision. "You know, Bill, when I came up first I felt as old as the hills beside Youie. Tried to explain to him that if he wouldn't let me stay on Wytaliba I'd bolt to the Argentine with Garry Macquarrie. But he looked so young and innocent, I couldn't hurt him. . . . It's being up here so long, and not knowing really how mean and vicious life can be, I suppose."

As grimly and sturdily as Mumae had ever worked, Phyllis rode and drove with Hugh, Coonardoo, and the boys during the dry, hot months of the long summer.

But play the game as she would, she began to flag in her stride, and lost weight on the hard salt rations which they ate, moving cattle. So skinny and leathern her face became, that she jeered at it when she caught sight of herself in a mirror unexpectedly.

"And I feel like the mulga looks," she told Coonardoo. "Withering up inside. My sap's gone dry."

"Phyllis not go," Coonardoo objected when, after a long strenuous journey, Hugh was packing the tucker bags to be off again in the morning.

Hugh glanced at Coonardoo; he knew her too well to imagine she would speak without reason. He looked over to where Phyllis was lying stretched on her back on the veranda. The utter weariness and shrinkage of her figure startled him.

"Here, Phyll," he called. "You got to stay in and rest a bit this trip. You'll be getting knocked up."

"What?" Phyllis was on her feet, game and fighting again at the idea she was to give in. "I'm as tough as nails, Youie."

Coonardoo scowled when Phyllis went off to the stock-yards next morning, stepping jauntily, with a swagger and jibe at Hugh for not getting a move on.

She knew very well, herself, that her strength was giving out. She was by no means as fit and keen for days in the saddle as she used to be. The drought was driving her as it was everybody else. She kept going for fear she would give in to some sheer female weakness. Phyllis told herself she needed to be up and doing: to keep moving and busy. She did not intend to give in to any sentimentality. There was too much to be done, shifting cattle on to fresh water. Then, too, keeping your nose to the grindstone prevented other things from plaguing you. A growing thirst for the sight and the sound of that damned Billy Gale, for one thing, and lying awake, thinking of him, feeling yourself being plucked all over and flickering to every thought of him, for another.

It was no good, Phyllis assured herself. No damn good at all. If you were being a son and a standby to the parent bird, be it for God's sake, and have done with this tommy rot. All the same she would have been glad to cry, say it was hot and she was tired. Both forbidden by the code she had set herself—which was to act chirpily, play cunning, and help Hugh pull Wytaliba out of the soup—if brains and spurs could do it. Soup! Lord, if only the mess were as watery!

But Coonardoo was not far wrong. She had measured and foreseen the end of the tether for Phyllis. Coming in from that trip Phyllis went down to an attack of blight, which kept her to her room for days. One eye was swollen and bloodshot; the other she could not open.

Coonardoo scolded Hugh when he had helped Phyllis into her room.

"She's run down with the salt meat and no milk or vegetables, I suppose," he said.

Phyllis lay stretched in her dark room, glad to be still, not to have to open her eyes, or move. Overwhelming weakness and sickness obliterated everything for her. She lay for days in the darkness, the hot stillness, knowing only that Coonardoo was there, holding a cool drink to her lips, bathing her face and hands, fanning her, murmuring with a comforting gentleness, insisting that she should have some stinging lotion poured into the swollen, bloodshot eyes. The pain of head and eyes, weakness and sickness left her; but for some time Phyllis was content to lie and sleep, eat what Coonardoo brought her, go along the veranda to the bathroom, and sleep again.

Hugh was to meet Don Drew coming down from Weelarra, and had left Coonardoo to look after Phyllis.

She was lying on the veranda the night Billy rode up, making the stones fly as he crossed the creek at a speed which Phyllis knew was the Blackguard's best.

Phyllis glanced at Coonardoo; and knew why he was there.

"Joey go walk about Nuniewarra." Coonardoo gazed ahead of her. "Tell 'm ask Billy Gale bring lemons for you."

"Oh, that's it, is it?" Phyllis exclaimed.

She covered her face with her hands as Billy came towards the veranda.

"You can't look at me," she said. "I've got a bung eye and I'm too ugly."

Billy had not swerved in his stride. Coming straight on, he took her in his arms with a gesture as reckless as it was final.

"I'm no great shakes, God knows, and your father's right, Phyll," he gasped. "But I want you like hell. If you don't want me, then go to blazes! But if you do—and I reck'n you do——"

"Do you?" Phyllis tried to lift her head.

"I'm kidnapping you, tonight," Billy said, "or——"

"Tomorrow, or the next day. Well——" Phyllis cried, "I don't mind if you do, Bill. I haven't another kick in me."

When Hugh came in, several days later, he had done a lot of thinking.

"It's no good, Phyll," he said, the same evening, when they had eaten their supper and stretched yarning. "You've got to go down and get a bit of colour into your cheeks again."

He had said that before, and Phyllis declared the sun would do all she needed, or a little pot of rouge which still hid in her suitcase. But this evening she was silent for a moment. Then she said slowly, "P'r'aps you're right, Youie. I believe I'd like to get into the sea for a while. . . ."

"That's it," Hugh declared. "Sea bathing. Just the thing, a loaf on the sands, tennis, young life."

"Will you come, too?" she asked. "Do. It would be good for you and I'd love you to."

Hugh shook his head.

"Everything depends on me staying, and doing what I can to save any stock that's left. You've been a brick, Phyll. Don't know what I'd have done without you. If only we'd switched on to sheep —when everybody else did. But I've been afraid of the dogs. . . .

We ought to have been able to pull through between us. But it looks as if somebody'll be carrying the monkey before long, now."

"I'm coming back," Phyll said. "But I've got to marry Billy, dad. I'm sorry. It can't be helped. That's the way I feel about it. I've got to. Out here, you can't live alone. You can't live on yourself."

"A slushie—damned rouseabout," Hugh groaned.

"I have heard," Phyllis murmured, "that my grandfather couldn't write his own name. Anyhow, I'll be quite near on— Catchy-Catchy." Her smile glimmered freakishly. "We can see each other often."

Hugh was not to be comforted, although he tried to make the best of this last back-hander Fate had dealt him.

In a few days Phyllis was standing on the veranda in the silk dust-coat she had worn when she stepped on to it that evening two years before. Winni brought the car to the gate, and Hugh took his seat beside Phyllis. He was going down with her as far as Karrara. Winni would follow with horses. Hugh intended to ride back after he had seen Phyllis off at Karrara.

Returning over the creek-crossing when he had said good-bye to Phyllis, a sense of desolation oppressed Hugh. There was nothing to do but work it off, and work he did. He worked as men drink, to gain oblivion. Extraordinarily tough, he plugged on through heat and dust storms, blazing sunshine which sapped the source and force of life in everything. Only Coonardoo sensed the forlorn obduracy of his conflict. Her face, heavy and sombre, reflected his depression, the dumb, unappeased hunger, thrown back upon itself. An old dog without a bone to gnaw, Hugh fought blindly, refusing to recognize disaster, or defeat.

Three months after Phyllis had gone down, Sam Geary brought a mail from Nuniewarra and a case of oranges Phyllis had sent. He said Billy Gale had gone south for a holiday, too. Hugh knew what that meant.

He was scarcely prepared all the same for the letter which came from Mollie, with a newspaper describing the wedding of Miss Phyllis Watt, eldest daughter of Hugh Watt of Wytaliba station, to William Gale of Nuniewarra and Catchy-Catchy Downs.

"My God," Hugh groaned.

His bitterness and disappointment were unreasonable, quite irrational, he admitted. He could not explain them to himself. Phyllis had come to him out of the blue. He had attached himself to her, and she had been absorbed into the blue again. He was left gazing at the place where she had been.

But Mollie was well satisfied with Bill Gale, it seemed. He had splashed money around, giving Phyllis and the girls a good time, before the wedding.

"Bill is really a success," she wrote, "though where on earth did he spring from and who is he? He seems to have money and that's a comfort, besides taking Phyllis off my hands. She was really a problem. I could do nothing with her, and it's probably the best thing that could have happened her, marrying a back-country man like this. Cora is very different and I daresay will be engaged to George Nott, of the Nott Proprietary Ltd, before the year's out.

"But really, my dear Hugh, you must increase the pittance you have been expecting us to exist on. How on earth you expect me to live, dress the girls, and give them a chance in life on the income you allow me, I don't know. Of course, the seasons are bad on Wytaliba. They always are when I want money. But, of course, you've only yourself to thank for staying there, when you could have sold out at a handsome profit years and years ago. However, now, for the children's sake—of course I know I don't count in your affairs and never have done—you might try to be reasonable."

Sam Geary was thoroughly pleased with himself and the news he had brought. He was looking upon Bill as a sort of protégé, the heir to Nuniewarra, and regarded it as a feather in his cap that Bill should have eloped with Hugh Watt's daughter.

"Nuniewarra and Wytaliba running in double harness, after all!" he chortled. "Well, I tried most ways—but I never dreamt of this one, Youie."

Geary looked little older than he had done ten years ago. Tall and ruddy, at sixty—he was as active and vigorous as he had ever been.

CHAPTER XXIX

H UGH was away mustering when the rain came. He had been out a week with all the men from the uloo, twenty horses and stores for three weeks.

Dust storms had swirled and inundated the uloo and homestead, promising a thunderstorm, and whirled off again. A cloud floated over the sky at dawn, shredded and drifted out in fluff. And still there was no rain; no crackling of thunder in the far, dim hills.

Coonardoo, watching the plains and the sky, knew rain was falling far away. She could smell it in the air.

For a week or so the clouds were loose and flowing, dingy and dirty as greasy wool. Rain fell beyond the Dog-toothed range. Fine slanting showers passed over the bluff and beyond the massed rocks of the Koodgeeda gap.

When the heat broke suddenly, shattered and scattered by a thunderstorm, thunder and lightning played all round Wytaliba, before rain fell, speeding outwards with a few scattered heavy drops.

Children ran from the uloo to the buggy shed, shrieking, trying to catch the great cool drops, which turned to hailstones, spitting and sizzling on the hot earth.

Thunder cracked, rumbled, a great skyey voice falling to earth among the ragged distant ranges. Lightning flung its long brilliant spears across wide spaces of the sky, flung them right into the eyes. And the rain fell quicker, splashing and spindling; quicker and quicker, steaming and sprawling, it fell, blotting out the hills.

In an hour or so the thick thready veil lifted and water was seen lying out on the plains. Wytaliba homestead, with all its houses, barns, sheds and windmills, stood in the middle of a shallow lagoon. The air was clear and cool, the sky pale and shining, the hills newly washed, raw, deep blue.

Down at the uloo, old Joey, Bandogera and Bardi's Polly were flooded out. The dogs prowled unhappily. Joey and his gins hurried down to the creek to pick branches. Coonardoo went with them, helping to patch up and mend holes in the huts through which

199

rain had poured. But everybody was gay and laughing about the bath they had got, revivified and chattering joyously, excitedly, because of the rain. Meenie began to sing the song Warieda had made when it rained like this, long ago.

It had been raining all through the ranges too, Coonardoo knew. She wondered whether as much rain had fallen on the far side of the hills, inland; and whether Hugh would come in from the muster.

Towards evening, when rain water had soaked into the earth, leaving shining pools round the crab-holes, a car came splashing through water along the track from the gap. Coonardoo's eyes darkened as she saw it.

The car was Sam Geary's, and a tall thin man, a miner, who had been out to inspect Cock-Eyed Bob's claim on the ridge, was driving. He and Sam Geary had gone through Wytaliba with Cock-Eyed Bob and his camels before Hugh went out.

Geary drew up at the little gate in the back fence and stamped on to the veranda.

"Hullo there!" he called. "Anybody at home?"

Coonardoo came from the kitchen.

"Youie not in yet?" he asked.

"Wiah."

Coonardoo stood stiff and majestic. Geary knew her resentment and distaste of his presence. He glowed with malicious enjoyment at the sight of her.

"Oh well, we're wet to the skin, me and Dick Crossley, my girl. Fix up some tucker for us. We're stopping the night."

"No meat. No killer."

Coonardoo spoke flatly, with authority.

"Now, look here, I'm not takin' orders from a blasted gin," Geary said. "You do as you're told, damn you. Come along, Crossley." He stalked along the veranda to the room where Phyllis had slept, and threw open the door. "You sleep here. I'll camp in Youie's room."

The tall man with pale blue eyes and fairish pointed beard smiled at Coonardoo as she stood scowling and staring after Geary.

Geary went on into Hugh's room and reappeared with a pair of trousers and shirt of Hugh's.

"Here you are, Dick!" he shouted. "See if you can get into these." He flung the clothes at Crossley and walked back along the veranda to Hugh's room. "I'll stick the bus up in the buggy shed. See you make a good fire, Coonardoo. And there's something to eat, pretty quick, or I'll know the reason why."

He went through the kitchen, down the steps into the yard.

Coonardoo watched him driving the car through the soft earth to the shed. The car stuttered, rocked, shot out from the oozing mud. Geary steered her under the high roof of the buggy shed, and swaggered down to the house. He came into the kitchen again. Coonardoo had gone to the fire and was raking the embers together as he came in.

"Great rain, eh, Coonardoo? Youie'll be pleased, eh? By God, it did come down out there be the gap. We was near drowned. Where's the whisky? No. I'll get it myself." Twisting the key from her hand, he went into the sitting-room and returned with a bottle under each arm.

When he had opened one of the bottles, Geary poured himself a drink.

"Hi, Dick," he called, "could you stop one?"

"Too right," the stranger's voice sang out.

He slouched into the kitchen; his keen hungry eyes travelled to Coonardoo.

"How about it, Coonardoo?"

Geary held the bottle over a glass invitingly.

He was in a crazy good-humour, because of the rain. Coonardoo was flattered to be asked to drink with a white man before a stranger. She knew the taste of whisky. Warieda had given her some to drink once. She could still remember the fiery quiver of the stuff. How she had laughed and sung, as the white men do when they drink it, and then how stupid and heavy she had been in the morning.

But whisky was forbidden. White people were not allowed to give this drink of theirs to the blacks, she knew. It was poison to them, Mumae said; made them do things they did not want to. Hugh had given Warieda whisky when he was sick to drive the bulya out of him; but he had died all the same.

"Come on, Coonardoo. Come on." Geary had walked towards her and taken her by the shoulder.

"Wiah."

Coonardoo flung away from him, her eyes fierce and afraid.

Bardi standing in the doorway watched her. She had seen the car drive up and the men walking about the veranda. That they were going to stay the night, she guessed; and there would be a meal to get.

"Hullo, Bardi! Back again? Been vamping all the boys on the place, they tell me. Bring those glasses and the bottles. Got a thirst on me like a wooden god!"

Geary led the way to the veranda and the chairs there. He and Crossley stretched yarning, until Bardi said the meal was ready.

With a face of thunder, lowering and overcast, Coonardoo had boiled a piece of salt beef and put some dried potatoes in the pot. For the honour of the station, and making the best of a bad bargain, she opened a tin of peaches and set them on the table in the kitchen. She did as Mrs Bessie, or Hugh, would have asked her to do; but sulkily, distrusting Geary, resenting his making free with Wytaliba like this in Hugh's absence. Disturbed and apprehensive, she moved out of the range of Geary's eyes. She saw in them what she had always seen.

With that consciousness came the stirred weakness and desire of her waiting for Hugh. She had been half dead in her sterility. Geary's grasp loosened instincts, which flamed greedily, clutching and swarming.

And Hugh did not want her. Coonardoo did not understand why Hugh did not want her. Why he did not take her.

Bardi giggled and whispered how the tall stranger had pulled her about. The men sat drinking and smoking, stretched after their food, before the fire in the kitchen.

Coonardoo could hear them laughing and shouting drunkenly, as they yarned.

She went out to the wood-heap; but the earth and wood were wet and cold. Creeping into the room Hugh had given her at the end of the veranda, she crouched there.

The men were drunk and quarrelling.

She could hear Geary's voice.

"No. No, you have Bardi!"

"Coonardoo! Coonardoo!"

It was the stranger calling.

Coonardoo hung back against the wall.

"No." Geary's voice, thick and insistent, soared and foundered. "Coonardoo's mine. You can have Bardi."

The voices fell away muttering and laughing.

Coonardoo could hear the men coming along the veranda. They had got Bardi.

Coonardoo heard her struggling, crying out, giggling and exclaiming.

Geary's voice bellowed, "Coonardoo! Coonardoo! Where are you, Coonardoo?"

Geary came along the veranda. He lurched against the door of the room she was in, and the door opened. Coonardoo hung power-less before him.

Heavy and drunken, in the doorway, his eyes glazed, Geary stood, swaying, an old man with his hair on end, his face red, swollen and ugly. Coonardoo could have moved past and away from him in the darkness. But she did not move. As weak and fascinated as a bird before a snake, she swayed there for Geary whom she had loathed and feared beyond any human being. Yet male to her female, she could not resist him. Her need of him was as great as the dry earth's for rain.

The morning was calm, clear and quiet; rain water lay out across the plains; crab-holes were full and glassy. The sun climbed the lower sky, a plaque of brilliance which played against the eyes. Mists, the mauve and magenta of wild flowers, which grow in candelabra on the river flats, hung before the bare red hills and tawny spinifex uplands. Kurrajongs in front of the house shook young bright-green leaves. A sky wadded with grey floating clouds promised more rain.

The gins were at work about the house, as early as usual. Geary and Dick Crossley slept on. Coonardoo made porridge and cooked meat for them. When Sam shouted for tea she took it to him, scowling, refusing to remember the night which had already become a dream, and hating Geary as she had always done.

Geary himself was sullen and bad-tempered. Dick Crossley groaned about the sore head he had got. He blamed Hugh's whisky and Sam went for him, said he had better drink his own whisky if he felt that way about it.

By midday they were ready for the road again. Geary was rather in a hurry to be off before Hugh came in. He was uneasy in his mind about how Hugh would regard the french leave he had taken with his house and women—particularly Coonardoo. Although over that he had got rather a shock. Drunk he had been, but not so drunk he did not hear and understand Coonardoo when she cried to herself, "Youie not want 'm!"

Sam was curious to know why she said that. Coonardoo had told him.

In the morning, before he left the veranda, Geary called Coonardoo. She came from the kitchen and stood before him.

"Come and be my woman, Coonardoo," he said. "I'll treat you better than Youie does. Give you silk gina-ginas, necklaces—a wristlet watch."

Coonardoo's eyes flashed to their anger and loathing. Very straight and dignified, her eyes took Sam Geary's. She turned her back on him and walked away.

CHAPTER XXX

A<small>GAIN</small> and again it rained, late in the afternoon, and at night, skies were still, pure and calm. Frogs, awaking in the crab-holes, yawped through the long hours. An owl moaned from the creek trees; mosquitoes, filling the air in clouds at dusk, kept their thin small song going all through the night.

Faint, thymey fragrance of nydee drifted out from bushes near the uloo, and the aromatic tang of a shrub with stiff resinous leaves, Coonardoo called thada-thada. The butcher-bird's notes before dawn flew pure and melodious; he chanted a stave or two, and the sun climbed the lower sky in white radiance. Serenity, unanimity, infinity, were in the clear sky and rain-drenched earth.

All day children from the uloo played in the crab-holes, sailing an old square box for a boat, toppled into the fresh water a dozen times, and trotted out shrieking delightedly, their bodies gleaming like the wet ironstone pebbles, or henna-dyed by soft mud. The gins laughed, calling to them; everybody was happy and good-tempered because of the rain.

Two days after Geary and the prospector had passed through, Hugh and the boys returned, straggling in from the ranges by the Five Mile gate. Rain had made it waste of time to try to muster. Water was lying everywhere. The men had been soaked through and through by the rain, over and over again. Everything they carried and had on was wet. But creeks were running, overflowing. Hugh was jubilant. He came in at the small gate, beyond the punti bushes, with a jaunty bounce and spring in his stride no one had seen for a long time.

Winni took his horse up to the yards to unsaddle and hang saddle and bridle on their pegs.

Hugh had not shaved for days, a coarse grey scrub was thick on his jaws; and his hair, when he took his hat off, showed rough and unkempt. His boots were thick with red mud, and his trousers held dust, which had caked with the rain on them. But his eyes were as blue and young as they had been years ago.

Coonardoo went from the kala miah towards the house, when he had walked with that sharp tinkling of spurs along the veranda. She stood in the doorway of the kitchen looking at him, confounded with the awe and joy of his presence. Youie had come. It was as if the sun had risen on a dark world again.

"Reck'n we'll get three inches out of this, Coonardoo. You should 've seen it come down on the To-Morrow. We were near washed away. And you've had it in here, too?"

Coonardoo nodded.

When he had changed and showered, Hugh cut up bread and salt meat for the blacks, put out a couple of tins of jam, measured liberal portions of tea and sugar into their quart pots. Bandogera and Meenie were there to carry the food over to the kala miah. Coonardoo stood waiting to move plates and pour fresh tea for Hugh when he sat down to his own meal in the kitchen.

"Met Cock-Eyed Bob on the road in," Hugh said. "Was bogged out by the gap."

"Eeh-mm!" Coonardoo murmured, a shadow falling across her eyes.

She waited for Hugh to go on.

"They got proper wet out there," Hugh said, and laughed over a mouthful of food. "Sam took the car out as far as the Fifty Mile well and left it. He had that long slab of prospector from the Bluff with him, Bob says. And as soon as it set in to rain, good and proper, blessed if Sam and Dick Crossley didn't beat it in, and left Bob with the camels. You should 've heard Bob cursing. But they came in here?"

"Eeh-mm."

"Winni picked up tracks of the car. Just as well they did beat it while they could. Car'd have bogged for a month if they'd waited. How long did they stay?"

"Camp here," Coonardoo said.

Her face had all the scowling heaviness it always wore at mention of Geary's name.

"I suppose they boozed up and you gave 'm all the food they wanted?"

"Eeh-mm."

Coonardo took the plates and dishes he had used to the bench beside the window, and stood there, washing and putting them away on the dresser again.

"That's right," Hugh murmured, and stretched his legs, smoking.

He could see herbage and grass the rains would bring; the plains under a flowing covering of salt bush, smoke-blue, and the emerald of wild spinach; the fat stock he would be mustering in a few months' time. His brain played over estimates of calves and prices for fats; the figures he had to juggle to bring the old prosperous peaceful days to Wytaliba. He would be able to reduce his over-draft; that juggernaut of numerals which mounted, piling heavier and heavier on his brain. Figuring and counting, he contemplated the miraculous recovery the station would make by means of the rains and cattle on the road. Almost he could count his shillings by the raindrops. It had been raining shillings, great heavy silver drops, and all those shillings on Wytaliba, sinking into the soil. . . . He fell asleep in his chair as he sat there thinking of them.

Waking with a start, he laughed and went off to bed.

Coonardoo had made a fire in a kerosene bucket beside his bed on the veranda, to keep off mosquitoes. It smouldered all night; Hugh slept like a log; slept with relief and weariness.

He muttered in his sleep, turning over, and smiled as he dreamt of Mollie and the rain . . . pelting her with shillings . . . and the little girls, those queer, disappointing little girls of his, who turned a knife in his heart.

So light a sleeper usually, he did not hear Coonardoo move to put cow-dung on his fire during the night. Dark and silent she stood beside him, then returned again to the other end of the veranda; and lay down to sleep on the ground near by, writhing against it, a prey to all the tugging and vibrating instincts of her primordial hunger.

Coonardoo asked to go out on the muster, when Hugh and the boys went out again, two or three months later.

It was a long time since she had ridden after cattle. No longer young, the lithe graceful girl, as Phyllis said, "any man would have fallen for", in a pair of Warieda's old blue trousers and a shirt of his, Coonardoo was still light and slender on a horse. She rode bare-headed, her short fairish hair blowing in the wind, her eyes gazing out over the plains.

Winni was pleased and proud to have her with the men.

"Best stockman on Wytaliba," Hugh said, after their first day's work.

Coonardoo's eyes lighted and filled with sunshine, as they used to long ago. She had become gaunt and silent through the long dry years. But she seemed happier out on the run like this, Hugh told himself. That scowling shadow had left her face. She did not like the house, the room he had given her; slept on the earth, unless it was very wet, out from the veranda, beside a small fire.

As he looked at Coonardoo riding before him, her straight figure, head erect and hair blown back by the wind, the steady face, dark as minnerichi wood or old bronze, with the broad nose and shadowy eyes of an aboriginal, Hugh wondered at the undertow of his feeling for her. Eyes hawk-bright and dreamy, Coonardoo looked out before her. Her small brown hands on the reins were almost unconscious of what they were doing. Her bare feet on the stirrup showed ivory bones through the dark skin. No longer young, in the hard spare way of a woman of some older world she was still as attractive as she had ever been.

When they camped for the night Coonardoo made Hugh's fire and looked after his food, brought him his tea, and meat boiled in a billy. She put it all down beside him and went off to the fire she had made for herself and for Winni, while the men watered, unsaddled and hobbled out the horses.

Hugh stretched reading beside his fire while the sky deepened from shallow green to the purple and indigo of berries on the wild emu-bushes, stars swarmed, sparkling and whitening across it. Beyond the glow of his fire he could see Coonardoo sitting near her fire, darkness and depths of the trees before, behind and round about, Winni lying stretched beside her. Sometimes she played with his hair, curling her fingers through it; they talked and laughed, and sang together. Rhythms and winding phrases of corroboree songs, Hugh had known as long as he could remember, swayed out and about them. Coonardoo would click two little sticks, and the boys join and follow the air of songs she was singing.

A wave of loneliness inundated Hugh sometimes when he could hear Coonardoo and Winni talking and singing together, at their camp-fire.

He was lying like that beside his fire, half reading from the book before him and looking out to Coonardoo and Winni, the night he heard a growing clamour at the boys' fire farther away. Voices rose shouting and screaming into the night.

Bardi and Chitali were having a row. Hugh heard a waddy descending, Bardi screeching. Coonardoo's name came and went across the rattle of words. Coonardoo . . . Sam Geary. Bardi was wailing and screaming. Was Chitali wringing her neck? Good enough for her. Chitali had been very patient, and she had played up with every boy in the camp since she returned. But still, Hugh thought he had better see what it was all about.

He strode over to the blacks' fire.

Chitali had Bardi by the hair, and was belabouring her with a stick, while she shrieked, complaining, explaining, excusing herself, and squalling as each blow struck her.

"Geary take Coonardoo! Long fellow grab me," was what Hugh made of her babble to Chitali. The men had been drunk. It was before the boys came in from the muster after the rain.

The words crossed Hugh's mind in swift jagged streaks. He stalked across to where Chitali was holding Bardi.

"What was that? What did you say?" he demanded.

Bardi shrank from his blazing eyes.

"What did you say?" Hugh repeated. "Geary . . . took Coonardoo that night he came into Wytaliba, after the rain. And Crossley, the long chap. . . ."

Bardi huddled herself together, mute resistance enveloping her.

Hugh seized and shook her.

"Did he? Is it true?"

Coonardoo had crossed from her fire and was standing there just beyond the glare, statuesque, part of the night.

"Coonardoo!" Hugh yelled, not seeing her.

"Eeh-mm." Her voice sounded near, on the other side of the fire.

Hugh walked over and stood before her, possessed by a rage, unreasoning and devastating.

"Is it true what she says?"

"Eeh-mm."

Coonardoo's eyes had the same level stare. There was no change in the steady quiet of her voice as he had always known it.

"It is, is it?" Hugh seized her by the shoulders and shook her. "You let Geary come into my house. You're my woman. You let Geary come into my house and——"

He dashed her away in his fury. Coonardoo scrambled to her feet crying out, unable to understand the madness with which Hughie had attacked her.

"You . . . Youie!" she cried, stretching out her hands.

The vilest words, the harshest, most bitterly cruel flood of language poured in a torrent from Hugh as he stood there beside the fire. He bashed Coonardoo across the face when she lifted her head to look at him, cry out, beg wordlessly.

The boys stood silent. While it was understood a black should treat a gin who behaved badly like that, they could not understand Hugh doing the same sort of thing. He was beyond himself in fury against Coonardoo and what she had done. Hugh was within his rights, the boys recognized. Coonardoo was his woman, and had given herself to Geary, whom Hugh hated. Everybody knew Hugh hated Sam Geary. Hugh might give his woman to Geary, or any other man and no harm would be done; but everybody in the camp knew Warieda, himself, would have punished Coonardoo for consorting with a stranger without his permission. Not as harshly as Hugh had done, perhaps. But the boys would not interfere.

As Hugh swung off, Coonardoo clung to him. She did not understand half he had said, or why he was saying it.

"You . . . Youie!" she pleaded, her eyes streaming.

"Get away from me. Keep out of my sight," Hugh cried. "Never let me see your face again. Go to Sam Geary. Be one of his gins. I'm done with you."

Coonardoo cried out, moaning and hanging on to him.

Hugh struggled with her, trying to wrench the thin, strong arms from about him. To escape her desperate grasp he dragged her across the fire. Screaming, as the fire bit into her flesh, Coonardoo clung to him. Flames squirted up from the dry rag of the trousers wrapped round her legs. Hugh twisted her wrist back, thrusting her away from him. Coonardoo fell back into the fire. He strode off among the trees.

Winni ran to Coonardoo, dragged her from the fire, and rolled her on the ground to put out the small flames, slithering up and down, and over her limp body. She lay moaning and unconscious for a while.

Chitali, Bardi and the others pulled charred clothing from her limbs. The flesh showed raw where fire had eaten into it. Coonardoo's loose flowing hair was burnt close to her head.

Bardi stooped over her whimpering. Chitali mixed ashes with a piece of fat from the salt meat hanging beside his saddle and plastered it over the burnt places on Coonardoo's body.

All night Coonardoo lay moaning, as if she were asleep, beside the camp-fire.

The embers died down beside Hugh's fire. At dawn he rode into the camp. He had caught the big chestnut he was working and straddled him bare-back. He saddled without looking at the boys, and went about preparing his own breakfast. When he had finished eating he called Chitali, handed out bread, tea and meat for the boys, Bardi and Coonardoo. But his face was hard and stiff, his eyes empty. The madness had died down in him. He was sane enough, too sane, and spoke harshly in a way no one in the camp had ever heard before.

"Send Winni and Toby along with me," he told Chitali. "We'll muster up to the soak. You spread out with the others. Meet at the old yards down by the gap. Bardi can look after the packs."

"Eeh-mm."

Chitali took the food and went back to the boys at the other fire.

There was no thought of failing to do as Hugh had commanded. In a little while Winni brought the horses and was waiting to roll Hugh's ground-sheet and pack his gear.

But the boy's face was heavy and sulky. Hugh rode off and Winni and Toby followed behind him at a little distance. A dead calm seemed to have descended upon him; he could not think. He felt wide awake, with a curious unsleeping quality of brain, as if he had been dragged of every emotion. He did not reproach himself. Could not feel ashamed; scarcely remembered the madness of the night before.

All day the boys riding with him averted their gaze. They were silent together, riding after and rounding up cattle, heading them from the hills to yards in the narrow valley of Koodgeeda gap. As though he were an evil spirit, possessed by a narlu, the boys kept out of Hugh's way, fear and mistrust in their eyes.

When he reached the gap stock-yards, sunset was flaming out beyond the purple bluffs of the hills and Chitali had his beasts yarded. Fires were going; the packs spread out.

As stars glittered, darkness closed in on the camp, Hugh realized, without searching, that Coonardoo was not there. Where was she? What had they done with her? He did not ask. She would be all right, he told himself. She was too tough to come to any harm. Her fortitude was equal to anything.

He was aware that for the next few days his instructions were being carried out, rigorously, with unsmiling exactitude. The boys worked silently, as a matter of course, without any of the usual gusts of laughter and good-humoured rivalry amongst each other. For the next two days Hugh branded and ear-marked calves, turned off cows and calves, and held fat bullocks for the road.

Still Coonardoo did not come into camp. Where she was he did not know. Her horse was missing. Hugh would not allow himself to think of her; to ask questions about her. But he began to remember what had happened by the fire: and to be ashamed of the brutal way he had treated her.

It was Geary he had to reckon with, Hugh told himself, coming along like that and making free with another man's house and women. Well, that was done with, anyhow. There would be no more talk of Coonardoo as his woman.

But what had the boys done with her? Where was she? Hugh slept lightly; but not so lightly that he heard Winni steal off, and make his way through thick scrub along the ranges to where Coonardoo had been left in the morning. Winni had ridden half the night to find her, take food and build up her fire.

He had found Coonardoo lying just where the boys left her; but with her eyes open and gazing up among the stars. Winni crouched beside her, trying to bring her mind from the dazed misery of her suffering.

He had ridden back and been in camp before dawn. Again and again he had gone back to Coonardoo at night; then Chitali had made him sleep and taken his place. Hugh guessed what had happened when he saw Winni sleeping on his stomach at midday. He looked over the horses, and saw that Dionysus was jaded as though he had been ridden hard, ridden all night.

Vaguely Hugh wondered whether Coonardoo would be in at the homestead when he got there; whether she would be standing on the veranda in a blue gina-gina, the dark, silent figure she had always been; and expect him to forget, never to refer again to that ugly nightmare of the ranges.

He did not intend she should stay there. He would order her off the veranda. Meenie could sweep and look after the place.

Hugh did not doubt, if she was not in when the musterers returned, that Coonardoo would come back to Wytaliba; wander out from the bush one day; very gaunt and hollow-eyed, drift down to the house or the uloo and sit down there.

CHAPTER XXXI

Hugh was droving the mob, mustered after the rains, to the railhead himself. The beasts mooched along feeding, though they were a wild lot and had rushed two or three nights running.

Billy Gale, with his boy Arra, rode into the camp below Nungarra rocks at sunset one evening. He and Phyllis were living in the shack of mud bricks roofed with corrugated iron he had put up on Catchy-Catchy, as Bill still called the country he held on Wytaliba boundary, north and east. Hugh had seen little of Phyllis since she was married. She had ridden over once or twice when Bill was going into Nuniewarra, which he still worked for Geary. But she was nearly eighty miles from Wytaliba homestead, and kept busy with the wells they were sinking, sheds and windmills which were being put up about her new home.

"How's the cattle going?" Bill asked when he stretched to yarn beside Hugh's fire.

"No good."

"Go on?"

Bill rode off in the morning. His hands were too full to attend Wytaliba muster this year, he said.

"Oh, well," Hugh conceded ungraciously, "the feed's good. You can pick up your brands later on, if you like."

He pulled in at the homestead for stores. The boys killed the night they came in, and Hugh himself saw to cutting up and salting of the meat. He refilled the tucker bags, and loaded his packs, gave Meenie stores for the blacks and put the keys in his pocket.

There was a curious heavy quietness about the women from the uloo; even the men looked sullen and resentful. Bardi had told her story of that night in the camp, Hugh knew. And where was Coonardoo? She had not come in as he expected. She was not down at the camp. He did not want to think about her, to feel she would not come along the veranda and stand beside him, knowing what he wished to do without his having to speak. He would not remember what had happened. The same heavy quiet was on him as on the blacks.

Deeper, more implacable than his anger, resentment had settled upon him. But he did not doubt Coonardoo would come in from the bush one day and live out the life of her people down there beside the creek.

No harm would come to her out in the ranges. Was she not part of the place and the life? But what a blank her being away made in life at the homestead where she had been! Could you believe it? Could anybody believe a man, a sane man, would feel like that about a gin?

Hugh started, sweating from his stretch on the veranda, at midday. Sharply, intolerably, he remembered how he had pushed Coonardoo away from him; how she had fallen into the fire. He had hit out at the dark pleading face, the anguished eyes. What possessed him? Was he mad? He could not understand the fury which had consumed him.

He was glad to be on the road again. Slept one night at the homestead, took the packs on and picked up the boys with the cattle. The bullocks were wild and restless after they left Wytaliba boundaries. When a night horse shook his saddle they were up like one beast, and raced for a couple of miles before they could be wheeled.

But hard riding and watchfulness were better to Hugh than time to stand and think; to lie and try to read, or sleep and dream. The boys muttered and glanced sideways at him. There was no doubt in anybody's mind that a narlu, some evil spirit, had jumped into and taken possession of Youie. He was not the man they had known. They had been used to a fellowship, jokey and good-humoured; a man who laughed and sang as he rode round the cattle with them. Sang his own long wailing rigmaroles and tried to sing theirs.

This morose and glowering fellow, with his gusts of ungovernable temper, was someone they did not know. The boys were afraid of him; that he would run amuck again as he had done over Coonardoo. They watched him from the side of their eyes, as he cooked his own meal over the fire at night, and sat brooding into the distance, smoking, or reading, and cursing the mosquitoes and ants.

Hugh slept poorly, waking at night with startled yells. The blacks could see him as they went round the cattle at night, sitting up to put wood on his fire, walking about, and always he was awake when Chitali came to him with his horse for the dawn watch.

When the cattle were restless he went on with the boys all night, and his eyes, during the day, were bare blue of the skies. Sometimes as he paced backwards and forwards on his horse under the stars, the boys heard him singing:

> *"Towera chinima poodinya*
> *Towera jinner mulbeena."*

Coonardoo's little song, that was, and they wondered to hear Youie singing it when he was so angry with Coonardoo. He sang in a thin, childish voice, as if it were Coonardoo singing when she was a little girl, and the boys exclaimed to each other, fear in their eyes. They began to think Coonardoo was dead, and her spirit was plaguing You for the way he had treated her. But Winni would follow Youie's singing, wailing and muttering. It was as if they were calling Coonardoo, Youie and Winni, both of them, calling and grieving for her, out there, as they went round the cattle.

More often, Winni was heard intoning a low, moaning melody with broken rhythm:

> *"Nungardie naju, karri chitar-aima warra naju*
> *Nieba-nieba kullinjarigo nuniewarra nyengo*
> *Murda-muddie, murda-murdidee."*

"What's it mean—that 'Nungardie naju' thing you're always singing these days, Winni?" Hugh asked him roughly.

"Means," Winni muttered, "Mother mine, I stand and wail for you, but I will return and bring something pleasing for you in the way of food."

"Oh, that's it, is it?" Hugh replied awkwardly.

The boys had heard him trying to sing "Nungardie naju" too; but he could never quite get the wavering air and broken rhythm of the little old song they all knew quite well.

In a rush, beyond Nuniewarra, forty beasts got away.

"Never mind," Hugh said. "Leave 'em grow fat."

But the mob had run off so much beef by the time it reached Karrara, he took £8 a head for the lot and, after a night at the pub, started back for Wytaliba again.

On Wytaliba, when Hugh and the boys returned, the grass was a foot high, beginning to fade and turn yellow already; wax-bushes had small faded pink flowers, the mulga tufts of new leaves. But down at the uloo old Joey and the women were having a bad time. Their flour and sugar had given out, and they had been living on bardis, bungarra and kangaroo, with only women and children to hunt for them. Coonardoo had not come in. The old women were wailing for her at dawn as though she were dead. They did not mention her name.

The house stood blank and neglected-looking. Fowls wandered over the verandas. Red dust lay deep on everything.

Chitali came to Hugh. Winni was with him; his eyes savage with misery and despair.

"Go find Coonardoo," Chitali said.

"Right." Hugh filled their tucker bags. He saw the boys, Chitali and Winni ride out, taking a couple of horses each.

It was three or four months since they had come in from the To-Morrow without Coonardoo. Hugh could not look at Chitali and Winni; he wanted to go with them. But he would not, watching them with bitterness and self-abasement.

"Rotten," he brooded. "Rotten, that's what I am. There goes my son to look for his mother . . . and I haven't the spunk to go with him.

"It's beneath my dignity. My pride won't let me. They're better than I am. Simpler, more honest and kindly. Warieda would have banged her about, perhaps; but not scared her to death, pitched her into a fire. Coonardoo, my poor Coonardoo, if you'd been a dog I wouldn't have treated you like that. . . .

"And I didn't even say to them, 'Bring her back. See that you bring her back, boys, no matter where she is, what she's done.'"

There was plenty to do in at the station during the weeks the boys were away. Hugh worked at the shed, tanning and stretching hides, repairing one of the mills which was out of order, making up his books and stewing over accounts.

He had to cook for himself, although Meenie washed and swept grudgingly, with a bad grace. Nobody forgave him really for the absence of Coonardoo. After Hugh left, taking the cattle down to Karrara, Joey and the women had gone out to look for Coonardoo. They had walked to the camp by the head of the creek where the boys left her, found her fire; but she was not there. They had followed her tracks along the creek and lost them where she crossed over. She was ill, and walking crazily, the tracks showed. Bandogera wailed for Coonardoo in the morning. Meenie and she would not mention her name.

It was a good season, the desert pea scarlet under the mulga. For miles it stretched, flowing, the colour of blood newly spilt, under the grey-green trees and over the plains, although there were stretches of country where not a drop of rain seemed to have fallen. Forests of dead mulga still stood, shining silvery in hard, dry earth.

Chitali and Winni returned, but Coonardoo was not with them. They had searched and tracked for miles, and could not find her. At the top of the range Winni had found the ashes of a small lonely fire and there were bird's feathers lying about. They had picked up a track again crossing the old northern stock route. Other blacks they fell in with had neither seen nor heard of Coonardoo. She had covered her tracks well.

Chitali was sure, however, she was not dead; they would find her some day. She had wandered a long way, joined an inland tribe or gone into the uloo of some station blacks. At the summer pink-eye, he thought, some news would be gleaned of her.

Hugh rode over to Nuniewarra. He took Winni with him; but would not go into Geary's house. Sam came out to meet him. There had been a row. Winni did not hear what was said. Hugh sent him down to the uloo by Nuniewarra well to find out whether Coonardoo was there.

But the Nuniewarra folk had not seen or heard anything of her. At musters, on all the stations along his boundary, Hugh inquired for Coonardoo. Winni asked every man he met, white or black, whether she had been seen or heard of.

Once or twice a rumour of her was caught, and lost again.

A teamster coming down from Roebourne had seen a tall gin with fairish hair.

"A dirty old swob come in from the bush to Monty Blood's place, a while back," he said. "He's got a hut back of Weelarra. The 'out station' they call it. All burnt she was, her wounds fly-blown. Monty washed 'em out with Condy's for her. Took him two hours a day. Beastly job. Made you fair sick to look at 'em. Monty said he'd heaved his heart out first time he touched her. You know Monty, damned old hard case, one of the hardest doers in the Nor'-West, but tender-hearted, by God. . . .

"The gin, oh yes, she lived with him for a bit. Then when Monty went off on a spree into Roebourne, she disappeared. Monty went real sour on it. 'That's the worst of abos,' he said. 'They've got to go bush or pink-eye every now and then. You can't depend on 'em.'

"But this one he called Esmeralda, she was a real good girl, could cook and sew. All the same there was something queer about her. She was a bit gone in the upper storey . . . the way she'd start, yelling and screaming sometimes, beside the camp-fire. You'd think she'd got the jim-jams or something. She was scared stiff of fire. But Monty was real fond of her. Queer, isn't it, how fond you can get of a gin? He was cut up all right when she went away."

Hugh rode over to Weelarra, taking Winni with him. He went to Monty Blood's hut to ask about the gin who had come in out of the bush. He thanked Monty for what he had done for her, having no doubt who the woman was. But Monty did not know where she had gone, or what had become of her.

CHAPTER XXXII

Y EARS moved at their slow even gait, but although Hugh and the boys searched north, south, east and west no more was heard of Coonardoo.

The bottom had fallen out of the market for horses. Mobs of three and four hundred roamed the plains and ridges. Hugh mustered to brand, geld and rough-handle the best of his young stuff: took what he needed for running the station, changed and worked fresh horses; but more and more, as cars and trucks made their way across the inland tracks, horses were eating their heads off, galloping in flocks as wild as birds, and depreciating in value.

Hugh tried shipping drafts of the hardy, well-boned Pluto and Hera strains to Singapore and the Straits Settlements. He and the boys took a mob to Port Hedland and shipped them on an old Dutch tub to an agent who had been inquiring for Australian horses. The horses brought a good price, but bucked and bolted mad with terror, at the sights and sounds of a foreign country. They gave the breed a bad name.

There was nothing for it, Hugh realized, but to send a man with the next draft to show what handling would do for fresh and spirited horses. And Billy Gale was the man for the job. Billy persuaded Sam Geary the game was worth the candle, and he and Phyllis went with the next shipload of horses from Nunie-warra and Wytaliba for British India. Hugh arranged to keep an eye on Catchy-Catchy while Bill was away, and Sam was pleased enough to demonstrate that he could manage quite well without Bill Gale if he felt inclined to.

Hugh shipped two or three drafts of horses to native rulers and English officials in the Straits and India.

Morose and sullen-eyed, he mooched along the wide streets of northern townships after he had been through with horses. As dirty as the boys, he looked, his trousers patched with the shark's teeth of gins' sewing, his wide-brimmed hat weathered and frayed at the edges, the band in shreds.

Men loafing about the whitewashed sheds and corrugated-iron

shacks, stores and pubs, looked after him as he walked, spurs clanking on the road. Hugh Watt of Wytaliba, they told each other, and gossiped about him and his down-and-out appearance. Teamsters and drovers who had been through Wytaliba pulled up to yarn with Hugh, and Hugh shouted drinks in bars up and down the town. He drank a good deal himself; but no amount of beer or whisky lifted the weight of his dour sobriety.

Wytaliba was having a tough spin, it was well known. Hugh was in up to his neck with the banks. There was even talk of foreclosure and of the place being sold over his head.

After one good season Wytaliba had registered no more than an inch or an inch and a half of rain for twelve months. Again and again Wytaliba missed the rains when almost every other station inland below the twentieth parallel got it. Or a storm had broken too early, sun and hot winds blasted and withered up the young grass and herbage which should have lasted a season.

It was enough to break any man's heart. Yet Hugh Watt slogged on; no veranda manager about him. He worked as few white men worked, droving night and day with the boys, through a dry season. Nobody understood why he stuck out life on Wytaliba without another white man or white woman to speak to and do odd jobs for him. Cock-Eyed Bob and Ben Alsop were about the only men who pulled into the homestead. The work of the place was done by blacks as it had always been, although Geary said even they were beginning to be fed up with Hugh.

He worked them too hard and was so surly, given to such outbursts of rage. The gins did much as they liked with the food and about keeping the place clean.

White cockatoos swirled around the house when it was empty, roosting in a tree beside the veranda. Hugh threw them scraps of food and talked to the cockies in an uncanny way, it was said.

For two or three years Geary and Hugh had not spoken. They passed each other on the roads, staring straight ahead, giving no sign of recognition. Hugh had sent his boys to Nuniewarra for any T7W cattle.

While Bill Gale and Phyllis were away in the Straits with horses, Geary was ill. In great pain, thinking he was going to die, he sent over to Wytaliba. The scratched, almost indecipherable scrawl Sheba brought begged for pain-killer of some sort, and Hugh returned in the car to Nuniewarra with Sheba, taking morphia and a hypodermic from his mother's old medicine chest. After an injection, he drove with Sam down to Karrara, where a doctor and hospital had established themselves. Sam weathered an operation for hernia and returned to Nuniewarra with a new lease of life. The hostility between him and Hugh seemed to die down for a while. They recognized each other when they met; exchanged a few words.

A tall, heavy man, wearing his belt under a loose flabby paunch, Sam still carried himself with a swaggering jollity, and liked to air his argument for polygamy in hot crowded hotel bars, and on sprees, up and down the river. He enjoyed nothing more than to rake a dilapidated Bible from his pocket and read aloud the story of Judah, or recite the number of Solomon's wives and female accessories.

The pub in Roebourne had a rowdy crowd of shearers and miners the night Hugh walked in with Big Otto whom he had met on the road. Sam was standing up against the bar, a huge new felt hat on his head, his face inflamed, raw-looking, pale eyes leaping under pink slatted lids.

" 'But King Solomon loved many strange women, together with the daughter of Pharaoh,' " Hugh heard him chanting as he had many times before. " 'Women of the Moabites, Ammonites, Edomites, Zidonians, and Hittites.' "

"Go on! Go on, Sam," the shouts resounded.

" 'He had seven hundred wives and princesses, and three hundred concubines. . . .' "

The laughter and shouts of the men, their oaths and exclamations, as they rocked and surged about Sam, drowned the rest of his reading.

Hugh ordered his drinks and stood with Otto But-Not-of-Roses, as the big Swede was called, at the farther end of the bar. Sam hailed them and called for drinks all round. He was well screwed and in great form, Josh Johnson the publican said. Hugh hung back. He had put away more whisky than usual himself, that night; but even in liquor, less then than at any other time, perhaps, could he fraternize with Sam Geary.

Seeing Hugh on the outskirts of the crowd, a sombre hostile figure, and knowing the wind was with him, Sam could not resist a malicious impulse to jab and annoy Hugh.

"Say, Youie!" he bawled, "who do you think I saw in the port the other day? Coonardoo! And you never saw such an old break-up. Never'd have known her, if she hadn't screeched when she saw me, and picked up a stone. Cripes, it near got me too! The boys tell me, she's been hanging around the port this couple of months. Come in on a pearling lugger. They say she's been up and down the coast for years, hanging round the Chinese quarters. All in now . . . rotten with disease, and booked for the island. I asked Trooper Andrews if there was any chance of getting her away. But he said they were shovin' her off next week."

Hugh swung over to Geary. His arm flew out, smashing across the red swollen flesh which was Sam Geary's face. Geary fell. Men started up about him, protesting noisily. Hugh staggered out of the bar, swaying, his mind darkened by his anger.

Winni found him lying on his face at the back of the hotel in the early hours of the morning. He went for Chitali and they dragged Hugh to the horse camp on the outskirts of the town. In the morning, before he had quite recovered consciousness, they were ready for the road. Hugh rode along beside them. He did not ask why he came to be leaving the town so early. Pink in the sky was as soft as the breast of galahs flying there against the horizon, rose and grey. Were they galahs flying across the plains, or feathers of clouds, flushed and sweeping like a flock of galahs?

A doped sickness and heaviness held Hugh's brain. He knew he was moving out and away from the town with its scattered and ramshackle houses, its sweltering iron sheds and seething human beings. A noisome growth it seemed to him, on the edge of the sea, like those fungi which melt away in stink and slime. As they rode on, there was only the wide empty country, grey fur of the trees stretching endlessly, hills lumped and undulating against a fading silky spaciousness, blue, fine and pure. Smell of the earth was good, heat of the sun, the clean brazen gleam on polished pebbles, taste of the red dust rising in mist from the horses' feet.

The boys rode ahead silently; Winni beside Hugh. Taking command, unconsciously at midday he said, "Camp here, Youie?"

"Eeh-mm," Hugh agreed, and sat under a tree while the boys made tea and brought him food. He felt sick and childish, his brain was clouded, as though a blood-vessel had broken; blood pressing heavily against sensitive tissue would not let him think or feel.

222

The boys believed he had been doped, as they had seen teamsters and drovers sickened and made unconscious by bad whisky, or cigar ash dropped in their drink.

At the homestead Hugh hung about for a long time brooding and gloomy, beginning a job and flinging it down, to sit staring over the plains. He had no pleasure or interest in anything, it seemed, though the routine work of the station kept him moving mechanically. A dull and sodden hopelessness dogged everything he did.

Phyllis and Billy Gale came over to see him when they returned from the Straits, and Chitali sent word that Hugh was ill. Billy had heard of Hugh's attack on Sam Geary in the hotel at Roebourne although he said nothing to Phyllis about it.

She had heard all there was to hear from Beilaba and Wanna when she went over to see Hugh. She could not make out what had come over him, and tried to jolly him out of his discouragement. Nothing seemed to rouse the old cheery, fighting spirit, which for so many years had kept Hugh going; indeed had been Hugh Watt of Wytaliba under all circumstances.

"I say, Bill," Phyllis exclaimed as they rode home together. "Ever hear of a chap named Jung?"

"Jim Young—keeps the pub in Carnarvon?" Billy asked.

"No. Not that one," Phyllis said thoughtfully, looking out to the hills folded together before her. Light striking from a cloudy sky drove the blue from their bulging sides into clefts and gullies, giving curled scrubs in yellowish mist for a moment. "Do you know, Bill, it's my belief our dear Youie took my mother like most men take a gin, and Coonardoo's been a sort of fantasy with him."

"I don't know what the devil you're driving at." Bill glanced at her, a little perplexed and unhappy at not being able to follow her thought.

"I'm not quite sure that I know myself." Phyllis's smile flickered, reassuring him. "It's so inexplicable this Hugh—Coonardoo affair. But there it is."

"Cripes!" Bill exclaimed irritably. "A man doesn't love a gin, not a white man."

"Doesn't he?" Phyllis reflected. "Some men don't love any woman, do they? They love women, look at 'em to lust after 'em, as the Bible says. That's Hugh. Just a good ordinary little man

223

who's tried to make a Galahad of himself. And his repressions have rotted in him."

Bill looked thoroughly miserable. "I don't know," he said. "I suppose you're right. It's beyond me, seeing under the skin like that —Galahad, repressions. . . .'"

Phyllis rode her horse in against his, her eyes laughing to him from the shadow of her wide hat-brim.

"I wouldn't for all the world destroy your illusion about love, all the tender sentiments, darling," she cried gaily. "You'll have to forgive me if I blither like that occasionally. Sing 'Till the sands of the desert grow co-old!' "

Bill sang until the hills were mauving in rosy garish light, and the first stars glittered brassily over a dark earth. Then Phyllis and he dismounted, made a fire, and camped for the night.

Down at the uloo they talked about You and how the station was going to pieces. Eight bullocks had been found dead round a water-hole where the pumping gear was broken. A sheet of iron, blown off the veranda in a storm, was lying out in the plains where it had fallen. Two old hens scratched about the garden and laid an egg occasionally in a corner of Youie's room. The shade miah had tumbled down and even the punti was dying where it stood in hard, rakish brushes before the house.

White cockatoos whirled, screeching and shattering the silence with their fierce, wild cries as they flew round the house and garden.

Mumae was concerned about what was happening to Wytaliba, the blacks believed. A curse was on the place since Coonardoo had gone.

"Close up finish 'em," Chitali exclaimed when Cock-Eyed Bob came in with his camels, late one evening, and looked about him, aghast at the neglected and gone-to-pieces air of the place.

"What's the matter? What is it?" Bob asked.

Chitali glanced over his shoulder at the blue coils of the To-Morrow ranges.

"Coonardoo," he said. "Youie send 'm away. Tell 'm never come back again. Coonardoo go."

Cock-Eyed Bob understood the blacks pretty well when they talked in their own dialect. He listened intently as Chitali's voice wavered off into an explanation of what he thought was happening on Wytaliba. Coonardoo's spirit had withered and died when she went away from Wytaliba, was something of what Chitali said. And that withering and dying of Coonardoo's spirit had caused a blight on the place. She had loved Wytaliba and been bound up with the source of its life. Was she not the well in the shadow? Had she not some mysterious affinity with that ancestral female spirit which was responsible for fertility, generation, the growth of everything? Bob did not understand; but something of Chitali's meaning reached him. The black's eyes flashed, there was a fervour in his speech. Bob remembered Mumae had said once, "Warieda's the poet and Chitali's the mystic of the crowd."

At any rate, Hugh was under the influence of Coonardoo's spirit, Chitali said. Not that she would wish any evil to befall him, or make magic against her own people and Wytaliba. Simply, the withdrawal of those spirit forces bound up with her made the place sterile. There was no secret source of joy, no growth for man or beast. The ancient native well, after which Coonardoo had been named, was drying up.

"Youie baba," Chitali murmured, touching his head.

"Aw, go to hell!" Bob exclaimed irritably. "The drought's got Youie down. That's all there is to it."

As he made his way to the homestead, slight and dapper, in his buff pants, white shirt and wide hat, Cock-Eye turned over in his mind what Chitali had said, all the same. He had no doubt that Hugh, being the sort of man he suspected, gentle and kind-hearted, was "chewing the rag", as he put it to himself, over Coonardoo. Bob had heard Sam Geary's story. But what sort of a man was Hugh, Bob asked himself, to let a thing like that prey on his mind, break him up? Most men treated a gin anyhow and never turned a hair.

Bob had letters in his pocket for Hugh which would put the capper on all this misery and desolation. From what had been said, Bob knew Sam's dream of roping in Wytaliba under his own boundary was nearing realization.

Sam had made the banks an offer for Wytaliba, and Hugh was to quit. How would he take it? Bob was afraid to hand over the letters. All the way over from Nuniewarra he had been wondering how to soften the jolt for Hugh.

After he had talked to Hugh for a while he put this proposition, "See here, Youie," he said. "You want to get away from this place for a bit. Come out with me. I'm on a real good thing. We can hang out for six months on the To-Morrow this time of the year, and you can pick up specks and bits of gold all round where I found that eight-ounce lump last year. Deposits in these 'ere jasper bars—it's a good sign. Might lead on to something big. At Mount Magnet, they come on to good gold in jasper bars. . . ."

Hugh listened as if he were more than half inclined to fall in with Cock-Eye's plan.

"Got some letters for me, Bob?" he asked, his eyes on Bob's pocket.

Bob handed over the letters and Hugh went off with them into the sitting-room where his mother's photograph still hung, covered with cobwebs. Hugh shut the door, and Bob stretched in a bag chair on the veranda. Then he went up to the shed, brought down his violin, and strummed all the little airs he knew to remind Hugh he was there.

When it was time for a meal Bob went into the kitchen, raked up the fire, looked into the cool safe, which no one had put water in for years, helped himself, and made tea. Hugh came along the veranda, looked through the doorway, a steadier, saner expression on his face than had been there for a long time.

"That's right, old man," he said. "Help yourself. I'll be along presently."

In the morning he told Chitali Wytaliba had been taken over by the bank. Sam Geary would probably buy and work the place from Nuniewarra. The men at the uloo could either stay where they were or go into Geary's and work for him.

Hugh explained the position to Winni.

"What'll you do, Winni?" he asked, confident that the boy would ask to remain with him. "I'm broke . . . done in, got nothing to give you, but a feed now and then, and a horse, or clothes. You're a fair mechanic and horse-breaker. You can make good money on any of the stations. I'm going out with Cock-Eyed Bob, prospectin' in the To-Morrow. You can come with me; or I'll give you a fiver and you can go anywhere you like."

Winni looked at him with deep dark eyes, lashes curled up from them.

"Give me the fiver, You," he said. "I got to find Coonardoo."

CHAPTER XXXIII

A TALL straight figure moved slowly through the stretch of drought-stricken mulga, on the plains stretching out from red flanks of the Nungarra hills.

Very thin, and darker than the trees, the figure swayed and drifted, making an arrowy track, as a kangaroo goes to water, across the rough, hard ground, towards the hills. A gin, naked and wasted by disease, carrying her clothes in a little bundle on her back, she stalked on, and on, and on.

All day she walked through the dead mulga, crossing the narrow pads of old cattle tracks which wavered over the dry hard earth, coming at sunset to ruckled ground at the foot of the hills where there were tussocks of spinifex, and bushes of thada-thada with thick waxen leaves. She made a fire there, threw a small piece of blackened flesh on to the ashes, ate it and, brushing the stones away, stretched to sleep on the sand.

At dawn she was walking again, steering with slow, flagging steps towards the breakaway which made a blue fissure in the wall of the hills. Up, up along its steep gravelly sides, she moved.

Day after day, for days, weeks, months she had been walking like that, eyes swung out before her, as if a magnet were drawing them across the plains; beyond blue backs of the most distant hills, drawing her to the dim edges of the pale-blue sky, although her eyes were quick to tracks on the earth as well, tracks of gin-arra, wild turkey, emu, dingoes and kangaroo, or cattle.

When that dark, straight figure came swaying and stumbling through the trees beside Wytaliba creek, just below the uloo, no dogs flew barking to greet it; there was no movement of beasts or people. Where were the children who should have scattered, with quick waving sticks of arms and legs?

Only white cockatoos, feeding in the garden before the homestead, flew away screeching, at sight of an old gin in a torn blue gina-gina, standing down there where the uloo had been, and staring out before her with thirsty bloodshot eyes.

The low brown huts were gone from the well near the creek.

Rusty iron, bleached bones, branches and sticks still lay about the ground. A piece of tin, struck by the sun, shone like a planet there in the dust. But the place was deserted. No breath of life went up from the homestead chimney, no white hens wandered about the verandas. Only fans of the big windmill moved slightly, now and then.

What had happened? Coonardoo wondered. They were all gone from Wytaliba, her own people and the people of Mumae who had made the house, the stock-yards and the windmills.

She walked a little farther up from the creek bank to where the camp had been. Scrawny hands reached for branches and sticks. A fire sprang from them before her, lipping and sipping at leaves and sheds of grass, making a smoke.

Coonardoo crouched over the fire. She had come a long way, all the way from the coast, and was very weary. Her arms went out to the fire, brown and twisted like minnerichi, showing the bone through. So withered and gaunt her face; the great eyes so sunken and bloodshot, who would have known this was Coonardoo? Flies swarmed and sang round her.

There was something of joy in those wild eyes, when she stood on the creek bank at the edge of the trees; but the joy had faded, leaving desolation, the black-out of despair.

Her feet were broken with festering sores, after the long rough journey, and she was so weak when she fell on the ground that she could not move for a while. Ants ran up and all over her, swarming, stinging.

Warmed by the fire, she sat up and looked about her, with vague tragic eyes, wondering, dismayed and remembering. She began to sing:

> *"Towera chinima poodinya,*
> *Towera jinner mulbeena. . . ."*

Faintly the melody and the words flowed. Coonardoo was back in her childhood, playing and singing with Youie, turning somersaults in the dust, Bardi and Youie and she. Mumae was there, calling the children up to the veranda for pieces of bread with jam on them.

Coonardoo sang on. Kangaroos were coming down from the range; their little feet dancing in the twilight. Dancing——

"Munyinbunna nunki-nunki chungee chungee!"

She shrieked cursing . . . was being dragged to a little boat on the river . . . the sea rocked under her, rocked and rocked.

"Wiah! Wiah!" Coonardoo wailed. She was screaming again, struggling against the great cruel hands which dragged her and nailed boots that kicked her in the belly.

"Wiah! Wiah!" she cried, lost in her agony, an anguish of consciousness.

Crowded shacks and white huts on piles, she could see them; a seaside town with its sweating, drinking, swarming crowds. Men, red-faced, lean, yellow, black, tan and tawny, streamed out of houses, smelling of rotting fish and the sea.

And then she was walking: walking away from the sea, the stench of pearlers and the close horrible places they live in. Away from the men whose faces were like corned meat, skin white beneath their filthy shirts and trousers; yellow men with small slant eyes, and the big trooper who blustered and threatened, finding her sick on the outskirts of the town.

Coonardoo listened again with the mask suffering and experience had taught her to wear when the trooper said she was to go away. Go to a place of horror beyond the sea she hated; the sea which was more cruel than anything human. Away, over and beyond the line it made against the sky; away from the earth which still held in its distances her own country and the uloo of her people. In her panic, a frenzy of fear, she had turned her back on the town and the sea; unconsciously, with the instinct of an animal making for her old feeding grounds, the haunt of her tribe, place of her birth and breeding.

There was happiness in finding it; looking at it again. To see the chalk-white trunks of trees beside the dry creek bed, and the square-topped hills of that red wedge against the western sky.

To breathe this air soothed and comforted her; to smell the earth where the uloo had spread, and the harsh fragrance of those strange trees Mumae had planted.

Coonardoo was glad to be there. She crouched over her fire, singing her little song about the kangaroos which came hopping over the range in the twilight.

She was "close up finish 'm", she knew, as the trooper had said. Her body was weakening and rotting away from her. When she had crawled ashore from the pearling lugger two or three years ago she had felt fouled and doomed.

Nothing was left of the clean straight aboriginal woman, nothing of her pride and dignity and grace. She was no longer Coonardoo, but Pearl, the "black pearl" of a pearler's crew, and before that she had been Esmeralda.

Esmeralda? Her mind wandered. She was remembering Monty Blood gratefully, how he had washed and bound up those wounds on her thigh and breast. But she could not stay with him. She had wandered away. Then there was the river and the pearlers.

With all her frail and flickering intelligence, Coonardoo wondered at the ways of white men with aboriginal women. She thought of Youie for whom she had waited and watched, who had taken her in his arms when he was a young man, strong fellow, wreathed his limbs about her. And then, was it true, what he said? That Winni was his son, not Warieda's? How could that be? Was she not Warieda's wife, given to him by her people, and had not Warieda sent her to Youie when he was alone and baba, grieving for Mumae?

"Warieda! Warieda!" Coonardoo's cry had the anguish of her widowhood. She wailed for her mate, the man of her people who had stood beside her with affection and confidence. The children she grew were his children, Warieda's surely? A whirlwind had put the spirit of the boy into her. Meenie was sure of that. When she was a child, Meenie and Bandogera had told Coonardoo how the whirlwinds and falling stars gave spirits for new babies to the women of her people.

And Youie had brought Mollie to live in his house. He had taken a woman to make children for him, and never again, even when she had gone, and Warieda; even when Youie said that she, Coonardoo, was to be his woman, never again, though they were all the time in the same place together, had Youie taken her to lie beside him. Coonardoo sorrowed and wondered, remembering.

What was it? What had happened to Youie, that he should treat her so? Did he not want her? His eyes said he did. The smouldering blue of his eyes, as they rested on her, had held her breathless, unable to stir.

Coonardoo thought of herself as if she were a child she had known; one of her own children perhaps. As if she had died; her Coonardoo existence had come to an end, that night when Hugh threw her into the fire.

She screamed, flaring to the memory of its old agony, the biting physical pain which had clasped her flesh.

Through all her troubled remembering Coonardoo could see Hugh, his figure neatly packed in white moleskins and blue shirt; that ruckled face so unlike Hugh's, distraught by the madness of his rage. Oblivion overwhelmed her as when Hugh had dashed his hand across her face. What had she done? Was it Youie to knock her about like that? She cowered away still from the memory, as if she would slink out of sight at his demand that never again should he see her face.

Youie had sent her away, driven her far from the place where she belonged, her place and the place of her people. She had gone; his will carrying her, when she did not know where she was going. Her feet, her legs, her arms and hands had been obedient to him; taken her away, wandering through the ranges, for how long she did not know, until she walked into Monty's camp, and he had looked after her. For no other reason could she have left her own country and the country of her people.

*"Towera jinner mulbeena
Poodinyoober mulbeena."*

The little song was driving Coonardoo, driving her memories. She was riding it as she had ridden her bay mare with the jetty mane and long flowing tail. And Winni, her fat little cooboo from the whirlwind, how she longed to see him! Had he not come to her under the stars when everybody left her in the camp near the head of the creek. Crouching down beside her, he had given her food. Coonardoo rocked herself, as if he were a baby still, and she were nursing him.

Where was he? Where were the girls? Charmi was dead, she knew; Beilaba had been given to Wanna long ago. She had cooboos of her own now. And where were they all? What had happened to them? Chitali, Wanna, Mick, old Joey, Meenie, Bandogera; Hughie and Phyllis? She would have liked to see them. Only Youie had said never again to let his eyes rest on her.

It was lonely down there by the creek. White bark of the trees gleamed with the faces of narlus. The trees looked very tall; their leaves swooped down, heavy and dark.

White cockies were settling to roost in the big gum-tree beside the house. Mumae was there, Coonardoo told herself. Mumae

would see and know that she, Coonardoo, had done as Mumae
bade her for Youie. She had looked after and obeyed Youie,
although in some way she had displeased him so; brought down
the torrent of his anger upon herself.

> "*Towera jinner mulbeena*
> *Poodinyoober, mulbeena mulbeena.*"

Little feet of the kangaroos were doing their devil dance in the
twilight. Coonardoo's voice fluttered out; embers of her fire were
burning low. Crouched over them, a daze held her. From that
dreamy and soothing nothingness Coonardoo started suddenly.
The fire before her had fallen into ashes. Blackened sticks lay
without a spark.

She crooned a moment, and lay back. Her arms and legs, falling
apart, looked like those blackened and broken sticks beside the fire.

GLOSSARY OF NATIVE WORDS

baba .... crazy (touched).
badgee .... sulky, cross.
bandogera .... wild turkey.
bardi .... grub (witchetty grub).
bucklegarro .... man-making (circumcision) ceremony.
buckunma .... come quickly.
bulya .... poison.
bungarra .... goanna.
coobinju .... baby.
cooboo .... baby.
coolamon .... wooden receptacle for food and babies.
coolardie .... bull-roarer.
coolwenda .... nor'-west butcher-bird.
coolyah .... kind of wild sweet potato.
cowa-cowa .... fool.
eeh-mm .... yes.
gina-gina .... dress.
jinki .... spirit.
kala miah .... wood-heap.
koodgeeda .... snake.
kylie .... a light boomerang.
miah .... screen, shelter.
milli-milli .... letter-stick.
minga .... ant.
minnerichi .... shrub with hard wood.
moppin, movin .... magic, a charm.
moppin-garra, movin-garra .. magician.
mulba .... young man.
nabi .... you, or you fellows.
namery .... reward (tobacco usually).
namma hole .... native water-hole.
narlu .... evil spirit.
noova, nuba .... (potential husband) lover.
nydee .... low-growing shrub.

punti .... wild cassia.

tani wali .... come quickly.

tarcoodee .... three.

tarloo .... totem, kobong.

tuckerdoo .... sweet stuff.

uloo .... native camp.

wallabee .... young man.

wiah .... no.

winni-carra, winning-arra .. whirlwind.

wongi .... applied to the tribes generally.

wongie .... a yarn.

wongo .... shelter (hut of bark and boughs).

wytaliba .... the fire is all burnt out.

yienda .... you.

yukki .... exclamation of surprise or fear.